PRAISE FOR MARY BURTON

THE SHARK
"This romantic thriller is tense, sexy, and pleasingly complex."
—*Publishers Weekly*

"Precise storytelling complete with strong conflict and heightened tension are the highlights of Burton's latest. With a tough, vulnerable heroine in Riley at the story's center, Burton's novel is a well-crafted, suspenseful mystery with a ruthless villain who would put any reader on edge. A thrilling read."
—*RT Book Reviews*, four stars

BEFORE SHE DIES
"Will keep readers sleeping with the lights on."
—*Publishers Weekly* (starred review)

MERCILESS
"Burton keeps getting better!"
—*RT Book Reviews*

YOU'RE NOT SAFE
"Burton once again demonstrates her romantic suspense chops with this taut novel. Burton plays cat and mouse with the reader through a tight plot, credible suspects, and romantic spice keeping it real."
—*Publishers Weekly*

BE AFRAID
"Mary Burton [is] the modern-day queen of romantic suspense."
—Bookreporter.com

CUT
AND
RUN

CUT
AND
RUN

MARY
BURTON

Montlake
Romance

Published by Montlake Romance, Seattle

www.apub.com

Amazon, the Amazon logo, and Montlake Romance are trademarks of Amazon.com, Inc., or its affiliates.

ISBN-13: 9781503902862
ISBN-10: 1503902862

Cover design by Caroline T. Johnson

Printed in the United States of America

CUT

AND

RUN

Did you notice the news this morning? Did you see the thirty-two seconds about the report on the missing girl? You did? That's good. Do you remember her name or what she looked like? It's hard to remember. Most people forget. But I don't forget the missing girls. I can recall each and every one of them, and I honor their sacrifice.

Everything I did. Everything. Was out of love.

And that happiness always requires a sacrifice.

Love,
Daddy

PROLOGUE

Exact Time Unknown

When the stairs leading down to the basement creaked, the young woman struggled to her feet. She pressed one hand to her very pregnant belly and gripped a metal pipe with the other as she listened to the steady, purposeful steps approaching the locked door. Keys rattled as mumbled curses echoed on the other side. She'd lost track of how many days she'd been waiting for him to return.

She took a step back, and her fingers tightened around the weapon, once a part of her cot's frame. For days, she'd been working on the screws holding her bed together. She'd used her fingernails and a small bedspring, tearing and ripping her nails in the process of loosening the screws. Last night the final screw and the metal rod had fallen to the floor with a loud ping. She'd wept, clutching her new best friend to her chest as she rocked back and forth. Months in this windowless box could come to an end today, if she was very careful.

The first lock turned. More keys rattled.

He had visited her every few days for months, bringing her food, magazines, prenatal vitamins, and larger clothes as her belly had expanded. He rarely spoke to her, occasionally asking how the baby was faring. *Did it kick? Did it move?* She'd never been pregnant before, so she had no way of knowing what normal was or wasn't.

A dead bolt turned, and the door swung open. He stood in the doorway, two bags of groceries in his hands. He vacantly gazed toward her and then to the small table by the kitchenette.

She smiled, her hand behind her back, her fingers gripping the metal so hard her knuckles ached. She had this one chance. One chance.

"Why are you standing?" he asked as he dumped the groceries on the table. "You should have your feet up. It's a matter of days before the baby comes."

"My belly has been cramping. Feels better to stand." That was true. The muscles in her stomach had begun to contract and release. At first she thought it was the baby curling into a ball and then stretching out. But she then realized time was running out.

"Is the baby kicking?" he asked.

"All the time." Also true. In the early weeks of her captivity, all she'd wanted to do was sleep and block out the baby and this room. Every kick to her bladder, cramp in her lower back, and bout of indigestion reminded her she'd been such a dumbass. And sometimes, when the loneliness overcame her, she wasn't sure if the kid was on her side or not.

"I brought you a few more magazines." He sounded proud, pleased with himself. "They're the current issues this time."

He carefully laid them on the small table in her room and fanned them into a neat arc. She studied the glossy covers and summoned a smile. He expected her to be pleased by this rare act of kindness. So she beamed, wanting him to believe she was docile and weak even as her mind buzzed with images of crushing in his skull. The bold magazine headlines skittered across her brain, barely registering. "Summer Beach Reads." "Hot Makeup Colors." "Short Shorts." "A Glimpse into Fall Fashion."

If anything, the magazines told her spring had given way to summer. "What day is it?" she asked.

He set the two plastic grocery bags beside the sink. "It's Friday or maybe Saturday. No more than two weeks until the baby is born."

The last time she'd seen the date displayed had been June 1, weeks after he'd locked her in this room. The paper had contained an article about her. In that piece she'd read the quote from her mother: "We don't think she's a runaway."

Think. Even her mother doubted that she'd been taken.

He'd left the paper with her, knowing it would fuel her doubts and fears that the search for her was dwindling.

After that article, she'd known there would be no savior. No one was coming. If she was going to be rescued, she would have to save herself.

"And then you'll let me go, right?" she asked.

"I told you I would." He carefully unpacked apples, bananas, bread, and packets of noodles. There were also eggs, milk, and cheese— everything for a healthy baby. And if she wanted to heat up her food or cook the eggs, there was only the microwave. No metal or glass. Just paper plates and cups. No pens or pencils. Nothing dangerous.

"Too much at stake now. Can't have you doing something careless," he said.

But she had already done the stupidest thing in her life. She'd believed his beautiful lies that had promised rescue from a nasty breakup and parents who did not want her or her baby. He'd baited this unholy trap with smiles and sweet words, and she'd stepped right into it. Now she and her baby would pay a steep price if she didn't make the first swing count.

"I also brought you more clothes," he said. "Your belly is getting so big, girl. You're straining at the edges of that extra-large T-shirt."

She mirrored his smile, hoping it would lower his guard just a little. "Baby's going to be a big one."

"Healthy and strong, just like the Lord intended. You'll thank me when it's born."

Thank him? For locking her in this room? "I haven't always been grateful for what you've done for me. But each time my baby kicks, I say a prayer of thanks," she lied.

"That's good. Real good. Feisty is a good quality in a child."

Looking satisfied, he turned and opened the tiny refrigerator and began placing perishables inside. First the milk.

She drew in a breath and gripped the pipe even tighter, picturing it striking the back of his head.

As he rummaged in the refrigerator to make room for the eggs and cheese, she took a step forward. He chatted about her needing to eat more, and she raised the pipe over her head, not making a sound as she lunged, focused solely on connecting metal to bone. She had one chance and couldn't bear to think what would happen if she failed.

Right before the pipe slammed down, he glanced up, and his smile vanished. Quick as a cat, he twisted to the right and raised his arm, and the pipe connected with his forearm.

He grunted in pain and snarled. "Bitch!"

Driven by pure panic now, she tried to raise the pipe again, but before she could, his left fist connected with her jaw, sending shock waves of pain through her head. She staggered, dropped to her knees. Her grip slackened upon the pipe, and it fell to the floor with a loud clang. It slowly rolled out of reach as her vision blurred.

His breathing was hot and quick as he picked up the pipe and, grabbing her by the hair, hauled her up to her feet. She could feel her hair tearing away from her skull as the pain in her jaw throbbed. She tasted blood, and her tongue skimmed over a broken tooth. She instinctively guarded her abdomen.

He raised the pipe, ready to strike. "I always thought you were just too kind and sweet. But you weren't nice at all. You were angling to get me to drop my guard. But I've been around this particular block before. I know how women like you lie."

"I'm sorry! I won't do it again!" she screamed.

He pulled her bloodied face next to his. "If it were up to me, I'd beat the living piss out of you. I'd punch every tooth down your throat." He shoved her onto the metal cot like a rag doll. He raised the pipe, reminding her how well he could inflict pain while safeguarding the baby.

"I won't do it again. I won't!" she pleaded, her trembling hands blocking her face.

"If you try that again, I will break your hands and feet. Do you understand me, girl?"

Tears streamed down her face as she tried to make herself as small as possible.

"Do you hear me!"

"Yes," she choked. "I won't move."

He hauled her off the cot and made her stand in the corner as he dumped the mattress on the floor, lifted the cot, and shoved it out the door. It landed in the hallway, forever out of her reach.

He left the room, slamming the door behind him. She didn't hear the lock or the rattle of keys. She sat a little straighter, listening to the thud of his footsteps, and wondered if she should dare make another escape attempt.

But just as quickly as the idea came, she abandoned it. The door opened, and he reappeared, gripping a chain with a manacle. "I should have done this on the first day. But I was trying to be nice. I don't like being mean. You have only yourself to blame."

He bolted one end to a hook wedged deep in the wall and reached for her ankle. Driven by reflex and fear, she kicked his hand away. But he gripped her leg so tight his fingernails bit into her flesh. He clamped the manacle around her ankle and locked it.

The metal compressed inflexibly against her skin and immediately began to chafe. "You don't have to do this. I'll be good."

"You had your chance to be good." He drew back from her, breathless and rubbing his forearm as if it still pained him. As scared as she was, she was glad she'd hurt him. It was worth the broken tooth and the pain still rattling around in her head to see him suffer.

"I want to get out of here!" she shouted.

He backed up toward the door, scooping up the metal pipe. "Oh, you will, darlin'. I'll let you go as soon as you give me a healthy baby."

The kid kicked her hard in the ribs, matching the beat of the heart hammering in her chest. "Why do you want my baby?"

"It's spoken for. A decent couple who can give it all it deserves." As he fished his keys from his pocket, a pen fell out and tumbled to the floor, rolling out of sight under the refrigerator. But he was too angry to notice as he rubbed his forearm and then slammed the door behind him. This time the dead bolt clicked into place.

She wrapped her fingers around the manacle and pulled at it, wincing as it scraped her skin. Tears welled in her eyes, but she refused to give in to the pure fear that threatened to swallow her.

She stood and walked toward the door, only to find out that her tether stopped several feet short of it. She had just enough slack to reach the toilet, the dresser, and the refrigerator. The microwave was inches out of reach.

She dropped to her knees and slid her fingers into the small space under the refrigerator. Her fingertips touched the pen, which for several tense seconds rolled just out of her reach. She pressed her bruised cheek to the refrigerator door, stretched her arm, and prayed for the pen, which miraculously came into reach. She coaxed it out from under the appliance and gripped it in her hands. It was a simple ballpoint pen. She pulled the blue plastic top off and tried to wedge it into the lock on the manacle. Unflinching metal quickly ate up the plastic, leaving her with a choice to now use the pen tip on the lock or save it for something else.

She sat for nearly a half hour before she made her decision and shuffled to the dresser, the chain clinking and rubbing as she moved. She pushed the cheap piece of furniture away from the wall, knowing exactly what she wanted.

She'd had months to explore every inch of this room, and she'd found initials on the back of the dresser.

JJ

OM

KS

If she'd ever had doubts that there'd been others before her, the initials proved she wasn't the first and probably not the last. She shifted her focus to the second discovery she'd made eight weeks ago. It was the air vent behind the dresser and two loose screws that were nearly stripped. Initially, she'd thought she'd found a way out, and hope had exploded so violently it hurt. But as soon as the vent cover had been off, she had realized it was too small for any human body. It wasn't an escape route.

But it was a hiding place.

She jostled the grate free, careful not to make a sound for fear he was still lurking outside her door, listening. As the silence stretched, she grew bold, stuck her hand into the dark vent until her fingers skimmed what she was looking for. Amazing what you could discover if all you had was time.

She removed the magazines, replaced the grate, and pushed the dresser back in place. She never knew when he'd return, and it was always smart to look guiltless.

She righted her mattress on the floor and then smoothed out her bedding and pillows. She settled on the bed, discovering it was even harder and more uncomfortable without the squeaky frame of the cot. She read the writing scribbled on the edges of the magazines she almost had memorized.

If you read this . . .

She'd have added her own, but there'd been no pen. And she'd spent too many hours searching for and wondering what had happened to the one they'd used. But now she had her own. Perhaps just a small victory, but she had to believe it was a lifeline. Now she could write her own thoughts in the margins next to the notes of JJ, OM, and KS.

She pressed her hand to her sore jaw and winced as she worked it back and forth. She clung to every win, knowing small victories like this kept her from going insane.

She carefully put the old magazines back in the vent and replaced the grate in case he should return. Picking up a newer magazine, she flipped past the magazine's title page to the first page with a lot of white space. She drew tiny circles in the upper left-hand corner until the blue ink flowed.

With a trembling hand she wrote,

If you read this . . .

My name is Paige Sheldon.

It's summer 2018.

What I like: binge-watching television. My smartphone. Chocolate ice cream.

What I hate: That my mom will never know that I am sorry.

CHAPTER ONE

Sunday, June 24, 4:00 p.m.
Texas Hill Country, Forty Miles West of Austin

Two buzzards circled overhead.

Their broad, pale wingspans caught the wind currents as they glided round and round in a tightening circle, dropping lower, zeroing in on what had summoned them. Like him, buzzards didn't have an elegant reason for being. Like him, they cleaned up the mess death left behind.

Texas Ranger Mitchell Hayden turned off the paved rural route onto the long dirt driveway that fed into Jack Crow's salvage yard. Hayden had not been in the Hill Country for a few years. Not since before his wife had gotten sick. Sierra used to coax him out here to visit wineries or browse the tony little shops. He'd always indulged her, grateful for her laugh and the smile she brought into a life dominated by so much darkness. She was gone now, and he'd stopped coming here.

The movement of the buzzards drew his gaze up again, alerted him that their target was on this property. The muscles banding around his skull tightened, and he knew that whatever was up ahead was going to be bad.

He'd received a call late Friday from an informant whom he'd worked with over the years. Jack Crow was a salty old man, every bit in his late sixties, who collected old auto parts, sold a few, but mostly let them pile up around him like a mountain of metal. Crow had been an army medic way back in the day, got caught stealing morphine, and earned himself a dishonorable discharge and a jail sentence. But he'd done his time and since then had been clean enough. Sure, he patched up people who didn't want to explain a gunshot or knife wound to an emergency room doctor, but he also stayed out of the very tempting human trafficking and drug trades of South Texas. Those who went to Crow knew he never snitched on the people he patched up, unless they were hurting women and children. In cases like that, all bets were off. Hayden assumed yesterday's call would lead him to another drug dealer or violent coyote.

Dust kicked up around Hayden's SUV as he drove through the salvage yard that to an outsider looked like chaos. He knew from experience, however, if you asked Crow where a part was in these rambling heaps, he could find it within minutes.

Two more buzzards joined the original duo, and together they squawked as an eerie quartet. Soon the buzzards would fill the bright-blue sky, rushing to beat the Texas heat that would eventually drive everything to find cover.

He drove toward the trailer Crow had called home for almost thirty years. He'd had numerous offers to sell in the past few years but had refused them all. The land was worth far more to developers now than a fading salvage business, but the old man had jealously guarded his territory. He had nowhere to go.

Hayden slowly rolled up to the trailer, came to a stop, and shut off his vehicle. He unfastened his seat belt and removed his weapon from its holster. Like the buzzards above, he smelled the very familiar scent of death.

Crow had a small deck out back that faced west and gave him a view of the sunsets. The old man liked his twilights, and he spent most evenings sipping whiskey from a saloon glass that reflected the sun's oranges and yellows in the amber liquid.

When Hayden came around the side of the trailer, he saw two buzzards pecking at a man's leg as he sat in his lawn chair, facing west toward a sunset that was still hours away.

"Get on out of here!" Hayden shouted. "Get out!"

The birds hopped several paces and then flapped their wings, landing on top of the trailer so they could watch until this new predator cleared out.

The old man was slumped back in his chair, and even from fifteen feet away, Hayden could see fingers bent and twisted at horrific angles. Several of Crow's fingernails were also missing, and puddles of blood dripped and pooled onto the deck.

Whoever had killed him had left slices in the flesh, knowing the smell would bring the buzzards from over a mile away.

Judging by the evidence, he knew Crow had been dead for several hours.

"Jesus, Crow." Sadness circled like the buzzards, but Hayden chased it away as well.

Instead of rushing toward Crow, Hayden searched the horizon for signs of an ambush. He moved around the trailer, scanning every angle before he climbed up the four narrow porch steps, crossed the wooden platform, and opened the front door.

Finger resting on the trigger, he switched on a light and peered inside. The place had been tossed. The cushions on the couch had been pulled off and cut open, the recliner had been upended, and the drawers from a small desk had been dumped out on the floor. A collection of pictures, mostly of a younger Crow and a little girl, lay crumpled in the center of the room, their thin black frames smashed along with the glass. Worn carpet muffled the sound of his boots as he moved deeper into the trailer toward the back bedroom, where he discovered an upended mattress hacked open, its white tufted innards scattered around.

Determining the trailer was secure, he returned to Jack Crow's body and found that two buzzards had landed back on the porch. He stamped his booted foot on the deck and yelled violent curses until the raptors left him alone to study the body.

The old man's rugged face was covered in white stubble, and thin lips twisted into a snarl born of pain and anger. His plaid shirt was unbuttoned, exposing a round belly protruding from a white T-shirt stained with blood and sweat.

This close, he could see Jack Crow's legs were turned at odd angles, as if someone had taken a hammer or crowbar to his kneecaps.

Hayden holstered his weapon, allowing the first flicker of sadness. The old bastard might have broken a few laws in his time, but under all the gruff and bluster there'd been a decent soul.

Hayden searched Crow's pockets, not expecting to find anything. However, in his front breast pocket, there was a playing card. It was the king of spades. It was clean, the paper slick as if it had just been removed from a fresh deck. None of the gangs who circulated in the area used cards like this, but it was clear. Someone was sending a message.

Hayden reached for his phone and called the local sheriff, then the state medical examiner's office. Crow hadn't given any hints about why he'd wanted to see Hayden. He'd just said it was real important. "Crow, what the hell did they want?"

CHAPTER TWO

Monday, June 25, 3:00 p.m.
Austin, Texas

Dr. Faith McIntyre of the Travis County Medical Examiner's Office stood at her autopsy station studying the body of the sixty-four-year-old male lying on the gurney against a stainless steel sink. Country music played softly from a small set of audio speakers next to a whiteboard covered with her daily schedule written in tight cursive. Beside it rested a **TEXAS** mug filled with red, green, and black dry-erase markers. Above the gurney hung a microphone as well as a large adjustable light that reflected on the stainless steel instruments on the tray.

According to the death investigation report, the subject of her examination had been found sitting outside his trailer in a lawn chair and had sustained multiple traumas to his joints. Paramedics had declared him dead at the scene.

When the body had arrived at the medical examiner's office and his clothes and shoes stripped, she'd immediately noted horrific signs of torture, including seven broken fingers, lacerations, and a shattered kneecap.

This was the kind of death reserved for those who landed on the wrong side of the drug cartels. "Did he have a connection to drug trafficking?" Faith asked.

Her question was directed at Texas Ranger Mitchell Hayden. His tan face, weathered by years in the Texas sun, was stoic and with no hint as to what he was thinking. Large hands weren't clenched at his side, but were primed to curl into fists in a blink of an eye. His large, muscled body, which had taken a gunshot directly into his Kevlar vest just three weeks ago, was as still as stone.

Hayden had a reputation for being decisive to the point of unfeeling, but she'd known him for a few years and recognized the quieter he was, the deeper his feelings ran.

"Why do the Texas Rangers care about Jack Crow?" she asked.

"Jack Crow contacted me on Friday. He never called just to chat, so if he had a story to tell, I listened. I couldn't get out to see him until yesterday, and when I did, I found him like this."

"Do you have any idea what he wanted to tell you?" she asked.

"He wouldn't say anything over the phone. He never liked them because he thought his calls were being monitored."

"Did he suffer from paranoia?" Faith asked.

"No. At least not any more than the average hermit."

"My death scene investigator said there was nothing in his trailer stronger than aspirin, though there was a prescription for OxyContin. There were twelve unopened bottles of beer in the refrigerator. There was nothing in writing from him that would indicate why he died this way."

"I know. I searched every square inch of the place, but it was clear someone had gone through it before me."

She lifted the dead man's wrist. "I can tell you he was restrained, maybe by handcuffs, and whoever put them on made sure they were painfully tight."

"No restraints were found at the scene, but Jack Crow was six foot two and maybe two hundred and fifty pounds. Even restrained, he wouldn't have been easy to keep down."

"I don't know about that. I think he was very sick."

"Sick?"

"My guess is cancer. His skin is jaundiced, and his belly is bloated. I'll know more when I get inside, but if it's pancreatic cancer, he didn't have long."

Hayden was silent for a moment, as if gathering his thoughts. Shadows of pain lingered in his eyes, reminding Faith that he still hadn't recovered from his wife's death four years earlier.

Hayden pointed to a faded tattoo on the man's arm and cleared his throat. "He was an Army Ranger when he was a young man. So cancer or no, he was a tough son of a bitch who wouldn't have left this world easily."

She ran her gloved hands over his scalp until she felt the hard lump. "There's a large hematoma. He was hit in the back of his head. Maybe also punched or kicked in the jaw before he was restrained, judging by the discoloration on his lower jaw."

"And then someone got to work on him," Hayden said.

"That's my thought."

"These injuries would have hurt like hell, but what do you think was the cause of death?" Hayden asked.

She opened Crow's eyelids and studied slightly dilated pupils and bloodshot, yellowed whites. "I'll know better once I open him up."

Faith's death scene investigator, Nancy Ridgefield, entered the room. Nancy was a five-year veteran of the medical examiner's office, and the pair had worked together since her arrival. Petite with black hair, Nancy was methodical and caring and had a wicked sense of humor.

"Doc, Captain." Nancy clicked on a computer screen and pulled up the first digital x-ray images of the right and left arms and hands. All were riddled with fractures. "The breaks are fresh. They happened shortly before he died. And his right kneecap, as you both first thought, was fractured in multiple places."

It took an incredible amount of blunt force to shatter bone. That kind of pain could have been enough to trigger heart failure.

Faith studied the victim's thick cheekbones and pale, rough jaw covered in white stubble. No one could have accused Jack Crow of being handsome, but she would bet he'd been striking when he was younger.

"Have you found his family yet?" Faith asked.

"I interviewed a man who lives on the property, a David Ledbetter," Hayden said. "According to Ledbetter, Crow has a son and a daughter. I haven't yet found the son, Dirk Crow, but I located the daughter, Macy Crow, and called her yesterday. She lives in Virginia. She said she would get the first flight out this morning."

"Leave me her contact information in case I need to call her," Faith said.

"Already gave it to Nancy," Hayden said.

Faith laid her hand on Crow's shoulder, feeling a stab of empathy for the guy. Maybe he'd not been a saint, but no one deserved to suffer like this.

She drew in a breath, trying not to picture the agony that would have filled the man's final minutes. Jack Crow had to cease to be a person for now. His body was evidence, and it had a story to tell that she would not hear if her mind was clouded with emotion.

She tugged the dangling microphone down a little closer and stated the patient's name, height, weight, and injuries.

Beginning her external examination, Faith lifted his right arm. Though the underside of the forearm was blackened from stippling, the settling of blood after the heart stopped pumping, she saw faint tattooed lettering that read DO NO HARM. She noted this find along with the Army Ranger tattoo into the recorder and then continued to search for other markings. There was a scar on his lower abdomen, likely from an appendectomy, and an old puncture wound on his shoulder as if he'd once been shot. She checked between his toes and fingers and checked the veins in his arms and inner thighs for signs of needle marks, but found none.

She lifted one of the victim's hands and studied the fingers, now blue at the cuticles. "Nancy, do you have paper?"

"Sure, Dr. McIntyre," Nancy said.

Faith scraped under three intact nails, and Nancy held the sheet of clean paper under the hand. Several scrapings fell onto the paper. "Maybe we got lucky and he clawed his attacker."

Faith rolled ink on the fingertips and pressed them to fingerprint cards. Hayden had made a visual identification, but forensic proof was also necessary.

"Ledbetter has worked with Crow for almost two years doing odd work around the salvage yard," Hayden said.

"Did he have anything to offer about the patient's health?" Faith asked.

"He said Crow had been slowing down the last few months, but that the old man never complained."

Faith reached for her scalpel and made a Y-incision that began above his pectoral muscles and went straight down his abdomen. She peeled back the flesh, reached for bone cutters, and snapped the ends of the ribcage so she could lift it away. She unpacked the organs, weighed them, and set them aside.

She noticed his enlarged heart immediately, and when she removed it from the body and dissected it, she found several severely blocked arteries. The right ventricle was badly discolored, as if blood flow had suddenly been stopped. His lungs had several lesions, and by feeling around in his abdominal cavity, she discovered a hard mass behind his stomach. She removed the stomach to reveal a tumor on the pancreas that she'd bet a paycheck was cancerous. Jack Crow had been a dead man walking for some time.

"He would have been in terrible discomfort," Faith said. "I'm surprised he didn't get the prescription for painkillers filled."

"Ledbetter said Crow passed out about six weeks ago, and he drove the old man to the doctor. The doctor wanted to run tests, but Crow refused." Hayden drew in a slow, steady breath. "Crow knew time was running out, and he knew he had a conscience to clear."

"Maybe," Faith said.

She continued to examine and weigh the organs, and when she'd inspected them all, she repacked them into the body and sutured the Y-incision.

"His heart failed," she said. "But clearly the torture, given his weakened state of health, triggered heart failure. I'm ruling this a homicide." Homicide didn't always mean murder, simply death at the hands of another human. Her ruling gave Hayden the green light to find the killer.

"Forensic technicians have pulled dozens of fingerprints from the trailer, but no telling who they belong to." His intense gaze softened a fraction. "I appreciate you working this case into your schedule this afternoon. I'll keep you posted."

"Thanks. I'd like to know what happened."

"Mr. David Ledbetter is here to view the body," Nancy said. "He also wants to see you, Dr. McIntyre."

"Legally there's not a lot I can say to him about the state of the body because he's not family, but I'll speak with him," Faith said. "Nancy, can you get Mr. Crow ready for a viewing?"

"Yes."

"Captain, would you like to join me?" Faith asked.

"I would," he said.

"Give me a moment to clean up and change." She glanced up at the clock, knowing she was now officially late for a fundraiser. "I've got to get out of these scrubs. Give me fifteen minutes."

"Sure."

Faith left the autopsy room, tugging off her gloves and the gown covering her scrubs. She moved into the locker room, but when she reached for the combination lock to her locker, her hand paused and it took another attempt before she could align the tumblers. The lock clicked open, and, grabbing her towel and soap, she headed to the shower. She ducked under the hot spray, washed quickly, toweled off, and dressed in the dark slacks, white silk blouse, and heels she'd worn to work that morning. She unpinned her hair, ran a brush through it, letting the ends fall onto her shoulders, and slid on her jacket. Ten minutes later she joined Hayden in the hallway, and they walked together down to the interview room.

A slim man who looked to be in his early twenties rose as they entered. He wore dirty jeans, a faded blue T-shirt, and boots that looked almost as old as him. His hair was long and pulled back into a ponytail.

Faith extended her hand to him. "I'm Dr. Faith McIntyre."

Ledbetter took Faith's hand, gripping with a strength that belied long, thin fingers. "I only got a glimpse of Crow, but he looked pretty torn up."

"I know you were rattled yesterday," Hayden said. "Have you had a chance to think about who might have wanted to hurt Crow?"

Ledbetter shook his head. "He kept to himself and stayed away from trouble. He ain't even had a patient in the last six months."

"When is the last time he saw his children?"

"Macy's been gone for years. I never met her. Dirk lives on the property, but I haven't spoken to him in months. He and Crow don't get along so well."

"Do you know why?" Hayden asked.

"Dirk wanted his dad to sell the land and enjoy his life. Crow wouldn't discuss it."

"And you saw no one around the yard who was suspicious?" Hayden asked.

"No. No one's been around in weeks."

"You took Mr. Crow to the doctor a month and a half ago?" Faith asked.

"Yeah, he was in bad shape. I rushed him into town, and he let the doctor poke and prod but in the end wouldn't let him do nothing."

"He had unfilled prescriptions?" Faith asked.

"Yeah. He said bourbon would do the trick. We stopped at the liquor store and got a six-pack and two half gallons of premium bourbon. He also had me stop at the drugstore and get a couple of burner phones and tobacco. He loved his dip."

"Two prepaid phones?" Hayden asked. "What did he want them for?"

"He didn't say. Only cared that they had a GPS map and a video recorder."

"Was he planning to go somewhere?" Hayden asked.

"He said not to worry when I asked."

"We didn't find any phones in his trailer," Hayden said.

"I don't know what he did with them." Ledbetter sniffed and shifted his gaze to Faith. "Can I see Crow?"

Faith nodded. "If you will follow me, I can take you to Mr. Crow."

Tension rippled through the young man. "Sure."

The three walked down the hallway to the viewing room, where Nancy waited with the draped body of Mr. Crow. When Ledbetter stepped closer, Nancy drew back the sheet just far enough to show his face. At first, Ledbetter hovered back; then, finding the courage, he approached the gurney. His face crumbled with a mixture of sadness and pity. "I didn't want to believe it was really Crow, but it is." Ledbetter patted Crow on the shoulder, turned, and left the room.

Faith covered the face, and with Hayden, followed the young man as Nancy remained with the body.

Ledbetter shook his head. "Everyone liked Crow. He kept to himself. Drank a little too much from time to time, but he never hurt anyone. Lord, he was beat so bad. He didn't deserve an end like this."

Hayden asked several more questions, got the man's contact information, and Ledbetter said his goodbyes before Nancy arrived and escorted him out of the building.

"I'll run tests for narcotics, and will let you know if anything is positive."

"Thanks, Dr. McIntyre."

"Here to serve, Captain Hayden."

Hat in hand he headed toward the elevator, passing Nancy as she headed back toward Faith.

As the elevator doors closed on Hayden, Nancy asked, "Dr. McIntyre, don't you have somewhere to be?"

Faith checked her watch. Damn. She was late.

There was now a ballroom full of people waiting for her. Tonight she was the lady of the hour and being honored by the Youth Emergency Board as their volunteer of the year. Awards didn't interest her, but she understood these events made the donors feel good and that much more inclined to open their wallets.

There would be no time to go home and change, so fresh red lipstick, a spritz of perfume, and another quick brush of her hair would have to do. Minutes later, she dashed out of the medical examiner's office with memories of Jack Crow close on her heels.

CHAPTER THREE

Monday, June 25, 5:15 p.m.

Faith left a voicemail message for Macy Crow on the drive to the Driskill Hotel. They'd yet to speak directly, but Ms. Crow had promised to catch up with Faith while she was in town.

As Faith crossed the marble lobby, she found herself playing back her late father's favorite saying. *"Keep your eye on the prize."*

And, for her tonight, the prize was the new youth shelter set to break ground the first of the year. The last hundred grand needed to be raised to ensure the opening.

As a string quartet played "Clair de lune," she moved past the white columns toward round tables decorated with crystal vases stuffed with fragrant white roses and place mats made from laminated drawings done by the shelter kids.

She headed straight to the bar, ordered a stiff martini, and took several sips, hoping it would blur Jack Crow's broken body and enable her to fake a smile and face the former peers of her parents.

Over the next few minutes she accepted the greetings of long-absent friends and regaled them with polite stories from the medical examiner's crypt. "Yes, Princess now cuts up dead people for a living." Reminisced about old adventures. "Nairobi was fabulous, but Paris was wicked fun." And accepted lunch dates from women she'd not seen in years.

"Faith, you're charming everyone, as usual."

Smiling, she turned toward the familiar deep voice of Peter Slater, PJ to his friends. She'd known PJ since they both had played hide-and-seek in the law office their fathers, Russell McIntyre and Peter Slater Sr., had maintained for over forty years.

Their fathers had met in college, attended the same law school, and hung out their shingles when they were in their late twenties. The families were intertwined to the core. PJ had mourned with her when her mother died a decade ago and her father five years later. In April, when Peter Sr. had died, she'd grieved as deeply as PJ and his mother, Margaret, who'd been a second mother to Faith.

Faith kissed PJ on the cheek, savoring the familiar brand of aftershave his father had also worn. "I'm sorry I'm late. Work. Where's Margaret? She's done a spectacular job of arranging all this." Margaret was a small woman in her sixties who was always immaculately dressed and had more energy than women half her age.

"My lovely mother is drifting around the room, deciding if she'll hold her stroke awareness fundraiser here next year. You know Mom, never satisfied unless she has twenty things going on at once."

"How is Margaret holding up? This is her first event since your father died."

"She has her low moments, but all and all she's doing well. And be warned, she's talking about inviting you onto one of her event-planning boards."

"I love your mother, but I don't think so."

PJ laughed. "Good luck refusing her. My father never could."

She surveyed the room and the bounty of flower arrangements, food, and drink. "For the cost of these kinds of events, it would be far easier for the board members to simply write a check to the shelter and call it a day."

"That will never happen. Not only do these folks like their parties, but also it would rob Mom of the chance to arrange an event. You know she loves this kind of thing."

"Don't tell her I said so, but I can barely stand them," Faith said. "I'm a fish out of water."

"You do a good job of hiding it. And your father and mother would be proud of your accomplishments."

Mother, yes, but father, maybe, maybe not. Her mother had supported her at every turn, whereas Russell McIntyre had been a man of few words and even fewer after her mother died. He had spoiled his little girl with every material item money could buy, believing stuff compensated for all the missed dinners, recitals, and vacations. Bottom line was he'd wanted sons and had had to settle for an adopted daughter.

Tina Walden, director of the youth emergency shelter, waved her hand to both Faith and PJ as she moved toward the stage. Tina wore a boxy navy blue dress that didn't quite suit her sturdy frame, new flats that, judging by her gait, were already rubbing blisters, and little makeup. However, for Tina, any apparel that wasn't faded jeans covered with magic markers, paint, or dirt was a step up.

"It's showtime," Tina said.

Faith sipped the last of her martini, knowing as much as she wanted a second drink, tonight was a work night and she had an early call in the morning. "Let's do this."

PJ escorted Faith up to the stage, and as she stood on the dais, he approached the microphone at the podium. He signaled for the quartet to stop and winked at his mother, Margaret, who broke off a conversation with a state senator to smile and wave at them.

Turning to the microphone, PJ said, "Good evening. I've finally corralled our very busy guest of honor, but she's not one to be penned long and won't stay long. As she likes to say, 'Death never takes a holiday.'"

Laughter rumbled over the room as the fifty or so guests took their seats. She searched among the faces but didn't see the one face she'd hoped for tonight.

"Dr. Faith McIntyre is a little shy about awards," PJ said. "I had to talk her into this. As far as she's concerned, if you never knew about her volunteer efforts, she'd be fine."

As Faith scanned the crowd a second time, PJ listed her professional and academic accomplishments and the list of high profile cases her work had helped solve.

It made sense Hayden wouldn't be here, Faith decided. The award she was receiving had been named after his late wife, and that was a wound that would never heal.

Clapping from the audience brought her back to the moment and to when PJ said, "It is with great pleasure that I present to Dr. Faith McIntyre the fourth annual Sierra Hayden Service Award."

Faith and Sierra had been good friends, and it had been Sierra who'd brought her onto the board five years ago. When Sierra had been stricken with ovarian cancer, everyone had been optimistic at first. But the universe had turned a deaf ear to everyone's prayers, and days before Sierra reached her thirty-sixth birthday, cancer claimed one of the planet's best people.

Faith accepted the crystal vase, etched with Sierra's name and her own. The award felt heavy in her hands, and its weight trod all over philosophical arguments about death being a part of life. It took a moment before she could speak.

She thanked the board, the shelter's director, Tina, and reminded everyone to "give until it hurts just a little, or better, a lot." She exited the stage, suddenly able to justify that second martini.

"Dr. McIntyre, want a snack?" The question came from Kat Jones, one of the kids who currently resided at the shelter. Kat had been in and out of foster homes until two months ago, when her pregnancy was discovered and she was branded as "difficult." For now, the shelter was all that stood between her and the streets.

Faith thanked the bartender and faced the young girl holding a tray of hors d'oeuvres. "Thanks, Kat. I'm not that hungry."

Kat wrinkled her nose. "I don't blame you. This fishy stuff smells like shark bait."

"It's wild salmon from Iceland and very expensive."

"I guess you need bait to catch big fish, right?" The girl's small, delicate face didn't quite jive with the dark-brown hair streaked with purple and green or the multiple piercings in each ear.

Faith laughed. "That's exactly what it is."

The kid was smart. If someone gave her a textbook, she would balk. However, when Faith gifted her with a reconditioned laptop, the kid had spent hours reading and working online. Despite her keen intelligence, Kat had been on a long and rocky road to a better life since the day she was born. And this pregnancy had heaped another huge obstacle onto her path. Happy endings for girls like Kat were few and far between.

"So that's your second drink," Kat said. "Craving liquid courage?"

Not courage, but maybe a brief respite from memories of today's autopsy. "I'm going to be calling it a night soon and will hire a car."

"But it's only nine."

"I've been up since five."

"I guess you could leave now," Kat said, leaning toward Faith a fraction. "But if you do, you'll miss the Texas Ranger standing at five o'clock. He's staring at you."

Faith didn't need to turn to know the Texas Ranger was Mitchell Hayden.

"Tell me you aren't in trouble," Kat said. "He looks like he wants to arrest someone."

"I'm not in trouble. But how about you? Are you still maintaining our noncybercrime pact? No hacking into systems to snoop around."

Kat shrugged a thin shoulder, as if they were talking about simply surfing the net. "I haven't broken any laws."

Faith didn't press. The kid was trying, and that was good enough for her. "Good. Would you offer that gentleman by the bar more food?"

Kat rolled her eyes. "That guy has eaten almost two trays on his own."

"He and his wife donated the land for the shelter. It would be nice to keep him happy."

Kat didn't move. "The Ranger doesn't look happy."

He never did. "I'll handle him."

"Fine. Whatever." Shrugging, Kat strode over to the judge.

Faith waited until the girl was out of earshot before she approached Hayden. "Good evening, Captain Hayden. I didn't think you'd make it."

The times she'd seen Hayden and his late wife together made her believe soul mates did in fact exist. After Sierra's death, he'd left Austin to work near the border, but now after four years, he was back with a new promotion that he was still trying on for size.

"Nice award," Hayden said.

She held it up so he could see Sierra's name. "It's an honor."

He studied the etched words with a silent, deliberate presence that made her skin tingle and her soul tinge with guilt.

Three weeks ago, she'd attended the site visit for this event. The committee had toured the hotel for almost an hour. After the group had dispersed, she'd been in no rush to go home, so she'd wandered into the hotel bar. She'd been sipping a martini when he'd tossed his Cattleman felt hat on the bar beside her. She'd waved away his apology for having missed the meeting, ordered him a bourbon, and made small talk. He'd never mentioned his Kevlar vest, which had caught a slug that morning, but after a long pause had said he was staying at the hotel. And, well, one thing led to another.

The sex had been purely physical. No kissing. No talk of affection. No one was looking for a soul mate. And it suited them both. Since then, they'd met at this hotel six times. Both had seemed to accept it wouldn't last, so each had taken care to keep the affair secret.

His dark gaze swept quickly over her white blouse and slacks. "Did you raise a lot of money tonight?"

"Yep, and then some."

"Sorry I was late."

"No apologies."

"Any word from Jack Crow's daughter?"

"I left her a voicemail message," she said.

Death was a constant factor in her line of work, but she never wanted to dwell on it.

"Room 701," he offered.

A tingle shot up her spine. "I hope you got a room with a view."

"It has a bed."

"That'll do."

Mitchell Hayden wasn't pretty boy handsome. His eyes were too deep set and his jaw too broad to resemble anything classical. Toss in a nose that looked as if it had been broken once or twice, and you ended up with a face that resembled a street brawler's. There was a sharp intelligence in those gray eyes that missed little. When Faith was in his sights, just for a little while, she forgot about the youth center, Kat's precarious future, and Jack Crow.

"I'll need another half hour here," she said.

"No rush."

Kat approached the two of them with a tray holding a fresh martini and bourbon. "Last call."

Faith drew in a breath as she swapped her partly drunk martini for the new. She didn't hide her irritation that this underage girl was thumbing her nose at state and federal law by serving alcohol.

Hayden took the bourbon. "How old are you, kid?"

"Twenty-six," Kat said without pausing.

He shook his head as he sipped. "What year were you born in?"

"1992."

He grinned. "You're quick. I'll give you that. But pick up another tray with booze on it, and I'll call your caseworker."

Kat rolled her eyes as if she hated the attention, but Faith knew the stunt was designed specifically to elicit a response. Negative attention was better than none.

"Roger that, Captain." Kat made a show of saluting. "The bus is leaving for the shelter. Thanks for the gig, Faith."

"Glad you could make it. Don't forget I'm taking you to your prenatal visit on Wednesday."

"Can't wait." A bit of Kat's attitude faded as it always did when the baby was mentioned. She left the two, sauntering across the room as if daring the bus to leave her.

"What's that kid's story?" Hayden asked.

He'd always paid close attention when Faith had made presentations at the board meetings, but he rarely asked questions about the kids at the shelter. Both he and his sister had made generous donations in Sierra's name, but they always remained on the periphery.

"She's smart as a whip. Knows computers inside and out. Mother used drugs, and father laundered money for a drug cartel. Both are now dead. The last foster family kicked her out after they found out about the baby, so the shelter is her best bet now. She'll turn eighteen in December, and then I'm not sure what's next for her."

"Who's the baby's father?"

"She won't say. And for the record, she didn't serve any booze tonight. That tray was her way of trying to provoke a reaction."

"Out of me or you?"

"Me. She's been needling me for a few weeks."

"Why?"

"She's looking for a lifeline. She knows she's drowning but doesn't know how to save herself."

"And you're going to save her?"

"If she'll let me."

The shelter director and Margaret motioned Faith forward as the local television station crew arrived to film her and a few donors. "I've a couple of details to wrap up. No need for you to stick around."

"I've nowhere to be."

"Suit yourself," she said. She crossed the ballroom to the reporter, spoke on camera for several minutes, visited with the guests, and kissed Margaret on the cheek. When she was finished speaking to the hotel staff, it was past ten.

She looked around the room, but she didn't see Hayden. His patience for the tedious side of her life had its limits. She left the ballroom and headed toward the lobby. Her heels clicked across the marble floor as she made her way to the elevator.

"Dr. McIntyre?"

She turned and saw a tall, lean man with a neatly shaved face and warm brown eyes. Midforties, smartly dressed in a gray suit and a shirt of a similar but lighter shade.

"Have we met?" she asked.

He held out his hand. "Kevin. I saw the event sign with your picture and thought you were someone else for a moment. Then I recognized the McIntyre name. I knew your father."

"Should I apologize now?" She accepted his hand.

White teeth flashed. "No. He didn't cross-examine me. Good thing, I suppose. He was known as a real tough nut in his time."

If by "tough nut" he meant "ruthless legal shark," then yes. "That he was, Kevin."

"I just saw you crossing the lobby, and I wanted to introduce myself. Would you like to grab a drink in the bar?"

"No, thank you. It's been a long day."

Rejection slid off him like water off a duck. "Maybe we'll catch up again some time."

"Have a good evening, Kevin."

"You, too, Faith."

Faith sensed that under all his sleek manners and polish lurked an ulterior motive. She'd dealt with several men like him since her father's death. Wearing nice suits, they came bearing law degrees and threats. And as she'd told them all, Russell McIntyre might have been worth a fortune once, but it was all gone. What she had now had either been left to her by her mother or she'd earned herself. Stones didn't bleed, no matter how hard you squeezed.

What most people don't realize about me is that I treasure all children. If I didn't love them as much as I do, I'd never have made the sacrifices that I did to create so many.

Love, Daddy

CHAPTER FOUR

Monday, June 25, 10:30 p.m.

When FBI Special Agent Macy Crow had arrived in Austin, she'd taken a taxi directly to her father's salvage yard. According to the Texas Rangers and the medical examiner, Jack had died in the early hours of Sunday morning under suspicious circumstances. The facts Ranger Hayden had relayed to her were grim. Jack had been beaten pretty badly before he'd suffered a massive heart attack.

Numb, Macy had thanked Hayden for notifying her as she sat in her small rented house near Quantico, staring at a picture of Jack and herself in front of the Chevrolet Impala they'd restored the summer she'd turned sixteen.

Immediately, she'd called her supervisor and cleared her schedule, stating she needed several days of personal leave. However, she hadn't been able to get a flight out until Monday morning and after several delays had made it to Texas.

During a brief layover in Atlanta, Macy had listened to a voicemail from Dr. Faith McIntyre, the medical examiner. Dr. McIntyre explained she had conducted an autopsy on Jack and had concluded if not for the heart failure, pancreatic cancer would have killed her father by the end of the year. Macy had sat in stunned silence, wondering why Jack hadn't called her earlier. Minutes before her flight, she had returned the doctor's call, promising to visit her tomorrow.

Despite the divorce, Jack had always sent his child support payments, and he never missed a birthday or Christmas. Her mother had never spoken a word against Jack, but as Macy had gotten older, she realized he had lived hard and occasionally put his medical skills to work for less scrupulous men. Her mother had once described Jack as complicated and regretted they hadn't tried harder to make it work.

Eight years had passed since she'd been in the salvage yard. It had been the spring she'd graduated from the FBI Academy in Quantico, and she had been driving to her first duty station in Denver. Austin hadn't been on the way, but she'd wanted to see her old man. When she'd arrived at the salvage yard, Macy and her father had spent the next two days rummaging through the yard for a radio and speakers for her old Toyota sedan. Though neither was a big talker, the visit had been kind of cool.

Now as the cab drove past the piles of crushed cars, bent motorcycles, and an occasional RV on blocks, an overwhelming sense of fatigue and loss hit her with the force and the finality of the salvage yard's hydraulic compactor.

Headlights slashed across the front of the trailer and flickered against the yellow crime scene tape wrapped around stakes positioned around the home. For an instant she couldn't move. When the cabdriver cleared his throat, she paid him, grabbed her backpack, and got out of the car. The evening heat hit her, and she thought about friends back east who were convinced dry heat was better than 100 percent humidity. She fished her phone from her pocket and turned on the flashlight.

Taking long strides across the dusty yard past Jack's late-model truck, she stepped over the tape and climbed the front steps past the lawn chair now roped off with red crime scene tape. She shone her light on the chair and its red, white, and blue woven straps and then on the cracked, sunbaked stained deck. Both were covered with blood.

The Ranger said Jack had been found in that chair, which ironically she had shipped to him two years ago for his birthday. She imagined him sitting in it, smoking a cigar, and then she pictured him in it screaming in pain and dying.

She pushed all the thoughts from her mind and read the orange seal placed over the doorjamb by the forensic examiner. It was dated yesterday and signed by someone named Ridgefield. The front doorknob and the wooden doorframe were covered with fine black fingerprint dust. On the deck beside her sat an overturned tented evidence marker.

She'd investigated enough scenes like this and wasn't intimidated by the **Do Not Enter** warning and the consequences listed in small print below it. She reached in her pocket, removed two of the black latex gloves always crammed in each of her jackets, and slipped them on. Using keys Jack had given her, she unlocked the door and broke the seal.

Careful not to touch the powder, she stepped into a dark interior that smelled of cigarette smoke, air freshener, and bourbon.

She switched on the overhead light, dropped her backpack by the door, and unholstered her gun. The place was trashed. A forensic team had come behind whoever had ransacked the place to dust windowsills, the refrigerator door handles, the broken picture frames scattered in the center of the room, and some of the now-crumpled and torn pictures. Jack had never liked strangers on his property, and this invasion added the final insult.

"I'm sorry, Jack." She tucked her phone in her back pocket.

Jack had called her a week ago, told her he'd stocked the refrigerator with a six-pack of Corona, her favorite. The call had been out of character, and when she had asked how he was doing, he had insisted everything was fine. She had instinctively known he wasn't *fine* and had promised herself a Texas vacation very soon.

One way or the other he must have known he was on borrowed time and that his call would be enough to ensure a visit from her. She reached for a cold beer, wedged the cap under a drawer handle, and with a quick jerk, popped the top off.

As she took a long pull, she returned to the broken picture frames, picked up one, and shook off the broken glass. It was a picture of her christening. The next picture she spotted featured her with Santa. A third captured the moment she'd taken one of her first steps. In this space, she was frozen in time as toddler, when she, her mother, and Jack had all lived together.

She crossed to the bedroom to find the mattress upended and sliced. The end table was overturned and the lamp smashed. More black powder everywhere, and evidence tents placed by one of Jack's pocketknives, his rotary phone now on the floor, and a newly shredded army-issue Bible he'd never gotten around to reading.

She holstered her gun and set her beer down on a dresser before straightening the table and setting the phone and Bible back on top. She pushed the bed frame away from the wall and peeled back a section of shag carpeting to expose a one-foot-square hatch. Jack had shown her the hiding place years ago. *This is where you look if I die, kid.*

She rooted around the small opening and pulled out a zip-top bag filled with twenty gold coins, a Sig Sauer, a spare set of keys to his truck, and a brand-new smartphone. She grabbed the keys, gun, and phone and set them on the nightstand before she returned the gold to its hiding place, closed the hatch, and replaced the carpeting.

When the bed was back in place, she dragged the mattress back onto the frame and dumped the blankets and sheets on it.

She sat on the edge, reached for the gun, and pulled back the slide just enough to confirm there was a round in the chamber. She tucked the Sig into her belt, picked up the beer, and took another long swig before reaching for the smartphone.

"Very tech savvy of you, Jack."

Her old man might have been able to take a car apart and put it back together, but he had been hopeless with computers and smartphones. As long as she'd known him, he'd always had a rotary phone. She turned on the smartphone and discovered it was password protected. Knowing Jack was a creature of habit, she typed in the numbers that corresponded to *Macy*—6229. The phone opened. If that hadn't worked, her next bet would have been 5225 for *Jack*. And her third bet would have been the year she was born, 1988.

As she searched the screen, she found no emails or, God forbid, texts. There were no apps that weren't standard with the phone or any kind of call history. "So why the phone, Jack?"

She double tapped the home button and discovered the Maps app and Photos app were running. She opened the Photos app first and saw the image of a post office mail receipt. Jack had sent a package to her by third-class mail on Friday. She'd not received it in Saturday's mail and guessed it was still floating through the post office system. "Curiouser and curiouser, Jack."

She opened the Maps app and found three saved addresses. When she pulled the first up, she discovered the location was twenty minutes west of here, and if her memory served, the area was remote. The second location was in East Austin. The third was in downtown Austin. "What the hell?"

If Jack had wanted to get her attention with the phone, he'd succeeded. He had left these addresses for a reason, and she sure as hell was going to check them out. The third address was 1213 Sabine Street and the least likely for Jack to visit, so she searched it first. The address matched the location of the Travis County Medical Examiner's Office. Interesting. She'd been in contact via voicemail with Faith McIntyre. Sometimes the world was a really small damn place. There was no staff page for the office, so she searched the site for "Faith McIntyre." Service was unreliable out here at the salvage yard, and the phone was slow to pull up any links.

As she waited, someone pounded hard on the front door of the trailer. She tensed and reached for the Sig. "Who is it?"

"It's Dirk Crow. Who the hell is in there?"

Dirk Crow. The brother she'd not seen since she was one or two. He was a stranger to her, but his voice had Jack's familiar deep notes, and for an instant, she thought Pop had come back from the dead.

"It's Macy Crow." She holstered her gun as she walked to the front door.

She turned on the deck light, flicked back the curtain, and saw the large man standing with his feet braced and his hand behind his back. She'd bet money it was curled around a weapon. Dark hair brushed off a face that reminded her of Pop's when she was a kid.

Dirk, nine years older than Macy, was the product of Jack's first marriage. He knew how to bend the law like Jack had and was as good at flying under the radar as their pop. Dirk, however, had no trouble breaking laws.

When she opened the door, she found herself indeed staring at a younger version of her pop. "The prodigal daughter has returned," she said.

He looked her up and down, his brown eyes wary. "Well, you sure are as white as I remember, *Snowflake*."

"So I am," she said.

Though they were Jack's legacy, there was no real connection between the two. They shared no childhood memories, or even DNA since she was adopted.

"Who told you about Pop?" Dirk asked.

"The Texas Rangers. And you?"

"Got a voicemail from Ledbetter." A small muscle pulsed in his jaw.

"You live on the property, and I bet the cops still had a hard time finding you," she said.

"They did." He shifted, his gaze narrowing as he looked at the lawn chair. "Ledbetter tells me Jack is at the morgue."

"Yeah."

"He wouldn't want a funeral."

"I know. I'll have him cremated."

"Why you?"

"Do you want to do it?" she asked.

"No. If you know anything about me, you know I don't like to get into town, and last I checked the funeral home is in town."

"Fair enough. That's why I'll do it." Her brother lived somewhere on the property and from what Jack said was good at keeping an eye on things and keeping the varmints away. "Where were you yesterday?"

He rubbed his temple. "I was in El Paso on business. I came back as soon as I got the message."

No sense asking what he'd been doing in El Paso. He'd not been here, and that was enough.

"Jack trusted you with all the paperwork," he said. "Is there a will?"

"That's the last thing on my mind right now. I want to know who killed Pop. Do you have any idea?"

Dirk's nostrils thinned and he drew in a breath, and then he scratched the black-and-gray stubble on his chin. "How the hell am I supposed to know?"

"Because you're the one who stuck around. You saw him all the time. And you'd know better than anyone if he'd done something to piss someone off."

"I hadn't seen Jack in over a week."

"And if Jack were into something he shouldn't have been, you wouldn't try to hide it, would you?" she asked.

"What do I have to hide from an FBI agent, sister?" he asked.

"I doubt we have time to talk about all that you're hiding, but unless it related to Pop, I don't care." She'd learned to bluff really well as an agent, knowing if she went in hot with a suspect and acted like she had the answers, they'd give up more than intended.

"Aren't you the badass agent?" He shook his head as he rubbed a splintered spot on the deck with the tip of his worn boot.

"When's the last time Jack went into Austin?" she asked.

"I have no idea."

"What about the local diner near here?" she countered. "Had he been there lately?"

"He barely left the yard in the last year. Why are you so worked up about where he's been? He was killed right here."

"Our old man was tortured and murdered. *Everything* he did in the last few weeks matters to me. What he did and who he saw is all a part of the puzzle."

Dirk shifted, as if he were trying to shake off the edginess that was eating at them both, but couldn't manage it. "Jack serviced a rough crowd from time to time. He patched up some dangerous people."

She'd warned Jack more times than she could count to keep clear of helping those who peddled in human flesh and drugs. "When was the last time he did that?"

"It's been a couple of years. Like I said, he's been a hermit mostly."

"Do you think he helped someone while you were gone?"

"How would I know?" He reached into his jeans pocket, pulled out a can of dip, and wedged a pinch between his cheek and gum. "You think someone like that killed him?"

"Or someone looking for one of his patients."

"He was stubborn. He'd not have ratted out anyone." Pride rang under the words.

"I know." She shook her head, some of the steam venting from her temper. "I'm going to find out who did this to Jack. I won't let his death go unsolved."

"That's good. Pop deserves as much."

She grabbed her backpack and walked out of the trailer, slamming the door behind her. She kept Dirk in her line of sight and a safe distance away, knowing a guy his size could beat the hell out of her without really trying. The truth was she didn't know or trust her brother.

He followed, holding up both his hands in surrender. "We got off on the wrong foot, Macy. I didn't come up here to stir trouble between us. I'm as upset as you, and I can be a blockhead like Jack used to be. Truce?"

Macy could play nice while she investigated Jack's murder. She crossed the deck and the hard red soil toward Jack's truck. "Sure. Truce."

"Where are you going?" Dirk asked.

"To a hotel."

She tossed her backpack into the front seat and slid behind the wheel before slamming the truck door and turning on the engine. As she pulled out of the yard, she glanced in her rearview mirror and caught Dirk opening the trailer door. If Jack had told him about the hidden compartment, he was in for a treat.

She drove for almost a mile before she hit a stoplight and pulled out the phone to check her browser for information on Faith McIntyre.

The pathologist's picture appeared, and the instant Macy got a good look, she did a double take. The woman was her age, she had blond hair, and they shared the same blue eyes. The likeness was so similar that she thought for a moment she was staring at her own picture. A closer look told her she wasn't. Faith's face was slightly rounder than hers, and her eyes looked a little less jaded.

The light turned green, and she drove ahead a few hundred yards toward a gas station. She pulled into the parking lot, not trusting herself to drive.

The close resemblance was unsettling. "What the hell?"

When she'd heard Dr. McIntyre's thick Texas drawl, she had never once thought it sounded familiar or even remotely like her own.

An unsettled feeling rolled through her, as if a quake were shaking the earth under her. Most kids might have fantasized about being adopted or wondered what it felt like, but she'd never had to wonder. Ever since she'd realized most raven-haired, olive-skinned parents didn't usually make blond-haired, blue-eyed babies nicknamed Snowflake, she'd assumed something was off. Now as she looked at Faith's picture, she knew if they weren't twins, there had to be a strong genetic connection between them. Her parents had come clean about her adoption when she was eight, but they'd never once mentioned she had siblings. Jesus, why hadn't they told her she wasn't alone?

Her head was spinning as the screen image glowed. She wasn't sure how long she sat before she drew in a steadying breath. "Shit, Jack. A simple conversation would have made better sense than all the secrets."

One way or another, she'd meet Faith McIntyre. But for now, the Hill Country and East Austin addresses waited. She typed in the rural address, and when it loaded, she took a right onto the road and drove past a lone strip mall and scattered homes before the turnoff to Blanco, Texas, appeared.

The moonlight was bright enough to illuminate sparse brown land covered with scrub trees and bushes. But the land and her surroundings barely registered as her mind spiraled around the idea that she might have a sister. Did Faith McIntyre know about her? One way or another, they would have questions for each other.

Which led to renewed questions about her birth mother, who had always been shrouded in *we-don't-knows* and mumbled comments about a closed adoption. If her mother or Jack really knew who she was, they'd never said, regardless of how often she'd pressed.

Her headlights cut into the deepening darkness. Hoping to settle her racing mind, she switched on the radio and found a country western station. She'd lived in Dallas growing up before moving east for college and then the academy, but despite all the bland apartments scattered across the country, she always felt at home when she heard country music. She cranked it, hoping the melody would drown out her thoughts.

The Maps app on Jack's phone reminded her of an upcoming turn, snapping her back to the present. She slowed as she searched the road for a sign. There wasn't one, and she was halfway past a small rusted mailbox when she realized she'd found her turn. She backed up and took the left, grimacing as the dry brown dust kicked up around her car.

Ahead, her headlights sliced over a brick house that faced east. The windows were boarded up, and the roof looked like it had taken a beating in a recent storm. It had a low porch that ran across the entire front and a single rocker that stood eerily still.

She stopped. As the engine idled, she studied the house bathed in moonlight. Out here unexpected guests could just as easily be met with the barrel of a shotgun as a welcome, a lesson she'd learned in the Colorado mountains her first year on the job. She'd been searching for several missing girls. The woman on the other end of the gun had demanded her name as her gnarled finger twitched above the trigger. Macy had grabbed the gun and twisted it out of her hands, but her supervisor had reamed her out for ending up in the tight spot.

After a few minutes and still no signs of life, she shut off her truck's engine, checked the gun holstered on her hip, and got out of the car. The day's blazing heat still hadn't dissipated.

Sweat beaded on her back almost as soon as she started walking toward the house. A rusted wind vane squeaked softly as her gaze swept the entire area a second time.

Climbing the front steps, she noticed the shades were drawn. There were also footprints in the dust scattered on the porch. "Was that you, Jack?"

She stood to the right of the door. Hand tightening on the grip of her weapon, she knocked on the front door and waited. Being out here alone at night wasn't the smartest maneuver and something she'd never dare if this wasn't so damn personal. A round object caught her peripheral vision, and she looked up to find a small camera covering the front porch.

The house remained silent, with no response to a second knock. She descended the stairs and walked around the back. Moonlight glittered on an old set of patio furniture. Windows facing the back of the barren property were also covered in shades.

She then walked to the back of the property. Dust coated her ankle boots and the hems of her jeans.

Other than the footprints on the porch, it looked as if no one had been out here in years.

Her gaze was then drawn to a row of three large rocks, arranged in a perfectly straight line. That kind of symmetry didn't happen in nature, and for some reason, the hair on the back of her neck rose. She realized what she was looking at. Grave markers.

As she unholstered her weapon, she moved slowly toward the stones and saw a set of large footprints that circled the first stone several times. The footprints trailed to the second stone and the third. She knelt by the first and placed her hand on the sunbaked rock. The stones had no markings, but they were spaced almost exactly five feet apart.

Jack had hidden this phone in a compartment beneath the carpet for a damn good reason. Using the Maps app was way out of his wheelhouse. "Pop, the phone tells me you were out here, but it doesn't tell me why."

She scrolled to the next address. East Austin. She was convinced her old man had left her a trail of bread crumbs, and in her entire career, she'd never been afraid to chase a lead. But this time, she truly feared what she'd find.

CHAPTER FIVE

Monday, June 25, 11:30 p.m.

Faith didn't give the man a second thought as she crossed the tiled lobby of the hotel. Laughter and the clink of glasses drifted out from the hotel bar as she stepped onto the elevator. Her attention shifted to room 701.

As the gilded doors slid closed, a hand reached between and pushed them open. She tensed for a second, thinking her admirer had followed, but then breathed a sigh of relief as Hayden casually stepped into the elevator.

He stood stock straight, staring ahead without acknowledging her. Broad shoulders, muscled thighs, and braced feet commanded most of the horizontal real estate, and over six foot two inches of height ate into a healthy portion of the elevator's vertical space.

"Looks like you made a new friend," he said.

Tucking her purse under her arm, she locked her gaze with his in the door's reflection. "Not a friend."

"He's been watching you for at least a half hour."

"As I'm sure half the people in that room were tonight."

Hayden was a foot from her, but his proximity warmed her skin. Touching him was tempting, but elevator cameras kept her gaze forward as overhead music reminded her of piña coladas and dancing in the rain.

The lighted elevator panel ticked off the floors until reaching seven. Hayden placed his hand over the open door and waited for her to exit.

She moved down the hallway, following the signs to 701. It felt good to be away from the crowds, the forced smiles and pretending.

Hayden's steady steps followed, and when they reached the door, he produced a key and opened it. She passed him and flipped on the lights.

The room wasn't fancy, but a shaving kit on the dresser, dry-cleaned shirts in the closet, and the closed curtains told her he'd been there earlier. He'd commented once that he lived out of hotel rooms for the most part and stayed on the go. She'd wager if she opened the curtains, she'd find a view of air-conditioning units or a brick wall. But then neither of them had come here for the sparkling view of Austin.

She sat on the edge of the bed and removed her heels as he tossed his hat on the chair. Next came his jacket and tie, which he hung in the closet. He stepped back, sat on the edge of the bed, and removed his boots as she pulled off her earrings and set them by the television.

This was how it had been with them. There was never a heady rush for either to get naked. Each took their time undressing, savoring the anticipation, looking at the other as if daring them to rush. It was sort of a game. Who would give in to temptation first?

She unbuttoned her blouse and shrugged it off before she turned her back to him and felt his calloused fingers slowly pull down the back zipper of her pants, exposing her lace underwear. He trailed a finger up her spine to the clasp of her bra, which he unhooked.

Her breath caught in her throat as her belly tightened. This was what she'd been craving since she'd last seen him four days ago. She wiggled the slacks over her hips and let them fall to her ankles. She stepped out of them and hung them and her blouse next to his clothes in the closet. Knowing he was watching, she slipped off her lace bra, panties, and lace-trimmed thigh highs. When she turned, he was no longer by the bed but standing inches from her. He still wore his khakis, but he'd stripped off his shirt.

Again, she didn't hurry. Let the anticipation build. Let the wanting grow so sharp that it cut away everything in her life.

He glided his hands along her waist, but instead of pulling her toward him, he turned her toward the mirrored closet door.

This was also how it went with them. Neither wanted to look into the other's eyes. She didn't want to see him as a person. And she guessed he was pretending she was the woman he still loved. His hand slid over her buttocks and squeezed hard enough to make her try to squirm away.

He reached around and cupped her mound, rubbing it until she was wet. When she began to wriggle, he drove his fingers between the folds. She sucked in a breath, not raising her eyes to his because she didn't want to see him. She only wanted to feel.

His zipper opened, she heard the rip of foil, and he fumbled only for a moment before he pressed the tip of his erection against her bare skin. She flattened her hands against the mirror and arched toward him. He spread her legs and pushed into her with one hard thrust so abruptly her breath caught in her throat.

He hesitated, allowing her body to adjust to him. Again, no kisses. No words. Just patience for her body to fully open. When the tightening eased, he moved inside her slowly as his fingers pressed against her now very moist center.

He'd learned very quickly which buttons it took to set her on fire, and he was pressing them all. A moan escaped her lips as he shoved into her harder with a fevered thrust she'd not experienced with him before. The tight control he always maintained had slipped, and she could feel a creature inside of him stirring.

He pushed into her faster, and she found herself racing toward the edge of an abyss that she so desperately wanted to tumble into. With him inside her, the world faded, and she could simply surrender to sensation.

A groan rumbled in his chest, and for the first time she opened her eyes. He was staring at her with a mixture of pleasure and pain.

She pushed his hand away and pressed her fingers to her clitoris. He gripped both her hips with his hands, and he thrust as she drew tighter and tighter circles around her core.

And then a fuse lit, caught fire, and the explosion propelled her over the edge into the void. Her eyes closed, she arched back, and he thrust into her one last time before his body stiffened and the muscles in his neck flexed.

Both stood still, breathless and savoring the last remnants of the climax. He smoothed his hand over her belly in a possessive, almost regretful way, as he slowly pulled out of her and stepped back.

He vanished into the bathroom, and as he discarded his condom, she reached for her panties and bra. She shimmied into both and sat on the edge of the bed as she pulled her thigh highs on. He came out of the bathroom and shrugged on his shirt. She stepped into her pants and tucked in her blouse. Without a word she turned away from him, and he zipped them up. She worked the left and then right shoes on, and then tipping her head and jostling her hair back, she put her earrings back on.

He was buttoning his shirt, but she could again feel him watching.

She picked up her purse, caught the rigid set of his jaw. "Keep me posted on the Ledbetter case. And be safe, Captain."

"Will do."

As she moved past him, he caught her arm and held her. She watched, uncertain. And then he leaned in and for the first time, kissed her on the lips. It was still hungry, but there was also something deeper entwined with the desire.

When he pulled back, she moistened her lips. "A kiss? Are we going steady, Captain?"

"There's nothing steady about us."

"Thankfully, no."

He released her arm. "Why'd you say yes to me the first time?"

"I don't know." She'd been very self-conscious that first time he'd entered her, and he must have sensed it had been a while.

Now without another word, she left the hotel room, the door shutting behind her as she made her way to the elevator. Wanting and loneliness trailed behind her, and she quickened her pace, knowing sooner or later they'd catch up to her.

***

In his car outside the Driskill Hotel, he tugged at the cuffs of his custom-made shirt, pleased that he'd blended so well with the city's finest in their swanky hotel. There was a time when he would never have made it past the front door. The bellman would have taken one look at his ripped jeans and dirty hands and called the cops. But those days, he kept reminding himself, were long gone. Not only would he never go back, but he would do whatever it took to keep them as far away from him as possible.

He'd have followed Faith if not for the Texas Ranger who'd caught the elevator just as its doors were closing. He had seen the Ranger arrive earlier and noted the two had exchanged a few words, but then they had appeared to go their separate ways. Until the elevators.

So Faith and the Ranger had a thing. Interesting. No one else had seemed to notice them. Attention to detail was what had gotten him off the streets and earned him a reputation as one of the best to call when a problem needed to be discreetly taken care of. Granted, this latest list of names was going to be a challenge, but that's why he got paid the big bucks.

The front doors of the hotel lobby opened, and Faith stepped out into the ring of light. She glanced at her phone as the bellman approached and a black four-door sedan pulled up. She tipped the bellman, slid into the back seat, and the car drove off, its taillights vanishing around the corner.

When he'd seen her picture in the lobby, he'd made a few inquiries about her in general. She enjoyed a solid standing as a forensic pathologist, had a curious mind, and had a reputation for being tenacious. He wasn't sure why the likes of Jack Crow and Faith McIntyre were on the same list, but it wasn't for him to question, only to execute orders.

He still didn't know how much she did or didn't know about the package, but that didn't really matter. She was on the list, so he would make the time to have a chat with her.

His phone vibrated with an alert from the camera he'd posted at the country ranch. As he glanced at the screen, he wasn't sure what he expected. A random coyote. A sagebrush's prickly arms reaching up toward a moonlit sky.

He sure had not expected to see a woman walking toward the stones in the dark. She knelt, ran her hand over the rock, and then looked to the other two as if she'd recognized them for what they were.

He stared at her face for a long moment. Then did a double take in the direction of the car that had just carried Faith away. The woman at the ranch looked exactly like Faith. Jack had been so mutinously silent during their chat, and now he knew why. There'd not been one baby on that night in 1988, but two. Twins.

When the phone vibrated with a text, he cursed until he saw the number.

He perched a cigarette on his lips and flicked the flint wheel of a gold-plated lighter until a flame appeared. He inhaled deeply, savoring the burn as the smoke flowed out of his nose and mouth.

Are we on track with our project?

He stared at the glowing tip of his cigarette and then typed. All is going according to plan.

Have you found it?

He hesitated. Not yet. But I will.

Watching the woman walk back to the truck that he knew belonged to Jack Crow, he could feel the skin on the back of his neck prickle the way it did when there was a problem. Who the hell was she? And then it hit him. She was Jack's kid. Macy Crow. She was the little kid in all the photos he'd smashed. When she had looked up at the camera, her gaze had been defiant and annoyed.

You need to wrap this up, his employer typed.

So you've told me. He was a professional and didn't need coaching.

All this needs to go away quietly and quickly.

The tone of the text reminded him that no matter how far he'd climbed, there would always be someone adding their two cents. Very annoying, and he had his limits. I'm on it.

Macy had been to the ranch, no doubt tipped off by Crow. If she was curious enough to go to the ranch at night alone, she was tenacious like her old man. He admired her grit.

Where would he send Macy next, if he were Crow?

When the answer came, he almost laughed.

CHAPTER SIX

Monday, June 25, 11:50 p.m.

Macy checked into a local, nondescript hotel that looked exactly like every other in the chain. With a pizza and diet soda and her backpack on her shoulder, she quietly slipped into a room near the staircase. Since she'd become an agent, she'd gotten more careful about knowing her exits and always having a retreat strategy mapped out in her head.

She tossed the pizza box on the bureau and her backpack on the bed. She grabbed a slice of pizza and turned on the shower. As she pulled off her hair tie, she bit into the pizza and toed off her boots. The first bite reminded her she'd not eaten in almost a day, and she polished off the slice in seconds. She stripped off her jacket, weapon and holster, shirt, and jeans and kicked her dusty clothes to the side as the steam rose up in the bathroom.

She stepped under the steaming spray, letting the heat sink into her muscles, and thought about what needed to be done. It was a given she would have to contact local police and let them know about the house and suspected old graves.

It would be easy to stay in the shower and drain every last bit of hot water from the hotel boiler, but that wasn't going to help Jack.

"Get it together, Macy." She shut off the water, toweled dry, and wrapped her hair and body in new towels. She grabbed two more slices of pizza, sat on her bed, and opened her computer. She went directly to YouTube and searched "Faith McIntyre, Travis County."

Several results appeared immediately. The top one was a news report from earlier in the summer titled SAN MARCOS'S BODY RANCH. She took another bite of pizza and clicked on the link.

The first camera shots were of a metal fence enclosing land covered by tall grass and grazing goats. A young reporter stood at the entrance by a crude gate and started spouting statistics about the Texas State University Forensic Anthropology Center in San Marcos. It was a research facility stocked with donated bodies, stripped of all their clothing and laid out on their backs so that scientists could study decomposition rates. The camera panned over several bodies protected by wire cages.

The reporter cut to a woman inspecting a sun-bleached skull as she began to speak in a husky voice tinged with a Texas accent. The voice Macy had heard on her voicemail.

The reporter introduced Dr. Faith McIntyre, and Macy leaned in and watched closely as the woman looked up toward the camera. Macy hit pause and stared at the face that could have been her own. Same blue eyes. Same cheekbones. Lips. Ears. Same everything.

She opened a new window and quickly searched social media sites, but found no trace of Faith. Like her, Faith had no presence. She did another search and found a reference to Faith, who had appeared in the paper yesterday promoting an upcoming fundraiser for a youth shelter.

If she wasn't this woman's identical twin, then she was related in some way. After all these years of not resembling anyone in her family, she'd found someone who looked exactly like her. That elicited a bone-deep satisfaction.

She brushed a tear from her eye—along with any temptation to call Faith right now. First, Jack.

Focusing, Macy searched the last address Jack had visited after he'd been to the ranch. The address matched a local bar in East Austin called Second Chances. On the bar's website she learned the place had been owned for almost thirty years by a guy named Danny Garnet. Garnet didn't look familiar to her, and she guessed his age to be a few years younger than Jack's. One of the postings on Garnet's social media page promoted a Memorial Day celebration at the bar where all veterans drank for free.

"Why did Jack visit you, Garnet?"

Maybe the two had served together back in the day. Maybe they were friends. There was only one way to find out.

She rose and redressed in a fresh pair of jeans and shirt she'd crammed in her backpack very early that morning, dried her hair, and reapplied some makeup. Staring at her reflection, she realized her hands were shaking slightly as she brushed on her mascara. She flexed her fingers, willing them to settle.

"Sure, the foundation of your life might have been shot to shit," she said to her reflection. "But you will deal like you always do."

What had Jack used to say to her? *Toughen up, buttercup.* The last time he'd told her that, she'd called him during her FBI training at Quantico. The O-course was kicking her ass, and she'd wanted Pop to lend a sympathetic ear. When he'd uttered the words, she'd told him to shut up. He'd laughed, and then she'd started laughing. The next day she had made it through under the six-minute deadline.

She snapped a picture of her driver's license, as well as her FBI identification, and then for good measure a selfie. She sent all three to her computer. She opened an email, dragged in the pictures, and typed in Faith's business email address.

> My name is Macy Crow. I'm Jack Crow's daughter.
> We've spoken only through voicemail, but we need
> to talk in person.

This might seem out of left field, but I believe we're related. I'm adopted and have been searching for my biological roots for several years. My adoptive father, Jack Crow, passed away on Sunday, and ironically, you were the pathologist who took care of him.

I've attached two addresses that Jack left me on a prepaid phone I found at his trailer. I've been to the one in the country, and I've got a gut feeling something very wrong happened there.

Macy Crow

P.S. A picture is worth a thousand words, so I've enclosed a few of mine.

Instead of sending the email now, she scheduled it for five p.m. tomorrow. The delay gave her an out in case she got cold feet or had a chance to have this conversation with Faith in person. And given she just might have found three graves, she had to at least make contact with Faith in case it went sideways at Garnet's.

She tugged her boots back on, but opted to leave her computer behind on her desk, along with Jack's keys and the phone he'd left her. Again, if it all went bad at the bar or the email failed to send or whatever else could go wrong, because Murphy's Law always bit hard, the cops would have the addresses.

Macy checked her service weapon before settling it back in its holster on her hip and pulling on her jacket. She checked her backpack for her wallet and ID as she always did and left the room. She placed the Do Not Disturb sign on the doorknob.

At one in the morning, she stood in the lobby and ordered a car, knowing the credit card purchase would create a digital trail that, God willing, any rookie cop could follow. The car arrived five minutes later, and she settled in the back seat, her backpack beside her. She watched the lights of the city race past as they drove east and toward the bar on Third Street.

When the driver pulled up, she found Second Chances to be fairly unimpressive from the outside. The windows were small, the front door solid, and a red neon **OPEN** sign flashed above the entrance.

Out of the car, she drew in a breath, crossed the street to the tavern's entrance, and pulled open its heavy wooden door.

It was a classic Austin bar featuring a funky decor that included local art. The ceiling was painted a deep blue and covered in white clouds and stars. The round tables were painted different colors, and the chairs looked as if they had been sourced from multiple locations. Every stick of furniture in the bar looked as if it had been repurposed. What might have looked shabby in the daylight passed for charming at night.

A country western song rumbled from a jukebox as the heavy scents of cigarette smoke and whiskey mingled. Conversation buzzed as a flat-screen television broadcast a boxing match as she crossed to the bar made of white oak and covered in a thick laminate.

Dozens of house-brand liquor bottles were shelved against a mirrored wall reflecting bright task lighting. Beside the bar was a corkboard that featured local sales, festivals, and even a reward for information on a missing girl named Paige Sheldon. Six years on the human trafficking squad had her studying the girl's face and name. The girl had vanished almost three months ago, and Macy knew from experience that the chances of finding her alive were almost nil. She tried not to think about what happened to pretty girls taken by monsters.

The bartender at the other end had his back to her. He was a big man with immense shoulders and dark hair pulled back into a ponytail.

Before he could turn, saloon doors separating the front of the house from the back swung open.

The woman who appeared was in her late forties. She had red hair fashioned into a topknot sprouting loose curls that fell across a pale face splattered with freckles. Her smile was quick and warm. She wore a black Second Chances T-shirt that stretched over large breasts and a full belly.

"Hope you haven't been sitting there long?" the woman said.

"Nope. Just arrived."

She wiped the bar with a clean rag. "Looks like Garnet is preoccupied. What can I get you?"

"I'd love a beer. Draft will do."

"Coming right up." She placed an iced mug under the tap and pulled until beer and foam spilled over the edge. She set a napkin on the bar and then the beer, all in one fluid move. "You new in town? I've never seen you in here before."

Macy took a sip. "I was born and raised in Texas, but I haven't been back in years."

"I can still hear a bit of a Texas accent."

She took another sip, deciding it was decent. "Raised in Dallas mostly by my mama."

"Once Texas gets in your blood, there's no getting it out." The woman filled a wooden bowl with salted peanuts and set it in front of Macy. "So what brings you back?"

"My dad passed. Cleaning out his things."

"Sorry to hear that, baby. My name is Heather."

"I'm Macy. I was going through my dad's things, and I found a note saying he had a good friend who worked here," she lied. "Danny Garnet."

The woman's smile didn't vanish, but it seemed to freeze. "Well, you found the right place. Garnet owns the joint. He's the lug over there."

"I didn't know my father that well, so I guess I'm trying to talk to anyone who knew him." It was always best to stick to the truth unless a lie was necessary. Made it easier to keep the stories straight.

The woman fiddled with a ringlet that coiled behind her ear. "Who was your daddy? I might know him as well."

Macy studied the woman's face closely as she took another sip of beer. "Jack Crow."

Heather's smile dimmed, and she dropped her gaze. Macy knew enough about body language to know the woman recognized Jack's name, and she'd looked away so she could compose an answer she thought would work best. "Jack Crow?"

"Yeah. He owned a salvage yard about fifteen miles from here. I barely knew Jack growing up, so I'm on this discovery tour. I only have a few days before I have to get back to school. I teach kindergarten."

Heather raised her gaze, and the smile returned. "I had to think for a minute. It's been a long time since I've seen Jack."

Maybe Heather had not been there the day Jack visited. Or maybe she was lying. "He's a hard man to forget."

Heather tapped her index finger on the bar as if pinning down a memory. "I remember a big bear of a man like Garnet."

"That was Jack. You think I could talk to Garnet?"

"Sure thing, baby."

Heather tossed a faltering smile and then moved down to the end of the bar. She placed her hand on Garnet's shoulder, and he looked a little annoyed until she leaned in and spoke. Garnet's body straightened, and his smile faded. Macy couldn't hear, but she guessed news of Jack Crow's kid arriving wasn't good.

When Garnet turned, he wore a broad grin on his face. He studied her as he moved closer.

She sipped her beer, meeting his gaze and doing her best to smile even as she wondered if he was the guy who had broken Jack's fingers and knee before her old man's heart had seized. "You must be Garnet."

"I sure am. And you're Jack Crow's kid. Heather tells me Jack died?"

"Heart attack on Sunday."

The lines on Garnet's face deepened. "I can't believe it."

"Yeah. It was out of the blue. No one saw it coming," she said.

She imagined the worry and sadness that had flashed in his gaze giving way to something more hard and calculating. But whatever she thought she'd seen was gone as quickly as it had come. "He said you two were friends back in the day."

"We sure were. He saved my ass a few times." That thousand-watt smile dimmed just a tad. "So how did you find me?"

"Saw a note with your name on it. Jack didn't have many friends, so I took a chance."

"Pretty savvy for a kindergarten teacher."

She laughed. "You've got to be quick to stay ahead of those five-year-olds."

His deep-throated laugh rang a little hollow. "I wouldn't know. I don't have kids."

She lowered her gaze to her beer, not wanting to put him on the defensive. She paused for effect before she slowly lifted her eyes. "Had you seen Jack lately?"

"It's been years. We always said we'd keep up after the army, but you know how it goes."

She nodded as she sipped her beer. "I was just hoping to learn more about my old man. Figured I'd try."

"I wish there was more I could tell you about him. All my stories are over thirty years old."

"I'll take an old story," she quipped.

He shrugged. "When we were in the army, I got into some trouble with the MPs. I think they'd have thrown me in the brig and tossed the key if Jack hadn't intervened. He could schmooze anyone when he put his mind to it. The MPs let me go, and Jack never told a soul. He was the kind of guy you could always rely on."

"But you two lost touch?"

"It happens. Life moves on."

She wondered if Jack had gone to his grave protecting Garnet's secret. "That was Jack. Loyal to a fault."

"Drink up. You've barely touched your beer," Garnet said.

She raised the mug to her lips. "No letter, no call, nothing recently? Just seems odd he'd write your name down and not follow through with a visit."

He grinned, shaking his finger at her. "Now you really sound like a cop."

She laughed as she patted her index finger against her temple. "Being a teacher, I'm saddled with an analytical mind that won't accept an unsolved problem."

"I guess you're a chip off the old block. Jack was like that."

Macy reached for her wallet, but Garnet shook his head. "How much do I owe you?"

His gaze sharpened as if he were either trying to pry behind her words or reaching for an old memory that danced in the distance. And then he smiled again. "Your money is no good here. Beer's on the house."

"Are you sure?"

"Positively."

"I appreciate the time and the brew." Her father had been murdered, and he'd left her three addresses. Jack knew there was trouble brewing. He'd called the Rangers and set her up as his contingency plan. Now it was her turn to call the Texas Rangers and let them know what she'd found.

"Sure thing, kid. Sure thing. Is there going to be a funeral for Jack?"

"No. He wasn't crazy about that kind of thing."

"You're right. He never liked a fuss." He shook his head as he studied her features. "You must take after your mother, because you sure don't look like Jack."

She grinned. "I get that a lot. My mom always said I looked like her mother." She recited her mother's lie because she'd heard it so many times, and it felt more natural than the real truth of her life.

"Brenda was your mother?"

"That's right. She and Jack split when I was two. Did you know my mom?"

"I met her once when she and your father were dating."

If he'd known Brenda, whose skin and hair were as dark as Jack's, and he had any inkling about genetics, he might wonder how the couple had grown Macy from scratch.

He filled a fresh bowl of peanuts for her and aligned it precisely next to the other bowl. "How is Brenda?"

"She passed eight years ago."

"Sorry to hear that. What was it?"

"Lung cancer. The smokes finally got her."

Before he could ask another question, a patron at the end of the bar waved Garnet over, and he told her to hold that thought as he refilled the man's mug.

She glanced in the mirror behind the bar, catching its reflection of the room, looking for signs that anyone was watching her. There were a few men checking her out, but with her bitch face locked in place, she had another minute or two before some crazy soul dared approach.

A man on her right took the bar seat beside her and drew Garnet's attention. She didn't bother a glance as his rusty voice ordered a scotch.

He didn't acknowledge her but reached in the bowl of nuts and scooped up a handful. He crunched on nuts as he waited for Garnet to bring him his drink. Finally, he asked, "Do I know you?"

"I don't think so, pal." A glance to her right revealed a good-looking man in jeans and a V-neck lightweight pullover. He'd pushed up his sleeves, revealing sinewy forearms.

"I could have sworn I saw you the other day," he said.

If she'd been feeling generous, she'd have given him a point for persistence, but she wasn't, so he got two strikes for his inability to read social cues. "Not me. I don't live here."

"What brings you to Austin?" he asked.

"I didn't come for conversation."

He laughed. "Ouch. Tough crowd. My name is—"

"I don't want to know." With her new friend sitting here, she'd have no opportunity to really ask Garnet anything and decided her visit was officially a bust. She pulled a twenty from her pocket and laid it on the bar, knowing she didn't want anything for free from Garnet.

She took one last long pull from her beer and slid off her barstool.

"Leaving so soon?" the man asked.

"I have an early flight in the morning."

"Back to?"

"An enchanted land far, far away."

He scooped up another handful of nuts. "It's a small world. My Spider-Man sense says we'll see each other again." He tossed several in his mouth. Crunch. Crunch.

She rose and left the bar. After crossing the street, she decided to cut down the side street as she fished her phone from her pocket and ordered another car. The driver promised to meet her on the street that ran parallel to this one near the park. When she wondered why, she then realized this section was one-way.

As she walked, she saw another poster of Paige Sheldon. This one was torn and weather-beaten, and someone had written a mustache over her smiling lips. When did a missing girl become a damned joke?

Without thinking she snapped a picture of it with her phone. Might mean nothing, but better to have the reference at her fingertips.

Walking away from the bar down Third Street, she searched her phone for Mitchell Hayden's phone number. Unlike Spider-Man's sense, she did trust her own, and it was telling her that the morning was going to be too late to call the Rangers.

Just outside the arched entrance of Comal Pocket Park, she saw a homeless man. He was wearing an army-issue jacket and when he looked up, their gazes locked. For a quick instant he reminded her of Jack, and she wondered where Jack would have ended up without the salvage yard. Knowing she'd given her last twenty to the bartender, she crossed the street to an ATM, pulled out sixty bucks, and returned to him. She gave him twenty.

"Thanks, pretty lady," he said.

"Don't drink it. Get something to eat."

"I will." He crumpled the bill up into a tight fist. "I was just dreaming about a hamburger."

"Now is the time to get one." She thought about the poster of the girl and pulled it up on her phone. "Have you been around here long?"

"Years. This is my home."

She showed him the picture. "Did you ever see this girl?"

"The missing girl."

"That's right. She vanished in May."

"I saw her around. She wasn't here long, though."

"Where do you think she went?"

He shrugged. "People come and go. That's the way it is."

"Did the cops ever talk to you?" Macy asked.

His eyes narrowed. "Are you a cop?"

"No, man," she lied. "Just a girl wondering if I'm even playing with the right puzzle pieces."

He laughed. "That happens to me."

She smiled as she studied the doodles made on the picture on the poster. "Seems like people have forgotten her. Like it's all a joke."

"People forget, but I don't."

"What do you remember?"

"She was nice. She was scared. She shouldn't have been on the street."

No kid should have. "When did you see her last?"

"I don't remember." He dropped his gaze and wrapped his arms around his folded knees.

Why the hell she was talking to a homeless guy in the middle of East Austin about this girl was beyond her.

"Okay, well, thanks anyway."

He didn't respond, and she figured the chances of him eating a hamburger were slim, but she kept moving down with her sights set on the car's location and her attention on the search for the Ranger's number.

What happened next came so fast.

Headlights flicked on and tires spun over the pavement, kicking up gravel. An engine revved and had her turning. She saw the headlights moving, the truck quickly picking up speed and aimed directly toward her. She started running and took a hard left onto Comal Street, pumping her arms, knowing the truck was gaining on her.

In the next instant, she felt metal crashing into the back of her left hip with such force it sent her flying to the right onto the pavement like she were no heavier than a rag doll. Her backpack flew into the shadows seconds before her head, back, and torso hit the ground hard. Brakes skidded and the tires kicked up rocks as the truck turned around.

Headlights glared on her broken body, and she knew one arm was bent at a sharp right angle and a femur bone jutted out of her thigh. A deep gash on her forehead oozed blood that dripped into her eyes, blurring her vision. Adrenaline rocketed through her body, but she knew it wouldn't last much longer. She'd been careless, and it was going to cost her her life.

In the distance, she heard the homeless dude screaming as pain shot through her body. She raised her head slightly and saw that he was waving his arms as she struggled to hang on to consciousness. She tried to drag herself away, but pain paralyzed her.

Truck wheels screeched in reverse, away from the approach of the flashing blue lights of a cop car. Agony hammered her body as she looked up at the stars, heard the man yelling now for an ambulance.

Macy thought about Jack, her mother, Faith, and the stones she'd seen on that barren stretch of land. She thought about the poster of the missing girl. Would she also die like that lost girl and just be forgotten?

As much as Macy wanted to say something, she couldn't form the words to whoever was now pressing two fingers to her throat.

"Hold on for me," the woman said.

But Macy's grip on consciousness was slipping fast as the darkness rose up around her, pried her fingers free, and sucked her under to what she accepted as death.

CHAPTER SEVEN

Tuesday, June 26, 4:00 a.m.

The early-morning air was humid and thick as Hayden pulled up to the flashing lights of three Austin cop cars parked on the perimeter of Comal Pocket Park. His partner's black SUV was parked across the street, and a collection of news vans had already gathered down the block on the other side of the yellow crime scene tape.

Out of his vehicle, he drew in a deep breath and took a moment to settle his hat on his head before he strode down the side street toward the crime scene and the female uniformed officer. "I'm Captain Hayden with the Texas Rangers."

"Yes, sir. Officer Holcombe. Ranger Mike Brogan is over at the impact site."

He'd worked with Brogan a few times. The tall, lean Texan, though only in his early thirties, was sharp and worked harder than any two men. He kept his brown hair cut short, his shirts starched, and his boots polished. The guy was all business.

As Hayden pulled on black latex gloves, he ducked under the tape, and his weathered boots crunched on the uneven paved sidewalk that ran along the park's chain-link fence. A series of yellow numbered cones marked several sets of skid marks. Preserving them would help tell the story later in court.

Brogan squatted by a large patch of blood and an ankle boot, a collection of used gauze pads, IV bags, and discarded syringes close by. Hayden gave his name to the forensic technician, whose job was to record every visitor to the crime scene. No one came in or out of a crime scene without leaving something behind, and all the comings and goings could be an issue at trial.

Hayden moved closer for a better look. "I was told it was a hit-and-run."

Brogan stood. "That's right."

"Is the victim dead or alive?"

"Alive, barely. But she's in bad shape, and there's a good chance she won't make it. Head injuries, broken leg, and a mangled arm."

"Where is the victim now?"

"She has been transported and is in surgery."

"Witnesses?" Hayden asked.

"A homeless man flagged down a patrol car. As the cop rolled up, the hit-and-run vehicle sped off. The officer saw the woman's condition and opted not to chase but give first aid." He glanced at his notebook and flipped through pages filled with precise notes.

"Do we know who the victim is?" Hayden asked.

"You're going to love this."

"Somehow, I doubt it."

"We found her backpack on the sidewalk. It must have flown off of her when she was hit. Her name is Macy Crow. She's an FBI agent."

"What?"

"Yeah. Card-carrying, gun-toting FBI agent. Do you know of any FBI operations in Austin? I know a few bank-fraud cases, but I doubt there's much bank fraud happening in this park at night." He handed Hayden the agent's badge.

"Macy Crow?"

"That's right."

"We had another victim of the same surname in the medical examiner's office late yesterday. His name was Jack Crow. I spoke to Macy Crow yesterday on the phone."

Hayden studied the picture for several moments. He could feel his expression hardening. Macy Crow had blond hair, a narrow face, and sharp blue eyes, but what seized his attention was her stunning likeness to Faith McIntyre. "Is this some kind of joke, Brogan?"

The Ranger looked at him as if he were a little insulted. "Why would you think it's a joke, Captain?"

Hayden studied the woman's picture again. The resemblance was too close to ignore. He knew enough about Faith to know she was the only child of parents now deceased. "She looks like our medical examiner, Faith McIntyre."

"I thought the same," Brogan said, shaking his head. "What do you make of that?"

"I don't know. When was Ms. Crow struck by the vehicle?"

"Two hours ago."

Hayden had left Faith not long before that. She'd been leaving the Driskill, and he'd seen her get into the car from his hotel window. Of all nights, he'd opted to splurge on a view, thinking she'd enjoy it. But the sudden jolt of concern had him reaching for his phone. "And you're sure the victim wasn't Dr. McIntyre?"

"Nothing to suggest she's the doc. Why do you ask?"

Hayden ignored the question and dialed Faith's number. She picked up on the second ring, and her voice was remarkably clear.

"Faith McIntyre."

"Doc, this is Mitchell Hayden. Sounds like you're up."

"Yes, I am. What can I do for you?"

He heard the curiosity in her tone, but she was too careful to make any kind of innuendo until she understood the true nature of the call.

"I'm at a crime scene, and there was some confusion. But it looks like it's been cleared up."

"Are you sure?" she asked. "If you need a body examined, I can come in."

Hayden glanced down at the blood and discarded bandage packets. "So far the victim is still alive. I'll touch base in the morning. Sorry to trouble you."

"Okay. Hopefully the victim won't be coming my way."

"Did you speak to Jack Crow's daughter?"

"We traded voicemail messages. We've not spoken directly. She was headed to Austin. Why?"

"I've got to run. I'll call you in the morning." One way or the other, Faith would have to be told about Macy Crow.

"What's going on?" she asked. "Something's off."

"I'll explain all in the morning. Trust me on this."

"Sure. But I want the full story tomorrow," Faith said.

"Understood." He hung up, realizing he was deeply relieved Faith had picked up the phone.

Brogan held up a bagged cell phone and handed it to Hayden. "Her last search on her phone was for the Texas Rangers."

"Did she place a call?"

"No. I also called Quantico, and the ASAC confirmed she's an agent, but he couldn't or wouldn't say what she was working on. Thought maybe you could give your sister a call and find out what she knows about Macy Crow."

He texted his sister, Special Agent Kate Hayden. She traveled with an FBI profiling team and had made it a standing policy that Hayden and his mother text rather than call. She promised to respond as quickly as she could and had always kept her word. In his text, he supplied the victim's name, description, and a request for information on her latest case. Moments later he received a curt Roger that.

Kate was brilliant, and though her specialty was forensic linguistics, she was a woman of few words. Some saw her silence as arrogance, but he knew Kate was always thinking and processing and often forgot about social niceties. They were two peas in a pod according to their mother.

"She'll get back to us." Hayden slid the phone back in his breast pocket.

"Where's your sister these days?" Brogan asked.

"No idea."

"A few buddies of mine in San Antonio say she's as charming as you."

Kate had solved a complex case in San Antonio recently but had ruffled a few feathers in the process. "I'm still the nice one."

"Shit." Brogan adjusted his hat, shaking his head. "Remind me to stay clear of your sister."

"Macy Crow is in town because her old man was murdered. Since she's FBI, I'm guessing she wanted to know more about what happened."

Brogan nodded. "Takes matters into her own hands. Something we both would have done. So what the hell was she doing in this part of town?"

"I don't know."

Despite what was portrayed on television, the FBI didn't just roll into town and take over investigations. They worked in conjunction with local law enforcement, and when they had an operation, they kept the Texas Rangers apprised.

"Did the responding officer say anything else?" Hayden asked.

"Said the victim tried to speak but was incoherent. She then lost consciousness."

"Is an Austin PD detective on scene?" Hayden asked.

"Detective Lana Franklin is en route. She's juggling two other homicides tonight."

"Where is Crow's backpack?"

"Over there in the shadows where it fell. No one other than me has touched it yet," Brogan said.

"Let's have a look at it." Hayden signaled to the forensic technician what he was doing and waited for her to follow with her camera.

As the technician snapped pictures, he moved around the bloodstain on the road and through the grass to the red backpack now lying up against the chain-link fence of the park. The backpack was marked with a yellow evidence tag. He knelt and unzipped it and found a wallet, a hotel room key, and several fast-food receipts.

"Where's the officer who responded?" Hayden asked.

"Officer Beth Holcombe is over by her vehicle," Brogan said.

He rose, asked the technician for pictures and an inventory of the bag, and then found Officer Holcombe. She was talking to an older man wearing disheveled clothes and carrying a large grocery bag crammed full of clothes and food.

Holcombe, midsized with an athletic build, had pulled back her black hair into a neat bun at the base of her neck.

Hayden extended his hand and introduced himself and Brogan. "Officer."

She shook his hand and then laid her hand on the forearm of the man beside her. "Rangers, this is Sammy Kent. He lives in the doorways up and down this street, which is my beat. Sammy and I cross paths a lot. Not much happens here without him seeing it."

Sammy hovered close to Officer Holcombe as his dark eyes shifted from Hayden to Brogan, sizing both men up. His green jacket looked to be army issue, as did his boots.

"Mr. Kent, my name is Mitchell Hayden."

Sammy locked eyes with him. "You a Texas Ranger?"

"Yes, sir, I am. Did you serve?"

Sammy gripped his bag closer to him. "I did. Operation Desert Storm."

"Thank you for your service, Mr. Kent. How long were you in?"

"Three years."

Three years meant he'd not finished his first enlistment, which ran four years plus. "Were you injured?"

"Medical discharge. But I wasn't injured."

Many of the homeless had mental health issues, which meant whatever Sammy told him could be suspect. "What can you tell me about what happened?"

"Lady was walking down the street, and she stopped and gave me a twenty. Told me to get something to eat."

"She say anything else?"

"Asked me about a missing girl. Showed me a picture."

"Who was the girl?"

"Paige."

"Were you able to tell her anything?" Hayden asked.

"Nope. The earth swallowed up Paige. It's done it before, and it'll do it again."

Hayden checked his rising frustration. It wouldn't help Ms. Crow. "Where was she going?"

"That way." Sammy shrugged, sniffed, and nervously rattled the change in his pockets. "Toward the park."

"How did the woman seem? Was she upset or worried?"

"Sad, maybe. But she wasn't worried or nothing. She passed me and wasn't more than fifty feet ahead when a dark pickup came out of nowhere. When the truck hit her, she flew through the air like a rag doll. She hit the ground so hard I thought she was dead. Freaked me out, and I went running toward her screaming. Officer Holcombe came to the rescue right away."

"You've met the woman before?" Hayden asked.

The old man shook his head. "I've never seen her before."

"And she just came up to you?" Hayden asked.

"Yep. Came out of nowhere."

"Did she say why she was here?" Brogan asked.

"No."

"We got more black pickups in Texas than I can shake a stick at," Hayden said. "Did you happen to recognize the driver?"

"No. Never saw the face. But I think it was a guy. Driver had on a baseball hat," Sammy said. "It all happened in seconds."

"Thank you, Sammy," Hayden said.

"Is she still alive?"

"So far," Hayden said.

"I saw a guy fly like that once," Sammy said. "After an IED blew up. He lost his legs. And he was screaming something terrible. But this woman that was hit tonight . . ." He paused to steady his voice and press fingertips to his tearing eyes. "She didn't scream."

Hayden patted the man on the shoulder, waiting for him to steady himself before he turned to the policewoman. "Officer Holcombe, are there security cameras posted along the street?"

Holcombe nodded. "Several of the businesses around here have them. And there's my body camera and dashcam footage."

"I'll want to see that right away." Hayden fished out a twenty from his pocket. "Officer, can you buy Sammy a meal?"

"Sure," she said.

"Thanks."

"Keep me posted on how she's doing?" Holcombe said. "She's one of us."

"I will." Hayden's phone rang, and he saw his sister's name on the display. He walked away from Sammy, Brogan, and Holcombe. "Kate."

"I made calls regarding Macy Crow." Her tone was clipped and sounded slightly annoyed.

It was always directly to the point with Kate. No "How are you doing?" or "How's the weather?" Small talk was foreign to his sister. However, when Sierra died and Kate had been in northern Maine leading an investigation, she'd driven three hours to the nearest airport and taken a red-eye so she could be present at the funeral. He'd not spoken to her or anyone that day. He'd been so broken and angry. After the visitation at their mother's house, Kate had left Austin. These days, he and his sister shared a mutual respect and had each other's backs, but no one would ever describe them as warm and sensitive.

"Give me what you have," he said.

"Macy Sunday Crow, age thirty, was attached to Quantico, Virginia. She's also spent time in the Denver, Seattle, and Kansas City field offices."

"She looks much younger than thirty." He'd thought the same about Faith and had been surprised when Sierra had told him she was a pathologist.

"For the last six years, she's worked juvenile sex trafficking cases because she can pass as a teenager. She broke a big case about two months ago and was just promoted. On Sunday, she called her boss, said her father had died and she was taking personal time."

"Does she have a boyfriend or other family?"

"No to a boyfriend and yes to a brother who lives in the Austin area. I have no address for the brother."

Neither did he. So far there'd been no sign of Jack Crow's son. "Any cases she was working that might have triggered this attack?"

"Like I said, that human trafficking case was big. According to the woman's file, she's not afraid to mix it up. She'll throw down with the best of them."

Kate could have been describing Faith. "Thanks, Kate."

"Of course."

"Have you called Mom lately?" He didn't get Kate on the phone often, but had promised never to let her go without trying to connect.

He could hear the gears in her very linear brain shifting from professional to personal. "She's on a cruise with three of her girlfriends from church."

"She's actually back. I saw her two days ago. She says she's left you messages."

"I'm working a case."

Kate was obsessive when she was working. "Call Mom, Kate. She worries."

"Understood."

"When are you going to do it?"

She sighed.

When they had been kids, he had teased her a lot, and he always knew he had gotten under her skin when she sighed.

"I'll wake her up if I do it now."

"She won't care, Kate. Call now."

"Will do."

"Perfect." He dropped his voice a notch. "Be careful."

"Back at you."

The line went dead, and he returned to Brogan. "Any sign of anything else she might have dropped?"

"Nothing other than the backpack. The paramedics did say she was wearing her service weapon."

"I'll check at the hospital and find out what was in her pockets. How long will Agent Crow be in surgery?"

"She won't be out for a while, and that's assuming she makes it that long," Brogan said.

"I want a look at her hotel room. And let's see if we can track down her brother. Maybe she made contact with him, and he can shed light on what the hell his sister was up to."

CHAPTER EIGHT

Tuesday, June 26, 4:30 a.m.

Faith hadn't been asleep when Hayden had called. She'd been fully awake, lying in bed staring at the ceiling, watching the shadows play overhead, wishing away the night.

But after his call, she immediately got out of bed, worried and sure something terrible had happened. Hayden was not the type of man to just call to hear the sound of her voice. That wasn't him. Or them.

Unable to shake the growing sense of worry, she called Tina at the shelter.

Tina picked up on the third ring. "Faith?"

"I'm sorry to wake you. Call it a bad feeling, but can you do a quick bed check for me. Is Kat where she's supposed to be?"

Tina cleared her throat. "Give me a second."

Faith paced her room as she waited for Tina's return. What was it that had torqued her up so much? Why did everything just feel so wrong?

"Faith," Tina said, sounding more alert. "All present and accounted for, including Kat."

The information didn't ease the tension banding the muscles in her stomach. "Thank you for checking. I'm sorry I woke you."

"You okay?" Tina asked.

"My brain is working overtime." She threaded her fingers through her hair. "Again, I'm sorry."

"No worries."

Even after she hung up, the sense of dread would not leave her, so she simply made tea and sat on the couch. Her feet curled up under her, and with a warm cup in hand, she watched a Home Shopping Network show advertising some new line of dipping bowls created by two Virginia-based designers.

For reasons she didn't understand, her mind kept drifting to Hayden's odd question about Jack Crow's daughter. He had actually sounded worried and a little unsure. She feared that hit-and-run victim would be in her office soon.

Finally, at five, she laced up her running shoes and went to the community gym, where she logged four miles on the treadmill. Work and life had gotten in the way of her runs lately, and it felt good to break a sweat and stretch. By seven a.m. she was showered, dressed, and walking through the front door of the medical examiner's office.

She spent the morning responding to phone messages regarding recent autopsies. She often received calls from family members who needed medical terms translated into plain English so they could better cope with their loved one's death. These people were vulnerable and emotionally distraught, and they relied on her professionalism and kindness to survive the grief.

The last message was from Kevin, the man who'd bumped into her at the hotel last night. He'd tracked her down. *"I wondered if you'd like to meet for coffee."* Amused, she hit delete.

She imagined Hayden kissing her, his hand to her breast and her heart beating a lot faster. "Sorry, Kevin, I have enough complications right now."

As tempted as she was to call Hayden, she left it to him. He'd said he'd call, and that was good enough for her.

She spent the next hour writing up her final reports on two autopsies she had performed two days earlier. The first patient had been a seventy-year-old woman who'd been on the golf course with her friends when she'd suffered a massive stroke. She was dead before the ambulance had arrived, and her children wanted to know if she had suffered. The subject of her next report was a fifty-three-year-old male, successful by all accounts, who'd died of an overdose of painkillers and alcohol.

She filed both reports and met Nancy in the autopsy suite.

It was close to noon when she checked her office voicemail and discovered another phone message. It was from the principal at Kat's school.

"This is Principal Boswell at the high school. Kat Jones hacked into the school computer system today. She didn't disturb anything, but she proved she could do a lot of damage if she chose to. According to our school records, you're her emergency contact." Kat hadn't mentioned this tidbit about assigning her as the emergency contact. *"We're sending her to the shelter. She has a three-day suspension."*

Faith closed her eyes as the principal rattled off her name and number. "Damn it, Kat."

"Did I hear my name?"

Faith looked up and found the girl standing in her doorway, backpack slung over her shoulder and two cappuccinos in her hands. She set one on Faith's desk. "A token."

Faith sipped the coffee, glad it was hot and strong. "Computer hacking? Really?"

Kat sat, tapping her finger against the side of her cup. "I didn't screw with anything. I was just nosing around."

"And showing others how to do it?"

"Teach the children, as they say." She sipped her coffee. "Besides, the next three days will give us bonding time."

"I have work to do. You have class assignments to turn in. You are going back to the shelter."

Kat's brow furrowed with frustration that went deeper than any worry over a school suspension. "I'm ahead of the teachers. I show them how to solve problems. Makes them feel threatened and challenged. And I get bored. And the kids at the shelter are fucking morons."

"Enough with the swearing."

"So now we're in 1900? Do you want me to wear a hoop skirt, too?"

"Wrong historical reference and we're in my office, so don't swear."

"So what do we do?" Kat asked.

"I take you back to the shelter. And then I return at 5:30 p.m. and take you to your ob-gyn appointment."

"I hate it at the shelter."

Faith reached for her purse. "Let's go."

"You're still wearing scrubs," Kat persisted.

"I'm coming right back."

They made their way through the building, and when they were seated inside Faith's car, her phone rang. It was PJ. "Buckle up."

More eye rolling as Kat clicked her seat belt.

Faith accepted the call. "PJ."

"So a little bird, meaning my mother, tells me you broke a few records with your fundraising last night," he said.

"I haven't had a chance to talk to Tina or Margaret yet, but I'm headed to the shelter now."

"You will be pleased. You did an amazing job."

"It wasn't me. You mother needs to take all the credit. No one organizes an event like that better than her." She put the car in gear and drove to the parking lot exit.

Kat turned on the radio and chose a rap station.

Faith turned it down, shooting her a badass glare that made the girl chuckle. "What else is up, PJ?"

"I also wanted to update you on something else. Remember when you asked me to look into your adoption?"

"Sure. Right after your dad died." As Kat reached for the radio dial, Faith tossed her a warning look that dared her to try. It did the trick.

She turned right onto the street and made her way to the first stoplight.

"Well, I found a name for you. I've been digging through your father's files for the last few months, and I found nothing. Then it occurred to me to check his old datebooks. I retrieved them from archives a few days ago. Your father was a stickler for keeping meticulous details of his appointments. The book I'm looking at now dates back to 1987."

The year before she was born. "Okay."

"Your father had a series of meetings with a woman by the name of Josie Jones. The first meetings were in July of 1987 to discuss a shoplifting charge she was facing. You remember he did a lot of pro bono work then?"

"I remember hearing Mom talk about it."

"Russell defended Josie and got all the shoplifting charges dropped."

A horn honked behind her, and she realized the light had turned green. She started driving. "Okay."

"She appears in his datebook ten more times after her case was cleared. The last entry was May 2, 1988."

"That was a month before I was born."

"I had a buddy in robbery pull her picture." PJ dropped his voice a fraction. "I'll text it to you. You might be a little stunned."

"Why?"

"Just have a look at it. I might have found your birth mother."

She glanced to Kat, wishing she were alone. "I'll have to call you back later. I'm on my way to the shelter with one of the kids."

"Sure. Of course."

She hung up, the phone still gripped in her hand. PJ was efficient and didn't delay. If he was sending a text, it would be coming soon. Within fifteen seconds the text arrived, and despite her lack of privacy, she glanced at her phone long enough to open the attachment and then back up at the road as the image loaded. When she looked back down, she drew in a sharp breath. She was staring at a black-and-white mug shot of a young girl who looked like her. Blond hair. Light-colored eyes. The face. The lips.

Too stunned and not quite able to process, she dropped the phone in her lap and focused on the road ahead.

"Texting and driving?" Kat quipped.

"I know. It's a bad combination."

As if sensing Faith's unease, Kat held in whatever comeback she had at the ready. "What's going on with you? You look like you've seen a ghost."

"I might have."

"Who is it?"

"Josie Jones. She could be my birth mother."

"Can I see?"

Normally far more guarded, Faith handed over the phone.

"Wow. You do look like her. I didn't know you were adopted," Kat stammered.

"You make it sound like it's a bad thing."

"I'm not sure if it's good or bad," Kat said.

"It can be a very good thing if handled properly."

Kat sat in silence for a moment and then handed back the phone. "You've never heard anything about your mom before?"

"No. My parents didn't like to talk about it. And when I was older, I tried to find her. Hit nothing but brick walls."

A frown settled on Kat's face, and some of her natural vibrancy faded. "So this Josie Jones just got erased like she never existed."

The girl's tone cut through Faith's own confusion and reminded Faith that Kat was completely dialed in to every word coming out of her mouth. "It doesn't have to be like that with you and your baby if you choose adoption. Adoptions can be open now. You can have contact with the child, if that's what you want."

"That's not what Mrs. Myers said."

"Who's Mrs. Myers?"

"She's with social services. She came to talk to me a few weeks ago. She told me it would be better for me to close this chapter and get on with my life because I'm so young."

Faith gripped the wheel, speaking with as much calm as she could muster. "You never told me about the visit."

Kat shrugged, as if to say, "Whatever."

"Going forward, don't speak to anyone about adoption unless I'm there. This is huge. You won't be doing this alone."

Kat flipped the sun visor up and down a few times, then reached for the radio and turned it up again. "Why're you being so nice to me?"

This time, Faith turned the radio completely off from the control on her steering wheel. "I like you, Kat. I can help you with placing or keeping the baby. I can also help with your college, if you'll let me."

"College. Might as well land on the moon."

"No. It's not that kind of a long shot."

"What if I don't want help with school or the baby?"

Faith turned a corner and then shot the girl a grin. "Then you're shit out of luck, kid, because I'm probably going to continue to butt my nose into your life until I know you're on solid ground."

A ghost of a smile tugged at Kat's lips as she turned the radio on again. They listened to a rap song that had Kat sitting a little taller and finally tapping her hand on her knee. Faith's mind drifted back to the image of Josie Jones. Could all this be as simple as a note in a datebook?

"Are you going to track down this Josie Jones woman, or what?" Kat asked.

"I just need a little time to digest it all. It's fairly overwhelming, but yeah, eventually, I'm going to get to the bottom of this."

CHAPTER NINE

Hayden and Brogan arrived back at headquarters to view Officer Holcombe's dashcam as well as the security footage videos that had been forwarded to Hayden's computer. The uniforms had tracked down three cameras that had captured a dark truck driving in the direction of Comal Pocket Park and Macy Crow's crash site.

Hayden shrugged off his jacket and brewed a fresh pot of coffee.

He handed Brogan a cup, and the two sat in front of the computer screen. The first block of dashcam footage showed the path of Holcombe's vehicle charging forward, lights flashing on the buildings of East Austin as her headlights caught the park's west side seconds before she came to an abrupt stop. The audio recorded the squeal of her tires as the visual captured Sammy Kent screaming by Agent Crow's contorted body lying on the ground.

Officer Holcombe sounded breathless, amped, the slight edge of panic contained when she called in the incident, requesting backup and an ambulance, and then offered a description of the situation. As she ran forward, the jostling image of her camera was hard to follow until she stopped and leaned over Macy Crow. Her hand was trembling as she felt the injured woman's neck for a pulse.

"She's alive, barely. Head trauma. Broken bones." A split second passed and then more calmly, *"Ma'am, the police are here. Just lie still. Help is on the way."*

"Oh, Jesus H. Christ!" Sammy shouted. *"That truck came out of nowhere and just mowed her down."*

"What truck, Sammy?" Holcombe asked.

"A dark-blue, maybe black truck."

"Did you see the plates?"

"ATX something. Oh, sweet Jesus, is she dead? There's so much blood! Sweet Jesus."

Blood oozed from the woman's scalp as the wail of sirens grew closer. Sounds gurgled in the woman's throat. Hayden could see Macy's lips moving.

"Ma'am, I need you to stay still," Holcombe said. *"The ambulance is almost here. You're going to be all right. Help is here."*

"Jesus, look at her arm," Brogan said, mostly to himself.

All Hayden saw was Faith. Intellectually, he knew it wasn't her, but that's all his mind registered. Beautiful Faith, broken and battered. He resisted the urge to call her a second time, even though he needed to hear the sound of her voice.

"Don't try to move," Holcombe said. Agent Crow tried to raise her head. She was trying to talk. Officer Holcombe lowered her head closer to the injured woman. *"Do you know who did this to you?"*

"Jack?" The woman went still for a moment, but the officer remained crouched close. Sirens grew ever louder. And then the woman moved again. *"Paige."*

The paramedic crew arrived, and the officer reported what she'd seen as they went to work on Agent Crow.

The audio captured Holcombe's desperate whispering. *"Holy shit. Holy shit."* The officer who'd been so steady when he'd spoken to her was struggling to get control of her own emotions.

"Jack is her father," Brogan said. "Who is Paige?"

"A teenager who went missing recently." Hayden rubbed his hand over the stubble on his jaw. "Let me put in another tape."

Security footage from the store across the street from the park captured a truck driving into the park at 2:01 a.m. Its lights were off, and it moved slowly toward a darkened corner and waited. Five minutes later Crow came into the camera's view as she passed. He saw her pause and talk to Sammy, move to the ATM, and then hand something to Sammy. Just as she left Sammy, the vehicle came out of the shadows and barreled directly toward her.

"You see that?" Hayden said. "That was no accident."

"I got a partial on the plate along with the make and model," Brogan responded. "Running it now."

Ten minutes later, they had the name of the owner of the vehicle, a 2008 Ford truck that had been reported stolen several hours before.

"The truck belongs to Randy Kelly. He lives in North Austin. He's been arrested for selling narcotics and is currently on probation."

"Let's have a talk with him," Hayden said, reaching for his jacket.

***

Hayden and Brogan drove to the North Austin neighborhood and to Randy Kelly's apartment building. They climbed to the second floor and banged on his door. Inside they heard footsteps, muttered oaths, and a lock turn. "Who is it?"

"Texas Rangers. We're looking for Randy Kelly."

Two more locks clicked, and the door opened. The guy who stood before them was shirtless, wore jeans, and his hair stuck up. "That's me. You find the truck?"

"Mind if we come in, Mr. Kelly?" Hayden asked. "I have questions."

Kelly nodded and stepped back. "Is my truck okay?"

"Your truck was used in a crime we're investigating."

"Shit," Kelly whispered as he pulled on a shirt that had been on the floor.

Kelly's one-room apartment had a Murphy bed, a small kitchen, and a bathroom. Several action-movie posters decorated the walls, a couple of pizza boxes were stacked on the kitchen counter, and dirty clothes were scattered on the floor around a card table holding a laptop.

"Where did you last park your truck?" Hayden asked.

"I work construction and odd jobs. I slipped into a bar to get a beer yesterday evening, and when I came out, the truck was gone."

"What is the name of the bar, and where is it?" Hayden asked.

"It's in East Austin. Rodney's on Linden. I parked the car on Seventh Street and went in for a couple of hours. I came out around eleven and no truck. I called the cops right away."

"You're sure about where you parked your truck?" Brogan asked.

"Yeah. I'd had a few beers, but I was in good shape when I came out. I know where I parked my truck. I was supposed to work today, so I couldn't get plowed. You said it was used in a crime?"

"In a hit-and-run accident sometime after midnight," Hayden said.

"Shit," Kelly hissed.

"Does anyone else have keys to your truck?" Hayden asked.

"No. It's mine." He scratched his head. "It's ten years old, and it doesn't run that well. But it's paid for and gets the job done. Who was hit?"

"A woman."

"Is she going to be all right?"

"I don't know. And you can prove you were here the entire time?"

Kelly shook his head slowly. "I called the cops, gave my report about eleven thirty, and then came home. There will be a record of the car service. I was asleep by twelve thirty."

"Where were you on Sunday?" Jack's murder and Macy's attack happening so close together couldn't be a coincidence.

"On a roof in north Travis County. I arrived at five a.m. and worked until sunset."

Hayden would check out the man's story but was inclined to believe him. "All right, Mr. Kelly. I might double back with more questions."

"What about my truck?" Kelly asked.

"If and when we find it, it'll be impounded as evidence. So we'll have to hang on to it for a while," Hayden offered with no remorse.

Kelly shook his head. "What am I supposed to do in the interim?"

"You'll have to make other transportation arrangements."

As they left to the sound of Kelly grumbling curses, Brogan made a call to dispatch, putting out a BOLO on the vehicle. His next call to the city's uniformed division was for a search of cameras near Rodney's on Linden. With any luck, they'd find footage of the car theft.

***

When Faith arrived at her office, Nancy was waiting for her with lab results from autopsies done three weeks ago, several messages from police officers with questions about pending cases, and the schedule for tomorrow.

"Good, you made it back," Nancy said. "It's going to be a crazy afternoon."

"What's happening?" The buzz and noise of the office normally excited her, but right now it felt like an annoying intrusion.

"We have a death that appears to be an ATV accident," Nancy said. "The victim is a twelve-year-old male, and the family is torn up and looking for some kind of closure."

Whatever worries had been plaguing her vanished as she focused on caring for this child. "All right. What about a possible hit-and-run? Female. Did she arrive here yet?"

"We've not seen any case like that yet. What do you know that I don't?" Nancy asked.

She was more relieved than she'd expected. "Good."

Nancy studied her. "You all right?"

"Long night. Bad sleep." She smiled.

"Let me talk to Dr. Ryland," Nancy said. "I might be able to talk him into taking the ATV case."

"No, I've got this. See you in the suite in thirty minutes."

After she changed and quickly leafed through the reports and messages, Faith met Nancy in the autopsy suite. Neither spoke as they performed the grim but necessary task of conducting the autopsy.

After she closed up his chest and pulled the sheet back over his face, she spoke to the bereaved family, answering their questions and listening as they cried and struggled to wrap their brains around the tragedy.

By the time Faith moved behind her desk, she was bone weary. Rolling her head from side to side, she released the tension in her neck. She wasn't sure how long she had been sitting there like that when she heard the knock on her door.

Mitchell Hayden stood in her doorway. "You all right?"

"Sure. Always. This is a surprise." Faith rose.

He entered her office and carefully shut the door. "I need to talk to you."

She remained behind the desk. "Now I'm getting worried. First you call last night, and then you show up to talk?"

He walked up to the other side of her desk. "Remember the hit-and-run last night?"

She leaned on the desk, knowing she might have been tempted to lean into him had it not been there. "Did the victim die?" Her breath caught in her throat, and she thought if a heart could actually pause, hers did. "Are you sending her to me?"

"She's still alive. She just got out of surgery an hour ago, but she's in rough shape."

An odd stillness settled around her, and her voice seemed to echo from far away. "Why're you telling me this?"

He fished his phone from his back pocket and selected a picture. "I snapped a picture of her identification badge, as well as of her driver's license. I'd like you to have a look."

"All right." She accepted the phone, studying his face as if somehow this mystery, which was now really scaring her, could be solved with one of his weighted glances or frowns.

When she could get no read from his expression, she studied the picture. She enlarged the image with her fingers and studied the eyes, nose, and quirky half smile that were all familiar. The hair was different, and she was wearing a necklace Faith had never seen. It was her, and yet it wasn't.

"I don't understand," she said.

"Neither do I. When I saw her identification, I thought someone had figured out we were sleeping together and was playing a sick joke on me."

Faith could do nothing but shake her head.

"But it wasn't you," he said. "Her badge says her name is Macy Crow."

"Macy Crow. I received a voicemail from her. This is Jack Crow's daughter?"

"The same."

She swiped to the next picture, which was of a Commonwealth of Virginia driver's license. The black-and-white image was no less unsettling than the color version.

"Are you adopted?" he asked.

She traced the shape of the face that was hers. "I am."

"How long have you known?" he asked.

"Always. But it's not the kind of thing that comes up in everyday conversation. My parents didn't like to talk about it."

Hayden shifted slightly and gripped the brim of his hat tighter. "Do you have any details about your adoption?"

"No. I contacted PJ Slater recently about it. I thought he might find something in the files. As a matter of fact, he called me just this morning and gave me the name *Josie Jones* as a possible birth mother."

"Do you have any adoption records? An original birth certificate?"

"None." Her head was spinning, and she was just trying to keep calm and find a rational explanation. "Do you think I have a twin?"

"A DNA test will confirm it."

Somewhere deep inside her, missing puzzle pieces snapped into place. "Where is Macy Crow?"

"ICU at Midtown."

She removed her purse from her bottom drawer, took off her lab coat, and didn't bother to change out of scrubs. "I want to see her, now."

"I'll take you."

"That's not necessary. I can drive myself." That was a lie. Her head was whirling, and she could barely focus as she fumbled through the keys on her ring.

"No, Faith. I'll drive. No arguing."

It was too hard to fight common sense right now. "Let me tell my office I'm leaving."

"Sure."

Later, she would think back on this moment, and she wouldn't remember speaking to Nancy about clearing her schedule, getting into Hayden's car, or driving to the hospital. Her first memories would begin with the hospital's fluorescent lights buzzing overhead and the rattle of a cart in critical care in the neuroscience unit as she and Hayden stepped off the elevator. Hayden showed his badge to the nurse, and they learned Macy Crow was in room 212.

Down another hallway, he punched the button for the ICU doors, and they entered another section, where patients had larger rooms to accommodate more equipment and staff.

The beep of a monitor had her pausing at the curtain drawn in front of one of the doors.

"Ready?" Hayden asked.

She wasn't ready for any of this. "Yes."

He pushed aside the curtain into Macy Crow's room. Her bed was positioned in the center and surrounded by machines. Her right leg was in traction, and there were pins in her thigh. Her arm was set in a cast, and her head was heavily wrapped in white gauze. Bruises and swelling made her face unrecognizable.

Faith stepped closer. Her mouth was dry and her body stiff as she leaned over the bed. In the autopsy suite, she'd witnessed human carnage, but this woman's injuries made her stomach roil. "My God."

Tubes fed into Macy's mouth and nose. Faith reached a trembling hand out and touched the woman's right wrist, which seemed to be the only spot uninjured.

Faith cleared her throat. "Macy. My name is Faith. I don't know if you can hear me, but I left you a voicemail yesterday about your father, Jack. And as it turns out, we might have something in common."

The beep, beep of the monitor picked up.

Hayden's presence behind her was calming, and she was glad he'd been the one to deliver the news. No drama. Just facts.

"Macy, I'm here with Captain Hayden of the Texas Rangers. He's working your case. He's going to figure out what happened to you and Jack. He's a pretty crackerjack crime fighter." The attempt at levity fell flat. "Concentrate on getting well, and leave the rest to him, okay?" Her voice cracked on the last word, but a deep breath settled the rising panic.

Faith studied the agent's hands. Like Faith's, Macy's fingers were long, the deep nail beds unpolished and short.

A knock on the door had her turning toward a man dressed in a white lab coat. The guy was young, and his head was covered in a shadow of dark stubble. "I'm Dr. Bramley."

Hayden removed his identification from his breast pocket. "Mitchell Hayden, Texas Rangers. This is Dr. Faith McIntyre. How is Special Agent Crow doing?"

Dr. Bramley rubbed his eyes and then moved toward the bed, automatically glancing at vitals on a monitor and then the drip from an IV. "She made it through surgery, and that is very encouraging."

"There is head trauma." Aware that Macy could be taking all this in on some level, Faith kept her tone clinical and tightened her mental grip on her trademark control.

"There is, but the good news is that we got her into surgery quickly and were able to relieve the cranial pressure. Once the swelling abates, we'll reevaluate. But as I said, she made it through the night, and that's a real testament to her strength."

Faith looked at the unconscious woman and had so many questions for her. The thought of her not making it was almost unbearable. "What are her other injuries?"

"Fractured femur and arm. Cracked ribs. When Ms. Crow came into the ER last night, I didn't think she'd make it through the hour. But as I've already said, she's hung in there. She's tough."

"Did she say anything in the ER?" Hayden asked.

"She was unconscious when she got to us," Dr. Bramley said.

"I've called city police," Hayden said. "A uniformed officer will be arriving soon to watch her room. No one gets in or out without clearing it past the officer or me."

"Her brother just arrived," the doctor said. "He's in the waiting room. We weren't able to let him see his sister because we were examining her, but I've agreed for him to visit for a minute or two."

"That's Dirk Crow?" Hayden asked.

"Correct," Dr. Bramley said.

"I'd like to meet him," Faith said.

"So would I," Hayden said. "I've been trying to reach him since Sunday."

"The waiting room is down the hall and on the right."

Faith reluctantly released Macy's hand. Drawing in a breath, she left the room with Hayden at her side, and they made their way to the waiting room.

There were several men in the room, but her gaze was instantly drawn to the large man cradling a crushed coffee cup in tattooed fingers. There was no missing the square jaw, thick brow, and muscled arms that so resembled Jack Crow.

When the man looked up, he stared at her with narrowed eyes glinting with wariness. "Macy, what the hell?" He tossed the cup in the trash and grabbed his cap as he stood.

"I'm not Macy. I'm Faith McIntyre," Faith said.

He didn't look convinced as he approached her, working his big fingers over the bill of a sweat-stained ball cap. "If you're not Macy, you look just like her."

"I know."

"How is it you look so much alike?"

"I'm not sure yet." The more people who noticed her resemblance to Macy, the more unsettling it was. "You're Jack Crow's son?" she asked.

"That's right. Dirk Crow," he said.

He barely glanced at Hayden as he stepped toward her. He smelled of motor oil, the hot sun, and Texas dust. "Jack kept up with Macy over the years but wasn't keen on me hanging out with her. I saw her for the first time yesterday at Jack's trailer."

"I've been trying to reach you since Sunday," Hayden said. "I had news about your father."

"Yeah, Ledbetter caught up to me," Dirk said. "He told me. That's why I went to the trailer. The place looked like holy hell. Did the cops do that?"

"We left the black fingerprint powder, but the rest was as we found it. Any idea who might have killed Jack?"

"Like I told Macy, not a clue. I've been in El Paso for over a week."

"Did you know there were two of us?" Faith asked.

"Not for sure."

"What do you mean?" she demanded.

"When Macy and her mother, Brenda, left for good, Jack commented it was better that Macy was gone. He said she was safer. I asked him why, and he said, 'As soon as someone started seeing double, there were going to be questions.' I asked if she was a twin, and Jack caught himself and said no."

"Did he ever bring it up again?" she asked.

"No. Never. Jack didn't trust anyone with whatever secrets he had." He went silent for a moment. "Hayden, do you have any idea who killed my old man?"

"Not yet."

Dirk flexed his fingers, making some of the tattoos on his forearms shift and move. "How is my sister doing?" he asked.

"She's holding her own. But she's in bad shape," Hayden replied.

"I want to see her," he said.

"In a minute. I understand from Ledbetter you and your father got into a fight a few months back. You wanted him to sell his land."

"He's sitting on a gold mine of dirt," Dirk said. "Land prices are high, and now is the time to cash in, but he was a stubborn old bull and wouldn't listen."

"You've been in El Paso for a week. When's the last time you saw Jack?"

"We hadn't spoken since we fought. So it's been a few months." He sniffed, cocking his head toward Hayden. "You think I killed him and then ran over my sister?"

"I didn't say that," Hayden said.

Dirk twisted the bill of his hat tighter in his fingers. "But you're thinking the money is motive enough."

"I do."

"I can give you the names of the people I was with in El Paso. They'll tell you I was there."

"What do you do for a living, Mr. Crow?"

"Construction foreman. I was in El Paso interviewing for a job. There are people that can vouch for me."

"I'll need those names and addresses before you leave here today. I'd also like your address."

"Sure."

"How old was Macy when your parents adopted her?" Faith asked.

"A couple of days old, I guess. She was small, and Pop and Brenda were worried she might not make it. But she was tough, even then." He shook his head and looked into her eyes again. "I'm not going to pretend we cared about each other. There's nine years between us, and I haven't seen her in almost thirty years. But she's still family."

"Did your father ever mention the adoption?" Faith asked.

"I asked him once about it, and he said he never thought about it and loved her like his own. I got to say, he kept up with her better than me. Those two always seemed more wired alike from what he said. He was proud as hell when she became an FBI agent." Dirk shook his head, a bitter frown twisting his lips. "Can I see my sister now?"

"The doctor said it'll have to be a quick visit," Faith said. "She needs rest."

"Of course," Dirk said. "Whatever you say."

The three went into Macy's room, and the big man stood silent, showing no signs of emotion as he moved closer to the bed and stood staring down at his sister. He didn't speak, and he seemed to be inventorying her injuries.

Faith wasn't sure how she expected a brother to react to a sister's grievous injuries. She didn't have a brother but expected something beyond the nothingness emanating from Dirk Crow.

A nurse entered the room and checked Macy's monitors. "Everyone, please leave now. You can come back tomorrow, but for now, my patient needs to be kept as quiet as possible."

When they exited the room, the uniformed officer was posted by it, and Hayden spoke to him briefly before the three moved silently to the waiting room.

Hayden asked for contact information, which Dirk supplied along with the names of the people he'd seen in El Paso.

"Is the cop going to stay outside her door?" Dirk asked. "Whoever did this to her must have been responsible for Jack."

"The cop is staying," Hayden confirmed.

"I don't know shit," Dirk said, "but it doesn't take a genius to see when a father is murdered and a daughter is nearly killed, it ain't just a string of bad luck."

"That's not lost on me," Hayden said. "No one will get in that room without me knowing it, and that includes you."

"Good," Dirk said. "Better safe than sorry."

"You sure you or your father weren't into something that got your sister hurt so bad?" Hayden asked.

"You sound like Macy," Dirk said. "Jack and I could never be accused of being choirboys, but we never did anything that would bring this kind of heat down onto the family."

Hayden studied him for a long moment, and Faith knew with a glance he didn't believe Dirk. But she'd picked up enough legal nuances growing up in the home of a defense attorney to know that unless there were outstanding warrants, pending charges, or probable cause, there wasn't much Hayden could do to hold Dirk until he had more evidence.

If the criminal investigations weren't center stage, she'd have been asking her own questions about Jack Crow, who clearly had known more about the links she and Macy shared.

"As far as the outside world is concerned, Macy Crow died from complications in surgery," Hayden said.

Dirk's grim expression mirrored the feelings jabbing at Faith. "To protect her?"

"Yes," Hayden said.

"No one will hear it from me," Dirk said. "I'll see you again soon, Faith."

"When we get the chance, I want to talk to you about your father."

"Sure. Whatever you want."

When Dirk's large frame vanished behind the closing elevator doors, she felt as if she'd been blindsided. But she didn't have the luxury of giving in to her emotions right now. "I need to talk to the nurses. I'm AB negative, and if we're twins, she will be, too."

"Good idea," Hayden said.

The whole point of her relationship with Hayden was that it was casual and neither burdened the other with anything too personal. Now he had a ringside seat at her life turning upside down. "You don't need to stick around, Hayden. There's nothing you can do here."

"I can stay."

Restless energy swirled around him, and she sensed ghosts of the past were circling. He'd spent a lot of time at hospital bedsides with his late wife. "I'd rather you didn't. I want you out there finding the sick bastard who did this," she said.

He lightly touched her arm. "I want you to be very careful, Faith. If I caught your resemblance to Macy in a split second, other people will as well."

"Fair enough. But how are you going to control what the hospital says about her condition?"

"I can keep it under wraps for a little bit and buy us some time."

"I also would not recommend releasing Macy's picture to the media. The last thing this hospital needs is a reporter snooping around."

"Will do." His expression softened a bit as he debated how to handle this very personal thing with her. If their relationship had been strictly professional or solely personal, it would have been straightforward. But they were in a gray area. Neither one wanted to overstep or crowd the other. "I know this has been a kick in the gut."

"It has been exactly that," she said. "I'm not taking this well."

"You look like you are."

"What other rational choice do I have?"

"Yeah, I suppose that's all we can do."

"Don't worry about me, Hayden. I'm a survivor."

Hayden took her hand, squeezed it. A kiss and a hug would have been welcomed, but again they found themselves stuck in that damned muddled middle.

She returned to Macy's room and walked up to the edge of her bed. She brushed her fingers over Macy's. A sudden surge of anger burned through her body.

Faith could explain the causes and results of death, but she'd never fully understood it. There were times when it was a blessing and other times a curse. The only constant was that it was always waiting for everyone.

"Macy, you're going to have to make that son of a bitch Death wait a long time if I have any say in this."

CHAPTER TEN

Tuesday, June 26, 4:00 p.m.

Hayden stepped into his office and pulled off his jacket. Anger and helplessness were tag teaming his ass, and he was running out of patience. He hated leaving Faith alone outside that damn hospital room, looking so hurt and lost. She was one of the strongest people he knew, but everyone had a breaking point. She'd insisted, however, and he knew she was right. He was of no use to anyone there.

"How did Dr. McIntyre take the news about Agent Crow?" Brogan asked.

"About as well as you could expect." He shifted his thoughts away from the memory of Faith's lost and confused look and back to the case. "I saw Macy's brother, Dirk."

"Where has he been?"

"In El Paso. I called two of the names he gave me. He was interviewing for construction work."

"That's pretty far to go for a job. He must really need the money."

"He admitted he was putting pressure on Crow to sell the land." Hayden rolled his head from side to side to release the tension.

"The financial statements for Jack Crow arrived. We also received several surveillance tapes overlooking the area where Randy Kelly's truck had been parked."

"Good. I also want to see Dirk Crow's financial records."

"Do we have enough probable cause to get a judge to sign that warrant?" Brogan asked.

"I'd say the attempt on Macy's life gives it to us. If she dies, everything will go to Dirk."

"That's motive," Brogan said.

"Let me see the tape."

Brogan keyed up the footage, and the black-and-white image that appeared featured a bakery located a few blocks from Comal Pocket Park. The camera caught the rear of Kelly's truck. At 7:05 p.m., Kelly pulled up and parked and then dashed into a bar around the corner.

Brogan sped up the recording, and over the course of the next couple of hours, several dozens of people passed by the truck. At one point a couple paused by the dented tailgate. The man kissed the woman, and as she wrapped her arms around his neck, he pressed her body against the side of the truck. His hand slid up her skirt, and though others passed, the two were oblivious to having an audience. Minutes later she adjusted her skirt, and they moved on.

It was at ten thirty p.m. when a hooded figure appeared. He kept his head down and hands in his pockets as he walked up to the truck, looked in through the front driver's side window, and then walked past, disappearing from view. Not long after, he reappeared, and this time with no one around him, he cracked the side window with a glass punch. Glass shattered into the front seat, allowing him to shove a gloved hand inside. He popped the lock.

The thief kept his head down the entire time, as if he knew there were cameras around. He leaned under the steering wheel to hot-wire the ignition and drove off like he owned it. Not once did the camera get a good shot of his face.

"This guy's good," Hayden said.

"He's likely scoped out this area before."

And why was the million-dollar question. "Pull footage from the last couple of weeks, and go through it. We might catch whoever did this on camera."

"Will do."

"Did you find anything in Jack Crow's bank accounts?"

"Crow had one bank account that he used for the salvage yard. He had one credit card that he rarely used," Brogan said. "The bank account received odd cash deposits over the course of each month. Nothing more than a few hundred dollars, but that fits with a salvage yard business. He couldn't have been laundering money through the account. The amounts are just too small."

Brogan shuffled through a stack of credit card statements. "According to the one credit card statement, he bought groceries infrequently, but again, he never spent more than twenty or thirty bucks."

"Any favorite haunts?"

"Maxwell's is a local diner. Looks like he ate out there a lot."

"I've been guilty of eating at the same pizza place for years," Hayden said.

"And you're telling me they know something about you?" Brogan asked.

"Maybe not me personally, but they have an idea of my schedule and if I ever ate with anyone. Same might hold true for Crow," Hayden said.

Brogan nodded. "Worth a shot."

"What about Crow's phone records?"

"He called Macy two weeks ago, and they spoke for about half an hour. And he called Dirk five or six times in the same time period, but they never connected. He called a few local auto parts stores, but that's about it," Brogan said.

"Not a sociable guy."

"Nope."

"If he was into something, then he was smart enough to operate in cash. Ledbetter said he bought two phones," Hayden said.

"He didn't use a credit card when he bought them," Brogan said. "I also did a background search on Crow. He joined the army when he was eighteen and stayed in a dozen years. That's when his first wife divorced him. When he got out, he hooked up with Brenda Hamlin, married, and opened the salvage yard. He and his second wife never filed for divorce."

"No jail time for Dirk?"

"None."

"Double-check with Ledbetter about where he bought those phones. I want to see the footage from that store as well."

Brogan grinned as he nodded. "'Be a Texas Ranger,' they said. 'There'll be nonstop action,' they said."

Hayden laughed, rose, crossed to a coffee machine, and refilled his cup. "Ninety-nine percent of the time, you'll be bored off your ass. It's during that one percent when all hell breaks loose that you can get your head blown off. What a rush."

***

He looked at the list of neatly typed names. Jack Crow's name was crossed out. Macy Crow's name had not been crossed out, but circled. As tempted as he was to strike her name, he could not. He'd hit her hard with the truck, and he'd heard the bones crunching as her body careened off the metal bumper and sailed through the air. She'd struck the ground with tremendous force, and he'd seen blood everywhere when he glanced back in his side-view mirror.

The chances of her surviving last night were slim, but he'd yet to see the body. Death could be a fickle bitch sometimes.

He circled Macy's name over and over, his pencil darkening the stark-white paper and then wearing it away. He should have squeezed her for information, but what was done was done.

Five names. Dirk Crow had also returned to town. Chances of him knowing much were slim, but he would leave nothing to chance.

After Dirk, that left three names, including Faith McIntyre. By rights she shouldn't know anything. The first time she'd met Jack Crow, he was dead. But the old man might have known about her, and if he did, he might have tried to reach out. Their possible contact meant she had to remain on the list.

She was also on that Ranger's radar, which meant he needed to be smart and bide his time. The Ranger was sharp and driven and could easily be trouble if not neutralized.

***

Faith was shaken and distracted when she arrived back at the medical examiner's office. Her mind swirled with so many unanswered questions about herself, her parents, and how she was linked to the battered woman lying unconscious in the hospital bed.

She dropped her purse in the chair behind her desk and tossed her jacket over the back. She sat, pressed her palms to her cheeks, which now felt as if they were on fire.

The halls were quiet, the daily hum of activity gone, and five pink message slips lay in the middle of her desk. Her phone's message light was blinking. It never stopped.

But more questions cascaded into her thoughts. Had Macy simply been dealing with her father's death when she got that drink at the bar? Or had Crow told her something that had put her on a dangerous quest?

Dirk's spotty knowledge of Macy's adoption reminded her of all the information swept under the carpet or just plain hidden by her parents. *Why don't I look like my cousins? What was it like the day I was born? Was I a difficult delivery?* Her mother had not come clean about the adoption until Faith was eleven. She remembered how stunned and then angry she'd been. Her mother had assured her it made no difference. Faith had wanted to believe that, but she realized now she had never fully released her anger.

Her phone buzzed, and she answered it absently. "Dr. McIntyre."

"Doc, this is Tina. Just confirming you're taking Kat to her appointment today. You're always early, and she's convinced you've forgotten."

She glanced at the clock on the wall. She had. "I was held up. I'll be there in twenty minutes. Can you let the doctor's office know we're on the way?"

"Will do."

The walk down the hallway, touching base with Nancy, and the drive to the shelter were a blur. She wasn't even truly processing when she walked up to the shelter and pushed through the front door.

Faith wove through the shelter's cobbled rooms searching for Kat, who had promised to be in the lobby waiting. She had to have the girl at the ob-gyn by six forty-five. She'd wanted to leave extra time so she could talk to Kat's doctor.

She found the girl sitting in the game room, a beanbag chair molded around her body as she frowned into the screen of the two-year-old laptop Faith had given her. It was now covered in dozens of stickers, including ones that read THINK DIFFERENT, GIRL POWER, and DO NOT DISTURB.

Kat lumbered up from the beanbag chair and closed her laptop. "Where have you been?"

"Dead people run my life." The words could have passed as a dry quip, but no truer words were spoken. What she would give right now for five minutes of living, breathing parents willing to answer questions.

Kat picked up her backpack and shoved her computer inside. "That's the best excuse I've ever had when someone flakes on me."

As they walked to the car, Faith cut her eyes to the kid who was acting like her tardiness was no big deal, when it was a big deal. "I didn't flake."

"Whatever."

"Ready to see your doctor?"

"No." Kat had had no prenatal care until her twenty-fourth week, when her foster mother had realized the kid wasn't getting fat but was pregnant. Her foster mother had no desire to deal with the pregnancy, so she'd turned Kat over to the shelter. Almost as soon as Kat had arrived, Faith had had her figured out. Though the kid seemed hell-bent on screwing up her life, Faith had taken her under her wing.

In the car, Kat buckled her seat belt and began immediately fiddling with the radio. She selected another station that made Faith's ears hurt and reminded her that as young as Kat still thought Faith was, Faith had aged out of the latest music playlist.

"So I've been doing a little detective work," Kat said.

"Looking into colleges?"

"God, no. Might as well be chasing unicorns."

More glibness. Had she been this difficult as a teenager? Faith found herself struggling to stay positive in the face of so much hormonal negativity and understood now why her father had sent her on so many lavish excursions during her high school summer vacations. "That's not true, Kat. I've told you that there are options if you want it."

The girl held up her hand with flair to silence Faith as with the other hand she rummaged in her pocket for a rumpled piece of paper. "I looked up your Josie Jones."

Faith was completely derailed by Kat's comment and swiveled her head around toward the kid, staring until she heard, "Watch out!"

Faith hit her brakes and stopped seconds before she rear-ended the car in front of her. She pulled into a gas station parking lot. It was several deep breaths before she attempted to speak.

"You did what?" Faith asked.

"I did a search for Josie Jones while I was killing time this afternoon."

"You shouldn't have done that," Faith said. "It's really personal."

"You're always up in my face about superpersonal things. Turnabout is fair play."

"It's different."

Kat looked ahead carefully, making a show of folding her piece of paper. "So you don't want to hear about what I found?"

Faith tapped her hands on the wheel. She was supposed to be the adult in this situation. She should remind Kat to mind her own business, but she knew the kid could find things on the Web that most could not, and her curiosity was stronger than her indignation. "I want to know."

Kat waved the piece of paper in front of her face like a fan. "Maybe I don't want to tell you now."

"You're killing me, kid."

The girl's laugh rang with a genuine brightness she'd never heard before. Carefully, Kat unfolded her paper. "I found out that Josie wasn't much different than me."

"What do you mean?"

"She had been in foster care on and off for several years before the system cut her loose when she turned eighteen. A couple of days before her nineteenth birthday, she was arrested for shoplifting, but the charges were dropped. Do you want to see a picture of her?"

"I've seen her mug shot."

"It's another one."

Faith's heart leapt. "How did you find it?"

Kat looked almost offended. "What kind of detective would I be if I couldn't find a basic picture?"

"Detective. Cute. More like a hacker."

"Such a harsh term." She dug in her pocket and pulled out a picture printed on regular paper. "This picture is from a Dallas paper. When Josie was fifteen, she won a science competition."

Faith held the picture, amazed at how already she was starved for details about this woman she'd only just learned about. The image wasn't high quality, but she could see the young girl standing next to the mayor and the secondary school principal. The headline read "Foster Child Wins Science Award."

A surge of outrage shot through her as she wondered why the reporter had defined Josie by her place in the social services system.

"Check out the headline," Kat said.

"I see it."

"She was pegged like me."

"You aren't pegged." Faith's attention shifted to the girl's bright smile, her blond hair, and tall, lean frame. Grateful there was no trace of the sullenness found in Josie's mug shot, she kept dissecting the girl's features, searching for any clues about her.

"The second I saw Josie's picture, I saw a resemblance to you," Kat said.

"Do you think so?"

"Oh, yeah."

She wrestled the excitement and sadness from her voice. "I wonder how she ended up in Austin."

"I haven't figured that out yet, but I will. I'm also searching for siblings, aunts, uncles, etcetera. I want to find out where she ended up."

Faith was surprised by how much she needed to believe that everything had worked out for Josie. "Any traces of her yet?"

"No, which is odd. Even back in the eighties, a.k.a. the Stone Age, people left some footprints. She left none. The world swallowed her up just like it's trying to do to me."

As quickly as Faith's hopes for information rose, they fell. "Kat, you're not going to be like Josie. The world is not going to devour you."

Kat looked up with tears glistening in her eyes. "How do you know that?"

"Because whether you like it or not, I'm not going to let it happen." She drove across the gas station parking lot to the entrance, looked both ways, and pulled back onto the main road. She drove the car toward the medical park on the west side of the city.

"Why are you nice to me?" Kat asked.

Faith had never stopped to ask herself that question. "I guess I've always liked your spirit. You're smart. A hard worker, when you care."

Kat fumbled with the zipper on her jacket, flipping it up and down. "And I threw it all away when I got knocked up."

"You haven't thrown anything away. But we can't ignore the baby. He or she deserves to be taken care of just like any other baby."

"I didn't say that it shouldn't have a good home." She continued to flip the zipper up and down. "The social services lady called again today. She wants to know what my plan is for the baby."

"It's a fair question. Babies are a lot of work, and you do need a plan."

"I don't want to give it to strangers."

"Then you won't. If you decide to find adoptive parents for the baby, you can meet them."

"What if adoption screws up my kid?"

Faith arched a brow but kept her gaze on the road. "Do I look screwed up?"

"No. You're pretty together." Kat seemed to chew on their conversation. "How old were you when you were given away?"

Given away. It sounded harsh when Kat said it. "Days, maybe hours old, I think. I don't know for certain."

This new puzzle sparked interest in the girl's eyes. "Why don't you know your own story?"

"My mother didn't tell me until I was eleven, and whenever I had questions, she made it clear she hated talking about it," Faith said.

"What if I give my baby to a couple, and they don't want to talk about me?"

"You choose people who will, and you have a legal agreement granting you regular updates."

"Why didn't Josie choose people like that?"

"I don't know."

Again there was more silence and brooding from the young woman in the passenger seat. "I can really do that?"

"Yes. Like I've been trying to tell you, you have a lot more control than you realize."

Some of the tension eased from Kat's shoulders. "I can keep digging for information on Josie."

"Let's just worry about seeing the doctor now. Then I need to get you back to the shelter."

"I hate seeing the doctor."

"Doesn't matter what you want. It's what you and the baby need."

Kat's doctor's visit confirmed she and the baby were doing well. She was thirty-four weeks into her term and on course to deliver at the end of July. "An August baby," Kat had quipped. "Probably going to be the hottest day of the year."

They drove in silence back across town to the shelter. When Kat looked at the brick building, she shook her head. "I hate the shelter."

Faith got out of the car and walked with Kat inside. She hugged Kat until the girl's tense muscles relaxed a fraction. "It's going to be okay."

It wasn't the first time she had regretted leaving the kid here. She had considered speaking to social services about fostering Kat but found she was just as afraid of committing as the girl was. No commitment had always worked for her. Hell, it was the cornerstone of her life, as well as her relationship with Hayden. But lately, instead of enjoying her freedom, she felt increasingly constrained and isolated.

Kat pulled away. "How do you know it's going to be okay?"

An odd sense of worry and tension swept through her, but she still smiled. "It has to be."

CHAPTER ELEVEN

Time Unknown. Maybe June.

Paige flexed her fingers in the darkened room, running a trembling hand over the slick pages of the magazine she'd written in. Writing without light, she doubted her words were intelligible, but it gave her comfort to write. The baby weighed heavily, and she could barely sleep at night now that all she had was the thin mattress lying on the concrete floor. An aching tooth was not helping, and since he had left, the baby had been constantly kicking, as if it knew its time was coming and it was scared shitless, too.

The manacle on her leg had rubbed her skin raw, and she could see the wound had begun to bleed.

When she heard footsteps on the other side of the door, she sat up and quickly tore out the pages with her handwriting, folded and tucked them in her bra. She shoved the magazine and pen under the mattress, her heart beating so fast she could barely think.

The lights clicked on, and she winced at the sudden stimuli onslaught. She blinked several times until her eyes slowly adjusted.

She looked up at him. He was frowning, something he'd been doing a lot lately. There had been a time when he had smiled at her. That smile, though welcome, was complete bullshit.

"Came to check on you, girl," he said.

He came every few days and so far had never returned this early. She drew her feet up as far as the chain would allow. Did he figure out he'd dropped the pen? Or that it was hidden under her mattress? If he found the pen, the papers stuffed in her bra, or the magazines in the grate, she didn't want to imagine what he would do next. "Why?" She spoke barely above a whisper.

"I was a little rough on you a couple of weeks ago. I lost my temper, and that's not right."

"I shouldn't have hit you," she said. "I'm sorry."

"No hard feelings. You got grit, and I like that. Will be good for the baby."

The nice words didn't hide the fact his mood could turn on a dime. "I brought you a hamburger, fries, and a chocolate milkshake. Didn't know if you liked chocolate or vanilla, so I guessed. Don't all women like chocolate?"

"I love it," she said, smiling.

Despite herself she edged to the end of the mattress. The burger and fries smelled good, and she was so tired of canned soup and cold cuts.

He unwrapped the burger and set the fries on the open wrapper. "Get it while it's hot."

She struggled to her feet and shuffled across the floor, making the chain rattle and rub. She took several bites and then drank from the milkshake. Chocolate. Soft. Sweet. It tasted so good she nearly wept.

"There was a woman. I saw her staring at your missing person flyer."

"They're still up?" She didn't mean to sound so excited.

"There aren't many left."

He tried to downplay this bit of good news, but hope still clawed at her chest. Someone was looking for her? She kept her gaze on the fries, trying not to let her raised spirits show. "What did she want?"

"I couldn't really tell. She can't know about you. I've been extra careful with you."

Paige knitted her fingers together so tightly the circulation nearly cut off. Could someone out there be looking for her? She had to believe, or else she'd go mad in this hellhole. "Are you worried?"

He leaned against the wall and surveyed the room. "How do you know I'm worried?"

"We've gotten to know each other pretty well." She nibbled a fry.

"Maybe you're right about that." He nodded thoughtfully. "In here, I can be honest and be myself."

In here, the lovely mask he wore for the world could be lowered. In here, the monster could roam free.

"I'm worried," he said. "But that's not necessarily a bad thing. Worry has kept me a couple of paces ahead of everyone all my life. Worry is what's going to get me through this last job."

"I'm a job?"

"That's right. My freelance job."

"And when the job is done?" She picked up the burger and tore it in half, staring at the ketchup oozing out over the pickles.

"Like I told you, I'll keep my word."

"You're selling the baby."

He shook his head. "There are people that'll be better parents than you. Besides, you said you didn't want it."

She'd been tired, depressed, and scared when she'd said that. Now, she was scared not just for herself but for the baby.

He inserted the key into the manacle's lock and twisted. The metal loosened, and he gently pulled it off her ankle, leaving a raw strip of flesh in its place. "That's got to smart."

"It does."

"I got some salve for that." He fished in his pocket and pulled out a tube of antibiotic cream.

She accepted it, fingering the fresh tube and wondering how she could use it to escape.

"Eat up, girl. That burger is getting cold."

She'd been nauseated with morning sickness the entire pregnancy, and it felt good to have an appetite again.

As she ate, he took the tube back and spread ointment on his fingers. He motioned for her to hold her leg out, and when she did, he carefully rubbed cream on the worn skin.

His touch was gentle, and it shamed her that she responded to his kindness. She was so starved for people and affection that even her jailer's touch was welcome.

"What if something goes wrong with the baby?" she asked.

"Don't borrow trouble. That baby and you are going to be just fine."

He was going to kill her. She'd feared this since the moment he'd locked her in here, but the instant she'd seen the initials on the back of the dresser, she'd known those women had not survived.

Without a word, he took her by the elbow and helped her to her feet. "Time to go."

She cringed. "Where are we going?"

"It's a better place than this. A bigger room."

When she didn't move fast enough, he grabbed her tighter and pulled her the rest of the way to her feet. "Let's go."

She dug her heels in. At least she was familiar with this hellhole. Here she at least had the pen and the two magazines containing the words of the other girls. "Where are we going?"

"Like I said, a new place."

"I don't want to die!"

He shook his head, grinning as if she'd lost her mind. "You ain't going to die."

Her belly felt heavy as she stood. "I don't have shoes."

"You don't need shoes. You won't be outside long." Taking her by the arm, he pulled her out of the room, past her discarded cot still tossed against a cement wall, and toward a set of stairs. She glanced back at the room. Every night she'd dreamed of escaping it, but now that she was leaving, she was terrified. That room was the devil she knew, not the unknown hell about to come.

As she tried to keep pace with his long strides, her gaze swept the room. There was a washer and dryer and even some of her clothes drying on a clothesline strung between two posts. There were shelves stocked with canned food, baby provisions, and medical supplies. It could have been anyone's basement. It looked ordinary. It was normal.

He yanked her and forced her up the stairs. She'd barely had any activity in the last few months and found by the time she reached the top stair, she was breathless with legs of rubber.

He yanked her through a kitchen equipped with avocado-green appliances that screamed 1970s retro. The smell of Clorox hung in the air.

"I'm afraid," she stammered.

"No reason to be worried. We're just getting you to a nicer room."

"Please, just let me go. I won't tell. I just want to go home."

His fingers tightened around her forearm. Not painful yet, but close. "I could shove sleeping pills down your throat, but you don't want me to do that. It's bad for the baby."

More questions sprang to mind, but she held them close, knowing he would make good on this threat. He always did.

He dragged her through a small living room covered in gold shag carpet and then out the front door. As her bare feet stepped onto the rough wood of the front deck, she was greeted by bright afternoon sunshine. Wincing, she had to look away from the sky, even as she savored the first lungful of fresh air she had inhaled in months. It smelled so sweet she nearly wept. Her face tipped toward the sun and absorbed every bit of its warmth. She'd been such a fool to take the sun, her mother, and her freedom for granted.

"No dawdling." He jerked her toward his truck, opened the front door, and ordered her inside. She struggled with her belly and unsure legs. She was still breathless when she climbed up into the seat. "Put your seat belt on. Don't want you getting hurt. And there are sunglasses in the glove box. Put them on."

She clicked the seat belt in place. "Where are we going?"

"I told you not to worry. It's a better place."

"Like as in dead? Like heaven?"

He laughed. "Like another house." He then pointed a meaty finger at her, and his tone changed instantly. "Get out of the car while I'm walking to my seat, and I will break your legs when I catch you. You hear me, girl?"

"I hear."

He came around the hood quickly, watching her, and before she could map out or process escape, he was behind the wheel.

He started the engine and drove down the graveled driveway. She glanced back at the house, thought about the initials carved on the back of the dresser and the other women who'd been held there. Was this what happened to them?

"Don't look so worried." He flashed her that dazzling smile.

He slowed at a stoplight on the main road that she guessed was west of Austin, somewhere near the Hill Country.

They drove in silence, and she stared out at the clouds and blue sky. Soon side roads fed into smaller and smaller roads. She leaned toward her window as the first car she'd seen approached them.

"Sit lower in the seat," he said.

When she didn't move fast enough, he grabbed her wrist, twisting her arm until she cowered down. They drove for almost a half hour, and soon the lights of Austin glistened around her. He exited the main road and took several rights and lefts before pulling into a little neighborhood and into the garage of a house.

When the garage door closed behind them, he shut off the engine and came around to her side of the car. He hauled her out of the car and into the house. She had barely seconds to register her surroundings before he dragged her down a set of stairs and toward another door. Another prison.

He opened the door and flipped on a light. "Go on, get inside."

This space was half the size of the other. The bed was a twin, and there was no kitchen table but only a side table with a microwave and packets of noodles and bottles of water. There was a toilet in the corner, but no bath or shower.

"This place is so small."

"Don't worry. You won't be here long." He grabbed a chain from under the bed. "Sit down. I need to put this on you."

"I don't need a chain. I won't run."

He shoved her toward the bed and forced her to sit, clamping the chain around her other ankle. "You fooled me once. You should see the damn bruise on my arm. So that's not coming off you until the baby is born."

Death in childbirth was rare in light of modern medicine, but that was in a hospital with doctors, nurses, and clean sheets. "If I have it alone, the baby's chances of survival are so much lower."

"I got it worked out. It's been a while, but I've delivered babies before. But you better hurry up and have that baby. If it doesn't come in the next week, I'll cut it out of you."

CHAPTER TWELVE

Tuesday, June 26, 6:00 p.m.

Hayden met Brogan at the Austin Police Department Forensic Science Division's forensic lab. Melissa Savage, a technician who favored jeans, flats, and brightly colored Hawaiian shirts, greeted them. Her dark curly hair was wound into a ponytail, and several pencils stuck out at different angles.

"Gentlemen, come on back to the lab," she said.

She walked with long, even strides as she led them toward a light table. She'd methodically arranged neat rows of Macy Crow's belongings, which had been found in her backpack and in her pockets. Her bloodstained clothes, which had been cut away by the EMTs and emergency room doctors, were also present.

Among the belongings were a hairbrush, lipstick, mace, PowerBars, and receipts for food and gas and a withdrawal from an ATM. There were also her cracked cell phone, breath mints, and a hotel key.

"What about that phone?" Hayden asked. "Any record of calls? I hear she was trying to call me."

"That's correct," Savage said. "But she was hit before she finished dialing. There's a voicemail from Dr. McIntyre's office."

"They were trading messages," he said. "What else is on the phone?"

"She also visited the website for the medical examiner's office and did a search on Dr. McIntyre."

"She saw a picture of her?" Hayden asked.

"It was on the page she pulled up."

How had Macy been tipped off about Faith? Had she learned something when she'd visited Jack Crow's trailer?

"No more calls," Savage went on to say, "but Special Agent Crow did snap a selfie in what looks like her hotel room, as well as a picture of a missing person poster, all on the night she was attacked." Savage opened the phone and showed the Rangers the pictures of the selfie and the missing person poster. "Remember Paige Sheldon?"

Paige. The name Macy had given the responding officer. "Sure. She was a pregnant teenager who vanished about eight months ago."

Savage pulled up the case on her computer. It was the same picture on the flyer, but this one was more vivid, in color, and showcased her stunning looks. "She's now nineteen, and according to the missing person report, she vanished in May," Savage said.

"Why did Macy take a picture of her poster?" Hayden asked.

"Missing girls, runaways, and black market babies are the exact kind of case Macy Crow specializes in investigating." Savage spoke the words as if she were saying Hayden's thoughts out loud. "She'd have been drawn to a poster like Paige Sheldon's."

These cases got under Hayden's skin because he remembered how Sierra used to talk to him about adoption. They had always known she couldn't have children, so adoption had been the plan. They had just been referred for a mixed-race toddler when she'd been diagnosed with cancer. Adoption was put on hold, and whenever she was sick from the chemo, he'd remind her that one day she'd hold their baby in her arms.

"Is there a geotag on the picture?" Hayden asked.

"Yeah," Savage said. "It was taken on Third Street outside a bar called Second Chances, which is two blocks from where she was struck by the vehicle."

"Her old man gets brutally murdered. Macy's in town less than five hours, visits a bar, takes the time to snap a picture of Paige Sheldon's flyer, and then an attempt is made on her life," Hayden said. "I want to talk to Paige Sheldon's family. Macy Crow saw something, and I want to know what it was. What else did you find?"

"Her Uber app showed she was picked up at a hotel at ten p.m. last night." Savage reached for the hotel key that was among Macy's belongings. "I called the hotel, identified myself, and told them to hold off on housekeeping until we can investigate the room. The manager said Macy wasn't supposed to check out until Friday and had put a Do Not Disturb sign on her door. The room should be untouched."

Hayden wrote down the hotel name and address. "I'll check it out." He looked at the picture of the Paige Sheldon flyer Macy had taken outside Second Chances.

"She might have left more information in her hotel room," Savage said.

"Which is exactly why we're headed there."

***

The drive to Macy Crow's hotel room took Hayden and Brogan just under twenty minutes. It was an average, nondescript chain hotel that could be found in hundreds of cities across America. They introduced themselves to the clerk, who ducked into the back and brought out the manager, a tall man with short, graying hair.

He came from behind the front desk and extended his hand. "I'm Jay Sanchez. You called about one of our guests?"

"That's right," Brogan said. "We'd like to see Macy Crow's room."

"It was a hit-and-run?" the manager asked.

"She passed away late last night, and we're trying to find out what happened." Brogan was sticking to the story that Macy was dead.

"That's terrible," Sanchez said. "Of course I'll show you the room."

As they rode the elevator to the third floor, Hayden asked, "When did she check in?"

"Yesterday," he said. "She was supposed to check out on Friday."

"Did you notice anything about Ms. Crow?" Hayden asked. "Did she have any visitors?"

"No visitors that I know of, but I don't work the front desk anymore." The elevator doors opened, and Sanchez extended his hand and waited for them to exit. "I did ask the gals that worked the front desk, and none of them remembered. I'm having the surveillance tapes pulled. As soon as I get the all clear from corporate, I'll turn them over."

The manager stopped at room 342, where a **DO NOT DISTURB** sign dangled from the door handle. He removed a passkey from his pocket, swiped it, and opened the door. "Ms. Crow checked in Monday, but she didn't have a reservation. I checked the room status myself when Ms. Savage called to confirm that housekeeping had not been inside. As you can see, they haven't."

"Did you enter the room?" Hayden asked.

"No. I didn't want to disrupt anything."

"Great. Thank you for your time, Mr. Sanchez," Hayden said. "We'll take it from here."

"Glad to help." Sanchez lingered a beat and then, accepting that Hayden wouldn't allow him inside, nodded and stepped aside. Hayden pulled on latex gloves, flipped on the lights, and closed the door.

Brogan worked his fingers into gloves. "Give us a clue, Macy."

The room was furnished with the standard two double beds, a desk and chair, a bureau, and a television. Both beds were still made, but judging by the towels on the bathroom floor and the open soap packets, she had showered in the short time she was here.

A blue zippered bag filled with cosmetics, tampons, toothbrush, toothpaste, and razor sat on the bathroom counter. In the shower, the shampoo and conditioner bottles were open.

Hayden looked at the blond strands of hair in the hairbrush, and his mind flashed to a memory of Faith running her hands through her very thick hair. She'd quipped once that sometimes the locks were like having a sheepdog on her head.

There was a coffee maker plugged into the wall, and beside it were two wrapped mugs and K-Cups. The trash can was clean.

Hayden stripped the top blanket on one of the beds and removed the pillowcases from the pillows before yanking off the sheets. He skimmed his hands under first one mattress and then the other but found nothing.

Brogan opened and searched the bureau drawers. The first was empty except for a Bible. None of the others held anything. He then crossed to the simple desk, where a computer and phone sat in full display. There was also a set of keys, which he guessed was for Jack Crow's truck.

"Here we go." Brogan opened the laptop.

Hayden rubbed the back of his neck and studied the stickers on the outside of the computer. "Hiking, a Hello Kitty sticker, a triathlon logo, and a literacy emblem. Athletic, quirky, and smart."

Brogan booted up the computer. A screen saver appeared featuring Macy standing atop a peak in a lush green mountain range that reminded Hayden of the Appalachian Trail. Her hair was tied back in a ponytail, her sunglasses were on top of her head, and she wore a blue puffer jacket. Straight white teeth flashed, and she had her hands in the air as if she'd crossed a finish line. He would have sworn on a stack of Bibles it was Faith.

"She worked for the FBI," Brogan said. "And yet she doesn't have a pass code on her computer."

"She wanted us to see this. One more precaution, just in case."

Hayden picked up the keys and walked to the window. Pushing back the curtains, he scanned the lot until he spotted several dark trucks. He began clicking the unlock button on the chain. The lights on the truck parked closest to the hotel winked.

Brogan picked up the phone. "Looks like a burner, like the one Ledbetter said Crow bought."

"Ledbetter said Crow bought two phones."

"The phone found on Macy was her own personal phone. There is only one burner that I see."

"Any activity on the phone?"

"No call, text, or email history," Brogan said. "But there are three addresses in the Maps application."

"Where are they?"

"The first is out in the Texas Hill Country, the second is in East Austin near where she was hit, and the third is for the Travis County Medical Examiner's Office."

"Jack Crow left Faith's work address for Macy?"

"Looks like it."

"That explains Macy's search for Faith. She had to have been floored."

Macy had been to Crow's trailer, but then she'd driven deeper west into the Hill Country, doubled back to this hotel, and finally gone to East Austin.

"She had a call in to me on her personal phone," Hayden said. "Because she found something out there in the country."

Brogan opened Macy's email account on the computer and scanned the received emails and then the sent folder. "You're going to love this. She sent an email message to Faith McIntyre. She scheduled it to arrive today at five."

"Put a call in to Savage. Have her people process this room and the truck completely. And tell them it's a priority."

He reached for his phone and dialed Faith. The call went to her voicemail. "Faith, check your email. There's a message from Macy, sent today."

***

It was nearly seven when Hayden and Brogan arrived at the Second Chances bar on Third Street. Stepping inside, they removed their hats, knowing there'd be no hiding the fact they were Rangers. But then, neither cared.

The bar had a decent-size crowd for a weeknight. Most of the patrons looked like working-class men. Only one or two in cheap suits were sitting in the booths. Behind the bar was a long mirror framed with barnwood, and in front of it were long shelves covered in countless liquor bottles. Hayden glanced at the flyers behind the bar and spotted the one for Paige Sheldon. Why had it caught Macy Crow's attention? This was the kind of work Crow did for the FBI, so maybe it had simply been reflex.

There were a few men at the bar hunched over their drinks, and standing before them was a tall man with gray hair brushed off a long, lean face tanned by the sun. He wore a bright-red T-shirt that read SECOND CHANCES, jeans, and worn cowboy boots.

He grinned when he spotted the pair. "How can I assist two of Texas's finest?"

Hayden made the introduction as each showed his badge. "You are?"

"Danny Garnet. I own the joint." He set the bottle of booze on the bar. "What can I do for you?"

"We're following up on a case lead. We had a hit-and-run at the park."

"I heard about that. Cops weren't giving out many details. What can I do to help?"

"Victim snapped a picture a block from the bar. Thought she might have come in here."

"Last night was hopping. We have a two-for-one special between eight and eleven, and that brings 'em out of the woodwork."

Hayden pulled out a picture of Macy Crow. "Ever seen her in here?"

Garnet studied the picture, nodding. "I do remember her. She's not the average gal that comes in this bar, and she stood out. There were several guys staring at her last night. One tried to hit on her." He handed back the picture. "How is she?"

"She didn't make it." Hayden watched Garnet's face, carefully searching for any hint that he knew more than he was saying.

"Shit." His face crumpled, and he looked down, shaking his head, rubbing the bar rag over an already-clean section. "Where was she hit?"

"Right down the street near Comal Pocket Park. And you were here the whole night?"

"I was," he said. "Slinging drinks. Like I said, two-for-one night is crazy."

"And you got people that can confirm it?" Brogan asked.

"Sure. Dozens. Say the word, and I'll find a few folks to back me up." Garnet shook his head and then seemed to think better of holding back. "Look, I don't like to share what my customers say, but Macy was here to ask me about her dad, Jack Crow. She told me he died on Sunday. Terrible. Crow and I served in the military together. He saved my ass a couple of times. Hell of a guy. And I told her so. I was sorry to hear he passed." He leaned in closer. "And for the record, I've been clean since I got out thirty years ago. Not even a speeding ticket."

"Did she tell you Jack Crow was murdered?" Hayden asked.

"Shit. No. She never said a word about that. What the hell is going on?" Garnet asked.

"That's what we're trying to figure out," Hayden said. "When was the last time Crow came by here?"

"Years."

"You sure about that?"

"Definitely. I wouldn't forget my old buddy. Maybe he dropped by, but I wasn't here. During the day I'm often off property dealing with suppliers."

"Did she speak to anyone while she was here?" Brogan asked.

"Just the guy who was hitting on her." Garnet twisted the onyx ring on his pinky finger. "I could tell she wasn't having any of his charm. She left less than a few minutes after he started hitting on her."

"Is there anyone else we can talk to here who might have known her?" Hayden asked.

"Sure. Heather was here. She's my manager, and frankly she notices more about what's going on than I do. As she likes to tell me, women are more astute."

"We'd like to speak to her," Hayden said.

"She's not here right now, but I can get you her contact information." Garnet went into the back and reappeared with a sticky note. "Here's her name and number. She's not scheduled to work until tomorrow night."

"Thanks."

"No problem. If you need anything, let me know."

"We will," Hayden said. And then as he turned he nodded to Paige's flyer. "Thanks for posting that flyer. Not all area businesses are as cooperative. And for that case, we need all the help we can get."

"We do what we can." Garnet again turned the ring round and round. "We're as much a part of the community as anyone."

Outside, as they got into Hayden's car, Brogan said, "He's lying."

"Yeah, I got that feeling, too."

CHAPTER THIRTEEN

Tuesday, June 26, 7:15 p.m.

Faith had put on her earphones and was listening to music as she spent the next hour typing up more reports that would have to be done eventually. As she slid into the facts of the cases she'd worked, she felt a sense of control returning.

When she finished the last report, Faith combed her hair back with her hands and then secured it with a band. She then shifted her attention to the queue of emails on her computer.

Several were from Margaret Slater. One was an update on the shelter fundraiser, and another invited her to be on a fundraiser for the brain trauma unit at the hospital. Her last line insisted they have lunch or dinner soon.

> Miss seeing you, kiddo.

Faith responded, promising to call her soon. And then remembering that Margaret had been a good friend of her mother's, she typed,

> I'd like to talk about Mom and my adoption when
> you get the chance.

For a moment, she hesitated to hit the "Send" button. She'd avoided these questions with Margaret for years, and as uncomfortable as they felt, they had to be asked. She hit "Send."

The tenth email down stopped her cold. It was from Macy Crow. She checked the time and saw that it had been sent at five p.m. today. How was that possible?

Dear Dr. McIntyre,

My name is Macy Crow. I'm Jack Crow's daughter. You left me a voicemail, but we need to talk in person.

This might seem out of left field, but I believe we're related. I'm adopted and have been searching for my biological roots for several years. My adoptive father, Jack Crow, passed away on Sunday, and ironically, you were the pathologist who took care of him.

I've attached two addresses that Jack left me on a prepaid phone I found at his trailer. I've been to the one in the country, and I've got a gut feeling something very wrong happened there.

Macy Crow

P.S. A picture is worth a thousand words, so I've enclosed a few of mine.

Faith studied the selfie and caught the wry expression that telegraphed, *"Ain't this something?"* For a long moment she stared at the picture, seeing herself but also noticing subtle differences.

Multiple reactions collided as she looked at what could have been her face. Joy. Curiosity. Anger. Sadness. She wasn't sure how long she sat just staring at the picture and reconciling it with the image of Macy lying in her hospital bed. Hands trembling, she tapped her index finger on her mouse.

She glanced at the clock. It was after office hours, and she realized the sounds of the office had faded as most of the staff had left for the day. She had almost an hour and a half before sunset. There wasn't much traffic now, and if she hurried, she could reach the ranch. As tempting as it was to go alone, it wouldn't do her or Macy any good if something happened. Hayden needed to have this information.

A knock on her door startled her for a moment.

Nancy poked her head inside. "What are you still doing here?"

"Like you, catching up on paperwork."

"Remember the autopsy you did last week? Miller was a thirty-eight-year-old male who suffered sudden death after a blinding headache. You determined it was an aneurysm?"

"Sure." Cranial examination had determined massive blood present in the brain cavity due to an arterial tear in the brain stem.

"His wife is in the lobby. She didn't realize how late it is, and I ran into her on my way out. She's still struggling and wants to talk to you."

As anxious as she was to get to the ranch, she knew this took precedence. "Send her in."

Faith spent nearly a half hour with the young widow and mother of two. She explained how her husband's death was due to genetics, and the weakness in the vessel would have been very likely inoperable even if it had been detected. It was terrible genetics.

After the meeting, she grabbed her purse and headed toward her car, checking her messages for the first time in a couple of hours. Hayden had called. She listened to his message and then texted him back, explaining she'd received Macy's message.

131

She reached her car and got in. She sat, absorbing the day's residual heat radiating from the seats. Her phone buzzed, and she glanced at the display. Mitchell Hayden.

She drew in a breath and answered the phone. "Hayden."

"Where are you?"

"In my car, but still at the medical center," she said.

"You've read Macy's email?"

She sat straighter. "I have. How did you know about it?"

"We found her computer in her hotel room. Why didn't you call me immediately?"

"I only just received it. It's been nonstop on this end."

Again, they were trapped between a personal relationship and a professional one. Distance and anonymity had worked well for them up to this point. But this case was twisting around them both, forcing them to interact with each other more than either had originally planned.

"I'm five minutes away. Stay put."

"Understood."

She grabbed her purse and got out of her car, and in just under five minutes, a dark SUV pulled up beside her and the passenger window rolled down.

Hayden nodded to the empty passenger seat. "Let's go."

She sensed his irritation as she got into the car. "I just planned to have a look around."

He shot her a glance. He pulled onto the main road and wove through town toward I-35. "Has Macy Crow sent you any other communication?"

"No."

"Are you sure about that?" An edge sharpened in his tone, and she sensed a line drawn between them. The Rangers were on one side and she on the other. Fine. So be it.

"I would know if a twin communicated with me," she said. "Those are the details that don't normally slip by me too often."

He drove in silence for several miles and then asked in a softer tone that radiated genuine concern, "How are you holding up?"

"Hayden, don't patronize me. That's about the one thing I can't take right now. I like you better when you're an SOB."

His frown telegraphed his own uneasiness with this new journey they were taking together into uncharted emotional territory.

"And for the record, I feel like I'm trapped in an episode of *The Twilight Zone*," she said.

"I've been there before. Not a good place."

"No, it certainly isn't."

She watched as the cityscape yielded to the rugged, brown countryside covered in scrub trees and cacti. She pulled up the email from Macy as he drove, referencing the map.

Strong, weathered hands, which gripped the steering wheel and looked suited for hard work or a brawl, were so gentle when they ran over her skin.

His watch was older, a throwback to the fifties. He'd always worn it, but she'd never asked about it. "Nice watch. You don't strike me as the type to chase the vintage look."

He didn't spare the watch a glance, but his pride was evident. "It was my grandfather's, then my father's. A tradition the oldest male inherits. Still keeps perfect time."

Faith countered, "My mother nurtured a deep reverence for her sixth-generation Texas lineage. Continuity was important to her. She and I would stand in front of the portrait of my great-grandmother, and she'd say, 'Generations of stern stock like us. One day you'll have a daughter and carry on the line.'"

Faith had been proud to be the descendant of a strong line of women. And when she found out she was adopted, she realized she would never be a genuine standard-bearer for the Wallace women whose lineage ended with her mother.

"And it bothers you?" he asked.

"Sometimes."

"You saw how Jack Crow died. I'd bet you my watch he did that for Macy, who by all accounts is not his flesh and blood."

A sudden surge of sadness wrapped around her voice. "Don't mind me. Feeling sorry for myself."

She clicked on the radio and selected a country song. They listened as he made his way through the still-congested evening traffic clogging up I-35. By the time he took their exit, there'd already been a fender bender up ahead and the sluggish traffic was coming to a stop.

He turned right onto a rural route that wound farther west, closer to the Hill Country. Another five miles and he slowed as he approached a rusted mailbox. He took a right and plowed down the dusty driveway. The SUV kicked up blooms of dust.

The driveway cut through fallow fields. In the distance Faith spotted a brick rancher surrounded by tall weeds, an old Ford truck on blocks, and several large oil drums.

Hayden parked, but he didn't get out right away. He studied the area. "Stay close to me. Don't wander off."

"I've worked my share of crime scenes."

"Like I said, stay close." He got out of the car, shrugged off his jacket, and tossed it in the back seat. His hand automatically went to the weapon on his hip. He touched it lightly as he appeared to go down a mental checklist.

Faith joined him at the front of the SUV. She studied the house, knowing from experience that the least remarkable places could hide the worst horrors.

"Let's have a look at the house first." He strode up the three front steps and tested the door handle. It was locked. The curtains were drawn over the large front display window, and the side windows were also covered. But the dust on the porch had been disturbed. And it wasn't just from the one set of footprints that he had expected after Macy's visit. He estimated there were at least three sets.

He looked up and pointed to what Faith suddenly realized was a very small security camera.

"A camera?" she said.

"Not only will they know we've been here, but also Macy."

He walked around back and stepped onto a patio made of cracked stone pavers. Off to the side was a set of rusted patio furniture.

Hayden's boots crunched on the gravel lining the patio as he stepped out onto the dusty earth around it. The sun had cooled, and its light was dimming quickly now. Soon it would dip completely from the sky, but tonight would be a full moon.

Hayden studied the land as if reading a book. He moved northwest thirty paces. Again he crouched and scooped up a handful of soil, slowly letting the dust trickle from his loose fist. "Have a look at this."

She moved up beside him and trailed her outstretched hand to the three stones spaced evenly apart. The land in front of each marker was slightly concave. "The soil is uneven."

"Yes, it is," he said.

She'd been to the sites of unmarked graves before, and she'd come to recognize the signs. When a body was buried and it decomposed, it bloated first; then when the flesh burst, it deflated. This rise and fall left cracks and indentions in the earth.

The burnt-orange light cast a glow over good-sized stones that were maybe fifty pounds each and natural to the area. They could have been easily overlooked. However, when she really studied them, she realized they were arranged in a perfect line.

"Gravestones?" she asked.

He reached for his cell and stood. "I don't know. But we need a team with ground-penetrating radar out here."

"We're out of daylight."

"I'm calling the sheriff's department, and I'll ask them to guard this area until we can return in the morning."

"I don't get it. Why did Jack Crow leave this address for his daughter? Why not just tell her?"

"Maybe he couldn't face her, but he needed to clear his conscience."

"He bought two burner phones before he died. We've only found one. We've got to find the other."

***

When Macy was four, she had gone on summer break with Jack to Galveston Island. She'd gotten tired of waiting for Jack to stop talking to the pretty lady at the snack bar and had gone to the edge of the pool. She had dipped her toe in, and the cool water had felt so good.

She had been sure she could jump into the pool and scramble to the edge just as she'd done with her father. So she'd jumped into the cold water. However, she'd landed farther from the edge than she'd anticipated, and panic had immediately set in.

She'd kicked against the cement bottom and clawed herself toward the sunlight flickering above. Her fingertips had broken the surface, and she had felt the air teasing her skin. But even as her little legs had kicked hard, they hadn't created enough lift to propel her face above the surface so she could inhale air.

She had sunk back down. Her fingers had slipped below the water's surface. Her lungs had screamed for air, and terror had sliced through her body. The chlorine had burned her eyes and filled her nose.

And then a hand had reached down from above and grabbed her by the back straps of her bathing suit and yanked her upward toward the blue sky.

The heat of the sun had warmed her face as her mouth had opened and she'd gulped in air. Fear had given way to relief as she'd blinked and stared at the face of her father, whose frown had revealed a kind of fear she'd never seen before.

"Pop!" She had sucked in more air as tears had welled in her eyes.

Tanned fingers had brushed the strands of blond hair from her eyes, and a grin had tugged at the edges of a glower that scared most grown men. "Don't you cry on me, Macy Crow. You're safe and sound now. No need to cry. Jesus, your mother will kill me if she even knew I almost let you drown." A sob had shuddered through her, and she had blinked back the tears. She'd sniffed and wrapped her arms around his neck.

Macy had forgotten about that day from twenty-five years ago. And she remembered it now because she was sinking again to the bottom of another pool that was far deeper and darker. Pop wouldn't be there for her this time.

She tried to open her eyes and focus toward the sunlight, but her lids didn't respond. She remained trapped in blackness. She wanted to kick her legs, flail her arms, push through the inky obscurity, and break the surface. But no matter how much she willed it, she couldn't.

In the distance, she heard hushed chatter and the beep of equipment. There were people around her. She wasn't alone.

Once she thought she heard her brother's low and angry voice. But it vanished almost as soon as she heard it and was followed by more poking and prodding.

"*Dirk, throw me a lifeline! Pull me up! I'm here! I'm alive! Don't leave me!*"

Macy couldn't remain in the darkness. She knew something.

Something important.

She couldn't quite remember what it was, but she was certain if she could reach the light and air, she could find the missing pieces and finish the puzzle.

"*Come on, Dirk, somebody, anybody. Pull me up! I'm right here, and I'm sinking fast.*"

***

It was just after ten when Faith pulled past the guard station at the entrance of her North Austin gated community. The townhouse development was less than five years old, and she'd taken out a hefty mortgage last year to buy her first adult home.

Her row of townhomes was located toward the rear of the property and backed up to woods. The building's sharp angles and modern lines could have been harsh and cold if not for the quirky combination of glass windows, tin roof, and wooden horizontal strips stained a warm honey brown. The building had an artistic vibe that blended with the water-efficient landscaping that provided touches of green cacti blended among rocks. There was a two-car garage space and metal steps that led up to the wooden front door with an ornate wrought iron handle. She'd been drawn to this home the moment she'd seen it.

As she pulled into her driveway, her headlights caught the silhouette of a person sitting on her front steps. Tensing, she slowed and rolled down her window to get a better look. The figure was slight and wore a hoodie.

"Who are you?" Faith asked as she reached for her phone. "How did you get past the guard? No, wait, don't answer that. Tell it to the cops."

"Chill, Faith. It's me, Kat."

Faith gripped her phone. "What are you doing here?"

"I came to see you," the girl said.

Faith's heart was still jackhammering. "You're supposed to be at the shelter."

"Well, I'm not. I'm here."

"How did you get here?" Faith asked.

"Uber."

"You don't have a credit card."

"I sweet-talked a visitor at the shelter. Said my mom was sick."

She liked the kid's moxie. "What's going on, Kat?"

The girl approached her car, her hand gripping the strap of her backpack. "We need to talk."

"Is something wrong with the baby?"

"We need to talk about DNA, Faith."

Out of her car, she closed the garage and climbed the front steps. She opened the door and clicked on the lights. "What about DNA?"

"You registered your DNA with an ancestry site," the girl said, following her inside.

After Peter Slater Sr. died, she'd lost what she'd thought was her last connection to her past. She'd wanted to broach the subject of her adoption with Margaret, but had been waiting for her to regain her footing after her husband's death. In April, in a moment of frustration, she'd tossed her DNA into the ever-growing pool of people searching for some clue about their family's past.

Faith had checked the site a few times, but she'd had no matches, which for now was fine. She had enough on her plate with work.

"How do you know that?" Faith asked.

"I'll explain after I eat." Kat looked from side to side. "I'm starving. Do you have anything you can whip up in the kitchen?"

As annoyed as she was at the kid for showing up unannounced and dropping one of her bombshells, she wouldn't press until Kat ate something. "Sure."

Inside, the foyer's cathedral ceiling crisscrossed with beautiful wood beams. Hanging on the walls was an eclectic mix of paintings, photographs, and etchings. She'd collected some from around the world, but the majority of it had belonged to her mother and grandmother, who'd both loved art. Since Faith had been a little girl, her mother had told her that the women in their family loved art. Faith had never quite had her mother's eye for it, but she'd inherited a deep appreciation.

Kat studied the artwork. Like most who entered, she stopped and stared. "Pretty sweet. Where'd you get all this stuff?"

"My grandmother, mother, and me collected this *stuff* from around the world. It's all I have left of them."

"Cool."

"Each piece tells a story."

"But the way you've put it all together tells a bigger story. That's kind of what I do with computers. I string a lot of code together to create something new."

Faith looked at the collection, realizing she'd never thought of the art as a whole. She'd always thought of the separate pieces and their unique stories. Now she realized she'd blended hers among her mother's and grandmother's and had told a new story.

She set her purse and keys on a side table and reset the house alarm. She made her way down a long hallway to a modern, open kitchen. It was outfitted with a spacious marble island illuminated by three industrial pendant lights, stainless steel appliances that she rarely used, and white cabinets stocked with mostly unused dishes from her mother and grandmother.

She opened the refrigerator and pulled out a loaf of bread, grapes, sparkling water, and several cheeses that had served as her dinner the last couple of nights.

Kat dropped her backpack by the island and sat at one of the barstools. Through the glass doors of the upper cabinets, she openly studied the collection of handblown glassware and platters made by a favorite potter in North Carolina.

Faith pulled the loaf of bread from its sleeve and sliced into it. She slathered mustard on the bread and then layered the bread with meat, cheese, and lettuce. She cut the sandwiches on a diagonal and arranged them neatly on plates with handfuls of grapes.

Kat took several bites. "I'm starving all the time."

"The baby is growing." She handed her a paper towel and then poured her a glass of sparkling water.

"Starting to feel like an alien invader is in my body."

"You have less than six weeks to go."

Kat set down her sandwich and wiped her fingers with the paper towel. "That reminds me. That lady from the adoption group called again. She wants to meet. But I keep putting it off."

"You can't do that," Faith said.

"I know. Will you come with me?"

"Yes. In fact, I can call her and set up the meeting, if that works for you?"

"Okay. Sure. Whatever," Kat said.

She took that as high endorsement and was gratified that the girl trusted her with something so important.

"Consider it done. Eat up."

Kat finished her sandwich and settled back in her chair. "When's the last time you checked the genealogy site?"

"I haven't." When she caught Kat's quizzical gaze, she sipped her own glass of water. "You aren't the only one who doesn't want to deal with adoption."

"Maybe that's why we have each other," Kat said. "You help me, and I help you."

"How's that?" Faith asked.

"You have a hit on your page."

She set her glass down carefully. "What do you mean I have a hit?"

"A half sibling."

"What?" A week ago she would have discounted the news as suspect, but with the arrival of Macy she knew anything was now possible. "Let's backtrack. How did you even know I registered for the site?"

"You strike me as the type. It's a very scientific and technical approach. And then I pictured you getting superbusy and forgetting to follow up. I watched you at the fundraiser and wondered if you even have time to sleep. But then I realized you aren't ready for the truth. I'm also a master of avoidance, if you haven't noticed."

The spot-on assessment was disconcerting. "And so you searched the most recognizable sites and hacked into them?"

Kat picked off a piece of bread crust and popped it into her mouth. "Hack is such a harsh word."

"What would you call it?"

Now that they'd shifted from the topic of the baby to computers and hacking, the girl came back into her own. "I had a look around on a few sites."

"And found me." She'd thought twice about sending her DNA into the site. She'd felt as if she was opening herself up to a world she wasn't sure she'd really wanted to know about.

"And a half sibling. She left you two messages in your account's inbox." Kat removed her laptop from her backpack, opened it, and pulled up the genealogy site. With no hint of apology, she logged into Faith's account. "You have a new password by the way. Can't be too careful these days."

"Do I?"

"Faith plus Kat equals exclamation point."

"Thanks for sharing."

"Next time make a password that doesn't just include the year of your birth and your initials. Very amateur."

"Good to know."

Kat tapped on the screen. "Her name is Marissa Lewis. She is a twenty-nine-year-old lawyer living in San Antonio. Less than an hour south of here." The girl folded her arms over her pregnant belly, looking pleased with herself. "You must come from very smart stock."

Memories of the country graves jabbed at her, and she wondered if she and Marissa Lewis were connected to any of them in some way. Her fingers trembled slightly, and she wasn't sure she could bring herself to reply to Marissa.

Could she really be biologically connected to this woman? And if they were half siblings, did they share a mother or father? It was possible that Josie could have had more children.

Again she thought about the three gravestones. Another darker possibility came to her, and her first thought was to reject it because it was so horrible. But if working in the medical examiner's office had taught her anything, it was that humans did unspeakably cruel things to each other.

"Do you want me to message her?" Kat asked.

One way or another, she had to find out if she was related to this woman. "Sure. Message her. What do I have to lose?"

Kat's fingers tapped quickly, and before Faith could even consider changing her mind, the girl hit "Return" and said, "Done."

"Thanks. I think."

"You don't sound very happy about it." Kat peered at her over the edge of her laptop.

"It's all a little much."

"But you want to know the truth, right?" Kat said. "You want to know your birth family?"

She heard the girl's fear. She was afraid of being forgotten by her own child. "I do. I want to know everything I can about them." They both were silent for a moment, and then she said, "Let me call the shelter and tell them you're spending the night here. We both could use a good night's sleep."

"We will find the truth, Faith."

The truth. Whether she wanted to know it or not, the truth was barreling toward her, and she had no choice but to meet it head-on.

CHAPTER FOURTEEN

Wednesday, June 27, 1:00 a.m.

Hayden had spent the better part of the evening on the phone, arranging for the state forensic team to inspect the land out in the country. When he'd told them he wanted a team in the field in the morning, there'd been some grumbles until he explained it was the case Macy Crow had been working.

Word of Macy's death had spread among law enforcement in the Austin area. One of their own had gone down, and regardless of which law enforcement agency Macy had been attached to, the Rangers and local police felt her loss personally.

He climbed the stairs to his one-bedroom apartment. He unlocked the door, stepped inside, and flicked on the lights. He rarely spent time here. He was either working a case or, when he was unable to face beige walls another night, staying in a hotel.

He locked the door behind him, and tossed his hat and keys on a small table by the door. He shrugged off his jacket and hung it on a simple peg.

This place was set up so that nothing in it reminded him of what he'd lost. The couch, coffee table, and end tables were standard and had been discounted floor models. The television was wide-screen with high definition, though he rarely turned it on these days. And the one bit of art was the Texas state flag, which he'd hung on the wall over the couch.

His mother had told him he would have to do better than a month-to-month lease overlooking dumpsters, and then told him to "hang a few pictures for God's sake," as she'd unpacked a new set of white dishes and a basic collection of pots and pans. When she'd discovered the cactus plant she'd left was nearly dead, she'd taken that back.

He strode into the kitchen and loaded the coffee maker with strong Mexican coffee. As the machine warmed up and gurgled, he grabbed a sausage biscuit from the freezer and popped it in a microwave. By the time it was ready, he was pouring his first cup of coffee.

In the next twenty minutes, he polished off the biscuit and downed two cups of coffee before laying his clothes on a neatly made bed.

He stripped and turned on the shower. As the steam rose up around the shower door, he looked in the mirror, loaded shaving cream on his face, and quickly whisked the blade around his jaw and up his neck.

Each day for the last four years, he'd wondered when the good Lord was going to release him from the purgatory of life. When he realized his maker was content to let him remain among the living, he'd taken matters into his own hands and embraced every fool risk a man could take. There were some Rangers who wondered aloud how he'd survived the bold chances he'd taken, but he was solving cases and getting results. Eventually those successes drifted up the chain of command and got him exactly what he did not want—a promotion.

Steam from the shower fogged the mirror, and when he wiped it away, a haggard face stared back at him. He realized he just might get his wish and how foolish it was. His life wasn't anything close to the one he'd had with Sierra, but for right now, he liked what he had with Faith, whatever the hell that was.

He stepped into the shower, letting the hot water wash away the remnants of shaving cream, fatigue, and the aches and pains in his ribs still lingering from a fight with a drug dealer last year.

Out of the shower, he toweled quickly. Fueled on caffeine, his body was so wired the chances of sleep were slim to none. But he lay down, knowing he should at least try, because he'd been a cop long enough to know even a little crappy shut-eye cleared the fog from his brain. He needed every advantage he could take. He closed his eyes, but his mind kept turning.

Faith. Macy. Jack. Paige.

There was trouble connected to that damn ranch. He didn't fully understand the correlation, but one way or another, he would get some answers in a few hours.

When his cell rang, it was four a.m. The cell's display read **MELISSA SAVAGE**. Clearing his throat, he sat up and on the third ring said, "This is Hayden."

"I have surveillance footage from several shops between Second Chances and the spot where Macy Crow was hit."

"I'll be there in twenty minutes." He dressed in the Rangers' trademark khakis, white shirt, boots, and string tie. He brewed fresh coffee and filled a to-go cup. He was fairly certain if he were cut, he'd bleed java.

The streets were quiet at this hour, as were the hallways of the justice center. He moved down the third floor hallway toward the light spilling out from the last door on the right. In the office, Melissa Savage was sitting cross-legged in her chair, cup of tea in hand, watching what looked like raw video footage. A coffeepot on the counter gurgled out fresh brew.

Hayden knocked on her door, and she looked up over her glasses. "Do you ever sleep, Savage?"

"Every Saturday whether I need it or not."

"I hear you. Mind if I grab a cup?"

"Help yourself. Brogan is on his way."

Hayden crossed to the coffeepot as the last bit percolated out. He pulled the pot and filled his cup. One sip was a jolt to the heart. "You drink it this strong?"

"I don't touch the stuff. But I've worked with cops long enough to know they run better on high-octane. I figured Ranger Brogan might want a cup or two to keep up with you."

"He'll get that."

As if on cue, Brogan arrived and wordlessly went to the machine and filled a paper cup. He all but drained the first cup before topping it off with more. "Weak coffee, Savage."

She didn't look up from her computer and deadpanned, "You're just bummed I didn't write your name on the cup with a cute smiley face like the local coffee barista downstairs."

Hayden wasn't in the mood to listen to one of Brogan's rare attempts at banter. "What did you find, Savage?"

She leafed through the pages of a spiral notebook until she found a note that had her backtracking footage to a different time stamp. "We know when Macy Crow was struck on Monday night per Officer Holcombe's body and dashcam footage. I was sent footage from three retail shops. All three picked up Macy Crow, and all confirmed what we already knew. So I backed up the dates and started looking for Jack Crow." She pressed a button. "Here is what I found on Wednesday, June thirteenth, at seven p.m."

The camera's lens captured black-and-white footage of the back alley that ran behind the main street.

"There was a lot of people coming and going from the back entrance of this particular bar," Savage said. "And it's always amazing to me how many people do what they do in public. Just about everything is on camera these days. Do they not realize someone is watching?"

Hayden thought about the moment in the elevator with Faith on Monday night. It had been all he could do to keep his hands off her.

Savage tapped her screen with her fingertip and stopped the footage. "What's so special about that seven p.m. time slot is that Jack Crow visits Second Chances."

"According to his son and assistant, Crow was practically a hermit," Hayden said.

"I talked to the owner of Maxwell's," Brogan said. "They said he used to come every night at five for dinner. Burger well done and extra fries. But about two months ago he started coming less, and they hadn't seen him at all the week before he died."

"Well, he made it to Second Chances on June thirteenth," Savage said as she tapped the screen. "We start with the first sighting at seven p.m. I found security camera footage of him entering via the alley entrance. The same footage showed him leaving through the alley door twenty minutes later."

What were the chances that Crow had not seen Garnet during those twenty minutes? It was possible but not probable.

Savage sped up the tape to 7:20 p.m. Crow's broad shoulders were slightly stooped and his face was pale, but there was no missing the anger in his expression. He paused by the back door and pounded his fist against the building's brick wall before he shoved his hands in his pockets and walked away.

"He's pissed," Hayden said. "And that kind of anger doesn't jive with showing up at a bar and not finding your buddy there."

"Note that no one follows him as he leaves the alley toward his truck." She pressed another button, and the image on the screen switched to a camera across the street. Crow was never picked up on this camera, but his truck could be seen in the background driving away. Seconds after, a hardtop jeep followed.

"Could be coincidence," Hayden said.

Savage froze the frame and tapped on the license plate. "I hear you. And I'd have bought into that as well if not for the third camera."

The third camera was mounted across from Second Chances, and it captured the jeep in full frame. The driver got out. He was wearing a hoodie and appeared to be male. His identity was hidden until, for a brief instant, the man looked up, and the camera caught a partial view of his face.

Savage froze the frame and reached for two printouts she'd made earlier. "Do either of you gentlemen recognize this man?"

Hayden stared at the shadowed profile and felt a rush of recognition and frustration. He'd had the guy in his sights. He'd had him.

"I can't say for certain if this is the man who killed Crow and also attacked Macy," Savage said. "But he was following Crow a week before he died."

"Want me to put out a BOLO?" Brogan asked.

"Yeah. I want Dirk Crow picked up as soon as possible," Hayden said.

***

Hiding in plain sight had always worked best for him. He found the more cloak-and-dagger shit people did, the more likely they were to be noticed. A change of shirt, a different hat, or a swap of coat or hoodie was all it took to change his look well enough so no one noticed.

When he heard the bar's back door close, he eased up in the back seat of Heather's car so he could look in the rearview mirror. As soon as he spotted Heather leaving Second Chances, he ducked down low, blending into the shadows. It was past one a.m., and she was leaving a little later than most nights, but he guessed she and Garnet had done the nasty as they liked to do in the back room. The later time suited him even better.

Her heels clipping on the paved alley signaled that she was approaching the car. The lights flashed as she unlocked the door and slid behind the wheel. The remnants of her perfume mingled with the scents of cigarette smoke, booze, and sex. She sat for a moment, allowing a deep sigh.

As she shoved her key in the ignition and started the engine, he rose up behind her and pressed the blade to her neck.

She jerked and sucked in a breath, ready to scream. "What the hell?"

He clamped his hand over her mouth, the razor tip pressed against her beating jugular. "I'll cut your throat right here, Heather, if you say a word."

She shook her head, looking into the rearview mirror at him. He didn't care if she saw him. He doubted she'd recognize him, and if she did, she'd never get the chance to tell.

"Now, you're going to be quiet like a good girl, or I'll end it right here. Understood?"

Her eyes shimmered with fear, but she did not make one sound. Slowly he removed his hand, and the knife tip released a little from her skin.

"Who are you?" she asked.

"Just a guy with a few questions. Now drive. Slowly and carefully. I want us to have privacy while we talk."

"If this is about money, I don't have much, but you can have it."

"I don't want your money, Heather."

His gaze didn't drop to the full cleavage but remained locked on her face in the rearview mirror. "Rape is not on the menu for tonight either. Now drive."

She put the car in drive and gently eased it forward. "Where are we going?"

"Toward the interstate."

She slowly wove through the streets, and when it looked like she was going to race through a yellow stoplight, he pressed the blade into her skin, making her bring the car to a stop. "I wasn't going to run it."

"I know you weren't," he said.

When the light turned green, he directed her on the southbound ramp of I-35, and they drove in silence for two exits before he ordered her off onto an unlit access road. He told her to stop under an underpass, cut the headlights, and turn off the engine.

Most exits were populated with too many businesses and too many lights, but there were a couple with undeveloped land that would work nicely.

He'd chosen this exit earlier in the day while scouting his route. Instead of stopping immediately, he had kept driving on the access road, just double-checking that no one was following him. He was paranoid that way. Always doubling back and going around corners multiple times. Meticulous. And now he was parked here with Heather and getting to know her better.

"You must have me mixed up with someone else," she said. "I'm a waitress, and I keep my nose out of everyone else's business."

"I know who you are. I know you're close to Danny Garnet, am I right? And I bet you know a few of his secrets."

The shift in her gaze lasted only a split second. "I work for the guy. But he doesn't trust me with secrets."

He released a long sigh, fearing she wasn't going to make this easy. "I was hoping we could avoid any lying." He grabbed a handful of her hair, wound it around his hand, and sliced the tip of his knife along her jawline. Blood immediately oozed from the open wound.

"Jesus!" she screamed. She cupped her hand to her cheek. "I'm bleeding."

"Don't get worked up. It looks worse than it is. Wounds on the face always bleed a lot. More for show than anything. But I did get your attention, didn't I?"

"Please!"

"I'll take you apart bit by bit, Heather. I don't want to, but it's up to you. Tell me where it is, and I'll walk away."

"I don't know where it *is*. What are you talking about?"

"I thought he'd given it to Crow, but the old bastard died before I could get anything out of him." Crow could have given what he had to Macy, and if he'd not reacted so quickly he could have grabbed her. Asked her questions. But she'd seen the ranch, and he couldn't have her calling in the troops. He needed more time to find this damn package.

He raised the blade to her eye. "Garnet is blackmailing my client. He has evidence. Where is it?"

Her breath was quick and rapid with fear. "I don't know what Garnet's got planned. He said I just needed to be quiet and patient. He's always kept me in the dark about the details. Even back in the day."

"So you knew about the ranch?" When she hesitated, he jabbed the tip of the blade into her cheek.

"I never been out there, but yeah, I knew what he was doing out there. But that was a long time ago. He hasn't done anything like that since."

"But he kept the ranch. All these years and he held on to it. Why?"

"I don't know why he kept it. He never told me. All I know is that Garnet has gotten jumpy in the last few months. I've never seen him like this before."

"If he'd been smart, he'd have let sleeping dogs lie. The past had been dead and buried until he dug it up." To remind her that she was living at his pleasure now, he lightly drew the tip of the knife over her cheek again. "You were around the first time he sold babies, weren't you?"

She swallowed, her gaze locked on his face. "Yeah. I was around."

"Did you help kill those girls?"

Panic flared in her eyes. "We didn't kill any of those girls. They all got paid for their time and were sent on their way."

"How do you know that?"

"He told me."

How easily people accepted a lie over a painful truth. "You're a smart girl, Heather. Do you really think that's what happened?"

She paled, as if facts she did not want to acknowledge had smacked her in the face. "He didn't kill anybody."

He wasn't here to debate this point. "That's neither here nor there. The bottom line is that Garnet is blackmailing a client of mine. He's got evidence that can prove what went on at that ranch."

"I don't know about that."

"You notice things. Did he give you any hints about where he could have put any evidence?"

"What kind of evidence?"

"The kind that could upset a lot of lives if it came to light. Why has he started returning to the ranch?"

"What?"

"I have a tracker on his car. Why has he begun going back out to the ranch?" He'd been watching Garnet come and go from the ranch for a couple of weeks, but he'd not investigated, fearful a search of the house would tip off Garnet, who would then expose the evidence.

"I didn't know that he was," Heather said. "Only that he was gone more and more."

"Really? I saw a poster of a missing pregnant girl in his bar. Did he have anything to do with her disappearance?"

"Why would he do that? She was already pregnant when she came into the bar."

Ah, more layers to the puzzle. "Why is that important?"

She hesitated, knowing not telling would cost her more now than telling. "The others weren't pregnant when they were handpicked. They were selected."

"To make babies?"

"I don't know. And I don't know anything about a new girl."

"It would explain why he's going out to the ranch, wouldn't it?"

"I swear he hasn't told me anything," Heather said.

A new girl made sense. Her baby would represent revenue flow, and Garnet was now in short supply of money since his last arrangement had ended. He had to pay those gambling debts somehow.

"Look, Garnet is older and more paranoid. He's always been worried about the cops. And then that woman came in the bar asking about Crow. She said her father had been a friend of Garnet's, but her visit freaked Garnet out."

The discovery of the graves wasn't a real issue. All DNA evidence on the property would have led to Garnet. And if anyone had found the new girl on the property, there'd have been a mention in the news by now. And even if the cop had the girl under wraps, whatever DNA she was carrying in her belly wouldn't trace back. Still, he was left with the problem of finding whatever evidence Garnet was holding against his client. "How long have you been with Garnet?"

"Thirty-two years."

"That's a long time."

"He loves me."

Maybe Garnet had some affection for dear sweet Heather, but he'd bet she was as disposable as the girls on the ranch.

"I swear I don't know anything, mister."

He loosened his hold on her hair. "I do believe you, Heather. But here is a truth, Heather. Garnet is using you just like he used those other murdered girls."

"He's not using me."

"Heather, you're smarter than this, I hope."

"Please, let me—"

Before she could finish the sentence, he burrowed the blade quickly into the side of her neck several times until he had opened a big hole in her jugular. Even a surgeon couldn't save her now.

As the air gurgled in her throat, she grappled with the door handle, and to her credit she was able to get it open. Killing Crow at his place had been easy. Not as fruitful as he'd hoped, but easy. Running over

Macy had been an impulse and poorly planned. He'd gotten the job done, but he'd taken too many risks. The knife was the best way to finish the task. Blades were far harder to trace than bullets.

But he'd not found Garnet's smoking gun, and until he did, he had to tread carefully.

He got out of the back seat and watched as she stumbled to her feet and staggered forward. He reached over and popped the trunk, walked around to it, and retrieved the gas can.

Heather stood still under the underpass. She wavered from side to side and then fell to her knees, grasping her throat. She rose up, her throat gurgling, and tried to crawl. Blood traced her path from the car to the spot where she fell.

He followed at a slow and steady pace, and when she collapsed, he came up beside her, set the can down, and gently rolled her onto her back. Unable to resist her plump, still-pink flesh, he gripped his knife and stabbed her arms, chest, and thighs. He loved the sensation of the knife piercing the flesh. Finally, he wiped the blade on her shirt and, pulling a cloth from his coat pocket, wiped his hands.

He stayed by her and waited another five minutes, listening to his heartbeat blend with the cars rushing above on the overpass. When his own breathing stilled, he checked her pulse and found none.

He brushed her hair out of her eyes and opened her shirt slightly so the knife wounds were visible. He removed a playing card. The queen of hearts. What better way to get the medical examiner's attention? *Like a version of a message in a bottle*, he thought, smiling.

He knew he shouldn't be playing games with Dr. McIntyre, but for some reason he couldn't resist. He was like a cat, and she was his mouse.

He doused the body and lit the match. The blue-white flames quickly engulfed her body. "Maybe Dr. McIntyre will help me find what I'm looking for."

CHAPTER FIFTEEN

Wednesday, June 27, 5:15 a.m.

Despite his lack of sleep, Hayden felt energized as he picked up Faith at her home. Her hair was pulled up, and she was wearing jeans and a fitted V-neck black sweater that hugged her breasts in a way that was downright distracting. He was certain the woman could've worn a paper bag and still looked fine.

The faint scent of her perfume drifted around him and reminded him she liked to dab the scent between her breasts and behind her right ear.

She slid into the front seat. If they were a legit couple, he would have leaned over and kissed her. But this was another one of the moments that simply felt like overstepping.

He looked her over, taking in every detail. "Where are you rushing from?"

She buckled her seat belt. "I just dropped Kat off at the shelter. She showed up at my place last night and ended up spending the night with me."

As she shifted in her seat, her sweater tightened briefly against her breasts. His heartbeat quickened, and he turned to the road ahead. As he left the parking lot, he said, "I need coffee. You want one?"

"Bless you," she said. "I would kill for a cup."

He pulled up to a fast-food drive-through and ordered a couple of coffees.

"Toss in a bagel. Cinnamon raisin, and I'll love you forever," she said. "I'm starving."

He ordered two bagels, refused the money she offered, and paid the clerk at the window. She took the cups, settled them in cupholders, and removed the drink tab on each. There was an odd intimacy in this moment. Sierra had done the same thing a million times.

She sipped her coffee while staring out at the city rushing past.

"How's Macy?" he asked.

"I spoke to the nurse this morning. She's hanging in there, which is saying a lot. No quit in her. And the nurse noticed she twitched when spoken to. It may simply be a reflex, but I'd like to think it was deliberate."

"Might have been. Just because someone's not awake doesn't mean they don't know you're there," he said.

"I know," she said. "And if she's like me, she'd want me focusing on the case, not her."

Hayden nodded. "We found a picture on Macy's phone that keeps coming back to me."

"What is it?"

"It's a snapshot of a missing person, Paige Sheldon."

She frowned. "The pregnant girl who vanished?"

"Yeah. I looked up her case last night. She was five months pregnant. Had an argument with her parents, moved out, and vanished two days later."

"And you've been to Second Chances?" she asked.

"I have. The owner, Danny Garnet, is smooth. He says he doesn't remember her."

"Maybe I should show up. My face is sure to spook the right person."

"Until I know what I'm dealing with and who tried to killed Macy, don't go Nancy Drew on me. Stay the hell away from Second Chances."

"I've helped solve a few murders."

"You've done it from the autopsy suite and lab. Not on the streets. And this case could end up being very personal for you."

"We don't know that."

He didn't believe that any more than she did. "Stick to the science, Faith."

"I've never been good at making promises."

She'd never made demands either. Never pushed. That had been just fine in the beginning, but it bothered him now. He wanted her to rely on him more.

He pressed the accelerator, cutting through the Texas Hill Country roads until he spotted the turnoff to the ranch. "The crew is meeting us out there," he said.

"Great."

"You're off the clock today?" he asked.

"For today. But there will be two days' work waiting for me tomorrow," she said. "PJ Slater called me yesterday. He's found multiple references to a woman named *Josie Jones* in one of my father's old datebooks. He thinks Josie might be my birth mother."

"Does he have any information on her?"

"Not much. She was arrested for shoplifting, and my father defended her in court." She wrestled with telling him about Kat's search and decided in for a penny, in for a pound. "Kat and I have been talking a lot lately, and I mentioned Josie to her."

"Was it really wise to tell her?"

"No, but we were having a moment. I was trying to empathize, and I told her about Josie. She did the search on her own. She not only found another picture of Josie but also a woman on a DNA site who might be my half sister."

"That kid's been busy."

"Maybe too busy. I have to be more careful with her. She's more fragile than she lets on, and her attaching herself to me and my drama can't be healthy."

"I can have our own people look into Josie Jones. The kid might have missed something."

"It would be interesting to talk to one of Josie's family members. They must have more information about her."

"Don't get ahead of yourself, Faith. You don't have hard evidence that this woman is your birth mother."

"Josie *vanished* thirty-one years ago, Hayden, about nine months before Macy and I were born. Crow sends Macy out to the ranch, and we find what might be graves. And Macy is snapping pictures of another pregnant girl who's missing. The coincidences are starting to pile up."

He shifted in his seat.

The sun grew brighter, chasing them as they traveled west toward the house Macy had found in Hill Country. Faith took one last bite of her bagel. Gravel spit out from under his tires as Hayden drove the last fifty feet and parked behind the forensic van.

As they got out, he could see that the recovery team had already unloaded a ground-penetrating radar machine, and two officers appeared to be mapping out their plan of attack on a paper grid.

He introduced Faith to a tall uniformed officer with dark hair and a football lineman's broad frame. "Dr. McIntyre, I'd like you to meet Officer Lance Pollard. He runs this equipment."

She extended her hand. "We worked together before, in a way. About two years ago. Remember the man who killed male prostitutes and buried them on his land?"

Pollard tugged his right ear and glowered. "I found them, and you identified them."

"That's exactly right," she said.

Hayden remembered the case. There'd been fourteen victims, and Faith had yet to identify all of them. In her press briefings, she'd promised she would not quit until every last one of the victims had been identified.

Pollard tugged on latex gloves. "Do you have any idea how many victims we're looking for today?"

"Judging by the terrain and those stones, I'd say there are three," Hayden said.

"We'll sweep the area in a grid pattern, starting by the house and working our way out," Pollard explained. "As you remember, the equipment puts off an electromagnetic wave into the ground. The signal keeps traveling until it hits any dense object such as rock, bone, or buried debris. The material will reflect the signal, and its image will show up on my display."

She folded her arms. "The medical examiner's van is on standby."

Pollard flipped the switch, and as it hummed to life, he studied the display console mounted at the top. Satisfied, he began to move in a straight line that ran parallel to the house.

"Hayden, do you know who owns the house?" she asked.

"We traced it back to a man by the name of Sam Delany. He's currently serving a lifetime sentence for murder. However, the property taxes are not in arrears," Hayden said.

"Who did Mr. Delany kill?"

"His girlfriend. They were fighting. He hit her. She stumbled, struck her head on a stone fireplace, and died."

"Were you able to get a search warrant for the land and the house?" she asked.

"I did. Utilities were shut off to the house years ago, but there's a generator there. It's relatively new, but it's almost bone-dry. We're refueling the generator, and it should be up and running soon."

Her gaze shifted to Pollard, and she carefully watched him complete his first row. "This could take a while."

"Very easily."

She shook her head. "What else have you found out about Sam Delany?"

"Not much yet. My partner is pulling his police record as well as financials."

The generator motor started up, and the lights in the house behind them switched on. The forensic team started to assemble their gear and move toward the front door.

The sun cast a brilliant hue over Faith's features, and Hayden found himself staring at the high slash of her cheekbones, the brilliant blue of her eyes, and the curve of her full lips. He'd always recognized that she was a stunning woman and, in the years after Sierra had died, acknowledged his strong sexual attraction to her. He'd thought that one evening in the hotel would have put to rest all the fantasies he'd had about her. But what he'd learned was that once was not nearly enough. In fact, he was finding it hard to envision a day when he didn't want to be with her.

Faith nodded toward the house. "I'd like to see inside."

"Sure. We'll get booties and gloves and have a look."

At the forensic van they slipped on booties and gloves, and he held back, allowing her to go first as they approached the officer positioned at the yellow crime scene tape perimeter.

They showed their identifications to the officer whose job it was to protect the integrity of the scene. He recorded both their names as part of what would be an ongoing log of anyone who visited the scene.

As soon as they crossed the narrow front porch and entered the front door, Hayden was struck by the musty, stale smell of the house's interior.

"Unpleasant but manageable," Faith said.

They both were acquainted with the sickly sweet smell of a rotting body that could permeate nostrils, clothes, and shoes. It was a scent never forgotten. However, as they moved closer to the kitchen, he detected the faint whiff of a cleaning agent.

"Do you smell that?" She threaded her long fingers together, working the gloves deep between her fingers.

"I do. Someone recently cleaned this room."

"The house looks in too good a shape to have been closed up for the past thirty years."

She stood back, studying the small living room with an oversize easy chair that had been patched in several places with duct tape. Beside the chair was an old end table with a large brass lamp.

On the end table was a picture of a woman standing beside a tall, lean man. Hayden didn't recognize him but wondered if he was Delany. Judging by the clothes and hair, he guessed the photo was taken decades ago.

The woman in the photo had shoulder-length blond hair, pale skin, and blue eyes. Like Faith.

"Who is she?" Faith asked. Her expression was pensive, as if she were reading his thoughts.

"I don't know."

Faith cocked her head, her gaze roaming over the woman's smiling face, which was vaguely familiar. "She's not Josie."

"No."

"I find myself looking into the eyes of any woman who's at least fifty and wondering if she's the one." Faith picked up the picture and turned it over. "I would like to talk to Garnet."

"Don't worry. I'll be returning to talk to him as soon as I leave here."

"I understand, but I want to be present. I need to know, and so does Macy." Carefully, she stepped back from the photo. "What's Jack Crow's connection to all this?"

"Still a mystery."

"He knew Garnet, so he must have had some idea of what happened here."

She crossed to the small L-shaped kitchen. No dishes in the sink; the counters, though covered in dust now, had been wiped clean; and the washed dishes were in the drying rack. She put her hand over her mouth and opened the refrigerator. Hayden braced, knowing it could be a capsule of revulsion. However, the appliance had been wiped clean, and the freezer emptied.

They entered the bedroom and found the bed made. The towels in the bathroom were hanging neatly on the drying rack, and the trash cans had been emptied. A fine coating of dust covered the counter and faucets.

Faith opened the closet in the bedroom and paused. "Have a look at this, Captain."

He came up behind her and saw five boxes of newborn disposable diapers. There were also several canisters of powdered baby formula, unused baby bottles, and packages filled with yellow baby blankets.

"An odd thing to be kept at an empty house."

"Yes, it is." Hayden opened the door from the kitchen and flipped on a light that illuminated a set of wooden stairs. "Watch your step."

Faith followed him down the dozen steps to a basement that stretched the length of the house. To the left was an upended cot, as well as a laundry room with clothes hanging on the line. She walked toward the clothes, inspecting them. "Big enough for a pregnant belly. They're dry."

He turned to the other side of the room and saw the next door. He tried the handle, but the door was locked, so he called up to the uniformed officer and asked for a crowbar. He banged on the door. "Paige, are you in there?"

They both listened but heard nothing. He didn't want to imagine the girl unconscious or dead, but the possibility was very real. Footsteps on the stairs had him turning toward a young uniformed officer carrying a crowbar.

The officer handed the bar to Hayden, and he wedged the tip under the lock. With a hard jerk, he popped the lock. The officer held the door handle and stood ready for Hayden to give him the word to yank.

"God, I hope we find her," Faith whispered.

The door swung open in one quick motion.

As the officer covered Hayden, he moved into the room and flipped on the light. He cut his eyes left, right, and up, making sure that no one had planned an unpleasant surprise. He continued to sweep the room, looking behind a curtain that hid a toilet and shower. When it was all clear, he motioned for Faith to come inside.

"She's not in here." He holstered his gun.

She entered the room, her posture tense as she looked around the small space. Her expression was stoic, but her eyes betrayed her distress as she looked at the tiny bath facility, what amounted to a kitchen, and the mattress. Her gaze settled on the chain and the cuff that lay open on the floor.

She knelt, hand outstretched, not touching the cuff but studying it closely. Tears glistened in her eyes before she blinked them away. "There's dried blood on the metal."

"We'll have it tested for DNA," Hayden said.

She drew her fingers back from the cuff as if they burned. "It doesn't look that old."

"I think when Macy came out here, someone was watching the camera feed and saw her," Hayden said. "Whoever was held here was moved."

"It has to be Paige. There are large clothes to accommodate a pregnant belly and baby diapers in this house."

"That blood will tell us if she's in our data bank."

"Jack Crow knew about this place, and he left that phone with the address for Macy. He knew he was running out of time and wanted to tell her something."

She crossed to the dresser and opened the top drawer. She inspected various undergarments before she moved to the next drawer, filled with more oversized shirts and pants.

He looked at the dust on the floor and saw that the dresser had been recently moved.

"Let me have a look behind the dresser," he said.

She stood aside as he gripped its sides and moved the piece of furniture. His gaze went first to the wall, which was solid cement. He then shifted to the back of the dresser. It was cheap particleboard tacked to the flimsy frame. But at the base of the board were letters carved into the wood.

"Officer, help me move this out more." Together they slid the dresser out several feet so that Hayden could stand behind the dresser. Faith joined him. He looked over the letters, his body tensing when he saw PS.

She drew in a breath. "Paige Sheldon. She was here. And there are three other sets of initials."

"And three stones outside."

JJ, OM, KS, PS. "Dear God." Her voice choked and dropped to a hoarse whisper. "He held them all in this room. JJ. Josie Jones."

Upstairs, voices of the forensic team drifted around, and he knew it was time. "We need to get out of here and let the technicians do their job."

She rose slowly as she studied the room again.

"Captain Hayden," an officer called down the stairs. "We have something." They climbed the stairs and found Brogan standing on the porch. "Might want to come out and see this."

Faith glanced up at Hayden, and he glimpsed fear and worry in her expression before she dropped her eyes, squared her shoulders, and walked out of the house. She stepped out with no hint of emotion on her face.

The warming sun was climbing in the sky now, and it reflected on a new red flag stuck in the ground and gently flapping in the breeze.

Neither spoke as they crossed the dusty yard to the ground-penetrating radar machine. Pollard turned on his computer display and showed them the image. Faith leaned forward, took one look, and instantly knew.

Hayden had seen several images like this over the years, and he knew the odd, apparently random waves demarked bones. "Do you think the remains are human?"

"Hard to say at this point," Pollard said.

It was easy to assume buried remains must be human, but people did bury pets—or perhaps it was a trash pit with animal remains. These bones were in close proximity, not scattered.

Faith said, "They were discarded in holes like trash."

Hayden had been to his share of horrific murder scenes, but hearing Faith's quiet outrage threaded with pain struck him to his core. She was hurting, and that bothered him.

"The spot was marked with a stone, correct?" Hayden said.

"Yes," Pollard said. "All the stones appear to have been pulled from the area. There's nothing special about them individually."

"But arranged as they are, they look like headstones," Hayden said.

"I know some serial killers like to return to the scene of their crimes and visit their victims," Faith said. "He would have had no problem remembering where he buried them."

"Two more stones doesn't mean two more bodies." He said the words for her benefit.

"You're wrong." Faith reached for her cell. "They're all headstones, and if Macy had been a few weeks later, there'd be a fresh hole with another dead girl in it."

"Jack Crow was tortured for a reason," Hayden said. "Someone was looking for something."

"This place?" she asked.

"Maybe."

"I'll call the medical examiner's office and have them send a crew so we can start excavating the sites."

Josie Jones, 1988

Things I like. Flip-flops. McDonald's french fries and hamburgers. Rain on my face. Cheers. My birthday. "I Wanna Dance with Somebody," Whitney Houston. My sister. And you, most of all. None of this is your fault.

Things I hate. Broccoli. English class. Parachute pants. Perms. My foster family. This room.

CHAPTER SIXTEEN

Wednesday, June 27, 10:00 a.m.

Faith leaned against the medical examiner's van, studying the collection of three red flags that now fluttered in the warm wind. Officer Pollard had found bones buried under each of the stones, and all appeared to have been in the ground for a long time.

The three grave sites were cordoned off, with a crew working on the first site. The team had decided to start at one end and work to the other, handling one grave at a time.

The excavation process was tedious because it wasn't a matter of digging up what the ground-penetrating radar had located. The soil would have to be carefully removed layer by layer so that no evidence, including clothing and jewelry, was lost.

The crew had dug down eighteen inches into the soil. The grave had been shallow, but excavating it had taken nearly an hour.

Hayden hadn't spoken to Faith for a couple of hours. He'd been busy searching the house and the grounds and coordinating a more extensive background search on Sam Delany. But she was glad for the solitude. So far she'd done a good job of controlling her emotions, but as Pollard had planted each flag into the ground, she had found it harder to keep her mind on point. Three sets of initials. And now three graves.

Pollard was working with Angie Chesterfield on the first site. Faith and Angie had crossed paths several times, and she'd found Chesterfield, a petite redhead, to be efficient and smart. While Pollard methodically scraped away the soil, she documented the discovery with her digital camera. She never looked in Faith's direction or spoke in tones louder than Pollard could hear.

The community that took care of the dead was a small one, and news had traveled quickly that the body in the grave might be related to Faith. She understood why they distanced themselves from her while they worked. She'd have done the same. But she didn't like it. It made her feel vulnerable.

Minutes later Pollard and Chesterfield stopped work. Stillness fell over the technicians as they leaned back and glanced at each other.

Faith pushed away from the vehicle, and as she tugged on fresh latex gloves, she strode toward the team. She looked into the eighteen-inch hole they'd dug to find an exposed human skull. Her breath caught in her chest. Everything around her vanished as she mentally juxtaposed the skull to the Josie Jones mug shot.

The tech gently brushed the dirt away from the bone with a soft-bristled paintbrush. Each swipe of the brush perhaps brought Faith closer to the secrets shrouding her birth. She'd always wanted to know, needed to know, her birth mother. Many times she'd imagined their first meeting, but the scenarios had never been anything remotely like this.

She was aware of Hayden moving beside her, and she knew if he touched her, she'd shatter. She may have looked cool and controlled, but she was barely hanging on right now.

Hayden didn't speak to her but watched as the tech unearthed the bones. He'd lived in a moment just like this one when Sierra had died, and though their losses were different, he seemed to understand that words, no matter how well intentioned, would fall short and ring hollow. Still, having him close was comforting. It made her feel a little less alone, less adrift in a life that now appeared to have been built on sand and lies.

Her breath caught in her throat as she watched the tech remove the top portion of the skull. The lower jaw, no longer attached by ligaments and muscle that had decomposed a long time ago, stayed anchored in the soil.

"Dr. McIntyre, would you like a closer look?" Chesterfield asked.

PJ's information, the mug shot, and the initials on the back of the dresser were all parts of an equation that added up to the harsh fact that this skull belonged to her birth mother. This calculation could of course be proven wrong, but deep in her bones she knew it wasn't.

That conclusion led to another argument. She was too close to this case and should not be present at the crime scene. And maybe sooner rather than later she would recuse herself, but for now, she felt an obligation to Macy, Josie, and the faceless women who'd been imprisoned in that forgotten basement cell to be here and bear witness.

"Yes, I would like a closer look," she said. Again, Hayden didn't speak, but she heard him shift his stance and felt the tension radiating from his body. He might not have liked her response, but he understood it enough not to challenge it.

As Chesterfield shot more photographs, Faith knelt down and held out her gloved hands, accepting the skull. Her heart raced, and she turned it around and peered into the eye sockets.

She didn't speak until she was certain her tone and inflections were carefully under control. She pushed aside her feelings and focused on the facts. "The nasal bridge and aperture are high and slim, respectively. This suggests the victim was likely of Caucasian descent."

"Hard to be sure with a look." Hayden played devil's advocate, a roll well suited for his analytical mind.

Professionally she understood it, and personally she appreciated it.

"You're correct, Captain," she said. "Though each race has its own unique characteristics, defining this individual's race with a cursory glance isn't scientifically sound. It will take more analysis in the lab to confirm the individual's ethnic origin."

But if he'd asked her to put money down, she'd have bet large. She ran her thumb over the brow ridge. "The bone is relatively smooth, and the brow ridge less pronounced, suggesting a female. The orbitals have a sharper ridge, which also suggests a woman. But again, the final call can't be made until we examine the pelvis." A female's pelvis was broader to accommodate childbirth. And if these bones were indeed female, there could be markers on the pelvic bones that would indicate childbirth.

"Any idea about cause of death?" Hayden asked.

"There's no damage to the skull," she said. Head trauma would have left cracks, but if the manner of death did not impact her bones, determining cause could be difficult, if not impossible. "I'll need the full set of remains to make a definitive statement."

Faith handed the skull back to Chesterfield and studied the faint outlines of the bones just below the thin surface. The woman had been laid in the ground in a fetal position. Had whoever buried her been rushed? Were they stunned by her death, or had her ending been planned since the day she'd been locked in the room?

"This is going to take some time," Hayden said. "We won't solve any of this today."

Pollard nodded. "We'll be out here today and the better part of tomorrow. We'll start sending the remains to the medical examiner's office as soon as we excavate each site."

"Yes, this can't be rushed. I don't want any potential evidence lost." Faith rose, brushing the dust from her gloved hands. "I could stay, but you have this under control. If you need me, I'll return to the site immediately."

She turned from the grave, grateful not to be hovering. She yanked off her gloves and wiggled her fingers, wishing she could forget the weight of the skull in her hands.

There was never any such thing as an easy death investigation. Death, even when it was a mercy, was never stress-free. She'd learned over the years to guard her emotions. Country music, Nancy's steady comments, and the exhaustion after a long run all kept her mind on an even keel. However, this site would require every tool in her bag of tricks.

"I'd like to show you something we found in the basement room." Hayden's long strides caught up to her easily as she reached the forensic van.

"What is it?" She tossed her gloves in a disposal bag.

"It's better if you see it," he said, giving no hint.

She braced, truly not wanting to return to that wretched prison. "Of course."

He guided her back toward the house and up onto the porch. They each paused on the front steps and pulled on fresh gloves as well as paper booties. This house was now an active crime scene and the less contamination they brought into it, the better.

Her eyes adjusted to the interior as she followed Hayden through the house and down the basement stairs. Inside the room a light flashed as a forensic technician snapped photos.

Hayden motioned for her to pause as he entered the room and spoke in low tones to the technician. The man soon appeared at the door, nodded to her, and stepped aside. Hayden stood behind him and signaled her forward.

In the room she noticed the dresser was still away from the wall. But she also noted that a ventilation grate behind it had been removed and was encased in a plastic evidence bag.

"What did you find behind the grate?" Her voice sounded so professional that for a moment she wasn't sure that it didn't belong to someone else.

"Two magazines," Hayden said. "They both date back to 1987. They're on the table."

She shifted her focus to the small round table and the two magazines. Both were fashion magazines and featured headlines such as "Beauty Blitz," "100 Ideas for Spring," and "How to Talk to a Boy." The smiling girl on the cover had rich dark hair and wore a red sweater, striped miniskirt, white tights, and flats. A thick gold chain with a heart dangling from it hung around her neck. A black-and-white composition notebook in her hand, she stared coyly at the camera.

Hayden carefully folded back the wrinkled cover of one of the magazines to the title page. Words were written in a teenager's loopy style all along the margins.

The first entry was dated 1988, the year Faith was born.

My name is Josie Jones. I'm nineteen. I am your mother, but you will never know me.

"Josie wrote messages in this magazine," Faith whispered.

"Yes," Hayden said.

Pain, sadness, and anger hitched in Faith's throat as she scanned the words scribbled in fading ink. She imagined the young girl sitting at this very table, locked in this room, pregnant, and alone. Somehow Josie had known she wasn't going to get out alive. "Does she name the man holding her?"

"She called him Daddy. He must have never told her his name."

"Does she say who fathered her baby?"

"I haven't gotten that far yet. It's going to take some time to go through this."

She turned to the next page, and in the white margin, the top line on the left page read,

I've begged and pleaded with him to let me go. He swears he'll let me go, but he has lied before.

She pressed her trembling hand to the page and felt the deep creases the pen tip made in the thin, glossy paper. "She never stood a chance once she entered this room. None of them did."

"No. But I'm hoping Paige Sheldon has a chance. She still might be alive," Hayden said.

"I know, but she's running out of time. Her baby has to be due any day, and who knows what will happen during a birth unattended by a doctor? Or what her jailor will do to her afterward?"

"You need to take a break. This is not a good place for you," Hayden said.

"You're right. I should leave. But this case has wrapped around me and frozen me to this spot."

He laid a hand on her shoulder. "I'll drive you back to town, Faith. Let's go."

"No, you're going to be needed out here," she said. "I can ask one of the uniforms to take me."

"There's nothing I can do here for the next couple of hours. No one is going to miss me. I'll drive you."

She dug her nails into her hands, focusing on the discomfort. "Sure. Thanks."

In his car, she buckled up. He paused to speak to several officers and then slid behind the wheel. He tossed her a pointed glance before he backed up the vehicle and pulled onto the main road. "Are you doing okay?"

Of course she *would* be okay, if not for her own sake, then for Macy's and Kat's. But the road between right now and okay would be a long one. "I'm handling it."

"That's not what I asked. Talk to me, Faith," he said.

"It wasn't an easy sight to see," she said.

"I suppose the day we get used to something like that is the day to worry."

She watched as the barren landscape raced past and was glad each new mile put distance between her and that place. She was suddenly anxious to get back to the city and see Macy. "Can you drop me at the hospital? I want to visit Macy. I can make my way back to the office after that."

"Have you received any new updates on her?" he asked.

"I spoke to a nurse this morning. She told me she's still unconscious. But I want to see her today. She's alone, and she's the one who led us to those graves." She thought about the date of birth on Macy's driver's license. It was her birthday. "Do you have any idea how odd it feels to think I could have a twin? From only child to having a twin sister and perhaps a half sister if Kat's right—that is one hell of a jump."

"Family is a good thing."

"You have a sibling?"

"A younger sister. She's with the FBI."

"Are you two close?" She was suddenly curious to know what it felt like to have a sister.

"We were as kids. We had a falling out when we were teenagers." He hesitated, as if the telling still troubled him. "Kate's ex-boyfriend turned on her and tried to kill her. She was with our father at the time, and he ended up taking a bullet to save her. He died in Kate's arms. For a long time, I blamed her for Dad's death. None of it was her fault, of course, but I wasn't seeing too clearly. After that, my relationship with Kate was strained. Sierra was the one who made me promise to fix it with her."

"I can't imagine Sierra allowing a rift between you and a sister to stand."

"As sick as she was, she was very clear and direct about that."

"Have you and your sister worked through it?"

"Neither one of us is good with talking through our feelings. I suppose any shrink would advise that we delve deeper. But we do okay. We have each other's backs."

Faith pulled her sunglasses from her purse and slid them on. "I'm not a fan of all the introspection. And I've done more of it in the last few days than I have in my entire lifetime."

"Maybe it's like anything else. The more you do it, the easier it gets."

"We shall see."

"What was it like growing up with your parents?"

"I was close to my mother, but she died when I was fifteen. Dad and I were never close but looked out for each other until I went to college. We kept up at holidays and during vacations after that." She traced the lifeline on her palm, noticing for the first time that its base was forked.

They drove in silence the remainder of the journey, and when he pulled up in front of the hospital, she removed her sunglasses and carefully replaced them in her purse. "Feels silly to sit and talk to an unconscious woman. No way of knowing if she can hear me, but I have to believe I'm making a difference for her."

Light caught the hard edge of his profile. "When my wife was dying and drifting in and out of consciousness, I talked to her a lot. Even the last few days when she never woke up. But I believed she heard me. I believed she knew she wasn't alone at the end."

Faith tightened her hand on the strap of her purse. "I miss Sierra. She had the most biting sense of humor. The shelter board meetings were always more fun when she was there. Whenever we had a budget meeting, she always brought doughnuts. Her favorite was chocolate glazed."

"I forgot about that." He gripped the steering wheel. "No one really talks about her anymore."

"If you ever want a Sierra story, ask me. I've got a few. We got into our share of trouble once or twice."

"Trouble?"

This conversation was more personal than sex, but Faith wasn't sure how she felt about bonding. "I'll tell you about it sometime."

"Counting on it."

June 1, 1988

I held you in my arms today, minutes after you were born. The stars in the sky were bright and clear as I carried you away from the ranch toward the future you were destined to have. I named you Faith, because I have faith that what I did was right. You will have a bright future, and I will always protect you.

Love, Daddy

CHAPTER SEVENTEEN

Wednesday, June 27, 4:00 p.m.

Faith got out of the car and hurried into the hospital toward the elevators to Macy's unit. She waved to the nurses in the small office behind the station as they gathered around platters of food. They were laughing, smiling. She nodded to one she recognized from yesterday and headed toward Macy's room.

Until a DNA test was run, Faith couldn't technically be considered Macy's family, but when the nurse looked up at her, she said cheerfully, "Your sister made it through the day. She's a strong woman."

Sister. The word felt natural.

"Good. Can I see her?"

"Sure. Don't stay long."

"Did she have any other visitors today?"

The nurse checked her computer. "Standard hospital personnel visited this morning."

"And they all checked in with the police guard?" Anyone could put on scrubs and blend into a hospital setting.

"I assume so. There didn't appear to be any issues with the guard on duty."

"Did anyone stay long?"

"They all stayed less than five minutes."

"Thank you."

As she turned she heard, "Faith?"

Margaret Slater was dressed in a pale pink skirt and matching jacket. Her graying hair was pinned into a stylish twist, and her delicate diamond earrings sparkled. Her gaze was quizzical as she stared at Faith. "Did we have a meeting here today?"

"No." She thought back to the email she'd sent to Margaret regarding the fundraiser, and it felt like a million years ago. "Are you here for the fundraiser?"

"You know me—I'm always planning." Margaret kissed Faith on the cheek. The older woman's trademark soft perfume wafted around them. "I'm meeting with the head of the department. We're setting a date for next year's gala. What are you doing here?"

"Visiting a friend."

"Who on earth do you know that's here?" Margaret glanced toward the uniformed officer in the hallway. "They're protecting someone. Is that who you're here to see?"

"I can't discuss this, Margaret."

"You've always been able to tell me everything."

"And I will when I can." She had been afraid to ask Margaret about her adoption but now was too desperate for answers to not ask. "Margaret, what do you know about my adoption? Mom and Dad never talked about it, and I just thought since you knew them then that you might know."

Margaret's face softened. "I remember when your mother called and told me a baby had been found for them. She was so thrilled. I made a point to be there when your parents met you for the first time at the law offices. The look of pure joy on your mother's face still could make me cry."

"Did Peter ever tell you about my birth mother?"

"She was young. Unmarried. Wanted a better life for her baby."

"Did you ever hear the name *Josie Jones*?"

Margaret frowned. "No. Do you think that is her name?"

"PJ found her name in my father's datebook. They met several times in the year before I was born."

Margaret's brow wrinkled as she slowly shook her head. "Honey, I don't know the name. Why do you think it's her?"

"I don't know anything for sure." What she did know about Josie was now part of an active crime investigation, and she couldn't discuss it.

Margaret took Faith's hand in hers and gently squeezed it. "You look tired. Are you okay?"

"I'm fine. Really." She leaned in and kissed Margaret's cheek.

"I will dig around in Peter's papers. I've only just found myself able to look at his things. But I will keep a lookout for anything related to your adoption."

"Thank you."

"We'll talk very soon," Margaret said.

"You promise?"

"I promise." Margaret kissed her. "Now I'm off to the hospital administrator's office. I have a fundraiser to plan."

She made her way down the hallway and nodded to the uniformed officer. He wasn't the officer on duty yesterday and, like the other one, looked incredibly young. Faith introduced herself.

"I'm going to need to see identification," he said.

She fished credentials out of her wallet and handed them to him. He checked the card against the very short list of people allowed to visit Macy and then stepped aside. "Thank you, Dr. McIntyre."

Macy's room was dark, with only the beep of the monitors to break the silence. Macy remained unconscious, lying so still that Faith had to look closely to prove to herself she was breathing. Under the bruises, Faith could see Macy's face was slightly more drawn.

There was a rumpled picture of Macy propped up on the shelf by the bed. The image must have been taken when Macy was one or two. She had a big toothless grin and was reaching for Jack Crow's beard. He was laughing.

"Hi, Macy. It's Faith. We met yesterday." She reached for the edge of the blanket and pulled it up a fraction before she sat. "This picture of you and Jack is remarkable. You looked so much like I did as a baby. When you get well, I want to compare more pictures. I ran track in high school, ran my first marathon last year, and finished in three hours and thirty-three minutes. Not a gold medal win but respectable."

A slight moan mumbled in Macy's chest. Faith replaced the picture and sat beside her, glancing at the monitors. Macy's blood pressure was low but not dangerously so.

She laid her hand over Macy's fingers, which were cold and didn't respond to her touch. "You're holding steady, Macy. That's good. You just need to keep hanging in there. You'll get better every day.

"I received your email, Macy. And I've been to the place you mentioned. The Texas Rangers are involved now. I'm involved now."

The heart rate monitor seemed to speed up, and Faith could have sworn Macy understood the wagons had circled around her and she wasn't alone.

"We went to the farm and saw the stones. You were right to be concerned. The Texas Rangers swept the land with radar." She drew in a breath, not wanting the news to upset Macy, but also realizing that if this gal was a top investigator at the FBI, not knowing what was in that ground would bother her more. "We found three bodies," she said. "We've only partly removed the first, but it appears to be a female."

The heart rate monitor picked up again by several beats.

"You can hear me, can't you?" Faith said as she studied the monitor. "Can you squeeze my hand?" Several seconds passed with nothing. "Macy, if you can hear me, move your fingers." More moments and then Macy's fingers jolted. It could have been involuntary and was hardly conclusive, but it was a good start.

"You do hear me." Faith was rewarded with more movement in her fingers. "That's good, Macy. I'm assuming you can hear me and you're listening. I'm going to talk to you like a medical examiner would to an FBI agent, okay?"

The fingers twitched.

"Good. I've always done better with facts rather than feelings, and I'm betting you're a facts-based girl, too."

The heart rate monitor stayed slightly elevated.

"So the graves are being processed. It's going to take a couple of days to excavate thoroughly. And when it's time, I'll be part of the team that examines the remains. Hopefully, we'll be able to determine manner of death. We also found a room in the basement of the ranch. Macy, these crimes may have spanned months or even years."

She detailed the discovery of the dresser. "I have a lead on JJ. She's a woman named *Josie Jones*. She vanished about the time we were born, and my father represented her in court." She didn't trust her voice to tell Macy about the journal written in the margins of the magazines. "Who knows? Maybe she's important to us and the case."

She sat for several minutes. "I've already spent too much time thinking about Josie and comparing her face, our faces. There are precious few details on her, but my imagination keeps filling in the gaps. It's not a particularly smart approach, and I know I'm setting myself up for disappointment."

She paused, catching her own breath, and then added, "But enough about me. You concentrate on getting better. That is your only job. I'll be back soon to check on you. Promise."

Faith rose, patted Macy's hand, and left the room, feeling like she was abandoning her.

***

Macy could hear the soft, steady voice and found herself transported back to an afternoon when she and her mother were living in the small Dallas apartment.

Her father had called that day, and when her mother had spoken to him, she'd dropped her voice to a hushed tone. When she had finally handed the phone to Macy, she'd looked worried but made an effort to smile. Jack had been upbeat and said he'd decided on a change of plans. They weren't going into Austin but east to Galveston during their summer vacation together. *"Sun, surf, and sand, kiddo. Gonna be great."*

After the call she had pressed her mother, wanting to know what Brenda and Jack weren't telling her. When her mother hadn't answered, Macy had argued, because that's what she'd done since the moment she could talk. Those days she had picked fights whenever she could. She hadn't known why she was always mad and in moments of clarity had wondered why she couldn't just shake it and be happy.

She'd always known her mother wasn't her birth mother. Most of the time it hadn't bothered her, but lately it had been driving her nuts. She didn't look like the stocky, olive-skinned parents who she knew loved her. She had felt like an outsider.

One afternoon when she'd questioned if her mother was real, Brenda had looked her squarely in her eyes. "I'm as real as it gets," her mother had said.

"You didn't give birth to me. What was my real mother's name? I want to see her!"

Her mother had been quiet for a moment and then, shaking her head, had said, "She's dead, kid. Buried in the cold ground when you were a baby. All you got is me."

The news had hit Macy like a slap to the face. She had stumbled back and run, her mother's apology chasing after her.

Later there'd been tears and an oath from her mother that she didn't really know what had happened to her birth mother. There'd also been hugs and a truce that had lasted until her mother's death.

The stones. The graves. And a young girl logically unconnected to the girls missing for decades who was still missing and ready to have her baby.

Faith had found the stones. The graves. JJ. She was getting closer. She was walking Macy's own path.

Words of caution rumbled just out of her reach. She had a warning for Faith. He was still out there. And she knew his face.

***

Hayden pulled up in front of the hospital, turned in his seat, and faced Faith. Sunlight caught her hair and highlighted her expressive eyes and the full lips he wanted to kiss. "Let me know if you need anything today."

She smiled and laid her hand on his arm. "Thank you."

There were so many things he wanted to say to her, but the words stuck in his throat. "I've asked Detective Lana Franklin to pull old missing persons cases that fit around the year 1987. I also want a list of pregnant girls that might have gone missing. There might be some answers there."

Her brow furrowed. "I hope so."

Unable to resist, he leaned over and kissed her. "We'll figure this out."

She squeezed his hand and kissed him back. "Thank you."

When she got out of the car, he waited and watched her vanish into the hospital before driving to the middle-class neighborhood in northern Travis County that was home to Paige Sheldon's mother and stepfather. The front lawn was neatly cut, the bushes trimmed, and the house freshly painted. There were two cars in the driveway, both American-made late models.

Now that they had evidence that Paige might be alive, he wanted to talk to her parents and find out more about the girl.

He rang the bell and heard a dog barking and then the beat of steady footsteps. The door opened to a midsize man with gray hair and brown eyes ringed with dark circles. He wore a collared long-sleeve shirt that he'd rolled up to his elbows, and his tie hung loose. He had the look of a man who'd had a long day.

Up came the identification badge. "I'm Ranger Mitchell Hayden with the Texas Rangers. I'm looking for the parents of Paige Sheldon."

The man's face grew grim. "Texas Rangers. Do you have news about Paige?" A small cairn terrier stood obediently beside the man's leg, sizing him up.

"And you are?"

"Fred Owen. Paige's stepfather."

"May I come inside?"

"Sure. Of course." He stepped aside. "What do you know about Paige?"

"Fred, who is it?" A woman wearing jeans and a sweatshirt stained with blue paint rounded the corner. "What's going on?"

"Texas Rangers, here about Paige." The man hugged his wife close. "This is my wife, Vivian. Please tell us what you know, Ranger Hayden."

Inside, Hayden was greeted with the scents of pine cleaner and baking bread. "You a cook, Mrs. Owen?"

"Never much to speak of, but since Paige vanished, I'm cooking her favorites all the time just in case this is the day she comes home." Vivian scooped up the small dog and then clasped her husband's hand, her knuckles turning white with tension.

"Smells nice," he said.

"Just say what you have to say, Ranger Hayden," Vivian said. "We've been expecting a visit like this for months, and now that you're here, I just want you to spit it out."

"We have evidence suggesting that Paige has been held captive since she vanished."

Vivian's eyes filled with tears, and she nestled close to her husband, who wrapped his arm around her. "How do you know?"

"We believe we found the location where Paige was being kept. But when we searched it, Paige wasn't there." He refrained from telling them about the manacle and the blood.

"Why wasn't Paige there?" Vivian asked.

"For whatever reason, her captor moved her. By what we found, it was fairly recently."

"What about the baby?" Vivian asked.

"There was no sign that she's given birth," Hayden said.

"Where was she held?" Fred asked.

"A remote location in the Hill Country. For now I can't say exactly where."

"How did you even know to look in this place?" Fred countered.

"Your daughter's name came up in another case. Another law enforcement officer was interested in her case."

"What does he say about all this?" Vivian demanded.

"The officer, a female, passed away before we could ask her." He hated lying to them about Macy Crow, but until he knew who was behind all this, he would stick to the story.

Vivian drew in a sharp breath, and tears spilled down her cheeks. "What kind of case was she working on?"

"I can't say." He chose his words carefully.

Vivian looked up at Fred, shaking her head as more tears fell. "Paige and I had a terrible fight. I was so disappointed when I found out she was pregnant. I yelled and said awful things. She finally lost her temper and left. What I wouldn't give to take back those words."

Fred patted his wife's shoulder. "Paige wasn't easy on you either. She wasn't perfect."

Vivian's eyes filled with tears and frustration. "But she's just a kid, and we can't find her, Fred."

"I know. The Rangers are getting closer." He hugged his wife tight as she struggled with the news.

"How long was she gone before you started looking for her?" Hayden asked.

"Two days," Fred said. "We thought she was at her friend Brittany's house."

"Why did you think that?" Hayden asked.

"First I called her cell and she didn't pick up. She also has the Find My Friends app, and I could see that she was at Brittany's," Fred said.

"That made sense because that's where she always goes," Vivian said. "Always."

"What's Brittany's last name?" Hayden asked.

"Russo. Brittany Russo."

Hayden scribbled down the girl's contact information. "Okay."

"We've told all this to the Austin police. Brittany told the police Paige never contacted her," Vivian said.

"What happened after you called Brittany?" Hayden asked.

"Brittany said she wasn't there, so I drove over, thinking she was lying," Vivian said. "I called the phone and heard it ringing in the bushes. That's when I really panicked."

"I started calling all her friends," Fred said. "No one had seen her, so I contacted the police."

"She's a teenager," Vivian said. "She lived on that phone. She would never have tossed it away like that."

"Paige can be headstrong, but it's not like her to ditch her phone and completely ignore her mother," Fred said.

"What about boyfriends, new friends?" Hayden asked.

"She broke up with her boyfriend last year, before she got pregnant. She said all along the baby wasn't his, but she never would tell us who the father was. Anyway, we went to see Derek, her ex-boyfriend, and he swore he'd not seen her in months."

"What's Derek's last name?" Hayden asked.

"Smith," Fred said.

"Did you check her social media accounts?" Hayden asked.

"We did," Vivian said. "It took me a whole day of trying to figure out her password, but I did. Buddy two thousand. Our dog and the year she was born."

"What did you find?" Hayden asked.

"Nothing out of the ordinary. The account is still open, and I check it several times a day, thinking she might post something there." She rattled off the username, which Hayden wrote down. "The account hasn't been active since the day before she vanished."

"What about before?"

"It all seemed normal. She wasn't out partying with friends because she was pregnant, and I think that was frustrating for her. You know how girls like to dress up and pose for the camera."

"What about friends other than Brittany?" Hayden asked.

"There's Su Morgan. The two of them liked to go out a lot." Vivian provided Su's contact information. "I've talked to her every day for the last three months, and she's heard nothing from Paige."

"And she never told Brittany or Su the name of the baby's father?"

"They swear she didn't," Vivian said.

"How far along would Paige be now?" Hayden asked.

"Thirty-nine weeks. The baby is due any day." Her eyes filled with tears. "I have dreamed of the worst possible scenarios, but I never thought in my heart that she might be dead. She's my baby, and I would know if she was gone." She closed her eyes and then shoved out a breath. "The last few nights I've worried about her giving birth alone. I had to have a C-section when she was born, and if we'd not been in a hospital, one or both of us would have died."

"All right, ma'am," Hayden said. "I'll have a look at your daughter's social media posts." He flipped the page in his notebook and then asked, "What about letters or threatening calls? Was anyone harassing her?"

"No."

"Did she use drugs?" Hayden asked.

"Not that I know of," Vivian said. "And after she went missing, I tore her room apart. There wasn't a square inch that I didn't search. I found condoms but no drugs. She was a good kid, Ranger Hayden. But I think not as grown-up as she believed she was. She was also very naive."

"Has she had any legal trouble?" Hayden asked.

"A speeding ticket last year, but we had an attorney take care of it."

"Okay," Hayden said. "One last question. She ever been to a bar called Second Chances?"

"When I went through her room, I found matches from Second Chances," Vivian answered. "I even went by the bar and spoke to the owner. He said he hadn't seen her but put up one of the flyers I gave him. Is the bar related to her case?"

That was an important tidbit Garnet hadn't mentioned. "I can't say yet."

"How does this help with your case?" Fred asked.

"I'll know better once I meet with local police tomorrow to compare notes." He especially wanted to know if there'd been other blond, pregnant teen girls who'd vanished. Healthy infants could be sold for a lot of money.

Vivian gripped his arm. "She's running out of time, Ranger Hayden."

"Yes, ma'am, I know. We're doing our best to find her."

CHAPTER EIGHTEEN

Wednesday, June 27, 7:30 p.m.

A quick search on her phone told Faith the Second Chances bar was on Third Street. It took only minutes to cross town and park near the small place that looked like the typical dive bar. Small windows and a plain front door led to a dimly lit interior that, combined with a collection of round tables made of reclaimed barnwood, fell short of cozy.

All the tables were full, and piped-in country western music added a buoyancy to a room that might not have fared so well in daylight. The woman behind the bar was young, with a shock of red hair pulled back in a ponytail that could not calm the curls. She was smiling as she pulled a draft and then poured a shot of whiskey, all in one fluid motion.

Faith found a spot at the end of the bar. If there was anyone who didn't look the part of a Second Chances customer, it was her. She settled her purse between her legs and tried to pretend she belonged.

The woman came up to her, wiped the wet bar, and set down a paper napkin. "What can I get you?"

"Bourbon, neat."

"Ah, the lady knows the wisdom of not ruining a good bourbon with water or soda."

"I'm a purist," she said, smiling.

"Be right back. And sorry for the delay. We're shorthanded tonight."

"No worries."

The waitress took her order to the bartender, who filled a shot glass. "We also have menus if you're hungry. Nothing fancy, but tasty."

"Thanks. Just a bourbon for now."

"You look familiar," the woman said.

"I've never been in here before."

"I could have sworn I've seen you. But then I'm new at all this and don't remember the faces as well as the boss."

Had she seen Macy? Or had she caught Faith on television a few weeks ago? "Maybe I've got that kind of face."

"The boss would know. He's good with faces. Never forgets one."

Then he would remember Macy. And he would notice her. She sipped her bourbon, certain if she asked about Macy or started showing pictures, she'd only raise suspicions.

The waitress was summoned by a customer at the other end of the bar, leaving Faith to stare into the mirror behind the bar and watch the crowd behind her. No one seemed to toss her a second look. She was just another woman at the bar.

Saloon doors that separated the front end of the house from the kitchen swung open, and a man in his late fifties pushed through. He was fit for his age and had a full head of hair. If not for the crow's-feet around his eyes and the deep laugh lines running the length of his face, he could have passed for a decade younger.

He crossed behind the bar, grinning. "I can take over, Jill. Why don't you check in on your tables?"

Garnet looked at Faith's drink and then her face and froze. That split second told her he'd seen Macy before. But he quickly covered up his shock with a very charming grin. "Can I freshen that up for you?"

"Still working on this one. Thanks."

"What brings you in here?"

"Heard friends talking about it and thought I'd stop in for a drink. Long day."

"Really. And what do you do?"

"I'm a medical examiner."

"Wow. That's an intense job." He held out his hand. "Danny Garnet."

"Faith McIntyre."

"I've seen you before, Dr. McIntyre."

"Not in here." She raised her bourbon to her lips and took a small sip.

"Maybe on television. I bet you get interviewed a lot."

"Occasionally."

He was studying her closely. Was he recalling Macy or simply flirting? "You don't look like a medical examiner."

"What do they look like?" she deadpanned. Any comment that could be made about her profession, she'd heard it.

He laughed, smelling the trap. "You're a beautiful woman, Faith McIntyre."

A woman in a red dress several spots down summoned Garnet. Promising to return, he moved to the woman and freshened her drink. The woman in red leaned forward, giving him a full view of her ample cleavage. He wasn't saint enough not to look, although whatever she was offering didn't seem to appeal at the moment. But he was charming in the way he shook his head and kept his eyes on her before he patted the bar in front of her and moved down the row to a cowboy ready to cash out his tab.

She could read the dead well, but with the living she was out of her depth. She pulled a twenty from her purse, set it on the table, and rose.

Garnet noticed her standing but was on the other end of the bar. That gave her time to leave before he could stop her.

She'd taken a big risk coming here. It was important to her to help Macy in any way she could. And if that meant flushing out whoever had hurt Macy, then so be it.

***

After Hayden left the Owens' home, he placed another call to Detective Lana Franklin. He checked on the status of the missing persons files.

"I'm pulling files now," Franklin said.

"Can you have this for me by morning?" he asked. "I know I'm pressing, but we're running out of time."

"It will be done."

"Appreciate it."

His next call was to Brogan, who had located Sam Delany at the Huntsville Prison, three hours northeast of Austin. If they hurried, they could be there before midnight and back in Austin before daybreak. Hayden picked up Brogan fifteen minutes later. They grabbed burgers at a drive-through and soon were on TX-290 toward Huntsville, Texas.

"Delany is a lifer," Brogan said as he settled back in his seat.

"So who's paying his property taxes?"

"He's clearly fronting for someone," Brogan replied.

"And our job will be to convince a lifer to give this guy up." The lights of Austin faded in his rearview mirror. Hayden pressed on the accelerator as he ate fries and sipped from a soda. "Any word on Dirk Crow's BOLO?"

"There's been no sighting of the man. The guy has lived in the middle of nowhere for years and knows every rock to crawl under. Hell, the guy could be in Mexico by now."

Hayden finished his burger, balled up his trash, and tucked it in the bag. "Think Melissa Savage is working this late?"

"Oh, yeah. She's a real night owl."

Hayden dialed her number, and she picked up on the second ring, sounding alert.

"I'm in the car with Brogan, and we're headed to Huntsville. You're on speaker."

"Understood," she said.

"Tell me you've found something on that surveillance footage."

"My eyes are crossing. I've reviewed ten days' worth of footage from a dozen different establishments near the Crow property and Second Chances."

"And?"

"Dirk Crow comes and goes from the salvage yard daily until two weeks ago, and then he goes AWOL."

"That fits with his story of being in San Jose."

"Maybe. Satellite imagery of the salvage yard property shows that it's not fully enclosed with fencing. There are patches that are large enough for a car to pass through. Your killer could have come in that way."

Hayden tapped a finger on the steering wheel. "Continue."

"Early Sunday morning a green sedan pulls onto the salvage yard lot. The driver is wearing a hat and sunglasses, and his face is turned. He knows there are cameras."

"The driver is male?"

"If I had to bet, yes."

"I came by the lot Sunday afternoon and found Crow dead," Hayden said. "We know from the autopsy that he'd not been dead long. So whoever this driver was, his arrival coincided with Crow's murder only a few hours before I arrived. Is the car seen exiting the yard?"

"It is at one p.m. I was able to enhance the footage and caught a partial plate. I've notified patrol, and as expected it was listed in the database as stolen."

"Whoever killed Crow and hit Macy is sounding more like a professional. The playing card with Crow suggests a type of signature. None was found with Macy because he didn't have time. Perhaps that attack wasn't planned."

"Maybe he didn't know Crow had kids," Brogan offered.

"Melissa, what about the cameras around Second Chances?"

"Based on Macy Crow's ATM receipt, I did locate her three blocks from Second Chances five minutes before she was hit. The dark truck that was identified as stolen passes behind her. I've taken a freeze-frame of the driver. It's only a partial and it's fuzzy, but I'm trying to enhance it as much as I can. That's going to take some time."

"Anything else?" Hayden asked.

"Still piecing it all together," she said.

"Keep me posted."

"Count on it."

Hayden hung up. "Brogan, see what you can pull up on Josie Jones."

"Will do." As Hayden drove, Brogan accessed the database for arrest records. "Not much in her file. She was arrested a day after her eighteenth birthday, and there is a note from the arresting officer, who noted that the judge of record was Ryder Templeton."

"I know Templeton. He was a buddy of my father's." At eighty-five, Judge Templeton was still active in Austin politics, never missed a UT football game, and met his buddies at his favorite bar every Thursday for a beer.

Hayden checked the time and, taking a chance, dialed Judge Templeton's number. The phone rang twice, and then he heard his father's friend say, "Well, as I live and breathe, Mitchell Hayden. How are you doing?"

"Doing very well."

"Glad to hear it. Let me say again how sorry Leticia and I were to hear about Sierra."

He didn't remember the judge and his wife of forty years at the funeral, but he didn't remember much of that day. "I appreciate that."

"So, boy, seeing as you're not one to call and just chat, what can I do for you?"

"I'm working on a case and came across the name of a Josie Jones. She was arrested for stealing in 1987, and her arrest records tell me she appeared in your court."

"I have a good memory, but you're going back thirty-plus years. I presided over thousands of cases."

"I remember you used to keep a personal log on your cases and sometimes made notes. I thought you might have a note or two about this woman."

"Leticia has been after me for years to throw out all those logbooks. They're taking up too much attic space, she says. Though what the hell else she wants to put in the attic is beyond me."

"Tell me you saved them."

"Of course I did. I can't throw out my logs."

Dogs barked in the background, and Hayden pictured two basset hounds, which had always been the judge's preferred breed. No doubt the judge was sitting on his back porch overlooking Lake Travis and sipping a whiskey. "Let me poke around. Might take me a day or two. And it would be nice to prove to Leticia that those old logbooks still have a use."

"Any help you can offer would be much appreciated," Hayden said.

"Mind telling me why you care about a case from the eighties?"

"We came across several graves on a Hill Country ranch. I think Josie Jones might be one of the bodies. Her name could very well be a dead end, but I've got to at least try."

"Understood." His chair squeaked as if he had leaned forward. "I hear you and Dr. McIntyre were friendly at the fundraiser the other night."

Austin was a big small town. "She and I are on the board of the shelter together."

"You two make a handsome couple."

A quick glance to his right caught Brogan now looking toward him with a renewed interest. He could have backed away from the comment and denied it, but he didn't. "I guess we shall see."

"Well, you're a fool not to chase that gal. Smart as a whip. If I were forty years younger, you'd have some real competition."

The comment wasn't lost on him. Faith might be his shot at a new life. "I'll keep all that in mind, sir."

"Okay. Now I'll get back to minding my own business and will call with an update soon."

"Appreciate it, Judge. I'll owe you one."

Two hours later, Hayden and Brogan arrived at the Texas State Penitentiary in Huntsville. Built in 1849, it was the oldest Texas state prison. It held the State of Texas execution chamber—the most active chamber in the United States.

"The warden knows we're coming and will have Delany up and ready to talk," Brogan said.

As Hayden stopped at the guard station and stated their purpose, each Ranger showed his identification badge before they were waved through the gates. Moonlight bathed the prison's red brick walls. They removed their hats and made their way through security, where they checked their weapons, and into the building.

The warden, Buddy Westchester, a short man with a round belly and dark-brown hair, met them just inside. They all shook hands. "Well, I can tell you Mr. Delany was not happy having his beauty sleep interrupted."

"That's a shame," Hayden said. "I know he's got to be worried about fine lines and wrinkles at his age."

Westchester laughed. "We'll make it up to him somehow." The humor quickly faded from his expression. "Brogan tells me Delany has Hill Country land and there are bodies on it?"

"That's right. We think we have three sets of remains."

"I read up on Delany's file while I was waiting on you two. As you would guess, Delany's a mean son of a bitch. Was in and out of prison, but a murder conviction landed him here."

"He killed his girlfriend, correct?" Hayden asked.

"That he did." They made their way down a tiled hallway toward the interview room at the end. "Beat the hell out of her. She'd just given birth five days before to their son."

"What happened to the boy?" Hayden asked.

"Social services scooped him up," Westchester said. "I suppose he was adopted."

"Did Delany ever say why he killed his girlfriend?" Brogan asked.

"Said he was hungry and she didn't have his supper made." Westchester shook his head. "Don't underestimate this convict, gentlemen. He's smart, and he's mean."

The warden opened the door to the interview room, which was divided by a thick pane of glass. Law enforcement sat on one side and the inmate on the other.

"I'll be standing right back here if you need anything," Westchester said.

"Thank you," Hayden said.

The two sat and had less than a minute to wait before the door on the other side of the glass opened and Delany was escorted into the room. His hands and feet were chained, and he wore a short-sleeve orange jumpsuit that showed off a collection of tattoos stretching from his hands to up under the sleeves. He had buzzed gray hair, a bushy white mustache, and a leery gaze that didn't hide his curiosity.

Delany straddled his chair and stared at the two Rangers. "Surprise, surprise. To what do I owe the pleasure?"

Hayden introduced himself and Brogan. "Your property tax on your ranch in Hill Country. It's been paid regularly for the last thirty years."

Delany glanced at his hands, inked with symbols and letters, and then slowly looked up at Hayden, a slight grin on his lips. "I forgot all about that place. Been years since I been out there."

"And yet someone has been looking out for your place," he said. "Also looks like someone has been using the place pretty regularly."

"How could I know that?" Delany said. "I'm here."

Hayden leaned forward. "I'm on a tight clock, so I'm going to cut to the chase. You help me, and life as you know it won't change. Whatever you have coming or going into this place will remain the same." He paused, rubbing his thumb against a callous on his palm. "But if you don't help me, you will spend the rest of your life in a stripped-down cell and will find yourself in solitary as much as the law will allow."

"Coming at me with both barrels, aren't you, Ranger?"

Hayden and Brogan let the comment lie there.

Delany sat back, studying the Rangers, and if he thought in any way this was going to be a negotiation, he was wrong. "And all I get is the same old, same old as my reward?"

Hayden checked his watch. "The deal is off the table in thirty seconds."

Delany sized up Hayden, seeming to realize Hayden would obliterate whatever comfort he had in this prison. "What do you want to know?"

"Tell me about a guy by the name of Jack Crow."

"Who's that?"

"Are we going to play games?" He was bluffing, acting as if he had all the puzzle pieces.

Delany was silent for a moment. "Oh, Jack Crow? Yeah, I know him. Shit, I haven't seen him in years. Tell me the son of a bitch is rotting in hell somewhere."

"Why do you say that?" Hayden asked.

"I'm pretty sure he's the one that tipped the cops off to my hiding spot when I went on the run after he patched me up."

"Why would he do that?"

He stroked his mustache and sat back. "He took exception to what I did to Susie."

"Susie Gallagher, your girlfriend," Brogan said.

"That's right. Sweet Susie," Delany said. "Crow could be a real high-and-mighty kind of guy. Always said he'd never hurt a woman, but his hands weren't clean either."

"What dirtied his hands?" Hayden said.

"You've been to the ranch, Ranger?" Delany said.

"Spell it out for me," Hayden said.

"I don't have firsthand knowledge, but I heard there might have been a grave or two out there."

"Who's in the graves?" Hayden asked.

"I don't know exactly," he said. "But I know for a fact that Crow dug at least one of them."

"Which one?" Hayden said.

"From what I heard, the first."

"Did Crow kill her?"

Delany's cuffs clinked as he rubbed his nose. "That I don't know. All I heard was that he dug the grave for a woman and a child."

"Who told you about the graves? Why did they end up on your land?"

Delany looked over Hayden's shoulder to the warden. Hayden caught Westchester's reflection in the glass as the warden shifted his stance.

"The Ranger asked you a question politely," Westchester said. "You can help or not."

"Are the cameras recording?" Delany asked.

"I'll switch them off." The warden made a call from a phone mounted on the wall and after a few seconds turned and said, "They're off."

"Who told you about the graves?" Hayden asked.

Delany stared at the warden. Hayden guessed the prisoner was as good at reading the warden as the warden was him. "My stepsister, Heather."

Heather. For a moment the name didn't trigger any memories and then, he asked, "Heather Sullivan? She works for Garnet."

"Is she still with him?" Delany asked. "Imagine that after all this time. That girl had nothing but blind loyalty for Garnet. She'd do anything for him."

CHAPTER NINETEEN

Wednesday, June 27, Midnight

Faith knew Hayden had mentioned Detective Franklin and he was reaching out to her to search missing persons. On the chance that the detective had found something, she called.

"Dr. Hayden," Franklin said after Faith introduced herself. "What can I do for you?"

"I'm working with the Texas Rangers on several missing persons cases."

"I spoke to Hayden a few hours ago. I have his files," the detective said.

"Do you? Would you mind if I came by and looked them over? The remains are arriving in my office soon."

"Sure. I can go over the cases with you."

"Thank you."

Fifteen minutes later she entered the lobby of the Austin Police Department and took the stairs to the third floor.

Faith found a short woman in a small conference room painted in a faded beige and furnished with a rectangular conference table, several worn chairs, and a whiteboard covered in head shots. Franklin was frowning over a collection of files. She wore black, slim jeans, a cotton blouse, and heeled boots. Her hair was tightly twisted into a bun, and her badge hung from a chain around her neck.

"Detective Franklin?" Faith asked.

"Dr. McIntyre. I took the liberty of pulling all the files that not only matched the initials the captain gave me, but also fell during the suggested time frame of 1985 to 1993. That actually narrowed it down to three files."

Faith set her purse on the conference table and rested her hands on her hips as she studied a stack of files the detective had decided didn't match the criteria.

"All those women are missing?" Faith asked incredulously.

Franklin tacked up one last photo and stepped back. "There are always women who vanish, but it's moments like this when I realize just how many."

The disappearances of these women likely had never made the evening news, and if they had, it had been a brief mention quickly forgotten by the public. The fact that many lived on the streets and near the margins was what made them such easy prey. A hunter could go on for years, choosing and killing, without ever being caught.

"I'm particularly interested in Josie Jones," she said.

Franklin tapped on the smiling face of a woman with feathered blond hair that skimmed her shoulders. She had bright-blue eyes and high cheekbones that could have been Faith's own.

"What do you know about her?"

"A majority of the women I initially identified as missing had been prostitutes. But interestingly, the women who corresponded to the initials the captain gave me had only minor legal infractions and offended once or twice. All were also runaways, with blond hair, Caucasian, and under the age of twenty."

"Tell me what you have," Faith said.

Franklin tapped her finger on Josie's face. "Josie Jones was the first to go missing, in 1987," Franklin said. "Next was Olivia Martin in 1988, Kathy Saunders in 1989, and of course, Paige Sheldon in mid-May."

Faith was impatient to hear about Josie but kept her thoughts to herself, allowing the detective to continue.

"Ironically, Josie Jones's sister was very involved in her sister's case until about ten years ago. Her name at the time was Maggie Jones. In the case of Olivia Martin, her brother, Ralph Martin, who's fifty now and runs a sandwich shop in Austin, last checked in with the department a decade ago. Kathy Saunders's father, Rex Saunders, also stayed up-to-date on his daughter's case. He died five years ago, but she has a sister now listed as a contact."

"Do you have addresses for these people?"

"I have last-known addresses for all these individuals, but I don't know if they're current." She handed her the family names written in bold ink on a yellow legal pad.

"Thanks. What can you tell me about Olivia Martin and Kathy Saunders?"

"Olivia Martin, aged nineteen, vanished in 1988. She'd left home after a fight with her parents, but by the time her parents tried to find her, she'd fallen off everyone's radar and whatever trail there might have been had gone cold. There were no hospital or arrest records for her. She'd been arrested the year before for trespassing and being drunk in public."

Faith moved closer to the board, studying the faces of the victims. Like Josie, Olivia had a slight frame and light-colored eyes and hair.

"And Kathy?"

Franklin sifted through the three folders until she found the files. "Kathy Saunders was seventeen and had dropped out of high school. She was originally from Waco, Texas, but after a fight with her mother hitchhiked to Austin in 1988 and was arrested for larceny in December of the same year. Police determined she'd checked into a hotel in East

Austin but vanished from there. The owner remembered her because she stiffed him a night's rent. That was the last she was ever seen."

"Were any of these women pregnant?"

Franklin flipped through several pages. "Not that any of their families were aware of."

"And they were all last seen in East Austin, correct?"

Franklin grabbed a handful of red pushpins and pressed each into the last known locations of all the missing girls.

Faith studied the pins tightly clustered in the area where she'd just been. "They're all within walking distance of Second Chances."

"I know the owner of Second Chances. He's kind of a bright spot in the community. Whenever the cops collect for kids in need, he always steps up. He's well liked," Detective Franklin offered.

"How long has Garnet had his bar?"

"I've been on the job fifteen years, so at least that long. Since I've known him, he's never had any problems with the law."

That made sense. Any arrest records would draw attention to him. "So how does a former enlisted army soldier come up with the cash to open a bar?" Faith asked.

"Good question."

"Maybe he sold two babies," she said, more to herself.

"Two?"

"Twin girls. If my theory pans out, Josie gave birth to twin girls before she died. The Rangers found the body of Jack Crow on Sunday, and Hayden believes Crow knew about the ranch and the twin girls." Jack Crow didn't appear to have the kind of money a black market baby would cost, but he'd ended up with Macy. What had Crow done all those years ago, and how had he gotten custody of Macy?

"Funny you should mention stolen babies. Hayden called and asked me to identify any pregnant missing girls. I found four. They don't look like these women, but they were in Austin and pregnant when they disappeared."

"They were never found?"

"Not a trace of them or their children."

Right now they had lots of pieces and few connections. "Who represented Olivia and Kathy in court?"

Franklin scanned the files. As she moved through the pages in each folder, mild curiosity hardened into suspicion. "Slater and McIntyre represented them all."

***

Paige's belly was contracting. Not hard and not often, but the pains had started to tighten and release, warning her the time for the baby was coming soon.

She rose up off her cot and walked around the small room toward the door. The cuff on her ankle stopped her from reaching the handle. Its metal rubbed her flesh raw. Blood oozed onto the floor when she stood.

He'd been saying from the beginning that he was doing all this for her own good. He said he was saving her immortal soul by forcing her to bring this baby into the world. She never once believed him. He didn't care about her soul, or even his. It was always about the money.

In a perverse way, she missed her initial holding area. At least there she'd had the magazines she'd found in the vent shaft on one of those early nights when she'd searched every corner for some kind of way to escape.

The notes had started with Josie, who of all of them had written the most. Olivia and Kathy wrote far less. But Josie had used up every available bit of space. And when she'd filled the first magazine, she'd used another until her notes abruptly stopped. Paige had read the notes so much she had memorized them.

Things I hate. Broccoli. English class. Parachute pants. Perms. My foster family. This room.

Paige glanced toward the door, listened to make very sure he wasn't close, and then pulled the torn magazine page from her bra. She stared at her words, which echoed the thoughts of the other girls, who'd understood the horror of being locked up, the isolation, and the fear of delivering a baby alone.

She didn't have her pen, but she glanced around the room until she saw a heating grate. She folded the paper and pushed it through the vent until it disappeared behind the grate. Then she flipped over a small wooden table. With her fingernail she started to dig her initials into the cheap wood because she needed to believe that someday, somehow, someone would realize she'd been here. The world was not going to eat her alive.

***

When he saw Faith leave Second Chances, he knew it was time to deal with Garnet, who was certain to panic after seeing a Macy clone staring him right in the face. He'd hoped to locate the evidence Garnet was holding over his client before he killed him, but it looked like it would be wiser not to delay. And who knew—maybe Garnet would be easier to persuade than Crow.

CHAPTER TWENTY

Thursday, June 28, 5:00 a.m.

Dawn was approaching when Hayden and Brogan made it back to Austin. They parked down the street from a closed Second Chances.

Climbing out of the SUV, Hayden glanced around the quiet street that looked dingy as dawn broke.

Two days' stubble darkened Brogan's chin, and the fatigue in his eyes surely mirrored his partner's. Murder investigations typically ran nonstop for at least the first forty-eight to seventy-two hours. Mix in the cold cases of three dead women and a missing teen, and they were now looking at a much more arduous investigation.

Brogan straightened his tie. "Do you think Jack Crow killed that girl all those years ago?"

"I'd like to believe not, but there's no telling. I do think it was that ranch that was weighing on him when he called me."

"But someone beat you to him."

"Yeah," Hayden said.

"If Jack Crow hadn't been tortured, I could have bought the theory that Dirk snuffed his old man and then tried to kill his sister for the land."

Hayden shook his head. "The old coot stirred up one hell of a hornet's nest. And we're going to keep stirring until all the bees are accounted for."

Brogan looked toward Second Chances. "I'd like to bring Garnet into the station this morning and ask him a few questions. Maybe he, Delany, or Heather have other properties we don't know about. There are none under Delany's name, but Melissa Savage is searching property records for Garnet, as well as for Heather Sullivan."

"He has Paige Sheldon's flyer in his bar," Hayden said.

"Hiding in plain sight," Brogan said.

Hayden drew in a breath. Neither Ranger expected Garnet to cooperate when they knocked on his door. But if they could link Garnet and Heather to the ranch, it would be enough for a judge to sign a search warrant for his financial records.

Hayden approached the front door and tried the door handle. It was locked. "I can't wait to hear what this guy has to say."

He peered through the front window, but didn't see any signs of activity. On the bar there were several cases of bottled beer that looked like they needed to be stocked. He reached for his phone and dialed the bar's number. As they stood there, the telephone rang, but no one answered.

"Do you think he took off?" Brogan asked.

"I don't know. Let's have a look around the back." They rounded the street corner and cut down the alley that ran along the building. They passed a dumpster piled high with trash and broken bottles. A lone rat scurried along the brick wall.

Hayden passed a black pickup with Texas plates registered to Garnet and touched the engine hood. It was cold. "If he's inside, he's been there awhile."

Brogan moved to the back door covered with chipped green paint and tested the handle. It didn't turn. "It could be stuck and not locked.

My toolshed door does the same thing sometimes. I just have to put my shoulder into it."

As Brogan tightened his grip on the door, Hayden nodded toward the security camera posted in the alley. "We need to be smart about this. If this case ends up in court, I don't want to see Garnet or Sullivan walk because of an illegal search."

Brogan released his grip on the handle, but a deepening frown telegraphed his frustration.

"I want to find Paige Sheldon as much as you do." Hayden reached for his phone again. "I'm calling for a search warrant so we can search that bar."

***

In Second Chances, Garnet heard the Rangers rattling the door, but by then his hands were tied to a chair in his basement and there was a gag shoved in his mouth.

He should have bolted right after Faith had visited the bar, but he thought the cops might be watching. He had played it cool as he'd gone to the basement, cleaned out his safe, and grabbed his passport. He had closed up the bar a half hour early and, when he thought the place was cleared out, had made a break for his car.

Jesus. He remembered the day Faith had been born, remembered handing her over. And he'd trusted Crow to take care of the dead woman and the other baby who had been on the verge of dying.

Fuck you, Jack Crow, was all he could think as the man who'd clubbed him unconscious two hours ago in the alley reached for a hammer. "They'll be back soon. I don't have much time, so with your permission, I'd like to start."

Garnet twisted his hands, trying to break the zip ties that were as unyielding as steel. The man was young, midforties, nicely dressed, and didn't look like the sort of guy who did this kind of work.

When the man pulled the gag from his mouth, Garnet rasped, "Who the fuck are you? And what do you want?"

A soft chuckle rumbled in his chest. "That's a fairly bossy tone for a man in your situation."

The hammer came down hard on his right index finger. Bone shattered and pain rocketed through his limbs like white lightning. "Where is it?"

"What the fuck are you talking about?" Garnet choked on a scream.

The hammer cracked over the knuckles of his left hand. More pain sliced through him, stealing his breath. His heart rattled so hard against his chest he thought he cracked a rib. "You know. The package. You didn't give it to Crow. If Macy had found it, we'd all know by now. And you didn't give it to Heather. Where is it?"

"Where's Heather? What did she say?"

"Sadly, not enough. Hopefully, you'll do a better job of talking." He slammed the hammer on another knuckle.

Garnet screamed as the pain vibrated up his arm. "Okay, okay," he wheezed. "I'll tell you."

The hammer skimmed gently over his broken and bent knuckles. "Thank you."

He tried to move his fingers but they didn't work, and any twitch or wiggle hurt like a bitch. "Look, I know that I got greedy with the money. I realize that. I won't ask for more."

Hot breath smelled of mint and cigarettes. "The problem is you asked for more money and then you got really stupid and you made threats. And threats cannot be ignored."

"I won't make any more threats."

"I know that," he said softly. "Where is the package?"

When he raised the hammer again, Garnet shook his head, his gaze on the blunt end. "You were right to go to Jack Crow. I gave it to him."

"What was it?"

"Recordings. I wore a wire when I met with my clients. I needed to prove I wasn't ever in this alone."

"Crow never said he had tapes."

"He wouldn't. That's why I gave them to him. Crow kept his word."

He paced back and forth, considering what he'd just learned. "Now the question is, If the tapes weren't in Crow's trailer, where did he put them?"

"He never told me what he did with them," Garnet said. "I told him to hide the package of tapes real well."

"And that is what Jack Crow did. He hid them so well there'll be no finding them." He gently tapped the hammer in the palm of his own hand. "Why did you return to the ranch?" he asked Garnet.

Garnet blinked and drew in a breath to fight unbearable pain. "What?"

"Don't lie. I know you were out there. I know about Delany and the land held in his name. Why did you go back there?"

Shit. How could he have been so stupid? As he considered an answer that sounded right, the hammer rose. Garnet sucked in a breath, braced as he shouted, "Okay, okay. I'm selling another baby." Sweat poured off his forehead, and he was pretty sure he'd pissed his pants. "When the money was cut off, I needed to make up the cash somehow. There was a girl. And I locked her in the same room that we used years ago."

"The cops didn't find her out there."

"I moved her after Macy came by. She said she was a teacher, but she had the look of a cop."

"She is a cop. FBI special agent."

"I knew she'd be trouble."

"She won't be trouble again. I took care of that." Without warning, he brought the hammer down on Garnet's left index finger. His scream echoed in the basement room. "I'm hoping we can be friends. And friends help each other, don't they? Are you my friend, Garnet?"

"Best fucking friend," he said.

"Exactly. I want to know where you've stashed your latest little baby maker."

Garnet looked up through bloodshot eyes. He was screwed every which way to Sunday. If he'd just kept his damn mouth shut, he could have gone to a new town. Heather and he could have found themselves another baby mama.

"Where did you get this one?" he asked.

Garnet shifted, wincing at the slightest move. "She came into the bar after she had a fight with her parents. I saw an opportunity, and I took it."

"How long have you been holding her?"

"Since early May."

He smiled as he scratched his chin. "Garnet, you're quite the businessman. How much do babies go for?" he asked.

"What?"

The man glanced at the hammer and then at Garnet. "How much for a baby?"

"A hundred grand if I do it right."

"Really? That's a hell of a lot of money. Do you have a buyer?"

"Yeah. In Arizona."

"A hundred grand from a client in Arizona? You really think you're getting that much money for a baby?"

Sweat stained his shirt, and Garnet realized he was losing consciousness. "Yeah."

"How much were you paid for the other ones?" he asked.

"I thought you knew," Garnet said.

"My client only gives me the bare-bones details. But I find it's to my advantage to fill in all the missing pieces."

Garnet stared at the guy, shaking his head. The client would do anything to keep the secret.

"Garnet, tell me how much you got for the babies. And remember, we're best friends and don't hold anything back from each other."

"Twenty-five grand for each of the first two and fifty grand for the last."

"Why did you get more for the last one?"

Garnet's entire body throbbed with pain and agony each time he tried to move a muscle. "It was a boy."

"But you didn't sell Macy? You said she was sick?"

"The mother had a bad delivery. I knew she was in trouble, and that's why I called Crow. He wouldn't ask questions. He barely had time to wash his hands before the first baby arrived. He laid the baby in its mother's arms, but then the mother started screaming again. And there was so much blood. He saw the second baby, who came out feet first. She was blue and barely responsive. Much smaller than the first."

"And the mother?"

"She bled out right there. There was nothing Crow could do to stop it. Crow took pity on that little baby. He didn't have to. He was always too soft for his own good."

"So you left with baby number one?"

"Yeah. Crow said he'd bury the mother and child."

"And the rest is history."

Garnet watched as the man pulled first a lighter and then a cigarette from his pocket and lit it. The man inhaled deeply a few times and then held the filter to Garnet's lips. Garnet drew in a lungful of air but found it impossible to hold the smoke in when his body hurt so much.

"Confession is good for the soul, isn't it, Garnet?"

"Yeah." Garnet swallowed, ready to sell his soul to get out of this alive. "Look, there's a bag by the door. It's got the down payment cash from the sale of the baby."

"I noticed that while you were unconscious."

"Take it. Take the girl. Sell the baby and leave me."

"Where is the girl?"

Lies sprang to mind, but Garnet chased them away. "There's a house in town. Not five miles from here. I have a basement room."

"How far along is she?"

"Less than a week from delivery."

"I need an address." He pulled out a pencil and paper. "Ready when you are, Mr. Garnet."

Garnet rattled off the address.

"See? None of this was hard. And I really enjoyed chatting with you." The man ground out the cigarette on the bottom of his boot and then pocketed the butt.

Without warning, the hammer landed on Garnet's kneecap. As he opened his mouth to scream, the man shoved a bar cloth into it, muffling the sound. The man waited patiently as Garnet sucked in a breath through flaring nostrils. For several minutes the world shrank away, and it was just him, the pain, and this crazy motherfucker ready to beat him to death.

The man studied the hammer and its gore as if it were a piece of artwork. "I want you to understand that technically this is business, but honestly, I like hurting people. Especially my best friend."

Olivia Martin, 1988

My name is Olivia Martin. I've read all of Josie's words so many times that I've memorized them. I hear Josie's voice inside my head, especially when I can't sleep and the baby is kicking. I am so afraid. I want out of this box. I want to live. I don't want you to read this after I'm dead. But I know the chances of living get slimmer every day.

Things I like. "Tell It to My Heart" by Taylor Dayne. "Wild, Wild West" by The Escape Club. Chocolate. Sunshine. The feel of grass. My mom's burned spaghetti sauce.

Things I Hate. The streets. Cold weather. Loud cars. Vitamins. Beasts that smile.

CHAPTER
TWENTY-ONE

Thursday, June 28, 7:35 a.m.

Faith was able to speak to the principal at Kat's high school and get the girl reinstated. Kat wasn't happy about it, but Faith wasn't trying to win a popularity contest with the girl. Kat might have had more innate intelligence than her teachers, but if she didn't graduate high school, there was no chance she'd go to college. If there ever was a kid who could thrive with a degree, it was her.

Faith's next stop was again the hospital, though this visit was quick because she had to get back to the autopsy suite. The first set of skeletal remains would be delivered today.

When she arrived at the medical examiner's office and passed by the break room, Nancy held up a fresh cup of coffee for her, which Faith gratefully accepted.

Knowing her possible connection to the case would come up sooner or later, Faith said, "There is a possibility this set of remains belongs to my birth mother."

Nancy stood stock straight for a moment as she processed what Faith had said. "How can that be?"

She could feel the foundation of her life rumbling and shaking. "I'm not exactly sure how all the pieces fit together. And when I do know how, I'll explain it all to you."

Nancy studied her. "You going to be okay?"

"Don't worry about me. Give me five minutes to change, and I'll meet you in the exam room."

Faith changed into scrubs and ten minutes later pushed through the swinging doors of the exam room. Nancy stood at the head of a sheet-covered gurney.

Nancy tossed one last quizzical glance at Faith, who didn't blink, and gently pulled back the sheet.

The skeletal remains were laid out in anatomical order, with the skull at her right and followed by rib bones, vertebrae, pelvis, femurs, and feet bones.

The bones were brown and brittle and looked as if they had been buried for years. Younger bones had a greasy feel and were sometimes referred to as green.

She stood beside the skull and stared into the sightless eye sockets. As she reexamined the skull's facial structure, she affirmed the individual had been Caucasian. Josie's mug shot showed she'd had a narrow face and high cheekbones, characteristics consistent with this skull. "I could take a snapshot of the skull and superimpose it over the picture I have of her."

"How many images do you have of the woman you have in mind?" Nancy asked.

"Two."

"Three would be better. The more angles we have for comparison, the better."

"I know. I'm looking for a quick affirmative to an identification that might take weeks."

"Mind if I do the preliminary evaluation?" Nancy said. "You can check behind me to confirm."

"Sure."

Nancy cradled the skull in her hands. "The molar teeth are intact, which is a good thing. If we can extract DNA, the lab can test for mitochondrial DNA, which can be cross-checked against your DNA, Faith."

"It's a longer process, but accurate," Faith said.

Nancy set the skull down gently and examined the lower vertebrae, searching for breaks, nicks, or fractures. She retrieved a magnifying glass and examined the ribs, again looking for signs of trauma. The thrust of a knife or blunt force could leave marks on the bone, but the cursory examination revealed no trauma.

"The victim's pelvic bowl is wide, also suggesting female."

The pubic bones separated during childbirth as the baby passed through the birth canal. It was during the birthing that ligaments could tear or bleed, and as the body healed, the bones remodeled, leaving small pits and marks on their surfaces.

"These bones are smooth," Faith said.

"She may not have given birth," Nancy said. "She may not be who you think she is."

"Or she died right after the baby's delivery, before her bones had the chance to heal. I can't imagine giving birth in a place like that basement room at the ranch," Faith said.

"Childbirth-related deaths are one in four thousand in this country, but out in the middle of nowhere with no medical equipment, the death rate would be so much higher."

Faith thought about the magazines with the young girl's handwriting crammed in the margins. Fury and frustration collided, but she now had to shift her focus to the victim's long femur bone.

Sensing her uneasiness, Nancy reached for a tape measure and ran it along the length of the femur. "It measures about twenty inches. Extrapolating from that number, I would estimate this person was five foot five to five foot seven inches tall."

Like her. Like Macy. "How old do you think this person was?"

Nancy returned to the skull and studied the line down the center. Called the sagittal suture, this line marked where the growth plates in the skull joined. Most people's closed up by age twenty-six, but everyone's was fused by age thirty-five. This line wasn't closed.

"I'm guessing she was seventeen to twenty-one," Nancy said.

"Agreed."

"Her teeth for the most part are in good shape. One deep cavity on the back molar that would have bothered her."

"What else do you notice about her?" Faith said.

"No signs of trauma. Cause of death is inclusive at this point."

Sadness clenched her chest as she turned from the table and pulled off her latex gloves.

"I want to see the other two sets of remains the moment they arrive. Understood?"

"Will do, Dr. McIntyre."

CHAPTER
TWENTY-TWO

Thursday, June 28, 7:45 a.m.

Hayden had been on the phone since before dawn with several judges until he found one willing to sign a warrant for Garnet's bar by early morning. In the interim, he ordered a patrol car to be stationed outside Second Chances and asked to be alerted if anyone appeared.

While Hayden and Brogan waited on the warrant, they headed to the law offices of Slater & McIntyre. Last night, Faith had texted him, informing him of her meeting with Franklin and the missing girls' connections to the law firm. The law offices opened at eight, and he planned to be on their doorstep when they did.

Before they cleared the parking lot, his phone rang. The display on his phone read **SPAGNOLO**, the forensic technician who'd been working the grave site last night.

"I'm with Brogan and putting you on speakerphone," Hayden said.

"Understood," Spagnolo said.

Hayden pressed the speaker button. "Go ahead. What do you have for us?"

"We were there until midnight and were able to remove the first set of remains," Spagnolo said. "It took longer than we expected because we sifted through each cup of soil to ensure there were no personal items that might have been with the victim. We did find a few metal snaps, but whatever fabric the victim had been wearing disintegrated a long time ago. We also found two pennies near the skull."

"Pennies?" Hayden asked.

"Best guess, someone was superstitious enough to think the victim needed the money to pay the ferryman," Spagnolo theorized. "Greek mythology said the mythical ferryman requires the pennies in exchange for passage across the river Styx from the earth to the underworld."

Crow had been superstitious. "Maybe he was more worried that she'd not cross over and would come back to haunt him."

"I can only hope," Brogan muttered.

"What's on the docket for today?" Hayden asked.

"We have two crews working sites number two and three simultaneously," Spagnolo said. "Barring any complications, we should be finished by the end of the day."

"Thanks for the update," Hayden said. "Keep me posted."

"Will do." Spagnolo ended the call.

Hayden pulled into the parking lot of Slater & McIntyre, located in a glass-and-brick building in downtown Austin.

Brogan checked his phone. "Just received an email from a buddy of mine at the state employment commission."

"Are you going to make me guess?" Hayden asked.

"Guess who worked for Slater and McIntyre in the mideighties?"

"Danny Garnet."

"Correct. So did Jack Crow."

"Interesting."

As they stepped through the front doors, they removed their hats, and Hayden's gaze was drawn to the portrait of a man with a round face and thick graying hair wearing a crisp, dark suit standing in a law library. The painting, hanging near the receptionist's mahogany antique desk, depicted only one of the firm's two founding principals, Peter Slater Sr., when he was in his early forties. All traces of Russell McIntyre had been erased after his arrest years ago.

From what he'd read about the two partners, Russell McIntyre had been the one with star power and the driving force behind the firm. Though Peter Slater Sr. had been competent enough, it had been McIntyre and his wife's family connections that had attracted the first big clients. Russell may have nearly ruined the firm with his financial schemes, but the fact was there'd have been no firm at all without him.

They showed their badges to the receptionist. "Mitchell Hayden. Mike Brogan. Texas Rangers. We need to see PJ Slater."

The woman rose, pulling the phone headset off. "He's in a meeting."

"We need to see him now," Hayden said, unapologetically.

"I don't think you understand who he is or who he's meeting with now."

"I don't think you understand how serious I am. This isn't a request," Hayden said.

She tipped her chin up a fraction. "I'll speak to his secretary."

She reappeared minutes later and escorted the pair to an office on the top floor in the back corner. The large plate glass windows overlooked the city of Austin. PJ came out from around his desk, adjusting his jacket. "Rangers Hayden and Brogan. It was good to see you at Monday's fundraiser, Ranger Hayden. What brings you gentlemen here?"

"Your mother did a great job organizing the shelter fundraiser. Hope you raised a lot of money."

"As always, she got everyone to give until it hurt," PJ said, grinning. "Can I offer you coffee or a soda? My assistant is bringing me a fresh cup."

"Coffee," Brogan said.

"Please make it two," Hayden said. "We've been going all night."

"Working a case?" PJ asked as he texted the coffee order somewhere.

Hayden grinned. "Yes, we are, and I'm hoping you can help us with it."

"I'll do what I can." He held out his hand toward the chairs and couch across from his desk. When the Rangers sat on the couch, PJ sat in one of the chairs.

The door opened and his secretary appeared with a tray of three cups of coffee in paper to-go cups, sweeteners, and cream. Both the Rangers took their coffee black, but PJ poured a liberal amount of sugar in his. "Hope you don't mind the paper. We're all on the go, and so are half our clients. Nobody sits and enjoys an entire cup of coffee anymore," he mused.

Hayden sipped his coffee, knowing he'd start slow and ask the easy questions first. "I'm looking for information on Danny Garnet. He worked for your firm in the mideighties."

"I'm not familiar with the name, but that doesn't mean you aren't correct. I can check with our human resources director and see what she has in her records."

"I'd appreciate that," Hayden said.

Slater picked up the phone on a side table and punched three numbers on the keypad. "Sharon, this is PJ. Can you pull the records for Danny Garnet? He would have worked for us in the eighties." He listened and nodded his head. "Pull whatever you have. And I'm going to need that yesterday if you don't mind. Great." He hung up and sat back down. "She'll be here shortly. We digitized our employee files about ten years ago, and that makes life a lot easier when old personnel questions arise. What has Mr. Garnet gotten himself into that requires a visit from the Texas Rangers?"

"Before I answer that, I have another question," Hayden said.

"Sure. Fire away."

"You told Faith McIntyre that you found the name *Josie Jones* in one of Russell McIntyre's datebooks, and you believe Josie might be Faith's birth mother."

230

PJ sat back, sipping his coffee. The jovial welcome didn't completely fade from his face, but it soured considerably. "That's a very private matter for Faith, and I don't see how that is the concern of the Texas Rangers."

"The reason I'm asking is that we think Josie Jones knew Danny Garnet back in the eighties," Hayden said.

"Again, I don't know how it relates to Faith's adoption. And frankly, I don't think she'd like me discussing this with you or anyone else. All I know for sure is that Josie Jones was a name I said may be a lead for Faith."

"Have you ever heard of Olivia Martin or Kathy Saunders?" Brogan asked.

PJ looked genuinely confused now, but Hayden reminded himself he was dealing with a very adept defense lawyer. "I have no idea who you're talking about."

"These are women who were represented at one point by Slater and McIntyre. They went missing in the late eighties."

"We have fifteen attorneys on staff and have been in business in our current and former forms for nearly forty years. Do you have any idea how many clients that means?"

"I'm guessing a lot," Hayden said. "But I'm betting you also digitized the client records along with the employee files. That kind of technology makes it so easy for you to find out."

"I could do that, but I won't. If we did represent those women, the work falls under attorney-client privilege."

Hayden's voice dropped as his patience thinned. "Well, for your own sake, I suggest you have a look."

"Are you suggesting someone here was responsible for their disappearances?" PJ asked.

"I'm not suggesting anything."

A knock on the door had PJ and Hayden rising as a woman in her late fifties with shoulder-length graying hair appeared. She nodded to

Hayden but moved quickly to Slater and handed him an iPad. "I've pulled up his file. This is all we have, sir."

"Thank you, Sharon." PJ sat back down and scrolled through the papers, not saying a word until Sharon closed the door behind her. "I don't want you to think that Slater and McIntyre isn't cooperative. But we are bound by ethics and laws."

"Understood. Just giving you a heads-up that we'll be circling back on this matter. What about Garnet? There shouldn't be any restrictions to talking about former employees."

"No, of course not." PJ studied the information Sharon had brought him. "Garnet was hired in 1985 as a private investigator. Back then the firm was small and had only a couple of attorneys other than my father and Russell. This day and age, I wouldn't work directly with a private investigator, but in those days, my father and Russell would have."

Hayden had searched PJ Slater on the Internet and learned he'd been born in 1990. He was the only child of Peter and Margaret Slater and according to the records was not adopted. "Do you have a list of cases Garnet investigated for the firm?"

That thousand-watt smile returned. "And we are right back to attorney-client privilege. Our private investigators often handle very delicate information that our clients would not expect us to ever reveal, even after forty years. I can tell you according to this printout that he handled dozens of cases. Why is Garnet so important to you now?"

"His name came up in an investigation, and we plan to interview him later today." Hayden always judiciously balanced how much to tell as well as withhold during an interview. Sometimes he had to give a little information to prime the pumps. "Have you heard the name *Paige Sheldon?*"

"I did hear the Sheldon name. Her story was in the news recently. She's missing, I think. Do you think Mr. Garnet is associated with the Sheldon case?"

"We don't know for sure yet, but considering this girl is still alive and about to deliver a baby, we want to find her as quickly as we can."

PJ glanced at his iPad screen. "As our firm has had no dealings with Danny Garnet in almost thirty years, there's not much I can do for you, Captain. And how do you know these young women didn't simply move on to greener pastures? They all could be alive and well in another part of the country and just be living under the radar."

Hayden decided to toss Slater a little more information. "The thing is, Mr. Slater, I've got three Jane Does in the morgue right now. Their bodies are nothing but bones, and it's clear they've been dead for at least thirty years."

PJ's expression didn't change. "Do you know for a fact that the three sets of remains belong to Jones, Martin, and Saunders?"

"I won't know until DNA testing is complete," he said.

"And Faith must know about this discovery?" PJ asked.

"She does."

PJ drummed his fingers on the arm of his chair. "I didn't realize this was a murder investigation."

"I don't like to use murder as part of my opening line. Has a tendency to put people on edge," Hayden offered.

"I can see why. And you think because the former Slater and McIntyre represented these women, someone here might have had a hand in their deaths?"

"Begs the question, don't you think?"

"Garnet did work for the firm during that time frame, but he could have been acting on his own."

"Possibly. And the answer might be as simple as that, but you did say in the firm's first years McIntyre and your father worked with Garnet. And you told Faith Josie Jones appeared in Russell McIntyre's datebook multiple times during the time in question."

"You really don't think respectable men like my father and Russell would do something as heinous as kidnap three girls and murder them?" Slater asked.

A smile played at the corner of Hayden's lips as he shook his head. "I learned a long time ago the capacity for evil stretches across all economic and social bounds."

"My father and Russell did a good bit of pro bono work in the early years as a way of *giving back* to the community. Maybe by representing these women we unwittingly put them in Garnet's path. How would we have control over what he did on his own time?"

"Does it say Garnet was a felon in his files?" Hayden asked.

"It says his offenses were nonviolent, nor were they felonies. My father and mother have always believed in second chances."

Funny he should say *second chances*, the name of Garnet's bar. "Ever met a Jack Crow?"

"No," Slater said.

"What about Sam Delany?"

"We can keep playing *do-you-know*, but the fact is I wasn't even born when these women disappeared, and since my father and his partner are dead, there is not much I can do for you."

"Faith said you checked McIntyre's datebooks and found Josie. I suggest you do the same for the other girls. I also suggest you read up on their files and find out who represented them."

"Most of Russell's records were seized during Mr. McIntyre's federal investigation. I was lucky to find the datebooks."

"Your father's records are intact, I assume."

Slater was young but he wasn't stupid, and he'd already shepherded this firm through his father's death.

If either Russell or Peter Sr. had a hand in these girls' deaths, he suspected PJ would find a way to hide it. It was easy to be high-minded and moral until your entire world was challenged. Hayden would have signed an oath with the devil to save Sierra, and he'd bet PJ would hide evidence to save his firm.

"I'm not releasing my father's records, especially when he isn't alive to defend himself."

"Those girls deserve justice, Mr. Slater."

"Of course they deserve justice. You aren't fresh out of the academy. You knew when you walked in the door I couldn't divulge my client names or discuses firm business." PJ tugged at the end of his monogramed cuff. "You were hoping because I'm young, I'd make a mistake, but I can assure you that you aren't the first person who's tried to test my mettle since my father's death."

"It never hurts to ask," Hayden said with a grin. "And you're right about me being on the job for a long time. But one thing all that time has taught me is to know when something isn't right." He leaned forward. "And Garnet's involvement with this firm does not smell right, Mr. Slater. So until you help, I'm not going to be far from your doorstep."

"You're wrong about us. I know my father and his partner did things differently than I do. I know they understood how far a law could bend, but I don't run the firm like that. We have nothing to hide."

"I hope you're right." He picked up his hat while he and Brogan rose. They all shook hands, and PJ walked them out of his office.

Brogan paused. "Hell, forgot my hat." He hurried in and out of the room in seconds, returning with his hat and a coffee cup. "You're right about these to-go cups. Very handy."

"Glad you like it," PJ said.

Despite Brogan's grin, they all knew they'd fallen on opposite sides of this case and would fight tooth and nail to protect their turf.

Outside, the two Rangers got into Hayden's SUV. As they settled, Brogan reached for an evidence bag from the glove box. He opened his door, poured out the coffee onto the parking lot, and dumped the cup into the bag. "I grabbed PJ's cup and left mine in its place. PJ's DNA may not be admissible, but I'm kind of curious to know who spawned him."

Hayden slid on his sunglasses. "Assuming all three of those girls had babies, he'd be the right age if he were one of the stolen babies."

"As I understand it, he's not adopted."

"I'll believe that when I see DNA results that do not link him with any of the three dead women," Hayden said. His phone rang as he backed out of the space. "Captain Hayden."

"Hayden, this is Judge Templeton. I got something for you."

"That was fast."

The old man's tone was serious. "You don't call in favors all that often, so I knew it was important. I did find Josie Jones in my daily journal. As you said, she was arrested for shoplifting when she was eighteen. According to my notes, she was very pretty and had a fancy lawyer defending her."

"Slater and McIntyre."

"How'd you know?"

"Lucky guess. Who was the attorney of record? McIntyre or Slater?"

"Peter Slater Sr. He saw to it she didn't do any jail time."

PJ had told Faith that Josie had been in her father's datebook. Was PJ lying, or was Russell's datebook misleading? "Thanks for the update, Judge." He ended the call and checked his watch. "Let's get that cup dropped off, and then we're headed to Second Chances, search warrant or not."

CHAPTER
TWENTY-THREE

Thursday, June 28, Noon

"I've got more information on Josie Jones," Kat proclaimed, suspending any salutation to Faith on the other end of the phone.

It was lunchtime, and Faith had spent the morning conducting the autopsy of a seventy-year-old male who'd accidently been shot by his neighbor. The buckshot had severed the femoral artery, and the victim had bled to death before the neighbor could get him in from the country.

Faith sat down behind her desk. "Kat, I thought you were in school."

"It's lunchtime. We get twenty minutes on the prison yard to ourselves."

She rubbed her fingertips to her temple. "You're back there because I sweet-talked the principal, and it's not a prison yard."

"Broom-Hilda is in her office. She can't see me. Do you want to know about Josie or not?"

Faith pushed aside the temptation to reprimand Kat about sticking her nose where it didn't belong. "Just spill it."

"I found Josie's older sister's address. Her new married name is Jones, and she lives right here in Austin." Kat rattled off the address.

The cops had given her the same name, but she'd not had the time or courage to follow up yet. "How did you find that?"

"Faith, *everything's* on the Internet if you know where to look."

"Apparently."

"So are you going to see her?" Kat asked excitedly.

"And just show up out of the blue?"

"Why not? Don't you think she deserves closure, too?"

"Sure she does. But I don't have any solid evidence for her yet about Josie, who may or may not be related to me."

"Do you want me to text this tip to Hayden?"

"No. I'll handle this." Faith typed in the address to the map app on her computer. The woman didn't live too far from Faith's office.

"You don't sound excited about the idea of seeing her."

"It's complicated."

"You're worried she won't want to see you." Kat's words echoed exactly what Faith was thinking.

"You're right, Kat."

"Don't be worried. She'll be glad to see you."

How could this child possibly know this? It had been over thirty years since anyone had seen Josie. Loved ones moved on and did the best they could to cope with the pain. A reminder about the past from her might not be welcome. "Maybe."

In the background a bell rang. "I've got to go. The prison matron is summoning us back."

Faith smiled. "Not that bad, kid. Graduate high school, go to college, and the world will be yours."

"School blows." Her words didn't have quite the anger and agitation they'd had before.

"Chin up, Kat."

The girl moaned and hung up.

Faith was familiar with the area Kat had mentioned. It would take her twenty minutes to get there.

Faith might not get a chance to meet the woman, but she could drive out there and see her house. Maybe spot something that would make sense to her.

Without overanalyzing, as she loved to do, she grabbed her purse, a couple of DNA test kits from supply, and made her way to the locker room to change. Ten minutes after Kat's call, she was driving north.

Maggie Stapleton's home was located on a cul-de-sac in North Austin. The one-level rancher was nestled under a large southern live oak tree that shaded the entire yard. There was a blue minivan in the driveway and a rooster weather vane perched on a pole in the front yard.

Drawing in a breath, she tightened her hands on the wheel, beginning to question herself. She had no way of knowing if Josie Jones was her birth mother or that the woman's body had been found. She had nothing definitive yet. But the need to know was overwhelming.

Before she lost her nerve, she shut off the car engine and crossed the aggregate driveway up to the front door. She rang the bell, almost hoping no one was home. She should have called first, but as soon as she heard the footsteps and saw the front doorknob twist, she had no choice but to stand her ground.

The door opened to a woman in her mid- to late forties. Immediately, she saw similarities between the mug shot and this woman. The face, the eyes, the lips all matched.

"Mrs. Stapleton?" Faith asked.

"That's right."

Faith dug out her medical examiner's identification from her purse. "My name is Dr. Faith McIntyre. I'm with the medical examiner's office, and I'm investigating a cold case. Was Josie Jones your sister?"

Mrs. Stapleton studied Faith's identification and then her face. Her head cocked slightly as if something she saw in Faith had registered, but she then brushed the thought aside as if it were too improbable. "Yes, Josie was my sister. Have you found her?"

"I can't say with any degree of certainty, but I was hoping to find out more about Josie."

Mrs. Stapleton's brow knotted. She didn't invite Faith inside, but she also didn't slam the door in her face. "It's been over thirty years. There are days when I have to look at pictures just to remember what she looked like."

"When did you last see her?"

"It was the fall of 1987. I was a sophomore in college and Josie was a senior in high school and working part-time. She was in foster care and I wanted to have her come live with me, but the judge said I was too young to take care of her." She moistened her lips and cleared her throat. "Josie was a beautiful girl, and she knew it. But she was always so restless. She was bored so easily. Was always looking for a new thrill. The first time she got arrested was for stealing her foster mother's watch. The second time, Josie was almost eighteen, and her foster mother felt like she needed a hard lesson. So she stepped back and let Josie face the police and courts. Tough love, she called it."

"From what I've learned so far, she was acquitted of the charges," Faith said.

"That's right. The day she turned eighteen, Josie came home like she could pick up where she left off. Her foster mother, who was having none of it, kicked her out. The woman told Josie to find her own place to live. Josie grabbed a few things and left. She said she had someone who said he'd give her a job and a place to live. I never saw my sister again."

"Do you know who that person was?"

"The cops asked her foster mother that question dozens of times. But Josie never told her or me." Mrs. Stapleton folded her arms over her chest. "Why, after all this time, are you here?"

"We've found a set of remains in the Hill Country. I'm trying to identify them."

Mrs. Stapleton raised her fingers to her lips. "What makes you think it's Josie?"

"There are several factors that I can't discuss right now."

Mrs. Stapleton's eyes watered. "To think you might have found Josie after all this time. I prayed for years that she'd show up healthy and whole, but as time passed, I lost hope."

"Do you have anything that belonged to her?"

"I have a few pictures." Mrs. Stapleton reached for the door, glanced at Faith as if she were trying to process all the information and emotion flooding her brain. "Does the medical examiner always make personal calls like this?"

"No. This is an unusual case."

Mrs. Stapleton stared at her and then pushed open the door and motioned Faith inside. The one-level house had a great room with a vaulted ceiling, bedrooms on one side, and the kitchen on the other. Bright light streamed into the room onto a large collection of houseplants. An artist's easel was propped against the wall along with some paintings.

"You're an artist?" Faith asked.

"I do portraits. Not getting rich, but it's a good business." She crossed to an intricately carved box on the coffee table and opened it. Inside was a stack of older photos that curled at the edges and were slightly yellow. "I wish I had more of Josie. Mom never took many, and neither did her foster mother, who had five other kids to care for."

Mrs. Stapleton gently handed the stack of six photos to Faith. Nervous energy burned through her body as she glanced at the first picture of two young towheaded girls standing by a Ferris wheel. She flipped to the next picture and found the two girls a couple of years older. Josie in these pictures was a far cry from the somber girl in the mug shot. Each image featured the girls a little older, until she reached the last picture. It was just Mrs. Stapleton.

"Can I snap pictures of these?" Faith asked. "We'll need it for the files."

"Sure."

Faith carefully laid each one on the coffee table and took pictures with her phone. "Thank you, Mrs. Stapleton." She handed back the photos, along with her business card. "I promise to keep in touch."

Mrs. Stapleton followed Faith to the door. "Josie did tell me the job she'd been hired for was a nanny position."

"Nanny?"

"Yes. She said something that was odd then. She said the man who hired her liked her looks a lot."

"He hired Josie based on her looks."

"Yeah. That sounded off to me, but Josie told me I worried too much. When she went missing, I relayed that comment to the police, but they never found any evidence that she'd interviewed for a job like that. I've always wondered if I had said something more to her, would she have been more careful and would she be here now."

"Josie wouldn't want you to believe that. No good will come of it."

"The guilt is all I have left of her, I guess."

"Did Josie say anything else about this guy?"

"She said he was handsome. Classy."

"Did she say anything about the baby or the wife?"

"No."

"Did she ever mention Russell McIntyre?"

"McIntyre. That's your name."

"He was my father. There is evidence that he might have represented your sister in court."

"Your father knew my sister?"

"Her name appeared in his datebook multiple times," Faith confessed.

"I don't recall the name." Mrs. Stapleton slid her hands into the pockets of her jeans. "Was she hired to babysit you?"

"She vanished a year before I was born." Faith cleared her throat. "When was the last time you saw Josie?"

"The day she was supposed to be meeting the child she'd be babysitting."

Anything could have happened to the girl that day, but she had one way of narrowing the search. "I brought a quick DNA test. Would you mind taking a cheek swab?"

"Sure. I'll take whatever test you have."

Faith removed the packaged test and latex gloves. Carefully, she slid on the gloves before breaking open the test. "Just open your mouth so I can take a quick swab."

Mrs. Stapleton opened her mouth and watched as Faith swabbed the inside of her cheek. When Faith was done, the woman ran her tongue over the area. "When will you know if the remains you found are linked to me?"

"Very soon." She replaced the swab in the glass vial and sealed it in a plastic bag. If she could prove that Mrs. Stapleton was her aunt, then she had proven her connection to Josie. But it would take a mitochondrial DNA test to prove the bones in the ground were Josie. "Thank you, Mrs. Stapleton."

"Call me Maggie."

"Maggie. I'm Faith."

Warm eyes studied her closely. "You look like Josie."

Faith stood perfectly still as her heart thumped in her chest. She wanted to explain everything, but she was in the middle of a police investigation and couldn't. "Do I?"

"The instant I saw you, I saw her."

She promised herself as soon as she could she would tell Maggie the entire story. "I guess I have that kind of face."

A half smile teased Maggie's lips as she shook her head. "No, you don't."

Faith felt an odd kinship with this woman. "One way or the other, you'll see me again."

She left, crossing quickly to her car and sliding behind the wheel. She was rattled, unsure, and nervous. But she was also exhilarated. She looked at the DNA test kit and then glanced up to find Maggie still staring. She waved and drove off. At her first stoplight, she called Hayden.

He answered on the first ring. "Faith, are you all right?"

"I've just visited Josie Jones's sister."

If he heard the tremor in her voice, he ignored it. "Does Nancy Drew ever go to school?"

A nervous smile tugged at her lips. "When it suits. Where are you?"

"At the forensic lab," he said. "I also have a DNA sample that needs testing."

"Who does it belong to?"

"PJ Slater."

"PJ? Did he give you a sample?"

"He left a cup behind," Hayden said.

"That's not going to be admissible in court."

"I'm looking for confirmation that he's the product of one of those girls, not court evidence."

"Why PJ?"

"He's the right age, has your coloring, and his father was at the epicenter of all this."

"But he wasn't adopted."

"So I've been told. Would you give me a DNA sample?"

"Sure."

"Good. Then we'll know soon enough, won't we?"

"Why would Margaret and Peter lie about their son not being adopted?"

"I don't know," Hayden said.

"I'll be there in a few minutes," she said.

Faith drove straight to the state forensic lab, and before she went into the building, she pulled a second test from her purse and swabbed her own cheek. Inside, she turned in Maggie Stapleton's DNA sample, as well as her own. She gave orders for her sample to be compared to Stapleton's and any one that Captain Hayden had dropped off today.

Rounding the corner, she saw Hayden standing at the end of the hallway. He was leaning against the wall, hat in hand, his right boot resting on the wall as his head tipped forward, cell phone to his ear.

She didn't know what exactly she had with him or even where it would go. But she was so glad to see him.

Straightening her shoulders, she moved toward him, and as her heels clicked on the tiled floor, he looked up, pushed away from the wall, and ended his call. He looked tired, but a small grin appeared as she approached.

"Everything turned in to the lab?" Hayden asked.

"Yes."

"Great. We could use some good news." He nodded toward the evidence-testing lab down the hallway. "The forensic tech has examined the two magazines," he said. "She said she'd like to go over some of the results. Thought you would like to hear."

"Thanks. I would."

"What did Mrs. Stapleton say about her sister?"

"She said Josie had a line on a nanny job and she was set to interview with both parents the day she vanished."

"When was that?"

"September of 1987. Nine months before I was born."

She felt his hand on the small of her back as they walked toward the lab room. They crossed the large room filled with workstations to a tech with salt-and-pepper hair wearing thick dark-rimmed glasses. His name was Doug Turner, and they'd met before. Turner looked up from his microscope. "Dr. McIntyre, I wasn't expecting you."

"I wanted to hear what you had to say," she said.

"Sure." He rose and crossed the room to a large computer screen. He pressed a couple of buttons, and the title page of one of the magazines appeared. "To save possible evidence and the integrity of the pages, I have photographed the magazine, and it's now in storage." He selected another file on his computer, and the next page in the magazine appeared, along with a fingerprint highlighted by black powder. "I pulled several prints from the magazine's cover as well as the interior. The large thumbprint you see on the right came from the magazine's cover."

"It's too big to be a young girl's," Faith said.

"Correct," the technician said. "I've already run the fingerprints against the AFIS database, and it's a match for Danny Garnet."

Hayden shook his head. "I've been on the phone the last half hour trying to light a fire under the judge. His clerk promises I'll have a warrant for Second Chances in the hour."

"This fingerprint should seal the deal," Turner said.

"Brogan and I were at Second Chances earlier, and from what we could determine from the outside, there was no one at the bar."

"I was also there last night," Faith said. And when she looked up at his hardening features, she said, "I can make all your logical arguments, Captain Hayden, so save the lectures. I wanted to see the place for myself. Unlike you, I went during business hours and got in."

"And?"

"The bar was packed, and Garnet was working hard to fill drink orders."

"When did you see him?" Hayden asked.

"About seven thirty last night."

A muscle pulsed in Hayden's jaw. "That was an unnecessary risk."

"Maybe." She deflected his ire back to the technician. "Garnet was taken aback when he saw me. I think he thought I was Macy at first. What else did you find, Mr. Turner?"

"I found more fingerprints on the inside of the magazines. Since all the missing girls had arrest records, I was able to match prints to Josie Jones, Olivia Martin, and Kathy Saunders. They were all there, and it appears each wrote notes in the magazine."

Faith watched as the technician slowly clicked through the photos of the different pages of the magazines. *What I like. What I hate.* Josie had started the trend, and each girl had followed suit.

She read through the notes, her throat tightening. The sets of bones all had faces and identities now. They all had stories.

"We also found several hair strands on various pages. I've bagged them and will run DNA against them." Easy to assume the hair found would just belong to the girls or Garnet, but there was no telling if evidence of another suspect was involved.

When they left the room, Faith said, "Test my DNA against Garnet's." The idea that that man could be her biological father was nearly unbearable.

Hayden stared at her a long moment. "All right. Did you ever test your DNA against Russell McIntyre's?"

"I did, as a matter of fact." He wouldn't have been the first man to father a child and then adopt it. "It wasn't a match."

***

Hayden walked Faith to her car, and he was glad to have her back in the sunshine. She'd been stoic in the forensic lab, but she'd grown paler as the technician had clicked through the photographed pages.

"Where are you headed?" he asked.

"Back to the office. I feel helpless at home or at Macy's bedside. At least at the office I'm doing something productive."

"You look exhausted."

"I could say the same for you, Captain."

"I'm used to the long hours."

Without thinking, she reached up and brushed the strands of gray hair over his temple. He liked it when she was close and fussed over him.

"If you have time, come by my house tonight and see me."

God, but that offer was tempting. He'd like nothing better than to bury himself in her. "I can't make any promises."

"I know. But if you get the chance, stop by. The chances of me sleeping are slim."

"All right." And then he leaned in and kissed her softly on the lips. She didn't pull away but held steady. She took his hand in hers and squeezed it gently before she got into her car and drove off.

In his car, he sat for a moment, savoring the faint scent of her perfume. Drawing in a breath, he glanced at his cell, expecting to see a text or call from the judge's office. When he didn't, he was ready to hit redial when the phone rang. It was Detective Lana Franklin.

"Detective. What can I do for you?" he said.

"I have a homicide you'd be interested in seeing." Her tone was clipped and adamant.

"Can you give me the stats? I'm on my way to another location."

"You'll want to detour to my scene. The victim's name is Heather Sullivan, age forty-nine. A pay stub in her car is from Second Chances. Her trunk is filled with baby diapers and supplies."

Heather Sullivan worked for Garnet. "I'll be right there."

He pulled up under the I-35 underpass to a collection of first responder vehicles. Blue and red lights flashed upon the concrete underside of the interstate. As he exited his SUV, he settled his Stetson on his head before walking toward the yellow crime scene tape where Detective Franklin stood.

"Detective Franklin," he said.

"Lana. Thanks for coming."

"What do you have?" he asked.

The forensic van was angled behind her, so the vehicle blocked his view of the body. A cement culvert ran under the bridge and, due to a few storms last week, remained dotted with puddles and trash. A forensic technician's camera flashed as she moved around the body. The cars on the interstate thundered overhead, oblivious.

"Tell me what you have," he said.

"An anonymous male caller contacted the 911 center about two hours ago. He reported the body's discovery."

"And he didn't leave a name."

"He did not. The phone he used appeared to be a burner. Untraceable."

"Okay." He reached in his coat pocket for black latex gloves and worked his hands into them as he followed her around the forensic van and saw the body of a woman who lay on her back, her arms outstretched. Her body had been burned over 70 percent, but her face remained intact. Through the black char, he deduced she'd worn booted heels, blue jeans, and a red shirt. Just above the burn line, he saw the tops of letters that spelled SECOND CHANCES.

Her throat had been cut multiple times, and the injuries had spilled out a halo of blood on the ground around her pale, almost translucent face. He could see her body had also been stabbed in multiple locations.

Hayden approached the body, careful not to step in the blood as he studied the victim's rough-cut nails, now bluing at the cuticles. Rigor had set, and the limbs were rigid. Rough guess, he'd say this woman had been dead twelve to twenty-four hours.

"Heather Sullivan has lived in Austin for the last thirty years. Her car is up ahead to the left. There's nothing remarkable about it except for the pamphlets in the trunk. They're all focused on adoption. She even has a scrapbook filled with smiling childless couples. Ms. Sullivan is not a social worker and has no affiliation with any adoption agencies. Last we spoke, we were talking about kidnapped women whose babies had been taken. Now I have a dead woman pretending to be an adoption counselor. Hell of a coincidence."

Neither of them believed in this kind of chance. "I should have a search warrant for Second Chances within the half hour, and if I don't, I'll be banging on a judge's door."

***

Notification of Hayden's search warrant arrived minutes after he left Heather's crime scene, and he immediately contacted Brogan, as well as local uniformed officers. Twenty minutes later, two Rangers stood on the sidewalk outside the bar as two marked cruisers pulled in behind them, their lights flashing.

The bar was still dark, and the neon CLOSED sign flickered in the window. While Brogan and Officer Holcombe offered cover, Hayden tried the door and discovered it was still locked. Holcombe returned to her cruiser and retrieved a crowbar and handed it to Hayden. Nodding, he wedged the end of the bar between the lock and the doorjamb.

As Holcombe moved back and drew her gun, he worked the back-and-forth prying at the wood until the front door popped open. The chime from a security system sounded but did not go off. Whoever left this place last had not set it.

Hayden set the crowbar aside and flipped on the lights. He pulled his service weapon and, along with Brogan, moved slowly into the main room of the bar, while Holcombe remained behind to cover their backs. Building searches could be a real mixed bag. Sometimes there was nothing, and all the hype was for just that. And then there were those times when someone was waiting on the other side of a door with a loaded gun ready to blow their heads off.

In these critical moments, all were aware that they were on the suspect's turf and anything could go wrong.

The scents of stale beer and cigarettes mingled as they crossed the wide-planked floor toward the bar. Hayden's gaze was drawn to Paige Sheldon's missing person flyer.

"I can't wait to find him," Brogan said.

"Odd to be closed," Hayden stated.

"Garnet's day isn't starting well, considering one of his employees is in a body bag on her way to the morgue." Brogan rubbed the back of his neck. "When the hair on the back of my neck rises, it's always a sign of trouble."

"What's it doing now?" Hayden asked.

"Dancing like demons."

Hayden looked behind the bar, making sure it was secure, while Brogan searched a small closet used for storing supplies.

Hayden pushed through the saloon doors into the kitchen. There were stacks of dirty cups, glasses, and plates on the counter next to a large stainless steel sink, as if someone had been interrupted before the evening cleanup could be completed.

They searched a pantry stocked with paper products, boxes filled with Second Chances matches, large jars of cherries and olives, canisters of peanuts, and extra cases of whiskey and vodka. A mop and several brooms leaned in the corner, and a box overflowed with a blend of Fourth of July, Saint Patrick's Day, Christmas, and Valentine's Day decorations.

"He's got to have some kind of an office," Brogan said.

Hayden moved toward the closed door on the far side of the kitchen, his weapon raised and body coiled. Brogan stood to one side of the door as Hayden gently pushed it open and found a long set of stairs that led down to a basement.

He clicked on a light and moved down the stairs. The deeper he descended, the stronger the coppery scent of blood and urine grew.

At the bottom, he glanced over his shoulder to the right and saw a large desk covered with stacks of papers, a half dozen coffee cups, a pizza box with one slice remaining, and an older laptop. No sign of Garnet.

He and Brogan shifted to the left, searching as they moved to an alcove behind the stairs, where they discovered Garnet's mangled body lashed to a chair.

Garnet's hands, still tied to the arms of the chair, were broken in several places. The dead man's left knee was twisted at a cruel angle, his right knee swollen and bruised. Blood and urine pooled under and around the chair. None of these injuries had killed Garnet. What had finally finished him was the slice across his throat. The cut ran from ear to ear.

Frustration rushed over Hayden as he stared at the dead man's gaping mouth and glassy eyes staring toward the ceiling. If he'd had any doubts that Garnet was the key to those graves and to Josie's disappearance, he didn't any longer. Someone else had figured out what Garnet and Heather were doing, and they'd dished out their own brand of justice.

He holstered his gun before reaching into his jacket pocket and pulling on latex gloves. Brogan did the same. The bar was now officially a crime scene.

"Wonder who got to him first?" Brogan moved to the back door that led to the alley and checked it. "It's locked, but that's easy enough to do as you're going out the door."

"The front door upstairs was locked, which means the killer had to have left through the back door. Let's hope the security cameras facing the alley recorded whoever it was."

Hayden cataloged the man's injuries. "He didn't die quickly, and it looks like he might have been trying to keep his secrets."

"That still might have given him time to kill Heather," Brogan said.

Garnet could have killed Heather, but in light of the torture he'd endured only a few hours ago, it was highly unlikely. "I don't think so. Garnet might have been taking the girls, holding them and even killing them, but there's another player in this game."

"He's cleaning house?" Brogan asked.

"Crow, Macy, Heather, and Garnet all had some connection to those girls in the basement."

"Dirk also might be considered connected to this," Brogan said.

So was Faith.

***

The pounding on Dirk's trailer door woke him from a sound sleep. He lurched to his feet, causing empty beer cans to rattle from his lap to the floor. He staggered forward and looked out the window to find a man in a dark suit, his eyes hooded with sunglasses. Fuck. The cops.

Rubbing his hands over his face, he blinked and sniffed in a lungful of what passed for fresh air in his trailer. He opened the door. "Yeah."

The man looked up at him, and even with dark glasses, his gaze felt cold and heavy. "Dirk Crow?"

"That's right."

"I need to ask you a few questions."

CHAPTER TWENTY-FOUR

Thursday, June 28, 9:00 p.m.

Faith poured a glass of wine and sipped it slowly, closing her eyes as she tried to forget the day. She carried the glass into the living room and sat in her favorite chair. She sipped again as she kicked off her shoes, leaving them where they fell.

The doorbell rang and she moved leisurely to the door, peering through the peephole. Mitchell Hayden towered on her front porch.

She opened the door. "Hayden."

He removed his hat. "Mind if I come in?"

She was glad to see him. "Sure." And when he stepped inside, she said, "Can I get you a wine or beer?"

"Beer, if you have it."

"Coming right up." She closed the door behind him. "Follow me."

She sensed his curiosity as he moved through her house, staring at her odd blend of artwork. He paused to study the oil painting featuring exquisitely detailed flowers in a vase done by a Russian artist in Washington, DC.

"Nice place. Some art collection."

She opened the refrigerator, selected a craft beer, twisted off the top, and handed it to him. "My grandmother started it," she said. "She and my mother introduced me to art when I was a child. A lot of what you see is their collection. I've only had the money in the last few years to begin collecting for myself."

He took a sip, his gaze on her. "I wouldn't know good art if it broadsided me."

"It's not complicated. If you like it and it makes you feel good, then that's all that matters."

"What pieces did you buy?"

"With my very own money?" She sipped her wine and moved to an acrylic seascape with a young woman and her two small blond children. The three all looked toward the ocean, their faces either turned away or covered with the brim of a hat. "When I think about it now, it's kind of prophetic. A faceless mother with two blond children."

His frown deepened as he looked at her. "How are you doing?"

"Me? I'm a champ."

"Seriously?"

This conversation felt more intimate in some ways than the sex they'd had. "Confused. Angry. Hurt. More confused. Where the hell did I come from?" She shook her head. "I always wondered why my parents weren't more honest about my adoption. Now I know."

"I can only assume they thought they were protecting you."

"Or themselves."

She didn't want to talk about herself or her issues any longer. "How is the excavation going?"

"They unearthed the last two bodies this afternoon. They're also female. We'll be viewing all the remains tomorrow. Now it's a matter of confirming they're who we think they are." He took a pull on the beer. She set down her wine glass, took his beer, and set it on the counter as well. "Garnet and his coworker were found murdered tonight."

"What?" Her first reaction was frustration. She feared now that it might never get sorted out.

"Neither one of them died easy. We still don't know who or why, but the forensic team is going over their murder scenes now. There were supplies for a newborn at both crime scenes."

She wasn't sorry for either one of them. That wasn't a very Christian thought, but she still couldn't begin to imagine the pain and suffering those two monsters had caused.

There was so much death and loss. And in this moment she was tired of trying to process it all. "Do you have to be anywhere in the next hour?"

"Nope."

She smiled. "Can I take your jacket?"

"Sure." He shrugged it off and handed it to her. She laid it on the chair. She'd never brought him back to her home. Up until now it had been hotel rooms, and they'd kept whatever it was between them at arm's distance.

She reached for his tie and loosened the knot. "You look tense."

He ran his hand up and down her arm. "Do I?"

She wrapped her arms around his neck and kissed him. She was tall for a woman but still had to stretch to reach his lips. He banded an arm around her waist and pulled her firmly against him. The malaise that had dogged her when she'd pushed through her front door faded away and was replaced by a delicious excitement that made her forget everything but this moment.

His full erection pressed against her, kicking up her heartbeat several clicks. Her fingers skimmed down his shirt over his flat belly, and she reached for his belt buckle. His breathing deepened as her long fingers unfastened the top button on his pants and slowly pulled down his zipper. She slid her hand down and wrapped it around him.

He sucked in a breath, kissing her again and cupping her backside with his hand. He squeezed, kneaded, and pressed himself against her.

"It's going to be right here and right now if we don't find a bed quick."

She considered the carpet on her living room floor but saved that idea for another time. She released him. "Down the hallway."

Faith started down the hallway, not looking back, knowing he would follow. As she moved, she reached for the hem of her sweater and pulled it off, the same as she had done, alone, countless times before. She let the sweater fall to the floor and reached for the hook in her bra. She paused at her bedroom door, unlatched her bra, and slid it off. It dropped to the floor.

When she looked up, he had paused to watch. "Still interested?"

"Yes, ma'am."

She moved into her bedroom, sliding off her jeans and tossing them aside. She loosened the clip in her hair and let it fall loosely around her shoulders.

The light from the hallway dimmed, and she knew he was watching her. Good. Just the idea of him watching her tip her head back and cup her breast lightly made her hot.

She heard his clothes hit the floor. She didn't turn, didn't coax him, but waited for him to come up behind her and pull her close.

She didn't have long to wait. Barely seconds passed before she heard the steady beat of his bare feet cross the hard wood. Strong hands rested on her shoulders. Next, he kissed her on the back of her neck. She closed her eyes, giving herself over to the sensations.

This was how it had been for them. She always faced away from him as he entered her from behind, never saying a word. She liked the impersonal nature of their sex. No emotion. Just physical sensation.

This time he turned her around. She considered making a joke about the conventional nature of the move, but when she caught him staring at her breasts, she forgot what she was thinking.

He kissed her nipple, sucking it until all she could do was tip her head back and give in to the firing nerve endings that threatened to short-circuit her brain.

He kissed her lips and cupped her bottom again, but this time when he took her hand, he guided her toward the bed. "Move to the center," he said.

She could have argued, but she didn't want any words to get between them. So she sat on the edge of the bed and very slowly scooted her bottom to the middle of the mattress. He watched, clearly savoring the sight of her slim legs and narrow waist.

"Put the pillow behind your back and lay back," he said.

Again the order excited her. So she pulled her pillows from under the comforter and stacked them on top of each other. She lay back, cupping her breast. "Like this?"

"Yeah. Like that."

He crawled up on top of the bed and smoothed his hands up and down her legs and then over her flat belly before teasing the nest of curls between her legs. She hissed in a breath, anxious for him to take her. She wanted an explosion of sensation. She wanted release.

But Hayden was in no rush. He nestled between her legs, kissing her breasts again as the head of his penis rubbed between her legs.

She moistened her lips and slid her hand to his erection, ready to guide him inside her.

"Not yet," he said.

"Why are you teasing me?"

He gently nibbled her nipple. "You don't like it?"

She closed her eyes, pushing toward him. "I didn't say that."

"Then what's the rush?"

"We aren't the type who linger."

"I've got a few extra minutes."

He spent the next twenty minutes teasing her body and bringing her so close to release she could see the edge of the abyss. But each time, he pulled her back, making her endure more of this sweet torture.

When she was so wet she was squirming, he straddled her and pressed into her just a little bit. She raised her hips, her body coaxing him deeper.

"Hold still," he said.

"You're cruel."

"Want me to stop?"

"God, no."

A devil's smile teased the edge of his lips, but it was mirthless and reminded her more of a hunter closing in on his prey. He pushed a little deeper into her and pulled out a fraction. This went on for God knows how long. He was moving in a little deeper and then retreating.

When she slid her fingers down, ready to send herself over the edge, he grabbed her hand and pinned it over her head.

"No cheating," he said.

He began to move faster, coaxing her again to the edge. He stared down at her with intensity like he never had before, and as hot as it felt now, she sensed something had shifted between them.

The thought was lost when his fingers slid to her moist center. Her breath caught, and his name rose from her throat as she moaned.

This time she was anxious for release and raced to the edge. And this time he was ready to let her fall into the abyss. She opened her eyes and discovered he was staring at her face, absorbing everything about her.

He thrust in and out of her faster and faster. The momentum was feverish and then a wave caught them both and release overtook them.

***

Kat was pretty sure that if she had to sit in the recreation room of the shelter five more seconds her head would explode. She'd done all her class assignments, she'd read half a book, but the giggle of the other kids blending with the beep, beep of the video games was driving her nuts.

When her computer chirped with a message from Faith, she was thrilled. Meet me in the alley. Parking a nightmare. We can get ice cream.

"God bless you," she whispered as she closed her laptop, shoved it in her backpack, and headed out the back door. When the door closed behind her, the quiet of the evening was a refreshing change from the noise inside. The baby kicked, and she tried to convince herself it was only gas. This was going to be a baby-free night. Just ice cream, like when she was a kid.

She saw the car down the alley flash its lights and hurried toward it. She had a couple of bucks in her pocket from the waitress gig, but she'd bet anything Faith was going to treat. Already she knew she'd order Rocky Road, with extra chocolate sauce and nuts.

She was steps from the car when she heard her name come from behind her. "Kat."

She looked toward the street, and there was a man standing in the shadows. For a second she thought it might be the Ranger, but then she decided he was too lean. The lights on the car flashed again, and she realized he was pressing his key fob.

"No way," she whispered.

A bad feeling settled in the pit of her stomach, and instead of talking to this creep, she turned and hustled back to the door. A year ago she could have outrun this clown, but with the kid weighing down on her frame, she could barely waddle, let alone run. But she did run, cupping her hands under her belly as her backpack thumped against her.

He was behind her in an instant, long legs eating up the space in seconds. Footsteps pounded directly behind her, and his fingers brushed and then squeezed her shoulder.

"Get off of me!" she shouted.

"Kid, don't panic. Faith sent me. I'm not going to hurt you."

Her chest burned with the quick exertion, but he sounded as if this chase was nothing. "Fine; I'll call her from inside and confirm."

She was seconds from reaching the door when he grabbed her from behind and jabbed a syringe into her thigh. The needle pinched, and whatever he had injected burned a little. She thought about what the drug would do to the kid. She might not want it, but that didn't mean she wanted it poisoned with drugs.

Immediately, her body turned to jelly and her tongue felt so thick she could barely speak. Her knees buckled, and he caught her, supporting her weight easily.

"Don't fight it, kid. What I gave you won't hurt you or the baby."

"Faith didn't send you." Her voice slurred as her eyelids closed.

"You're right about that. She didn't send me."

"Then who?"

"Doesn't matter, kid," he said. "Only thing that matters is that Faith cares about you, and she'll jump through all kinds of hoops to save you."

He lifted her into his arms as she tried to draw in a breath to scream, but nothing came out. From what felt like a distance, she heard the back door of his car open and then he laid her gently on the soft leather seats that had that new-car smell.

***

He set Kat's computer on the kitchen counter and carried the half-conscious girl down the stairs, following the directions that Garnet had finally shared with his new best friend. He punched the code in the door lock, and when it clicked, he pushed it open.

The girl moaned and tried to pull away from him. "Shh," he said. "Just a few more steps, and then I'll put you down."

"Wh-where are we?"

"That's a good question, Kat." He looked around what amounted to a nondescript home. It was on a half-acre lot, and though there were neighbors, none were right on the property line, so he had ample privacy. "Looks like another hideaway for Mr. Garnet."

"Who?"

He hoisted her closer to him. "I doubt you know him. But I'm sure if given the chance, he'd have brought you here."

She looked up with unfocused eyes. "Why?"

"To take your baby and sell it, silly."

Fear registered in her gaze, and it excited him. God, but he loved fear. He opened a door to a basement, switched on a light, and helped her down the stairs. He spotted another door, also outfitted with a security pad.

"The man liked his basements and high-security locks," he said.

Killing Paige and then Kat was the wise move.

It was the smart thing to do.

But it wasn't what he was going to do.

He punched the keys, and when the lock clicked, he pushed it open.

He saw the girl lying on the bed, rolled on her side. Her legs were drawn up, and she moaned slightly. A manacle attached to a chain was wrapped around her ankle. When she looked up at him, her eyes were hazy with pain and fear. "Where's Garnet?"

"He's not coming." He walked Kat inside and lowered her onto the end of the bed. He tried to sit her up, but she slumped over. "But I brought you a friend."

Paige pushed up, wincing as she straightened. "Who is she?"

He grinned. "Paige, this is Kat. Your new best friend." He realized the bed was wet and that Paige's water had broken. Anxious to be out of the room that smelled stale with the heavy scent of birthing, he prepared to head back up.

"Are you going to just leave us?" Paige said. "My baby is coming."

"I know. Don't worry. I'm betting the cavalry will be here before you know it."

"Who?" The chain rattled as she shifted.

"You'll see."

She screamed for help as he closed the door. He didn't bother to lock it. Paige wasn't going anywhere, and Kat would be lucky if she could stand in the next twelve hours, considering the juice he'd shot into her veins.

He opened Kat's backpack and removed the computer. Opening it, he logged in to the Wi-Fi account he'd created.

"Come and find us, Faith," he whispered.

CHAPTER
TWENTY-FIVE

Friday, June 29, 5:00 a.m.

When Faith awoke, Hayden was gone. She glanced toward the pillow where his head had lain. They weren't the cuddling kind of couple, but this time they had slept beside each other. Neither had spoken, but she'd felt an odd sense of peace that she assumed was part and parcel of her orgasm.

The room was bathed in shadows and darkness as she reached for the digital clock on her nightstand. It was almost five a.m. She'd been asleep for nearly three hours but had no idea how long ago Hayden had left. For a big man, he was proving to be more agile than one might assume.

Pushing her hair out of her eyes, she swung her legs over the side of the bed, aware that Hayden's scent still clung to her skin. She rose and headed to the shower.

Thirty minutes later she was showered and dressed in dark slacks, a black V-neck sweater, and cowboy boots. Downstairs, she made coffee and a bagel. When the coffeepot gurgled out the last of the coffee, she opened the fridge for milk. Attached to the milk carton was a note written in bold block letters.

I'm headed out to Dirk Crow's trailer. I'll contact you about the autopsies in the morning. MH

No sweet words from her Texas Ranger, but then he'd put his note on the milk carton. She'd commented once that she always had milk with her coffee every morning. "Good memory, Captain Hayden," she said, smiling as she reached for the carton.

She called the hospital and asked about Macy. The nurses reported her vitals were slightly improved and there were times when she was restless. The doctors thought she might be coming out of her coma.

She checked texts and emails. Nothing yet on the arrival of Garnet's and Sullivan's bodies, but they'd be first on the docket for an autopsy.

Remembering what Kat had said about a possible half sibling, she checked the ancestry site.

> My name is Marissa. I'd like to meet you.

Faith sat for a long moment staring at the message and then before she lost her nerve, typed back.

> I'd like to meet you as well. When?

Marissa's response was almost instant.

> I'm free later this morning, say about eight a.m.
> If that's too soon, I get it. But I want to meet you.

Faith looked at the time of Marissa's reply. *So you are a night owl like me.* She offered the name of an Austin coffee shop that she knew opened at six. Marissa answered back.

> See you then.

She drove into work in the predawn hours, parked in her regular spot on the deck, and then made her way through the building toward her office. She switched on the lights and spent the next couple of hours studying the photographic images of the notes written in the magazines. Could Marissa be related to one of these girls? Marissa hadn't given her age, so for now there was no way of knowing.

Faith arrived at the trendy coffee shop fifteen minutes early. She was nervous and didn't know what she was going to say to this Marissa woman. She ordered a latte and sat in a corner, adding extra packets of sugar, a thing she did when she was nervous, and wondering why sugar took the edge off her fear.

She sipped, glancing toward the door each time the bells above jingled. Even at this early hour, the shop was filling quickly. Some customers were dressed in hospital scrubs, others in suits, and all looked rushed to get to work.

Twenty minutes passed, and Faith worried that she'd gotten the day and time wrong. Or maybe her abrupt agreement to a meeting had scared the woman off. That kind of response would have scared her off even a couple of weeks ago.

The bells over the door jingled, and she spotted a late twentysomething woman with dark hair and an olive complexion. She watched the woman, but she quickly crossed and met up with a man wearing a dark suit. Was Marissa going to be a no-show?

And then from behind her she heard a woman say, "Faith?"

Faith looked up to find a young woman with light-brown hair and green eyes. She searched for similarities between them and decided their noses were the same. "That's right."

"I'm Marissa."

Faith rose, jostling the table and her empty coffee cup. "I didn't think you'd come."

"I was here earlier, and when you came in, I freaked and left. I've been walking the block for the last half hour. And now I'm back."

"Do you want a coffee?"

"God, no. I mean, maybe later. I'm too nervous as it is."

What conversation starter broke this kind of tension? "Want to have a seat?" If she'd thought biology would trump any kind of initial nerves, she'd been wrong.

"Sure." She settled in a chair, but kept her purse in her lap and her hand firmly on the strap, as if she could bolt in any second.

"This is so weird," Marissa said. "When I put my profile on the ancestry site, I thought a match was going to be a long shot. And then you popped up as a half sibling."

"I'm sorry I didn't see your message right away. Life has been crazy the last couple of months. And honestly, as much as I wanted to know the truth, I was afraid of it."

"I know. I had started to think I'd made a mistake when I didn't hear from you. First few days I checked the site twenty times a day, and then I had to pull back because I was driving myself crazy."

"You sound braver than I have been. I put up my DNA and didn't have the nerve to check back." Their shared fear chipped at some of the ice.

"So you're adopted?" Marissa asked.

"I am. I found out when I was a kid."

Marissa was staring at her, and Faith knew she was searching for similarities just as she was. "Was it a shock?"

"I didn't really understand it when I was a kid, but by the time I was a teenager, it was pretty overwhelming. How long have you known?"

"I've always known. I have four older brothers, who are Mom and Dad's biological children. I call them the Bio Boys. Mom always wanted a girl, and my dad started looking into an adoption. They found me and brought me home when I was two days old."

"Do you know anything about your biological family?"

"Mom said the lawyer told her my birth mother was a medical student and that she chose career over motherhood. She thought we'd both be better off going our separate ways."

"Do you have the name of your biological mother?"

"No. It was all closed. And I'm still trying to wrap my brain around my bio mom having a medical background. I'm a painter. And the sight of blood scares me. What about you?"

"I'm a doctor. A pathologist. I have no information on my biological family."

"I was hoping you did."

"Who handled your adoption?" Faith asked. "My father handled mine. He was with the law firm of Slater and McIntyre."

Marissa leaned forward. "For real?"

"Yeah. Why?"

"That's the firm that handled my adoption," Marissa said.

"What year were you born?" Faith asked.

"I was born May 1, 1989."

In the magazines, that was the year Olivia Martin had been held captive. Faith recalled the words Olivia had written.

Things I like. "Tell It to My Heart" by Taylor Dayne. "Wild, Wild West" by The Escape Club. Chocolate. Sunshine. The feel of grass. My mom's burned spaghetti sauce.

"Do you think we have the same mother or father?" Marissa asked.

It would take DNA testing and more investigation. But if Faith had to guess, Marissa and she had been born to different women and they'd both been fathered by a monster. "I don't know yet, but I have a few lines in the water. As soon as I know more, I'll be happy to share it with you."

***

Hayden arrived at the Crow salvage yard less than an hour after he left Faith. As he drove through the piles of scrap metal and cars, he caught the flash of several cop car lights near another trailer. Three sheriff's deputies' cars greeted him when he pulled up.

He placed his Stetson on his head, got out of the SUV, and walked toward the trailer as Brogan stepped out. Hayden paused to shake hands with the deputies on duty and then crossed to his partner. "What did you find?"

"Dirk's dead. Someone roughed him up pretty good before his throat was cut. There was also a playing card on his lap. It was the ace of diamonds."

Hayden removed his hat and slid on black latex gloves as he stepped inside the trailer. It was almost a mirror image of what they'd found at Crow's, only Dirk was sitting in his recliner. His fingers were broken and one knee was shattered. The place appeared to have been ransacked.

"What the hell is this guy looking for?" Brogan asked.

"He knows who's responsible for taking those girls thirty years ago," Hayden said. "And he knows there's evidence that could ruin him or he's protecting someone."

***

Faith arrived back at the medical examiner's office midmorning. She found Nancy in what was now called the bone room with the remains from the ranch. The first two sets had been arranged in anatomical order, and the third was partly complete.

Faith grabbed a fresh set of gloves and took in the sight of the three gurneys arranged side by side. All likely had been young girls held in that basement room, murdered, and then buried.

"Any idea how long sets two and three have been in the ground?" Faith asked.

"Rough estimates are at least twenty-five years, but it could easily be longer. At this stage we're only guessing," Nancy said.

"That timetable matches with forensic evidence found in the room in the ranch. We have an idea of who we might be dealing with here, but so far no confirmed identification."

"We might have caught a break with victim number three," Nancy said. "She has a metal plate in her right femur."

"Did you reach out to the manufacturer?" Faith asked.

"I contacted the surgical implant company late yesterday, and I heard back just a few minutes ago," Nancy said.

"What did you discover?" Faith asked.

"The plate on the femur of victim three was indeed surgically placed in a young girl by the name of Kathy Saunders. In 1985, Ms. Saunders, age fifteen at the time, was involved in a bad car accident. She suffered a broken femur requiring the plate."

Faith felt a surge of satisfaction as she always did when the pieces of a case fell into place. She walked up to the second gurney and picked up the brittle white femur with the metal plate. She tried to imagine this was once a living, breathing young woman.

"Oddly," Nancy said, "the forensic team found a ballpoint pen with this victim. Most of her clothes have long disintegrated, and they theorize it might have been in her pocket. It's going to take more testing, but they believe that's the pen the girls used to write in the magazines."

She was accustomed to the dead telling her stories through their remains, but there was something far more sobering and disturbing in reading their thoughts. "Were there any signs of fetal or infant remains?" Faith asked.

"None. If their infants didn't survive the births, they weren't buried with their mothers. The pelvic bones also don't show signs of childbirth, which tells me if they did deliver, the mothers died very soon after."

The utter insult to these girls sent tremors of rage through Faith, and it took her a moment to corral it before she could speak in an even tone.

"The Texas heat coupled with vultures and wild animals could have turned these bodies into bones in a matter of days," Faith said. "Out there on that isolated ranch, they could have been scattered and rendered into dust. But the killer chose to bury them."

"I can't believe it was out of respect," Nancy said.

"I'm not defending the killer. I'm trying to understand why he didn't just leave them out in the open. Why put grave markers?" She thought about Marissa, who, if the ancestry site was correct, was her half sister. Marissa's birth date fit with the disappearance and death of Olivia Martin. "Maybe he fathered all the babies."

"Why would you say that?" Nancy asked.

"There was no evidence suggesting any of the three girls that went missing were pregnant. Just thinking out loud," Faith said. "There are sociopaths who are obsessed with passing on their DNA."

Nancy shifted her gaze back to the bones. "This was his own little baby farm?"

"I think so." The idea was too disturbing for her to consider right now. "Any signs of trauma to the bones?"

"None," Nancy said.

These girls could have died any number of ways that would not leave a mark on the bone. Drowning, suffocation, poison, or hemorrhaging could be detected in the tissue, but once it had decomposed, the clues that would have solved the manner of death would have been lost.

"Check all the teeth and see if you can get mitochondrial DNA. That might help if any offspring are identified later."

"How would we even begin to find these kids? They would be adults now."

"We'll worry about that later," Faith said.

The walls of the room felt as if they were shrinking, and her head felt light. The idea that she was the product of a madman and an imprisoned runaway made her physically sick. "What else is on the schedule for today?"

"The bodies of Garnet and Sullivan have also arrived," Nancy said. "They're both ready to be autopsied."

"When it rains, it pours," Faith said. "Did the detectives say which body they wanted us to begin with first?"

"Captain Hayden asked that you start with Heather Sullivan." Nancy shook her head. "I've seen a lot of gruesome deaths in my years here, but the last week has taken it to a whole new level of evil."

"It's not been easy. Hopefully we can help stop the killings."

Both women knew they had to do something, and do it fast.

"Set up a room," Faith said. "I'll be ready to go in a half hour."

"Will do, boss," Nancy said.

Thirty minutes later, both were in the suite ready to begin when the swinging door opened and Mitchell Hayden, now gowned up, entered the room. He moved with quick, purposeful strides, his gaze holding hers only for a second before he nodded and said hello to them.

Faith tugged down the overhead microphone. "Captain Hayden, is a detective from Austin police joining us?"

"Their detectives are running down surveillance tapes and witnesses." He tugged on latex gloves. "Ready?"

She nodded to Nancy to pull back the sheet.

"According to the police report, her name is Heather Sullivan, age forty-nine," Nancy stated.

Faith studied the round face etched with deep lines around the eyes and mouth. Age spots darkened portions of her forehead and the sides of her cheeks.

"I've run a toxicology test," Nancy said. "She has the look of a drug user."

When Heather Sullivan had been dressed, she'd looked trim, but here on the table Faith could see she was painfully thin.

"X-rays of her lungs showed a couple of questionable spots," Nancy said.

Faith turned her attention to the victim's neck, which had been stabbed and sliced. Judging by the angle, she guessed her killer had been behind her.

"Nancy, did you get a liver temperature?" Faith asked. Rigor mortis gave an approximate time of death, but either a rectal or liver temp was the most accurate way to go. After death, the body lost heat at a rate of thirty-four degrees per hour until it reached the temperature of its surroundings.

"I did," Nancy said. "It was taken as soon as she arrived here. The temp was seventy-eight degrees, which almost matches the air temp at the crime scene. Her body was burned so that might throw off my estimate, but best guess, she's been dead less than twenty-six to thirty-five hours," Nancy said.

Faith inspected her charred skin. "The burns occurred after death."

"We think the same person killed Sullivan, Garnet, and Crow," Hayden said. "In Crow's case, he used a hammer before the man suffered a heart attack and died. With Garnet the killer used a hammer first and then sliced his throat."

"He didn't use a hammer on Heather," Faith said.

"Maybe she was frightened enough and talked before he had to."

Faith continued her external exam, cataloging scars and any signs of old injuries. She found nothing else that might hint that there'd been trouble in this woman's life.

She reached for the scalpel, made her incisions, and removed the rib cage. She took out and weighed each organ.

The uterus showed no sign of pregnancy, but there was significant scarring. "I doubt she could have had children. I believe she may have had a botched abortion or a miscarriage that wasn't treated properly."

She removed, weighed, and cataloged all the organs and then repacked them back into the abdomen. She opened up the throat and noted the damaged jugular.

As she tipped the head back and studied the throat, she saw what looked like a white piece of paper. She adjusted the headlamp hanging above, picked up tweezers, and used them to pull out the card.

Both Hayden and Nancy watched as she carefully unfolded it. It was the queen of hearts.

"A card. Just like with the Crows and Garnet," Hayden said.

***

Macy felt the warm embrace of the long fingers that reminded her of her mother's. There was a calming voice hovering over her, and she could make out sporadic words now. "Getting better. Sleep is best. Vitals good. I never knew about you. I wish I had. It would have all been different."

She couldn't nail down who was speaking, but she felt calm when the person was close. As much as she wanted to tell this person she was alive and only trapped in her body, she couldn't get her eyes to open, regardless of how hard she tried.

Macy's frustration grew with this broken body of hers that refused to cooperate. If she could just open her eyes, she would see all the answers that were so close.

***

As Faith returned to her office after visiting Macy, she pulled the rubber band from her hair and rubbed her scalp. She drew in a breath and rolled her shoulders, trying to chase away the tension. With a solid identification in hand, she called Detective Lana Franklin in Austin's Homicide Unit.

Franklin picked up on the second ring. "Franklin."

"Dr. McIntyre at the medical examiner's office. We have a positive identification on the third victim. It's Kathy Saunders."

Franklin shoved out a sigh. "Good. We at least have a confirmation."

"I'd like to talk to the family. What was the contact information for Saunders?"

Papers rustled in the background. "After we met, I tried to update the info on family members. As luck would have it, Kathy's sister is still in Austin. Her name is Diane Saunders and she lives in the Hyde Park neighborhood."

Faith jotted down the address. "This is perfect. Thank you. I'll let you know when we have more on the other two victims."

"After all these years."

"The girls are finally going home," Faith said.

"Thanks, Doc."

Faith hung up, changed, and within fifteen minutes was driving to a neighborhood that had been originally built in the 1890s. The homes were modest, but the area's proximity to the university made it desirable, and many of the older homes were being purchased at a premium and renovated. Diane Saunders's address was a bungalow tucked back on a wooded lot.

She parked and got out of her car, noting the modest red car in the driveway. She hurried to the front door and knocked. Inside she heard violin music and a small barking dog. The music turned down as a woman shushed the dog. The woman who appeared had gray hair pulled up into a loose bun. She wore glasses, and the deep lines around her mouth and eyes suggested she either laughed or worried a lot. Maybe both.

"Diane Saunders?" Faith pulled out her medical examiner's badge.

"That's right."

"I'm Dr. Faith McIntyre, medical examiner. I'm here about your sister, Kathy Saunders."

"Kathy has been gone for almost thirty years."

"I know." A car drove behind her, and she hated that she was having this conversation on the porch. "Do you mind if I come inside?"

Those lines around her eyes and mouth deepened. "It can't be good if the medical examiner is here."

"It's not good news."

An old dog wobbled up to Diane, stared up at Faith, and then barked. Diane snatched the dog up. "I'm sorry. She's protective."

"It's okay."

Diane and her dog stepped aside, allowing Faith inside a house that couldn't have been more than a thousand square feet. There was a main living room with an overstuffed couch, a flat-panel screen mounted on the wall, and several bookcases that hugged every spare square inch of wall space.

"I teach history at the University of Texas," Diane said. "I'm a bit addicted to books."

"They're impressive. I don't get as much time to read for pleasure as I'd like."

"You must stay busy if you're a medical examiner." Diane held her hands together so tightly her knuckles were white.

Sometimes the small talk helped families brace for the news they knew was coming. "It does keep me on the go, but I love the work most of the time."

Diane drew in a breath and motioned for Faith to sit. Faith settled on the sagging cushion while Diane pulled up a wicker chair, cradling her dog in her lap.

"But this is one of those times that you don't enjoy your job?" Diane asked.

Faith nodded. "There was a ranch outside of Austin," she said. "We found several sets of remains. We know that one set belonged to your sister, Kathy, because of the metal plate in her leg."

"The hit-and-run settlement was supposed to help her through college." She rubbed the dog between the ears until it settled on her lap. "She was fifteen when it happened. She wasn't at fault. The company that employed the driver settled, and the money was more than enough to repair her leg and cover college. Unfortunately, my divorced mother met a new beau, who in turn convinced her to take the money and run. I was a senior in college and barely scraping by. I tried to help Kathy, but she was strong-willed. She wasn't interested in college and told me she had a new boyfriend who was going to take care of her. I was heartbroken."

"What happened?"

"She vanished. One day she was working, and the next she was gone." She rubbed the dog's delicate ears. "How did she die?" she said, her voice barely above a whisper.

"We don't know for certain yet. But we'll keep you updated."

The dog seemed to sense Diane's pain and climbed up on old, rickety hind legs to lick her face.

"Do you have any pictures of the boyfriend? Any clue as to who she was hanging out with around the time she vanished?"

"I have a few pictures taken toward the end. I always held on to them because I didn't want to give up hope." She rose and, carrying the dog, went to a desk piled high with papers and opened a small drawer. She retrieved a thin collection of pictures and sat on the couch next to Faith.

Diane settled the dog in her lap and handed Faith the first picture. "I only have four pictures. I wish I had more. This one was taken right before the accident."

Faith lowered her gaze to the smiling girl who was standing with another young woman who looked so much like her. "This is you?"

"I was in school, and she came to visit for the day."

"You two look a lot alike." As she studied Kathy's features, she had an odd sense of déjà vu but could not place why she felt like she knew this girl.

In the next picture Kathy had coiled her hair up into a fashion-able twist that she must have thought made her look older and more sophisticated. She wore a slinky black dress and high heels. "When was this taken?"

"December of 1989. She vanished four days later."

Marissa had been born in May of 1989, so she couldn't have been Kathy's child.

Diane handed Faith the next picture. "Kathy sent me this picture and the next because she wanted me to see she was doing well." It featured Kathy standing with a young Danny Garnet, who actually looked dashing in a tux. The bastard was like a damn cancer. He was everywhere. But the last picture was most telling.

Kathy was dressed in a waitress uniform, and she appeared to be working at a country club. Faith recognized the club. It had been her father's club. In the background there was a banner that read **HAPPY BIRTHDAY, PETER**. Peter Slater—her father's law partner. In 1988, he'd have just turned forty.

Before she could fully process, Faith's phone rang. It was Dr. Bramley at the hospital. It went directly to voicemail.

"Diane, I'm going to have to return this call, but can I snap pictures of these photos?"

"Sure. Do you have any idea who took Kathy?"

"We do. But it's going to take more evidence to fill in the entire picture."

She snapped each photo and then fished out her business card. "I'm going to be in touch."

"I've waited thirty years. Don't make me wait much longer."

"I won't. I promise."

Diane rose and from her desk picked up her card. "This has all my contact information. Whatever you need, just call me."

Faith stood. "I promise to get back to you soon."

She called the hospital and asked for the nurses' station on the neuroscience floor. "This is Dr. McIntyre returning your call."

"Yes, Doctor. I have good news. Macy Crow is awake."

Faith closed her eyes, almost fearful to ask. "Is she coherent? How is she doing?"

"She's responding to basic questions. And she seems alert."

"I'll be there in fifteen minutes," Faith said.

She was so focused on getting to the hospital that she barely remembered the drive. She parked in the spot closest to the entrance and raced across the parking lot and up the elevator to the second floor. She tossed a quick wave to the nurses and dashed down the hallway.

When Faith entered Macy's room, Dr. Bramley was standing by Macy's bed checking her pupils with a small light.

Faith couldn't see Macy from this vantage point, and as much as she wanted to insist the doctor get out of her way, she held back, waiting for him to finish his exam.

The doctor had said Macy was awake, but with a brain injury she could be facing a whole host of problems that affected her memory, cognitive skills, emotions, and even her ability to walk and move.

The doctor glanced over his shoulder and then stepped back. "Dr. McIntyre. I understand you and Ms. Crow have not met."

As Faith gripped the strap of her purse and came forward, Macy's eyes were not only open but also alert. The instant Macy saw Faith, she blinked and looked to the doctor, back to Faith, and then nodded as if she remembered.

"She's real," Dr. Bramley said. "Her name is Faith McIntyre. She's visited you every day. We believe you two might be related."

Faith set her purse in a chair and stepped forward. "Hi, Macy. We've not formally met. But Dr. Bramley is right. We might be sisters." Telling her about Marissa would come later. For now, it was about the two of them.

Macy shrank back a fraction before she nodded. She tried to speak, but the words came out garbled. Her brows knotted, and the fingers of her good hand clenched into a fist.

"I was just having a talk with Macy," Dr. Bramley said. "She's come out of her coma better than we'd hoped, and she's responding to questions, light, and small pinpricks. Finding the right words may be a challenge initially. She has a lot to recover from. But I'm very hopeful."

Macy tried to find words, but the sounds she made were unintelligible.

Faith took Macy's hand. "You're doing great. It's just going to take time for the speech to return."

As Macy looked at Faith, her grip tightened.

"We know about Garnet at Second Chances. And we found the house in the country and the graves."

A clear presentation of facts calmed Macy. Faith understood that Macy had comprehended every bit of what she had just explained to her. She would want her case solved.

"She's going to fatigue very quickly," Dr. Bramley warned. "It won't take much to tire her out."

Macy shot an annoyed glance at the doctor.

Faith couldn't help but smile. "Can I talk to her? If she knows what's going on, she'll be more likely to rest."

"Keep your visit short," he said.

"I understand. Thank you."

When the doctor left them alone, Macy looked closely at Faith. She moved her lips and then drawing in a breath said in a hoarse voice, "P-P-Paige."

"We haven't found her yet. But the Rangers are digging through all of Garnet's records hoping to. We think she was at the country ranch house you found, but Garnet moved her."

Macy closed her eyes, and Faith thought for a moment it was all too much.

"It's a lot to take in."

Macy opened her eyes and shook her head.

"Do you remember who hit you?" Faith asked.

"Yes. I don't know him."

"Garnet was murdered," Faith said. "He was tortured like Jack. Someone was looking for something."

Macy shook her head. "Jack. A package."

"Where did he send it?" she asked.

"Arlington." Her voice was barely a whisper now, and no doubt force of will had enabled her to speak this much. "Mailbox."

"Do you know what was in it?"

"Guessing evidence against Garnet."

Satisfaction mingled with excitement. "We'll send someone from the FBI to open it," Faith said.

Macy nodded.

"Whoever killed Garnet knew what he did thirty years ago. Do you have any idea who it could be?"

"No." Her voice was barely audible now, and as Dr. Bramley had stated, she had fatigued quickly.

Faith patted her on the hand. "It's okay. You've told us how to find this package, and from there we can figure out the rest."

Macy eyes closed.

"Just rest. I'll be back very soon, okay?"

Macy nodded.

Faith sat for a moment, grateful that all the pieces of this nightmare were finally falling into place.

As she was leaving the hospital and crossing the parking lot, her phone rang. It was Tina, the shelter director.

"Dr. McIntyre, is Kat with you?"

"No, she's not. I haven't seen her since I dropped her off at school yesterday."

"I know you're generous with that kid, and I also know she has a tendency to press boundaries. I've talked to all her friends at the shelter, and none of them have seen or spoken to her since last night. Please tell me she's with you."

Mary Burton

Faith glanced at her cell phone and quickly scrolled through the messages. None were from Kat. "Is her computer at the shelter?"

"No. But she's never more than a foot away from it."

"If I don't locate her in the next few minutes, I'll call the police."

"I know she's been stressed about her baby. But you're the one person she's really gravitated to in the last month."

"Let me look into this. I'll call you back." She opened the Find My iPhone app and selected the computer she'd given Kat. At a glance she could see that it was online and twenty minutes away. Rising, she grabbed her purse. "Kat, what are you up to?"

I held you in my arms today. You have golden-blond hair and the cutest little frown. You gave me a start when I heard you'd been born early. No one expected you to be this soon. But here you are.

Not a boy, but a perfect little baby girl.

Love, Daddy

CHAPTER TWENTY-SIX

Friday, June 29, 3:15 p.m.

As Faith followed the map on her phone and got closer to the Travis County residential neighborhood, her sense of unease grew. Why would Kat come to an area like this? The girl talked often about how she hated the burbs and that she'd never end up in a one-story ranch. Faith was trying to help the girl make something of her life, but the bones found at the deserted ranch left her with the fear that the girl was going to end up dead if she stayed her course.

As she spotted the entrance to the neighborhood, she dialed Hayden's number. The call went to voicemail and she almost hung up, believing she was overreacting. But when his recorded voice told the caller to leave a message, she heard herself saying, "Hayden, this is Faith. Kat is missing, and I've activated the Find My iPhone app. Maybe I'm being paranoid, but something is not adding up. I'm going to continue to the location, but, like I said, it doesn't feel right."

***

When Hayden saw Faith's message hit his voicemail, he hit redial, knowing she wasn't the type to call and chat.

Faith answered with a breathless and agitated, "Hayden. Thank God."

The agitation in her voice set his nerves on edge. "Explain to me what happened again."

"I received a call from the shelter. Kat is missing. I'm at the house where her laptop is supposed to be."

"When was the last time she was seen?"

"Yesterday. I dropped her off at school. I spoke with her at lunch but not since."

He heard the tension in her voice. "She always has her laptop with her, correct?"

"Yes. That's why I came here. But none of this looks right. I know Garnet is dead, but after seeing the bones of the three girls, I'm afraid Kat is going to make more bad decisions and end up like them." The barely whispered words sounded as if she were afraid she'd break down.

"We'll find her. Text me the location of the laptop, and I'll meet you there."

"Hayden, I think Garnet was working with Peter Slater." Her voice was a raspy whisper filled with dread.

"Why do you say that?"

She was silent for a moment, and he knew she was focusing on fact patterns and logic. "I visited the sister of victim number three, Diane Saunders. She had a picture of Kathy waitressing at Peter's birthday party at the club."

It was another link to the girls and the law firm. "We don't have the results of PJ's DNA yet. Once it's cross-checked against yours, we will know for certain."

She expelled a deep breath, as if she was struggling to deal with an unraveling world. "Peter used to say how much he loved children. He said if he could have he'd have had a house full of them. Did he love children so much he'd have someone like Garnet make them for him?"

"Why would he stop after making three babies? He could have kept on for a long time."

"You're right. There could be more. But Margaret said once she was proud she'd given her husband a son. 'A man needs a son,' she used to say. Maybe he was waiting for his son, and once he had his boy, he didn't feel the need to keep going." Pain and sorrow laced around the words.

"Maybe. Or there are more dead girls and stolen babies to be found."

God, she prayed that wasn't true, but she had no guarantees there weren't more. "Margaret would have done anything for Peter. She loved him so much. If she couldn't give him a son, she'd have accepted his son from another woman to make him happy. She'd have also been content to let him keep doing whatever he wanted to girls like Josie." Another sigh leaked over the line. "If the last girl gave Peter his son, then there'd be no more need to keep taking girls. He had PJ."

"Once I receive your text, you need to stand down. I don't know who is tied up in this, and until I do, you have to let me handle this. This can go sideways very quickly, Faith. You got it?"

"I've known PJ all my life. We practically grew up together. He's the one who gave me Josie Jones's name."

Jesus, she was stubborn. "Faith, stand down. Agreed?"

"Yes."

"I mean it, Faith."

"I'm texting the location. Move your ass."

He hung up and found Brogan jostling a jar of pills in his hands. "There's another pregnant girl who's gone missing. It's Kat, the girl from the youth shelter. She's been gone since yesterday. Faith thinks she's found her location."

"If Kat vanished yesterday afternoon, then Garnet couldn't have taken her."

"Kat might have run away. The kid has a history of running. Or the guy who killed Garnet, Sullivan, and Crow might be behind it."

"It's been thirty years since those women on the ranch died. Assuming Garnet doesn't have another burial ground, he sat dormant for thirty years. Why pick this up again?"

"Peter Slater died three months ago. Maybe whatever deal he had ended, and he didn't like it."

"So he decides to kill the players in the original crimes?"

"Possible. Or maybe he saw it as a chance to blackmail money out of the firm or family. What I do know is that we've got a clock on us, Brogan. Paige doesn't have a lot of time, and Faith is not going to wait long for us."

***

Paige rocked back and forth, wrapping her hands around her belly as it cramped and twisted. The pains were getting closer together, and she was finding it hard not to panic. When this latest round finally released its grip on her, she crawled over and looked at the girl.

Kat's body was so still that for a moment she thought she was dead. She poked Kat in the arm, but she didn't move. A hard pinch to the back of her hand brought a slight moan.

She wasn't dead. Which Paige supposed was good in the short term, but when she woke up and realized where she was now being held, she just might wish she were dead.

Another contraction grabbed Paige, stealing her breath. She was forced to retreat to her fetal position as she waited out this latest wave. When it passed, she kicked the girl in frustration. "You've got to wake up! He's going to kill us if we don't figure this out!"

The girl sucked in a breath and opened her eyes. She looked around, startled, and her fists were clenched as if she was ready to fight. She staggered to her feet but fell back against the cot as her legs gave out from under her. "What the hell is going on?"

A contraction twisted Paige's belly, forcing her to pause before she could speak. "I wish I knew."

Kat turned to the door. She pounded on it with her fist and started screaming.

"It won't do any good," Paige said. "I screamed for days when I first got here. No one ever came."

Kat darted around the room looking for any way out. She was petrified and for good reason.

"You're going to have to pull yourself together. Otherwise we're both dead. That's the only thing I'm sure of right now," Paige said.

Kat took a deep breath and slowly sat down next to Paige. "I'm listening."

"Garnet brought me here. I know we're in Austin."

"Who the hell is Garnet?"

"His full name is Danny Garnet. He owns the Second Chances bar."

"Was that Garnet who was just here?"

"No."

Kat blinked and shook her head. The drugs were wearing off. "I've heard that name before."

"He's very charming. Evil," Paige offered.

Kat narrowed her eyes. "You're Paige!"

"You know me?"

"I saw your picture. Everybody thought you ran away."

Tears welled in her eyes. "I thought I had all the answers. I was so stupid."

Just that moment, the door slowly swung open. Neither girl had heard footsteps or voices. It was just open. The one prayer Paige had been asking for was answered.

Paige felt another contraction and closed her eyes, breathing in and out as she'd seen on a television show once. Finally when she could take a deep breath, she said, "I can't leave. Get help."

Kat stood, and after looking at Paige and ticking through her options, she pushed through the door and vanished into the hallway.

***

Faith saw the flicker of movement in front of the large glass window and realized it was Kat. She shut off her car and got out, locking it behind her. A part of her was annoyed with the kid for giving her such a scare. What the hell was she doing out here?

When the front door opened, Faith was halfway up the walkway. She saw immediately that something was wrong as the girl wobbled and dropped to her knees.

Faith raced up and knelt beside her, immediately searching for injuries. "Kat!"

"There's a girl." Kat gripped Faith's arm. "She's in the basement. Her baby is coming right now."

Satisfied Kat wasn't bleeding or injured, Faith helped her to her feet. Relief and fear collided as Faith struggled to keep her voice steady. "Can you make it to my car? It's parked across the street."

"I think so."

"Sit in the car and lock the doors."

"What's going on?" Kat asked. "This is so messed up."

Faith heard the girl's screams coming from the basement. She pressed her keys into Kat's hands and pushed her out the front door. "No questions. Don't come back into the house."

Kat nodded and then took a couple of halting steps forward, gripping the keys as she staggered toward Faith's car.

Faith followed the sounds of the screams through the house into a kitchen and down a flight of stairs. It took a moment for her eyes to adjust to the darkness. She followed the hallway toward the light that streamed out of the door. Faith ran to the open door and found Paige Sheldon lying on her back. She was drenched in sweat and gripping her belly. Panic radiated from her eyes.

Faith ran to her side. She then spotted the chain. Jesus. Hayden couldn't get here fast enough.

"Paige, it's going to be all right."

The girl was silent as a contraction racked her body. When it finally eased, she was panting and pale.

Faith hurried to the small sink and washed her hands quickly before returning to the girl and lifting her knees, pushing up the folds of her loose skirt, and removing her panties.

"Paige, I'm Dr. McIntyre. Let me examine you."

"Please," she whispered. "It hurts so much."

Faith had not delivered a baby since medical school, but she knew it would all come back to her.

"Paige, I want you to take a deep breath. When the next contraction comes, draw in another deep breath and push as hard as you can."

The girl closed her eyes, bearing down as she cried and pushed. The top of the baby's head crowned before the contraction ended and she collapsed back.

"You're doing a great job. The next one is going to come fast, Paige. I want you to push as hard as you can."

Tears streamed down Paige's face. "I can't!"

"Yes, you can. You don't want your baby stuck in this godforsaken place forever. We need to get the baby born and get you two out of here."

As Faith expected, the next contraction came even faster, and again the girl pushed and screamed.

This time the baby's head emerged enough for Faith to see that it had ink-black hair. "I need one more push. Your baby is almost here!"

Paige screamed as Faith firmly tugged on the small head enough for it to slip out until the face was fully exposed. She quickly swiped the baby's mouth and opened its airway. "One more push and your baby will be born."

Paige's face was drawn with fatigue and pain. "I can't. I'm so tired."

"You can and you will. Now get ready. Let's do this together."

The girl gritted her teeth and pushed. This time the infant's head, neck, and shoulders slid out enough for Faith to get a grip and pull the child the rest of the way.

"Your baby girl is here, Paige. You did a great job."

Paige collapsed back against her pillows as Faith focused on the baby girl. She placed her on her side and rubbed her tiny back with her knuckles. The child's mouth opened and let out a cry.

"Is she all right?" Paige asked.

"She looks good." Faith turned the baby over. "Your daughter is beautiful, Paige."

Faith laid the baby, still attached to her umbilical cord, on Paige's belly and shifted to delivering the afterbirth, which appeared to come out whole. Later doctors could confirm this and deal with the minor tearing Paige had suffered. The girl was incredibly lucky considering the conditions and lack of prenatal care.

Paige continued to lie against the pillows, exhausted, making no move to hold the child. Faith didn't have clean scissors to cut the umbilical cord and accepted she'd have to wrap the afterbirth with the baby and have the separation done by the paramedics. As the baby cried, she found a clean bath towel and wrapped her in it.

"Paige, I've got to get you out of here," Faith said. Holding the baby, she fished her phone from her back pocket and dialed Hayden. He should have been here by now, she thought.

Paige looked up, glancing toward the door. She cried out and she shrank back.

Faith felt the presence behind her and, bracing, turned and saw a shadow of a man hovering at the threshold. He had a tight grip on Kat's arm and was pointing a gun at her belly.

"Let's go, Faith," he said. "You and the baby, now. We need a quiet place to talk. I have a few questions for you."

The voice sounded familiar, and when he stepped into the light, she knew she'd met him before. For a moment her mind scrambled to place him, and then she remembered the fundraiser. Fear snaked up her spine as she pictured his easy smile and hard eyes. She hugged the baby close. "I've seen you before. At the hotel."

"Good memory."

Faith thought about the smooth, friendly smile he'd presented to her at the hotel. He'd asked her out for a drink and then called her office. "That meeting at the hotel wasn't random, was it?"

"Smart lady." He pointed the gun at Paige.

She moved forward, quickly placing herself in front of the gun. "You don't have to kill her. Just leave her be. She's suffered enough."

"And she's seen me."

Faith had no doubt he would kill that girl and never lose a moment's sleep. She had to give him some kind of distraction or the girls would die. She raised her chin. "Macy Crow is alive."

He stood straighter. "Is she?"

"She's awake, and I talked to her," she said quickly, knowing she had his interest. "She knows where the package is."

"Does she?" His eyes sharpened with interest.

"If you kill them, I won't tell you."

He looked amused. "I can be persuasive."

"Apparently not enough. You didn't get Jack Crow to talk." Faith was doing her best to unsettle him.

"I've learned a few new tricks since then."

"You and I leave now, I'll tell you where the package is."

"Fair enough. Bring the baby. Like I said, I've learned some new tricks." They stepped out of the room, and Faith, holding the baby tight, followed. He closed the door behind her, locking it, and then motioned for her to climb the stairs.

Faith's mind was spinning. Hayden was close. All she had to do was buy a little time.

As she reached the kitchen, she started toward the front door.

"No. Back door."

She pictured Hayden rolling up in the cul-de-sac, seeing her car, and being distracted long enough for this man to get away with her and the baby. And if she died, he would surely double back and kill the girls. The baby began to fuss. "Aren't you worried about the neighbors?"

"Keep it quiet, or I'll kill it right here."

She put her pinky in the baby's mouth, and it suckled. Blood from the afterbirth had stained her shirt and was now dripping on the floor. "The baby needs to see a doctor."

The wail of police sirens echoed in the distance, and he glanced over his shoulder. For the first time, he looked worried.

"Leave the girls," she said. "I'll tell you everything you want to know if you leave them."

The sirens grew louder.

"We don't have much time," she said.

His jaw tensed. "They can identify me."

"Does it matter? You get the package and you'll get paid, right? Then you can vanish."

***

Hayden's lights were flashing as he and Brogan raced to the location. He saw Faith's car parked in the cul-de-sac and moved in behind her. "Damn it. She doesn't wait for anyone."

Out of his car, he drew his weapon and hurried toward Faith's car. The front door was ajar, and her purse and keys were on the passenger seat. He'd seen so much violence working for the Rangers, but he'd never thought about it touching Faith. He couldn't entertain the thought of losing her, or he wouldn't be able to function.

"She's got to be inside. Call in marked units. I want this area surrounded."

"Consider it done," Brogan said.

The Rangers raced to the front door and heard the distant screaming and pounding from the basement. They hurried into the kitchen, and as Brogan moved cautiously down the stairs with his weapon drawn, Hayden glanced toward the back door and saw the small droplets of blood. "I'm heading to the backyard," he said.

"Roger that," Brogan said.

Hayden went out the back door and saw the trail of blood running down a narrow sidewalk leading to a back exit in the tall privacy fence that banded around the yard. He heard a car door close and ran, kicking through the privacy fence door. More blood droplets led to the side street that backed up to the house. He had only a split second to assess the situation. Blue four-door. Blood, woman in the passenger seat, and a man in the driver's seat. The car wheels started to roll.

He leveled his weapon and fired, hitting the back right tire. As the car gained speed, he trained his weapon onto the left rear tire and fired. As much as he wanted to fire at the driver, he couldn't risk hitting Faith.

But when the man in the front seat raised a weapon toward the passenger, a clear and calculated rage overtook him. Hayden drew in a breath as he lined up the sights on his weapon with the driver's head. *Don't move, Faith. Don't move.* The car gained more speed even with the blown-out tires deflating quickly. He squeezed the trigger. His bullet blew out the back window and slammed into the jaw of the driver. The car swerved, careening left into a tree. He didn't allow satisfaction as he raced ahead, desperate to see Faith alive and well.

When he reached the car, he kept his weapon drawn, his finger beside the trigger, ready to shoot again. Adrenaline pumped through his veins as his focus zeroed in on his target.

When he saw the man slumped over the wheel, Hayden yanked open the door and hauled the man out of the car. He heard a baby cry, saw a flicker of movement in his side vision, but kept his focus on the man.

The events that came next felt like they happened in slow motion, each critical action and reaction weighted with life and death.

Hayden threw the man face-first onto the grass and drove a knee into the small of his back as he kept his weapon trained on him with one hand and reached for his cuffs with the other. He snapped one cuff around one wrist and then, hauling the second wrist toward the first, clamped the cuff around it.

The baby's cry grew louder, echoing its fear and panic as Hayden rolled the man on his back and pressed his fingertips to his carotid artery. There was no pulse. He recognized the guy. He'd tried to make a play for Faith the night of the fundraiser.

He then shifted his focus to the passenger seat. Faith was slumped over in the front seat, her body folded over the baby. Holstering his weapon, he raced to the passenger side and yanked open the door.

His heart sank as he thought about Faith dead and lost to him forever. He could not bear it. He could not.

Gently, he took her by the shoulders and carefully leaned her back, freeing the baby underneath. He could see a gash across her forehead and her lip was bloodied, but there seemed to be no other injuries. The baby cried. Faith blinked and moaned. She wasn't unconscious, but badly stunned.

"Faith!" Sirens wailed around him.

Slowly she nodded her head. "I'm here."

Jesus. A tangle of emotions clogged his throat, and it was all he could do to keep his voice even. "Faith, I don't want you to move. The paramedics are here."

"Kat and Paige are in the house," she said. "They're alive."

"Brogan's inside. He's got it under control." Hayden tried to take the baby from her.

Her grip tightened around the small bundle. "I have her."

"You're unsteady. Let me have her."

She pushed back the towel and stared at the squalling infant and then handed the little girl to him. He cradled her like a football.

She looked over at the man lying on the ground. "His name is Kevin. I've met him before. He didn't want Kat, Paige, or the baby, but used them to lure me to him. He was going to use me to get to Macy and whatever he thought Jack Crow had left her."

"What would Crow leave Macy?" Hayden asked.

"She thinks her father had evidence against Garnet and he mailed it to Macy."

"How do you know?"

"She's awake. She told me." A sob caught in her throat. "Jesus, Hayden, who would hire a monster like that?"

"I don't know. But we'll find out." He kissed her lightly on the forehead. "I'm just so damn glad you're okay. I wouldn't have made it if I lost you."

Instead of answering, she kissed him softly on the lips as the first of the paramedics stepped in to administer first aid.

Kathy Saunders, 1989

Josie and Olivia are dead. I know it. He says they are not. He says they've gone on to better lives. But he lies. He always lies. And I will be dead soon, too.

Things I like. Country music. High-waist, stonewashed jeans. My teddy bear, Boo. Starry nights.

Things I hate. This room. Not seeing my sister, Diane, again. This pen running out of ink.

CHAPTER
TWENTY-SEVEN

Friday, June 29, 9:00 p.m.

Faith had spent several hours in the emergency room with Kat, Paige, and the baby. Doctors had also done an MRI and determined Faith did not have a concussion. The gash in her forehead hadn't required stitches, just a couple of butterfly bandages.

Once Hayden had heard from the doctors she was going to be fine, she had insisted he return to the crime scene. It had taken her several tries to convince him to go, and finally, he had left.

She'd been able to wash the blood from her hands and face, but her blouse had been a total loss, so the staff had lent her a pair of scrubs and flip-flops.

Now as she sat in the exam cubicle, she pushed back her hair and straightened her shoulders. All she could do was mull over the unanswered questions that still lingered. Hayden had discovered that Kevin was Mark Canada and had done jail time for assault. It was assumed Canada had been hired, but the question was, By whom? What was in the package that he was so willing to torture and kill for?

"Where's Faith McIntyre?" Kat's loud, unsteady voice cut through the buzz of the emergency exam cubicles.

Faith pushed off the gurney and drew back the curtain. Kat was standing in the center of the room, dressed in a hospital gown, her pregnant belly protruding, and pulling her IV pole with her.

"Kat. You should be in your exam room."

The girl's face crumpled, and tears streamed down her cheeks as she rushed toward Faith, still pulling her IV. "No one would tell me where you were."

Faith smoothed back the girl's hair and smiled. "I'm right here. We're all fine."

She sobbed. "When I got here, my head was spiraling and I couldn't think. But when I shook off those drugs, all I could remember was that man taking you away."

"I'm fine." She glanced past the girl to see several nurses moving toward her. One was pushing a wheelchair.

Kat gently touched the bandages on Faith's forehead. "You're hurt."

"No. I'm really no worse for the wear. But you need to get back into your room and rest. They're going to have to take you to the maternity ward and check out you and the baby."

"It's kicking the crap out of me," Kat said.

"Good." Faith helped the girl lower into the wheelchair.

"Where is that Paige girl?" Kat asked.

"She's in the maternity ward with her baby."

"Can I see her?" Kat asked.

"Her parents are with her now, but I don't see why not. If it weren't for you, we might not have ever found her."

Kat wiped away several tears. "He said he was going to use me as bait."

"I know." Faith laid her hands on Kat's shoulders. "But it didn't work. We're all okay, and he's dead."

"The Ranger got him, didn't he?" Kat asked.

"Yes, he did."

Kat sniffed. "He's pretty cool. You should keep him."

Faith laughed. "I'll keep that in mind."

"What are you doing? Can you come with me to maternity?"

"I'll visit you as soon as I can. I have a few other things I have to take care of first. Don't worry; the nurses will take good care of you."

Kat gripped her fingers. "You promise?"

"I surely do, kid."

Faith stood and watched as the nurses wheeled Kat away, and when she turned to figure out how the hell she was going to get out of this place, Hayden stepped into view.

He strode toward her, his hat in his hand. Without a word, he gripped her arm in a firm but gentle hold. "You're like that kid. You don't listen."

His touch always made her feel alive. "I always hear you."

He shook his head as if he were arguing with a teenager. "You just do what you want."

Without hesitating, she said with pride, "I do what is right."

He settled her on the gurney, pulled off her flip-flops, and covered her feet with a white cotton blanket. He kissed her on the forehead, his fingers gently brushing the butterfly bandage.

"I thought you were at the crime scene."

"I was. I received a call from the forensic lab. The DNA results are in."

He handed her the printouts and sat silently as she read them.

She looked up. "Our theory was right. Marissa and PJ share the same father as Macy and I."

"Yes, you do. Look at the DNA results of Kathy Saunders compared to PJ."

She flipped the page and read and then reread the results. "It's a match."

"Yeah."

"I need to see PJ now."

"You're hardly in shape to do much."

"I'm fine. And I need to know who would hurt those girls. I need to know what he might know or what Margaret might know."

"Faith, you can't."

She shook her head. "Like you said, I don't listen. So one way or another, Captain, I am going to the Slater house tonight, with or without a change of clothes."

***

Hayden drove Faith to the gates of the Slater home. He was not happy about this scenario or the fact that she had insisted on going inside alone. "I'm giving you twenty minutes, and if you're not out, I'm coming in."

She touched the small wire that ran up her shirt to a tiny microphone. "I can handle PJ and Margaret. As far as we know, they both might not know the entire truth."

"You don't know who you're dealing with. That's why I'm here." He kissed her on the lips, got out of the car, and moved to Brogan's SUV, which was parked behind them.

She slid to the driver's side, pulled up in front of the tall brick house next to the circular driveway, and put the car in park. The light from the dashboard illuminated the sharp angles on Hayden's face.

"You're sure about this?" he said.

"Very." She straightened her sweater and smoothed her hands over her jeans, clothes Nancy had brought from her locker at the medical examiner's office. She got out of the car, climbed the front steps, and rang the bell. Even though Hayden didn't want her taking this chance, she had to. There was too much at stake now for her to simply sit on the sidelines.

She heard heels inside the house clicking against the floor she knew was white marble. The door opened to a petite blonde dressed in Chanel, who smiled the instant she saw Faith.

"Faith, how are you?" Margaret's smile faded when she saw the bandage on her head. "Is everything all right?"

"I need to see PJ, Margaret. I have some questions for both of you."

"Sure, of course. Come inside. PJ is in his study. I just opened a bottle of wine. Would you like a glass?"

"No, thank you."

The older woman frowned. "You're scaring me, Faith."

Faith didn't have the energy to allay her worries as they walked along the tiled foyer with glistening chandeliers overhead.

"You know where the study is, Faith. I can't let you visit without coffee or something. I'll be right back."

Faith was almost glad to have Margaret out of the room while she had this conversation with PJ. She made her way to the study and past the portrait of Margaret holding PJ when he was less than a year old.

This house had belonged to Margaret and Peter, and PJ had moved out almost a decade ago. But after Peter's death on the first of April, PJ had moved back home to be close to his mother, who he knew was having a hard time being alone.

Faith had always loved this house. It had been a second home to her growing up and most especially after her own mother died. When Peter had died, she'd also returned to the house for almost a week so that she could help Margaret.

She knocked on PJ's office door. He glanced up from a stack of papers and rose immediately. "Faith, what brings you here on a Friday evening? Mom and I have had dinner, but we can certainly have the cook warm you up something."

She hugged him, savoring the familiar scent of tobacco she remembered on his father. "You've found your father's cigars."

"Guilty. I inherited his taste for Cubans. Mother is not thrilled, but she turns a blind eye."

Genetics was a powerful thing. She closed his study door. "There's something I need to talk to you about."

His grin faded. "Sounds serious."

"It is."

He offered her a seat on the leather settee, and when she sat, he took the chair adjacent to it. "What is going on?"

She shook her head, trying to make sense of it all.

"Did you hear about that FBI agent who was killed?"

"Was she killed? Mother heard at the hospital that she might have survived."

Hayden had said keeping a lid on Macy's status wouldn't last forever. Faith moved closer to the edge of the settee. "She's alive."

"That's good to know. What does that have to do with us?"

She reached for her cell and found the picture Macy had emailed her. "A picture is worth a thousand words."

He studied the image and then looked back at her. "This is you."

"No. It's Macy Crow," Faith said softly.

"Faith, this is you."

"DNA just confirmed we are identical twins," she said.

"There are two of you?" PJ pressed his fingers to his temple, rubbing them as his father had done when faced with a dilemma.

"I'm as blown away as you are." She watched him closely, searching for any tells that would hint to lies. He was so much like his father, and she knew behind the easy smiles was a cunning, keen mind. "Have you found anything regarding my adoption?"

"Nothing more than the entries in your father's datebook. What did you say the FBI agent's name was?"

"Macy Crow."

"Crow?"

"Do you know the name?" she asked.

"Captain Hayden asked me about Jack Crow. I had human resources look through the old personnel records, and we did use Crow for a few odd jobs in the mideighties. He was referred to us by Danny Garnet."

"Do you know what kind of cases Crow was working?"

"Divorce cases mostly. He did surveillance and took pictures that we could use in court. He quit after six months. According to his exit interview, he said it wasn't the kind of work he wanted to be doing."

"Have you seen Crow in recent years?" Faith asked.

"I wouldn't know the man if he walked in the room and shook my hand. And I'm still not sure how all this relates to me."

As tempted as she was to tell him about the graves in the country, she hesitated. "Slater and McIntyre, specifically your father, represented three women between 1987 and 1990. Their crimes were petty, and soon after they were dismissed, they vanished."

"I can't help you. I wasn't born."

"But you could pull their client records, couldn't you?"

"As I told the Rangers, I can, but I won't. Attorney-client privilege."

"For your own sake, you should." She pulled the DNA printouts from her purse and handed him the first.

He read the results, and though he was young, he was proving himself to be a very savvy defense attorney who could pick up technical details quickly.

She pulled out the second sheet of paper. "Marissa Lewis lives in San Antonio and is adopted like me. As it turns out, we are half sisters."

PJ frowned, and this time when he read the report, he made no comment.

She studied the last sheet before extending it to him. "I also have a half brother."

He raised his chin but hesitated before he took the paper. This sheet he didn't read as he had the others.

"You are my half brother," she said. "According to a DNA test, we share the same father." The quick DNA test had proved they were half siblings, and PJ's DNA was not a match to Josie's. Faith pictured Peter Slater, the portly man with a thick shock of gray hair and a smile that could light up a room.

"I never consented to giving a sample of my DNA."

She would save this argument for the courts later. Now she just wanted him to hear the truth. "The three girls I mentioned were found in graves out in the country. They'd all been held against their will, and the Rangers believe they were forced to give birth to children before they were killed."

He set the paper down and shook his head. "No. That's not correct. My father might have had affairs, but he would never do anything so horrific. He wouldn't."

"We are already in the process of testing the mtDNA of these women against mine, Marissa's, and yours. It's not as quick a process, but mtDNA will prove or disprove if we are their offspring."

He stood and shoved his hands in his pockets.

The door to the study opened, and Margaret appeared with a tea cart filled with cups, a fresh pot of coffee, and cookies. "What is going on in here? You two look so serious."

"It's nothing, Mother," PJ said.

Margaret filled a cup and handed it to Faith and then filled another and handed it to PJ. "Faith, my son is overprotective. He thinks I'm fragile china and can't handle hard news."

"Margaret," Faith said. Peter had always protected Margaret, and she'd been happy to live in his shadow and to dedicate herself to him and their son. "It brings me no pleasure to deliver this news."

"I know, dear. You would never hurt anyone," she said. She drank her coffee and watched as Faith took a sip of her own.

There was a sharpness in Margaret's gaze that rivaled the intensity of her late husband's and son's. "Maybe I can help this along. Is this about the police officer at the hospital?" Margaret asked. "I know you've been visiting her."

"It turns out, Mother, that the police officer is Faith's identical twin."

"A twin? Good Lord, Faith," Margaret said. "Who hurt that poor woman?"

Faith shifted in her seat, feeling more uncomfortable about this conversation. "The police have a name, but they're still trying to figure out what motivated him to kill."

Margaret set her cup down. "Kill. That's terrible."

Faith felt suddenly dizzy and wondered if being here now had been too much. "The thing is, Margaret, we have DNA tests linking me to two other half siblings."

"We don't need to get into that tonight, Faith," PJ said. "My mother doesn't need to be subjected to your theories."

"You're the one that told me about the first missing girl, PJ. Josie Jones."

His lips flattened into a grim line. "She was listed in Russell McIntyre's datebook, not my father's. That leads me to believe he might have been behind all this."

"Behind what?" Margaret asked. "I can see you are very upset."

PJ began to pace.

Faith felt her stomach flip-flop and was certain now she was going to be sick.

"Faith, you look pale," Margaret said.

She stood and looked toward the door. Her vision blurred, and she staggered.

Margaret stood and hooked her arm in Faith's. "PJ, would you go and get some water from the kitchen? Faith does not look well. Maybe even a ginger ale."

PJ shook his head. "Sure."

When he was gone, Margaret guided Faith back to the couch. She carefully brushed a blond strand from Faith's eyes and smiled.

"I know about the graves," Margaret said.

Faith began to sweat as she stared into the face of a woman she'd known all her life. Margaret's smile had hardened in a way that hurt more than it frightened her. "How?"

She dropped her voice a notch and said, "Because I handpicked all those girls. I chose them to give my husband children after I discovered I couldn't."

"You did this for Peter?" Everyone had a darker side, but she realized now that this couple, who'd always made her feel welcome in their home, were monsters.

"A wife is duty bound to give her husband a son. And I couldn't. Broke my heart. The first girl gave us you and, as it turns out, Macy. I thought she had died the day she was born along with her mother, but she's tough, isn't she?"

Faith tried to stand but just a little pressure from Margaret now was enough to keep her in place. "That girl bled to death. You see, Garnet and my husband had a financial arrangement, and when Peter died, Garnet came to me and demanded more money. He thought I'd be shocked, overwhelmed, or terrified or whatever it is men think we women do when faced with a problem. He said he had evidence and would go to the cops if anything happened to him. I told him to leave my house, and I called Mr. Canada that day."

Faith's vision blurred. For an instant she thought it was related to the car crash but then as she stared at Margaret, who put her own coffee cup aside, an idea dawned on her. "Did you put something in my coffee?"

"A strong sedative. It will be enough to put you to sleep. It'll give me time to talk to PJ. Once I've spoken to him, he'll understand everything we did was out of love."

Faith shook her head, hoping now that Hayden was listening closely. "Peter always gave the impression he was the master of his castle."

"That's what everyone believed. But in reality, Peter made no important decision regarding business or this family without me. PJ knows his father and I bent the rules from time to time. He knows when to look away."

The front door slammed open, and she heard Hayden's distant voice. He was demanding to see her. She could barely focus or bring herself to call out to him. She tried to stagger to her feet but couldn't. She collapsed back against the couch as he stormed into the study. Hayden called out her name, and when she didn't respond, he called for a paramedic.

Faith's vision cleared enough for her to see Margaret's face tighten with concern and worry. "Thank God you're here, Captain Hayden. Faith is not doing well."

Hayden took Margaret by the arm and pulled her away from Faith. She wanted to tell him that Margaret had poisoned or drugged her. She wanted to shout and scream for him to be careful. But the words wouldn't form. Her eyes wanted to close, but she struggled to keep them open. The distant sound of wailing sirens grew louder.

Hayden's voice was sharp and cutting as he read Margaret her rights. Margaret was calm when she demanded to see her son. And when that request was denied, she insisted on a call to her attorney. Faith felt a mix of satisfaction and sadness as she watched Brogan lead her away. She still couldn't reconcile the woman she'd loved as a second mother with this monster.

Hayden touched Faith on her forehead and lifted her in his arms. "I heard everything she said."

Faith blinked, struggling to speak clearly. "She's put something in my drink," she said.

"I know." He carried her to the front door and down the steps. In his arms, she felt safe. He was the only thing in her life at this moment that made sense. She only hoped Margaret hadn't poisoned her. She hoped she wasn't going to lose the man she loved.

"You're not leaving me, Faith," he said, as if reading her thoughts. "I love you too damn much to lose you."

Lights flashed around her as she passed out in his arms.

EPILOGUE

Restless sleep and nightmares had plagued Faith since her confrontation with Margaret. Her mind continued to replay the scene featuring Margaret's almost serene face. Later, after Hayden had interviewed PJ, he'd relayed to her how confused PJ had looked, how he'd quickly recovered, and how in the end he'd sided with his mother.

A knock on her bedroom door yanked her from the terrifying replay, and she sat up to see Kat standing in her room. The girl had moved into Faith's house immediately upon discharge from the hospital. So far the two were still getting to know each other. Like most teenagers, Kat wasn't always easy. Throw in the stress of the adoption, and well, sometimes it was a study in patience.

The bright spot had been Nancy Ridgefield, who had proposed the idea of Nancy and her husband, Mike, adopting Kat's baby. Faith had presented the idea to the girl, and the four of them had sat down and had several lengthy discussions. In the end, Kat had decided she liked Nancy and Mike Ridgefield and had agreed.

"My bed is wet," Kat said. "I'm soaked."

Faith tossed back her covers, surprised at the rush of panic and worry shooting through her body. She considered herself cool under fire. Crime scenes, autopsies, even a grilling from a defense attorney in court didn't faze her. But this moment felt entirely different.

"Don't worry. It's your water breaking," Faith said. "We just need to get you changed and to the hospital."

"Is the baby going to fall out?" Kat asked, sounding panicked.

"No, it's not going to fall out. We've got time. Let's get you changed."

She helped the girl change into clean clothes, dressed herself in jeans, a pullover blouse, and sandals, and then grabbed the go-bag she'd packed when the girl had moved into her house.

"Paige was in so much pain," Kat said as Faith drove through the dark streets toward the medical center. "I remember her crying."

"It won't be like that for you. I've told you there are medicines that will help. It's going to be fine. I promise."

Each time Faith remembered Paige's anguished cries in that drab room, she thought about Josie, Olivia, and Kathy. They'd not had any help. They'd suffered alone, or worse, with Danny Garnet offering his ham-fisted help.

But Paige was back home with her parents and her baby girl. She was trying to put her life back together. She'd survived.

Faith tightened her grip on the steering wheel, forcing a smile for Kat's sake as she pressed the accelerator and sped through a yellow light.

"Where's the Ranger?" Kat's voice sounded strained as she shifted in her seat.

"Hayden is south of San Antonio. He's working a case."

"Top secret."

"It must be," Faith said. "He didn't want to leave until the baby was born, but there was no avoiding it."

"Shouldn't you call him and tell him?" She grimaced and pressed her hand to her belly.

"I will as soon as I get you checked in to the hospital."

"And you need to call Nancy and Mike. They're going to want to see the show."

"Let's just get you to the hospital."

"You look worried," Kat challenged.

"Nope. Not. A. Bit."

Faith pulled up in the circular entrance to the hospital, dashed inside, and returned quickly with a wheelchair. As a nurse pushed Kat toward labor and delivery, Faith parked the car and then ran inside with Kat's bag.

Fifteen minutes later, she was changed into scrubs and in the room, the worried girl's contractions rapidly growing closer. She called Nancy first, who answered on the first ring. Nancy sounded calm and focused and promised that she and Mike would be there soon.

The next call was to Mitchell. He answered quickly as well, and she discovered hearing his calm, even voice settled her own jitters and worries.

As it turned out, Kat delivered Baby Boy Jones three hours later, with Nancy and Mike looking on. The boy was healthy, perfect, and squalling in a way that reminded Faith a little of Kat when the girl was complaining.

Faith took lots of pictures of mother and son. She texted several to Hayden.

Nancy and Mike held back, watching nervously as the nurse laid the baby in Kat's arms. For a long moment, the girl stared at the baby boy and then cried. "Nancy, come and get your kid."

Faith took the baby from Kat and laid him in Nancy's arms. The couple cried, thanked Kat over and over, and then stared at their son with such love. After the Ridgefields moved into their own room with the baby, Faith stayed and held Kat as she cried.

Had Faith's adopted parents looked at her with the same devotion? She'd met Marissa's parents, and they'd listened quietly as they'd learned the circumstances of their daughter's birth. An investigation into the

Lewis family revealed that the wife, Caroline, had been a member of Margaret Slater's tennis club. It had been Margaret who had come to Caroline and told her about a baby girl who had been born. Caroline and her husband, Kyle, had agreed immediately to the adoption. Slater & McIntyre had handled all the paperwork.

When Kat was finally asleep, Faith went to the lobby café, bought sandwiches and soda, and took them back upstairs to the physical rehabilitation step-down unit, where Macy had been staying for the last two weeks.

Faith stood at the door of the floor's rehab gym and watched as Macy wrangled with crutches. Macy's now very short blond hair caught the sunlight coming through the window.

Her sister was getting stronger every day, and her doctors often commented on her drive and determination. But Macy set high standards for herself and when she didn't meet them, often got frustrated.

"This is crap," Macy said to the therapist. "I used to run a sub-six-minute mile. And now I hobble around like an old woman."

The therapist, a practical, no-nonsense woman who only smiled when her patients excelled, raised a brow. "Work harder, old woman."

"It's looking good to me," Faith said.

Macy shot her a look, a blend of annoyance and hope. "You're always positive."

"It's a curse," Faith said. "I got us a couple of sandwiches. Turkey on rye, your favorite, and those baked chips you like. Are you almost finished?"

The therapist nodded. "We are."

"Great. See you there."

"Aren't you going to push my wheelchair?" Macy asked.

Faith looked to the therapist, who shook her head. "Boss says no can do. I suppose you'll have to wheel yourself."

"You are a slave driver, just like the PT Goddess of Pain."

Faith laughed. "If you want to eat hospital food, then by all means stay here."

Macy muttered a curse but held up a hand. "I would crawl for a sandwich right now."

"I'm hungry, so you better hurry," Faith teased.

As she left her grumbling sister behind, she had to smile. It was nice having family. They were far from perfect, but that suited her just fine.

She set the sandwiches on a round table in the break room and then put a straw in each cup. She grabbed napkins from a dispenser.

The click of Macy's crutches had her standing, pulling out a chair, and helping her settle. Faith stacked her crutches against the wall beside them.

Macy grabbed a half of a sandwich and took a bite, her eyes closing with pure pleasure. "You're in scrubs, which means Kat had her baby. Boy or girl?"

"Boy. Healthy with a strong set of lungs," Faith said.

Faith was pleased by her sister's speech and cognitive recognition. Like Faith, Macy was having trouble sleeping. She also suffered from headaches, but her memory and recall were now almost perfect.

Macy picked up a napkin and wiped her fingertips. "And Nancy and Mike now have the baby as planned?"

"They do. It was bittersweet."

Both were silent for a moment, and then Macy said, "Kat had a choice. And that counts for a lot. She'll also get to see the boy from time to time."

"Yes. She'll be a big part of his life."

"Are Nancy and Mike still calling the kid Alexander?"

"I suppose. We didn't get that far today."

Macy and Faith fell into silence as each ate her sandwich. The fate of Josie, Olivia, and Kathy was never far from their minds, the story of their deaths becoming clear as the details unfolded.

Forensic examination of the bones had revealed that Olivia and Kathy both had broken hyoid bones. The horseshoe-shaped bone was found in the neck, and its fracturing generally indicated strangulation.

Special Agent Kate Hayden, using Macy's key, had retrieved Jack Crow's package from her mailbox. She'd returned it to Austin and, with Hayden, Brogan, Faith, and Macy in attendance, had opened it.

Inside the padded envelope, they'd found the second burner phone, as well as several cassette tapes and pictures taken of a very pregnant Josie, Olivia, and Kathy, all chained in the ranch's basement room.

On the burner phone had been a video made by Jack Crow for Macy. They all had watched the phone's video image as it captured Crow's recliner and then his off-screen cussing as he appeared to wrangle with the phone and turn on the selfie mode.

"Jesus, I never thought I'd be glad to see this ugly mug." He sniffed and sat straighter in his brown recliner.

"Macy, if you're watching this and we haven't had a chance to talk about what you're about to hear, then it means I'm dead. Either the cancer has gotten me or my past sins have finally caught up to me." He laughed. *"Bet on the past sins.*

"My doctor looks like he's fresh out of middle school, but he seems smart. He told me he had all kinds of things he wanted to try, but I told him to save his voodoo treatments. I'm not dying in a damned hospital, hooked up to machines." He reached for the bourbon on the end table and took a healthy slug. *"You should have found the Coronas in the refrigerator. I don't know how you drink that shit, but I know you like it. Hopefully, you've finished your first beer and are working on your second."*

The first time through this video, Macy had cried. Faith had wrapped her arm around her as Hayden and Brogan stood by silently. There'd been questions for Macy about Crow and his most recent conversation with her. She'd wiped away her tears and answered the questions as the professional she was.

Macy had explained that once she'd joined the FBI, Jack had called her less and less. He loved her, he had said, but it was best each stayed on their side of the fence. She'd always known the salvage business wasn't his primary occupation. She had known he patched up gunshot wounds, broken bones, and overdoses, but she'd not thought his sins went much beyond that. Sadness, loss, and too many unsaid words had sat with her as she watched the recording.

"And you better not be crying for me, kiddo. Don't shed one damn tear. I lived large, and I crammed a lot into sixty-plus years."

In the image, Jack reached for a hand-rolled joint and the lighter Macy's mother had given him for Christmas twenty-five years earlier and flicked the flint until it sparked. He held the flame to the joint's tapered tip. He puffed several times, drawing in a deep breath and holding it before releasing it slowly.

"I can almost hear you grousing at me now, Macy. You were right about the butts. They're what did me in." He puffed again. *"But this,"* he said, studying the joint, *"this is medicinal. Doctor's orders."* He laughed and took another hit. *"And I'm not turning in any of my sobriety chips.*

"I'm going to cut to the chase," Jack said. *"Your mother never wanted to tell you, but of course you found out when you were eight."* Another long hit on the joint and a more serious tone.

The next time Faith and Macy had watched the video together, they'd been alone. Macy had then truly let her guard down. Faith had snuck in a couple of Coronas to her hospital room. Neither had seemed to care if one of the nurses caught them as they had pried off the tops and drunk.

Air had whooshed past Macy's lips as she'd stared at the image of her pop's face and then had pressed the cold beer to her flushed cheeks. "I'm not sure if I'm pissed or relieved to hear him talk about my adoption."

"If your mother weren't dead, I'd probably not have told you. But it doesn't seem right to let the secret die with an old man.

"You were always a smart kid, and I think on some level you knew. I know you stopped asking your mom about why you were so different. You were sensitive enough to know the questions upset her. As far as we were concerned, you were ours. And I know I'm not Mr. Rogers, but I always wanted to do right by you.

"The details aren't pretty, kiddo. It has never been my style to confess, but it's now or never, right?" He drained his bourbon glass. "I had a buddy from the army. Danny Garnet. He was a wily kid that I kind of took pity on and looked out for when we were locked up. We both got out, moved on, I thought, and then one night he called me. He said he had a medical emergency. He needed help.

"I followed the directions he gave me, and when I arrived at this old ranch, I found a woman. She was in labor, screaming like her insides were ripping apart. I had just enough time to wash my hands before I was delivering the baby. It was a girl.

"Garnet wasn't pleased, and immediately made a call. I couldn't hear what he was saying because I was too busy. The woman started to bleed out as a second baby was born. That baby was blue and appeared stillborn. I couldn't save the mother. Garnet had a home for the first baby. And since no one was expecting a second, he said we'd bury it with the mother. He paid me three grand and told me to keep quiet. He left with the first baby and asked me to bury the rest."

Jack looked off in the distance for a moment, as if he were watching the scene replay all over again. "I should have called the cops, but shit. Your mother and I really needed the money. We were about to lose the yard. That's a shitty excuse, because I could see this girl had been locked in that room for a while. I hated Garnet for what he'd done.

"I dug a hole out back, and I laid the woman in it. I went back to get the second baby, and the little one twitched. Scared the shit out of me." He looked up at the camera, his gaze wistful. "Garnet didn't want the second one. I was already carrying enough sin that night without the weight of a dead kid on my shoulders, so I took the baby. That baby was you, kiddo."

When Faith had turned off the recording, both had sat in silence for a long moment. They were twins, but both were still getting to know and trust each other. Family ties took time to build.

Faith tore a piece of crust from her sandwich. "Are you going back to the FBI?"

"I have to. I've still got the damn dreams, but the headaches are better. More than ever I have to make my work at the bureau count for something."

"For Josie and the other girls."

"Yes."

"Selfishly I'd like you to stay here."

"I won't be a stranger." Macy reached for her sandwich. "So what's the deal with old Margaret and PJ?"

"The judge set the bail at one million dollars for her after he heard the tape and saw the pictures. He also took her passport."

"She shouldn't have gotten any bail."

"No, but there are many who still don't quite believe the stories. She and Peter have very deep roots in this community."

"She could still run. A woman like that who planned so much evil, she must have an exit strategy. She could slip over the border into Mexico without anyone knowing."

"The ankle bracelet might slow her down," Faith said.

"You got her on tape," Macy said. "You got her full confession."

"PJ is arguing diminished capacity," Faith said. "He's saying his mother is confused, and that she doesn't have any idea what she's saying."

"I've seen her kind drag out litigation in court for years. And she's got the money and resources. She'll fight this so long old age will get her before she sees prison time."

"I know."

"Has he accepted his DNA is a match to Kathy Saunders?"

"No. And he's arguing the DNA sample was unlawfully obtained."

Faith still grappled with the two faces of Margaret Slater. What perplexed her was that Margaret truly had been kind to her over the years. Margaret believed bringing Faith, Macy, Marissa, and PJ into the world had been just and right. If not for Margaret's evil act, Faith and Macy would not be here now.

"That bitch killed those girls and would have killed you if not for Hayden." Macy's voice faltered. "I'd be talking about your funeral as well as Josie's with Maggie Stapleton."

Since Faith had visited Maggie, she'd kept her updated on Josie's case. Maggie had visited Macy at the hospital and spent hours talking to them about Josie. Faith and Maggie had attended the funerals of Kathy Saunders and Olivia Martin, and Maggie had delayed Josie's funeral until Macy could attend.

Macy lifted her chin. "Canada killed my dad and brother to keep her secret."

An investigation into Mark Canada had found that he had worked for Slater & McIntyre for five years. He had done private investigative work at first, but quickly had become known as a man who made problems go away. He had come from very humble roots and had sold his soul to reach his station at the law firm. He had no prison or arrest record, but interviewing neighbors and an ex-girlfriend had revealed a love of poker and womanizing.

"Mitchell is working closely with the prosecutor," Faith said. "Margaret might have a great legal team and money, but he's like a dog on a bone. He isn't letting go until she's in jail."

That prompted a satisfied smile. "I'm liking that guy more and more. Speaking of which, does he know about Kat's baby?"

"I texted him updates and pictures, and he texted back 'Roger,' which he does when he's working. He's in San Antonio."

A knock on the door had them turning, and Hayden strode into the room, his white Stetson in his hand. "Macy, you're looking sharp."

"Kicking ass and taking names," Macy said. "I'll be running a six-minute mile by the end of summer."

"I have no doubt." Hayden leaned over and kissed Faith. It had been a week since they'd seen each other, and she could feel a hunger rumbling under the kiss. "How are you?"

"I'm well. Been a crazy night."

"I checked in on Kat when I arrived, and she's sleeping," he said. "And the boy looks like he's going to give Nancy and Mike a run for their money."

"The hard part is yet to come for Kat, but I'll help her figure it out," Faith said.

"And me, too," Macy said. "The docs say I get sprung in two days and can move in with you, Faith, if the offer still stands." She reached for the bag of chips, set them in her lap, and released the brake on her wheelchair. "Which means if you two want some alone time at Faith's place, you better get cracking. It's going to be a full house pretty damn soon."

"We can stay longer," Faith said.

"Get out," Macy said, smiling.

"Are you sure?" Hayden asked.

"Yes!" Macy said. "See you two lovebirds another day."

Faith rose and kissed her sister on the head. "You don't have to tell me twice."

They followed Macy out into the hallway. When she vanished into her room, Faith said, "I'm ready to be done with this place. It would be nice to get to know my sister in a normal setting."

"How about I drive you home?" he asked.

She kissed him. "I'm parked out front."

"I'll bring you back in a few hours." He took her hand, and they walked to the elevators. They stepped into the car, and when the doors closed behind him, she wrapped her arms around his neck and kissed him, not caring about any security cameras that were watching.

"Have I told you that I love you?" she asked. Her policy of noncommitment felt worn and outdated. All the pieces of her life had fallen into place, and he was the cornerstone.

His expression softened in a way that telegraphed his feelings for her more than words. He traced his thumb over her moist lips. "You have not."

He had told her he loved her, but she hadn't said the words back to him. "Well, I do. I love you."

He kissed her on the lips with an intensity that took her breath away. "I never thought I'd ever feel love again, Faith. I'd accepted that. And then you proved to me how very wrong I was. You saved me."

She smiled. "I will save you anytime."

ABOUT THE AUTHOR

Photo © 2015 Studio FBJ

New York Times and *USA Today* bestselling novelist Mary Burton is the popular author of thirty-five romance and suspense novels, as well as five novellas. She currently lives in Virginia with her husband and three miniature dachshunds. Visit her at www.maryburton.com.